Taming of the Fire Sword

Nikki Root

Stories Like That

Published by Stories Like That
www.storieslikethat.com

Cover design by Lee Anderson and Alyssa Harris.

ISBN 979-8-9905363-0-2

To those of you who know you have it in you. You do.

THE CURSED

CHAPTER 1

DEATH AND THE SCORTH Empire ravaged the Vigilon Galaxy, and Mic Rorren knew the peace that followed would never come for him. As the desert planet Desandor rotated in the ether, Rorren combed its dunes. Hunting for deposits in the sand took his mind from the burden he carried. He survived the war with a knowledge few possessed: how to tame the power of the fire sword.

Mic Rorren bent to one knee and cut into the white core of the buried sandfruit, but not even a successful harvest could erase the past.

His trench coat flapped in the wind, the collar upright against the scarred flesh of his neck. He surveyed the barren landscape with a wisdom and physical strength unusual for a man of thirty-five.

A gust of Scorth magic cut across his square jaw and whistled through his hair on the tails of a dust cloud.

A shabby motor cruiser came into view. Exhaust from the hover pads tore grooves in the sand, destroying Rorren's crop.

"Aklaren. Worse than desert rats," he said because his father would have.

Rorren sprinted away from the dunes to the edge of the red cliffs. He wedged into a crevice. Head tilting, he adjusted the veer rifle and took a long, apprehensive look through the scope.

Raids on outlying farms were getting more common.

Today was his turn.

He didn't mind. Better him than his helpless neighbors.

For thirty seconds he didn't move. He waited for his breathing to settle as he honed in on his target.

He squeezed the trigger.

Bam! Bam! Bam!

He hit the fuel tank. Exploding gases blasted a horde of marauders across the dunes.

Rorren tore himself out of the rocks and skidded over the cliff. He reached the gangsters to find half of them retreating. The other half attacked, swinging crude weapons, murderous sneers on their sunburned lips.

Most stood seven and a half feet tall, making Rorren's six foot-two inches insignificant by comparison. Few weapons could penetrate their hides, though Rorren never dared get too close to spare an encounter with the rows of spikes on their arms and necks.

"Why can't any of you scumbags ever be a beautiful woman?"

Rorren cracked his Galactic Order staff over heads and torsos. He questioned the wisdom of taking on six Rocbulls alone. He preferred the cunning Rodilians to the massive muscle of the Rocbulls.

The sandstorm came on fast and, leaning into it, Rorren chuckled as a burst of dust swallowed them. He vanished into the blowing grains and waited for the scumbags to stumble into his trap. He thrashed three of the Aklaren using the storm as cover and tracked the other three.

He maneuvered to attack again, but exposed his position and the Rocbull took advantage. The gangster bashed Rorren over the head with some kind of cage. The blow stunned Rorren, but he recovered and launched at the attacker. A bird flew up into his face.

Incessant cawing and the flap of wings broke Rorren's concentration. He took a steel-hard fist to his abdomen.

The impact dropped him to the ground, but rolling onto this side, he dodged a death blow from the spiked end of a mallet. The Rocbull wound up for another strike, his partner joined him and Rorren regretted leaving the veer rifle behind. He was out of time and options.

A whiff of that Scorth magic he smelled earlier came again, emanating from the injured raven across the sand.

Particles of sand conglomerated into a crude, sword-welding figure. The sand woman charged, protecting Rorren and the raven from unrelenting Aklaren death blows, matching them strike for strike.

The demon sufficiently freaked out the Rocbulls and they abandoned their crusade. Rorren found himself alone with the raven and fading remnants of magic from a war he wished to forget. He pushed to his feet as if Desandor's gravity had become too heavy to shoulder.

He approached the bird but stopped cold in his boots when the hide of a sabretooth tiger emerged from the dying winds.

Kencats were native to Desandor but almost as rare as fowl.

The beast growled and licked his chops as he sniffed the raven in intervals. The bird tried to flee, but its wing hung at a twisted angle and blood oozed from its chest.

Rorren crouched, level with the kencat and shook his head.

"Now you show up. I could have used you ten minutes ago."

The kencat tilted his head and then bounded to Rorren, sticking his wet snout against Rorren's cheek and slopping his tongue all over.

The smell of Brawn's breath told Rorren all he needed to know about where his pet had been.

"You've been eating sunwarts again, haven't you?"

Rorren scanned the horizon for traces of the desert rats—a nuisance to all farmers on Desandor.

He scratched Brawn by the scruff and then, lingering over the raven, pondered whether to mess with things he knew better than to mess with.

The winds vanished and across the moonlit dunes, he saw the world reflected in the cab of the sandcrawler. After a storm, the air went so clear that Rorren's senses turned everything hyperreal. That uncomfortable moment in the solitude when he suspected big things still waiting for him up there in the stars.

He cut straight across the southern crop on the way to the farmhouse. Even after eight years, the sight of the barn and rustic lodge got to him not for their quaint charm, but because they were still standing—something he hadn't destroyed.

After he parked the sandcrawler between unused stalls in the barn and, cradling the raven, he avoided tripping over Brawn on the way up the porch steps.

The front door swung closed behind him and he kicked off his boots inside the thinly furnished room. Sand coated his denim trousers. He didn't bother brushing them off.

Rorren shoved aside tin soup cans, old books and tools and cleared a place on the kitchen table. He tossed an old towel on the stained wood and fashioned it into a nest.

He could feel the rapid pump of blood giving life to the raven in his hand.

Wrapping and cleaning the wound reminded him of those brutal days on the battlefield, patching up his injured soldiers.

The bird screamed as he dabbed at the gash on its chest with disinfectant. A black eye froze, watching him with malice as if the bird resented his help.

Rorren shrugged off the odd sensation and secretly congratulated himself on another excellent deed on his path of penance. He dropped the gauze and rolled the knots out of his shoulder.

The encroaching harvest meant the giant machines that processed the crop had to be repaired. Before the Aklaren attack, Rorren spent the day hammering at pipes and pulling out wires. His shoulder ached from constant swinging and he longed for a cold shower.

Satisfied with his patch job, he moved the old towel and bird under the kitchen window, then peeled off his dusty clothes.

He rinsed off and pulled on shorts and a shirt missing most buttons, grateful the smell of Brawn's sunwart breath was gone.

He opened a tin food can and set it on a rusted heating plate. He chewed on the bland noodles as he watched the raven sleep. The sheen over black feathers looked translucent under the light of Desandor's moons.

"Where did you come from?" Rorren swallowed the last bite and set the bowl in the sink. He retrieved a cold glass of water from the fridge and went outside. Brawn was asleep on the front porch under the table. His ear flinched every so often against the breeze.

Rorren sat on the swinging bench just beyond the kencat and propped his feet on the porch railing. One of the slats sagged under his weight. One more thing that needed fixing, but he didn't mind.

Better to build up than tear down, his father always said.

Sunsets after a storm were breathtaking. Vibrant colors spilled over the desert in pillars that broke through patches of puffy clouds.

The cool liquid washed away the grit from Rorren's mouth.

He lived for these moments—a hard day's work accomplished, a peaceful sunset and a barren desert around him. There was no audience to stare at the scars on his neck. The pretty picture almost made him forget the monster storm that took everything.

He lingered on the front porch until exhaustion won out.

On his way to the bedroom, he passed the kitchen window to check on the raven. Its chest scarcely moved, but it was still alive. She was still fighting, just like him.

In the morning, he would visit the widow, his favorite neighbor and local mystic. She'd probably have some crazy opinion. He could already hear it. *Rorren, that raven is as cursed as you are.*

Dust trickled through the cracked window as Rorren drove up the sagebrush-lined driveway to her homestead. He spotted her on the porch, waiting like she knew he was coming, hands wringing the apron tied at her waist. Her eyesight deteriorated rapidly in the last few years, but her sixth sense grew stronger.

This routine was their ritual. Metra would have cooked all day, using too many of her meager supplies to flood him with pies and cobbler. Generous as her intuition was uncanny.

She predicted drought and sandstorms with alarming accuracy.

Rorren's leather trench coat kept him cool as he climbed out of the sandcrawler and into the hot suns. The high collar, his protection from gawkers, itched and constricted. Metra never spoke of his scars, but he couldn't give up wearing the coat to visit her.

He climbed up the steps and greeted her with the raven cradled to his chest, a sandfruit sack slung over his back. Her dull eyes brightened and a smile parted her lips. She was old as the hills, stalwart in stature, and her white hair gave her a trace of majesty.

"Come here, little birdie. Let's see what we can do for you." She took the black feathers between her wrinkled hands and tottered inside. The new bounce in her step made Rorren follow her with one of his own. He deposited the food sack in the usual corner next to the coat rack he had never used.

"Mic Rorren has a kind heart, as you've realized by now," she said to the raven. "You'll be right as a trivet in no time."

She put the bird on the kitchen table and Rorren sat in his favorite chair, the one missing the slat. A trove of baked goods and homemade sweet water stretched before him.

"What do you think a bird is doing on Desandor?" He asked and then gulped down the juice. Delicious. Probably made from the last batch of sandfruit he brought her.

"I'm of a mind to ask the little birdie itself." She bent down, extending her hand to reveal some seeds in her palm. The raven gobbled them down, then pecked at the air for more.

"Little birdie, what is it you want?"

The widow seemed half off her rocker to talk to the raven as if it understood, but he did the same thing to Brawn occasionally.

The raven cawed at them and surprised Rorren as it fluttered from the table on its one good wing.

Something about the way it hobbled into Metra's bedroom, about the way it rummaged through her personal belongings, got Rorren thinking maybe it was—

The raven knocked over a vase on the dresser and squawked when it shattered. Metra owned next to nothing and he knew that ornament was a family heirloom. He moved to intervene, but Metra's soft hand landed on his arm.

"Wait a twig," she said as the raven vanished into the closet. Each rustling sound and thud tensed Rorren's shoulders until the raven reappeared. He held his breath, expecting something less mundane than what he saw.

The raven clutched in its beak a glittering necklace of gemstone.

"Is this what you want, little birdie?"

The way she said it, Rorren knew she would part with the treasure, though he could see it pained her. That was a charity he couldn't abide.

"Drop that and come here." Familiar words he said to Brawn many times.

The raven cocked its head, jewels swinging beneath its beak. He swore that beady eye was cursing him.

"Now."

The raven obeyed but with loud cawing and a rough flight into the kitchen.

"Let me clean up this mess," Rorren said.

"Nonsense, you get back to your pie."

The raven hobbled to the food, but Rorren chased it away before it damaged more of Metra's hard work.

He heard the front door open as he took the first savory bite.

"Bird stirs a ruckus, but I think I'll keep it," he said with a mouthful.

"Alturen see tos kira," Metra said.

"Holy ginger, grams, you speak Scorth?!" Jon entered the kitchen holding an icepack to his bruised eye. Blood oozed from a split lip and the brown curls on his head twisted up in a fluster that mimicked his entrance.

"What happened?" Metra bumped into the table on the way to her grandson, squinting to examine the damage.

Rorren knew the answer before Jon explained.

Aklaren. Another Scorth word. Made twice as vile because it was also the chosen moniker of the most dangerous gang in the universe.

"They jumped a bunch of us on the way home from the dock." Jon tried to bat Metra away as she lavished him with ointments and bandages.

Rorren stabbed his fork at the pie hard enough to dent the tin.

"We fought them off, but they got what we had on us. Next payday, we will pool our money and send a message to Galactic Order HQ. Maybe the Premier will send help."

The kid had stars in his eyes and hope in his tone. Rorren knew the truth. He'd already sent a dozen messages to Tagion Krave, Premier of the four Cardinal Worlds and leader of humanity in the galaxy, and received no reply. If Tagion couldn't bother answering Rorren, there was no way some unknown kid from the sticks would have better luck.

It might be time to take matters into his own hands.

"You're quiet, Mic Rorren," Jon said after he escaped Metra's nursing. "What was it you two were talking about and what the heck is that?"

"The Scorth call it tos kira. The raven," Metra said.

"I've never seen a bird like that before. And since when do you know Scorth?"

"It's a line from an outlawed book about the Scorth." Metra sent a knowing glance to Mic Rorren. His brow tightened and he hoped Metra would keep his connection to that book to herself.

"I've seen Scorth writing before. The symbols look like Mic Rorren's neck tattoo," Jon craned his neck to glimpse beneath the coat collar. "Did you get that during the war? I always wondered what it says."

Rorren stood and the chair with the missing slat tipped over.

"It's not a tattoo," he said. He inclined his head at Metra, "I should be going."

He hated that look of disappointment in her eyes every time he left. When Jon was there, Rorren found leaving her came easier.

"Take some pie with you. Lands sakes, but you don't eat well enough. You need to find yourself a good woman."

Rorren adjusted the coat collar with a flick, gathered the wounded raven and headed out the door. He heard Metra talking to Jon, her voice fading into the distance.

"...and alturen means gift, but, mark my words, that raven is no gift. The poor little birdie is bewitched."

CHAPTER 2

RORREN WEDGED HIS HEAD inside the fuse box and peered into a tangle of wires and motherboards. He noted scorch marks where lightning had broken through the outer edifice of the tower. The reflective plating had saved most of the parts, but the energy conductor looked fried.

He switched on his flashlight, and the beam penetrated deeper inside the forty-foot tower, illuminating a vast network of complex connections. Though the towers would stand for a thousand years, the interior parts were delicate and constantly needed repairs.

Felt odd to use a flashlight with the suns burning his skin through the linen of his shirt.

The damage seemed confined to the generator.

Rorren withdrew from the opening and put his hat on. A thick heat weighed on his body at the tower's top section, and his shirt was soaked through. He leaned against the harness, one hand gripping the metal rod of the ladder and looked down.

Brawn patrolled the base of the tower. He'd circled enough times that a path had been worn into the sand. The raven swayed with the movement of Brawn's lithe muscles, riding his back like a snobbish noble carried by a servant.

"That wing is healed now. Stop using Brawn as a crutch."

Caw.

Rorren grunted, put the flashlight in his mouth, and ducked into the darkness. He reached for the generator with a screwdriver, his upper torso suspended above the abyss. Wires sparked and a flash of flame burned his fingers. He bit on the flashlight, whacked his head, and dropped the screwdriver.

He shook out the sting, hat falling off as he leaned into the sunlight. Brawn hurried over to the round-rimmer and the raven squawked.

"You must hate the desert to punish it like that with your singing."

That the two animals formed a bond seemed natural to Rorren. There were few of Brawn's kind left and no ravens on Desandor. The unlikely pair proved the best company because neither questioned his scars.

Without his hat, he knew he wouldn't last in the heat. He pulled an extra screwdriver from his utility belt and replaced the panel, wiping his forehead twice between motions. Sweat and sand made the climb down the vertical grips dangerous. He worked methodically, rung by rung, and let his brain do the same with the problems ahead.

He kept thinking about the two crops he'd lost. If he succeeded in restoring the towers at each corner of the farm, he might never have to leave the comfort of the wasteland.

He retrieved his hat and glanced up into the cloudless sky. The shipping lane to the spaceport crossed over his land, so there was almost always air traffic. Had the vessels used a lower orbit, he might have worried about the outside world looming too close to his corner of paradise. As it was, they couldn't see anything from such vast heights.

"Brawn, we're going to town."

He needed expensive parts to get the towers working again.

Brawn loved the town. The kencat bounded to the sandcrawler and ejected the raven from his hide. The bird extended its wings and hovered above the sand, cawing in irritation. It landed half a stride from Rorren.

He knelt and said, "Come here."

The bird flailed at Rorren, but he waited. Something he learned from the desert. If he stood still long enough, the entire landscape could change. He knew it just required patience.

With a twist of its neck, the raven hopped once toward him and then stopped. Now seemed like the time to teach the raven who was boss, especially since the bird seemed inclined to stay.

Rorren extended his arm.

The raven closed the gap between them, flapping its wings once to get enough lift to land on Rorren's forearm. Its talons were sharp but did not break his skin.

"Was that so hard?"

The raven made a noise, not quite a full squawk, and turned its head away.

He closed gentle hands around the body of the bird. The feathers were softer than when he first retrieved it—a few weeks out of the sun and sand had eased some coarseness from them.

"You can't tell how far a raven will fly by the size of its wings." He lifted the raven to his chest. "But I'd reckon you can go pretty far."

The body in his hands stiffened.

He pushed the raven into the sky and let go when the momentum was right. Black feathers flew forward.

Its wings didn't spread. It tumbled to the ground head first and temperamentally cawed at Rorren.

"Not yet, then. That makes two of us."

The bird shuttered off the sand and hopped to the sandcrawler. Not so easy for Rorren.

Rather than dwell on it, he checked his wallet. No grubmite flew out, but he growled and slammed the door. Negotiations at the market were dangerous and his trench coat stood out in a crowd.

———

Desandor Dock welcomed the locals with a crooked sign next to the salvage yard. A mangled pile of metal rose from behind a rusted fence and intermittent sparks spilled onto the unpaved street. The road led past a cluster of houses to a Sandorian church. The church was comprised of four wooden beams supporting a roof made from sage and straw. There were no windows or walls. The only indication of its purpose was a textile banner strung between the beams. It was said to depict the time the Great Spirit visited an ancient nomadic tribe.

Thanks to Rorren's intervention, the nomadic tribes were still allowed to sell their textiles at the market, though it made the Sandorian government officials unhappy. The beautiful and affordable designs out sold the bigger manufacturers tenfold.

Grinning as he thought about that, Rorren moved beyond the church. The street opened to the large market square.

Vendors stood beneath canopies of tattered cloth, peddling their overpriced goods. Only foot traffic was allowed beyond the church, so Rorren parked beside the quaint structure.

The kencat was at his side when he stepped out of the crawler. Brawn's size kept the riffraff away, but the noise and commotion hypnotized the kencat and he often wandered off to seek adventures.

The raven nestled into the utility pouch at Rorren's side.

"Never pegged you for the shy type."

As they entered the bustling marketplace, the raven's beak stuck out from under the pouch's flap.

Above the tops of the vendor canopies, Rorren could make out the wall of the docking port. Hagglers shouted over the rumble of spaceship engines.

Rorren pushed his way through the crowd, a task made easier by the presence of Brawn. Mothers pulled children in close at the sight of the sabretooth tiger. Rorren didn't bother telling them his pet was mostly harmless.

He made inquiries at a few vendor stations, his leather coat and physique intimidating them into giving quick and efficient answers. They directed him to a brothel down one of the offshoot alleyways.

"Stay." He pointed at the wall just outside the front entrance. The last thing he needed was Brawn mixed up with the unsavory types roaming about. Brawn landed on his haunches with a snort. Rorren gave his pet a warning glare and ascended the steps.

Light blinded him briefly when he pulled open the curtain. Dive bars at the space dock prided themselves on illuminating every newcomer while concealing their patrons in near darkness. Hidden in the pouch at his side, the raven squirmed like his stomach.

That was the way at Desandor Dock. The rarer or more expensive the item, the seedier the place Rorren had to go to get it.

He ducked out of the entry light without drawing too much attention.

Rorren pegged the most dangerous man in the room sitting at the bar. Aklaren marauders frequented dives like this one. The one at the bar barked his order and kicked out the stool from the creature next to him. Bony fingers grabbed the cup and strings of white hair touched the dented body armor on his shoulders as he tilted his head to drink. He wiped his scaled mouth with savage intensity and then pinned his oily eyes on Rorren.

With a single motion, he propped his loot bag on the counter and jewels and dodd dribbled out into the dim light. Pillaged goods he used as a dare. The Aklaren gangster must have pegged Rorren, too.

Rorren cracked his knuckles, told himself now wasn't the time to settle vendettas and approached the bar.

"Looking for Jagmar the Rocbull."

The barkeep motioned to a booth in the far-right corner. Rorren nodded and put his hand to the weapon concealed beneath his coat as he marched forward. There would be many surprised looks if he revealed the Galactic Order staff that hung in a compressed tube at his side.

"Hiya handsome," a woman said as she cleared drinks from a table.

Females rarely ventured to Desandor and the few that did show up were not hardy stock.

Rorren needed hardy. A robust female who could withstand the heat and still cook, clean and wash for him and rear his children.

Another female at the bar lifted her drink toward him.

Above all, he needed a woman who didn't mind being with a murderer. Not many of those around.

Ignoring both flirtations, he identified his contact.

The seller, also Aklaren, was a Rocbull from the untamed Ullur system east of Cardinal World Beta. He stood two heads taller than Rorren and his shoulders were twice as broad. Ribbed spikes ran down his neck, arms and the bridge of his nose. His leathered skin could stop the bullet from a veer rifle, as Rorren had learned from experience.

"Farm boy!" He slapped a callused hand between Rorren's shoulder blades. With the other, he pulled a square cube from his pocket. "Energy conductor is hard to come by. They say you in need."

Rorren slipped into the booth opposite the Rocbull and examined the circuit that might save his farm.

"How much?" Rorren asked.

"Ten thousand dodd."

"Ten!?" Rorren scoffed. "I'll give you three. And that's generous."

The seller smiled, revealing thick yellow teeth.

"Farm boy, starfruit crop will bring millions of dodd. Ten is cheap."

Most space travelers called the local sand crops "starfruit" because the food lasted in deep space for decades and lost none of its flavor or vitamin content.

The raven wiggled inside the pouch, distracting Rorren as two more Aklaren Rocbulls entered.

Aklaren in Scorth meant 'to plunder.'

Rorren hated the marauders almost as much as the Scorth. They were cut from the same bad space matter. Meant trouble if either species got comfortable on Desandor.

"Three thousand dodd," Rorren said again.

The seller shook his head and gestured toward the scaled gangster.

"Look, farm boy, my boss over there, Hevcar Duronilan, you hear of him? He likes the profits. Now, you do me favor, you do him favor and we don't forget. Seven thou."

Rorren ran his hand over his chin.

"Five, and I'll throw in a case of starfruit."

The seller leaned forward. His stomach, exposed beneath is armor, squeezed over the top of the table.

"Because I like you, farm boy. Deal."

Rorren reached across the table to shake the massive hand, but the raven shot out of the pouch.

The Rocbull reared and the table overturned.

A dozen hands grabbed for the animal as it shrieked and fluttered up to the rafters. A living bird on Desandor would fetch a premium price, so Rorren fought off unsavory treasure seekers.

The raven dove for the loot bag on the bar, the worst mistake it could have made.

Talons scooped up a jeweled pendant, but Hevcar Duronilan caught it by the legs.

Rorren took a blow to the chin, ducked and squeezed through the brawlers, coming out on the other side to see the raven stab Hevcar with its beak. The animal refused to let go of the jewel.

Hevcar lifted the bird over his head, aiming its body at the bar to bring it down in a killing blow.

Rorren caught the marauder by the elbow. The gang boss locked black eyes on Rorren. They sparkled with murder.

"You have a death wish, aux rand?"

Rorren didn't let go.

"That belongs to me."

The raven flapped its wings, futilely attempting to escape Hevcar's hold.

"Sent your pet to steal from me?"

"To steal what you stole? Not a bad idea, but I prefer the direct approach," Rorren said as he untangled the cursed bird from Hevcar's bony fingers. He wrenched the pendant out of a sharp talon.

Caw! Caw! Caw!

Rorren handed the jewel to its keeper, ignoring the thrashing complaints of the bird.

"Stop," he said and the raven shut up.

Hevcar pocketed the pendant and spat on Rorren's boots. His two Rocbull henchmen drew up on either side, causing the other bar patrons to scamper into the shadows.

"You kiss your mother with that mouth?" Rorren asked.

"I see that bird again and it will be the last time you ever do," the gang boss said.

Rorren stood his ground, fingers itching to draw his staff.

Hevcar sneered, but with his property restored and Rorren's boots soiled, he must have lost interest in a real fight.

Rorren didn't move until the gangsters vanished beyond the spotlight. He shoved the raven into the bag and sought out Jagmar the Rocbull. He paid and took the energy conductor with the promise he would send two cases of fruit for the trouble.

The raven perched itself in the passenger seat of the sandcrawler, preening its feathers and Rorren caught another whiff of dark magic.

A flash of memory distracted him. Scorth faces mixed with those of his dead friends. The remains of war—like entrails from a hideous carcass—spanned the galaxy.

"Must be loco to keep saving your hide," he told the bird.

Worse than loco is the man who deceives himself, Rorren remembered his father saying.

Mic Rorren started the engine, hoping never again to smell the dangerous sorcery that decided the Scorth War.

The problem was the planet reeked.

Chapter 3

Somewhere in the Galaxy

70 years ago

V ESTA DESCENDED FROM THE skies, shedding her raven form and turning Scorth, inserting herself into the raid at the perfect moment.

She ignored the surprised hiss of the hairy four-legged resaurs and the shouts of the Aklaren who rode them. All that mattered to her was the drawstring pouch clutched between the trembling fingers of a child. Vesta couldn't remember finding such a place in all in the galaxy. Precious metals were never so plentiful that children used them as pocket change.

The child's pouch sagged under the weight of gold. Vesta thrashed it out of the girl's hands. The contents burst, making delicious clinking sounds as coins scattered in the dirt.

"Pick that up!"

Vesta saw her reflection in the child's eyes. Her dark hair fell over spiked spaulders and her form-fitting armor glistened beneath a feathered cape meant to terrify. The spikes were a new addition to her regalia. She liked them almost as much as the stolen diamonds embroidered in the cape. The gems sparkled when she moved, swirling around her like a starry night.

Other species often mistook Scorth for human—incredibly insulting. She was far more magnificent and radiant than the pathetic human child before her could ever hope to be.

Trembling hands offered the trinkets to Vesta.

She swiped them and shoved the child into a transport crate. The girl fell into her mother's arms, crying and making a pathetic spectacle.

"Away with you, naset," Vesta hissed.

One of Vesta's Aklaren comrades slammed the crate shut.

As he rode up on his resaur, Zarog, their Rodilian leader, surveyed the victory with visible arrogance. His eyes, a pale wintery grey of the eastern ice, darted to Vesta, freezing her in place at his feet.

"Another successful raid. I suppose Scorth witches do have some uses."

Everything Zarog said to her was laced with disgust. Vesta hated him for it. He hated her. They found their truce in mutual dislike.

Overthrowing him to lead his gang of Aklaren marauders sweetened her every thought. Vesta was a fugitive from Ragora and that limited her options. She owed him for taking her in which forced her to grovel.

Over the last forty years, she'd done enough groveling to sour her stomach.

Vesta fingered the crown jewel around her neck, replacing ugly thoughts with lighter ones. She had the purple stone inset in a silver necklace she raided from a wealthy village several years ago. It was her mother's jewel, stolen from the Queen's Rishka. Smiling, she thought about her mother's face, relishing the stricken look of horror when her mother realized who had bested the Queen and taken the treasure.

"Now you prove yourself again," Zarog said. "At dawn, we take the sanctuary."

Aux rand idiot.

Aklaren always did go after more than was wise. When she joined Zarog and his band, it was with the promise she would have equal weight in deciding targets. She had become nothing more than the disrespected hench-witch to the boss.

"A moment to ponder, wise-one. My head still attached to my neck is worth more than any baubles we might find inside."

Zarog never looked at her directly. Just as well. His cratered skin reminded her of the crusted rock formations on Ragora's diamond moon. Balding with a few greasy strands of white hair, some braided, that fell to his shoulders, he was as repulsive as she was beautiful. The zealot often used her beauty to his advantage, leaving her feeling debased and annoyed.

"All you need do is open the gate. You can stand there like the useless sage hen you are while we take care of the guards."

He dug his spurs into the beast's hide and it squealed.

"Move out!" he ordered.

The cart lurched forward and the weeping villagers packed inside were lulled into silence by the churn of the wheels over the forest floor.

Aside from abundant precious minerals, the strange outlying planet possessed a magnetic field strong enough to disrupt electronics and detour advanced spacecraft from venturing into orbit. It explained why there was so much left to steal.

Vesta climbed up the resaur, thinking about the Betanese steam bath she would treat herself to once off the loathsome planet. An indulgence courtesy of the gold coins in her pocket.

As she rode to catch up to her smelly, foul-tempered boss, she passed the cart, overhearing the mother consoling the girl.

"Scorth witches have lips of deep red wine, faces fair as polished bone and blazing eyes of ice fire. They are beautiful as they are cruel."

"Why are they?" The naset asked, wiping away dried tears.

"Because when you lose your soul to greed, nothing is left but evil."

Sneering at them as she passed, Vesta pretended the words meant nothing to her.

At the fork in the road, the cart was taken to base camp, where the captives would either be made to work or sold for a profit. The cart drifted out of sight, leaving Vesta to tally all the treasure she had taken from the peasants.

Instead, she found something taken from her.

Her peace of mind. Rationalizations of her actions over the past forty years were distorted through a new lens. Had her child-eyes gotten to her mother the way the eyes of the naset lingered with Vesta now? Is that why her mother punished her?

Zarog left her no time to contemplate further.

She was grateful.

They camped on a cliff overlooking the expansive valley and the trees surrounding the sanctuary. The steeples and towering brick gave the religious epicenter of the region the feel of a well-fortified fortress.

Zarog told them they'd strike at dawn. He outlined a rough plan which all hinged on her. Any successful raid, however small, always went to his head. Made him cocky. Given the terrain and the armed guards, Vesta doubted their ability to confiscate the treasures inside the sanctuary.

With the morning sun came a painful grip on her arm.

"Now, witch, time for you to turn."

Glaring at him, Vesta sighed, then rose to her feet, fingers wrapping around the jewel at her neck. She hated transforming in front of him because he always confiscated the jewel afterward. He said it was for her protection, but she knew it was because he liked her trapped.

With a plume of smoke flaring her cape, her essence funneled away and she became the raven.

Her wings caught the winds to the upper air, carrying her over the forest with the majesty of a shooting star. Flying teased her into thinking she belonged with the stars, but then it slapped her. High above worlds, looking down on inhabitants she did not understand, she knew she didn't belong anywhere.

Her soul soared as light as her body. Not lost. Not evil as the mother accused.

Sailing into an open window at the top of the sanctuary, Vesta navigated the stone corridors until she found the control room. Technology on the planet was primitive due to the magnetic field. She found the chain and pully system that operated the drawbridge.

Vesta perched on a high beam, not drawing attention while she studied how to open the fortress. It would have been much simpler if Zarog allowed her to keep the jewel. She could transform, incapacitate the guards and use her hands to lower the bridge.

She'd have to work twice as hard to accomplish her mission in raven form. For Zarog, a Rodilian she detested, and for money. The thought didn't satisfy her like it usually did.

Soaring from the rafters in secret, Vesta readied to implement her plan and draw the attention of one of the guards.

It started insignificantly.

A wisp of thread.

A small tug.

A net spiraled around her, capturing her before she could react.

She flapped her wings, cawing, but the ropes pulled tight.

As she hung in a ball of feathers and talons, her raven eye watched the guard captain saunter toward her.

"I recognized you, Scorth witch," he said. "We've been expecting an attack."

He barked orders and one of the guards pushed the lever. The draw bridge lowered, welcoming Zarog into a trap.

If she had her voice, she would have laughed.

Served him right.

Maybe it served her right, too.

The captain tossed her into a cage. She heard the sounds of the fight echoing in the corridors. Hours passed. No one came for her. She didn't need to see the battle to know the outcome.

Zarog and her mother's jewel were long gone.

———————

Desandor
Present Day

The new energy conductor had been installed and Rorren stood with his hand poised over the ignition panel.

He watched clouds piling against the horizon, inching nearer to the farm's borders. The dune beneath his feet blazed as hot as melted gold from the vaults of Ragora.

A clump of sand wedge between his toes, a nuisance growing ever more present against his skin. Ignoring it and the crop-killing storm in the distance, Rorren glanced at Brawn and the raven.

"My dad always said, when in doubt, hit the red button and run."

He flipped the switch and the guts inside the tower rattled the outer walls, vibrating the sand where metal met the ground. Columns of light blasted to the top of the four-pronged spire, gathering into a triangle churning with voltage.

Strings of electricity splashed over the spires, powering the shield with a rumble so furious Rorren forgot all about the sand clump between his toes.

The power grew, reaching out with strands of energy like deformed skeletal bone and Rorren waited for the real magic to erupt.

Prongs of light decomposed and vanished.

Electricity faded into smoke like Rorren's hope for anything miraculous.

Cursing, he tore off his boot and sock and chucked them at the tower. After more cursing, he found Brawn and the raven watching his meltdown. Lucky for him, animals couldn't talk.

Standing on one leg between Brawn's ears, the raven's bead-eye blackened, appearing not the least bit puzzled by the outburst. The kencat tilted his head and the raven wobbled.

"I don't know why it won't work," he said to Brawn.

A crack of lightning accentuated his statement:

Inside the turmoil of the storm, more flashes of light made Rorren's spirit sink further.

He tore open the control panel and started pulling wires. Fused them together. It wasn't an act of desperation; he knew what he was doing. He kept telling himself that over and over. The intestines of the control panel spilled over the side in a twisted hack job of ingenuity.

"You're worse than a foul-tempered woman."

He kicked the console, sending a silent prayer skyward, and flipped the switch again.

The wind picked up, darting sand particles against his skin with increasing force.

The tower sputtered to life and Rorren watched with less hope but more faith as the triangle formed between the prongs.

Caw! Caw!

The raven flew from Brawn's head, gusts of wind tossing it off course as it veered toward Rorren. He lifted his hand to shield himself from impact, but the raven turned at the last moment.

"You finally fly," he shouted. Not precisely the miracle he hoped for.

The annoying cackle faded upward, winds lifting the bird higher into the storm. Rorren craned his vision to the towers.

The unexpected happened.

The raven flew straight into the prongs, vanishing into the triangle of light, swallowed whole.

Feathers, wings, and beak, there and then gone.

Rorren's shirt and trousers flapped around him while sand pelted metal and flesh. He was frozen in astonishment—all that effort, saving the raven twice, teaching it to fly, all so it could suicide itself.

Brawn stood on his hind legs, front paws pressing to the tower, body stretched upward as he pined for his missing friend. The sound of the approaching storm muffled Brawn's whimpers.

The tower hadn't shut down yet and Rorren prayed harder as strikes of lightning hit dangerously close to the crop.

Eight long years of fighting the land for his place and failing in the end.

He sunk to his knees and grabbed a handful of harsh, hot sand. His crop moved beneath the storm, dropping under the clouds like the prow of a doomed ship. Nothing left but to watch his future scorched under a barrage of killing lightning.

A beam shot beyond the tower prongs across the dunes, forcing the storm to cower. Rorren scrambled to his feet, but the beam vanished into an endless wasteland before he could see what triggered it. A new spark flared up on the horizon, too far away for him to make out anything significant.

He waited, and then, with the beam barreling over his head from the tower at the south end of the farm, it connected with the west tower and closed the loop.

A floating net of light filled the sky, covering his crop, instantly fending off the storm's electric threat.

The raven tumbled out of the light beam.

Racing across the sand with one booted foot, Rorren caught the bird mid-fall. Its feathers were coated in wet sand from the storm. He brushed them off and the bird swelled until its normal, annoying voice returned. He couldn't help but grin.

"I'll admit, maybe you're a little impressive."

Caw.

"My saving angel."

He ran his fingers down the bird's sleek chest and it puffed, tamed if just for an instant.

"Don't let it go to your head."

Lightening hit the shield and in reflex, Rorren ducked for cover. The net absorbed the energy from the strike and transferred the charge to the tower, making the lights brighter. It was a rare moment of triumph. As Rorren climbed into the sandcrawler, raven in tow, he almost forgot about his father.

No storm lasts forever.

CHAPTER 4

THE SMELL OF FRIED desert moss pulled Rorren through the vendor stands. He scanned the market for the source and saw a neon sign flashing *Moe's Moss Hut* halfway up the main square.

Lunch wasn't what he was after, but it dawned on him that he hadn't indulged in a bit of fast food for months. Craving it now, he walked to the shop, anticipating an afternoon treat.

The stand was old and paint-chipped, but there was a line, and, from the smell of things, they had to be the best at port.

Food trays under glass panels held an assortment of mosses, reds from the southern dunes and every shade of greens commonly found under rocks and sage brush.

Three stools beneath the tattered canopy were occupied. Two old nomads played checkers at a picnic table across the street at the food court.

He approached the register.

When the teenage Sandorian with a studded piercing in her lipless mouth noticed him, he detected a flicker of annoyance in her round brown eyes.

Was she trying to see the scars beneath his trench coat?

In the reflection of a rusted mirror behind the counter, he saw some commotion and understood her look of disgust.

Hevcar Duronilan, looking as menacing as a snake on the hunt, upturned the scales around his mouth in a sneer. Hevcar was Rodilian and unlike his henchman, Rorren knew he was as cunning as ruthless.

His clawed fingers wrapped around the long wrist of a Sandorian woman. She clutched her young child to her side but didn't hold to her purse as tightly.

Hevcar opened the satchel strapped across his armor and she emptied her precious few dodd inside. The money she most likely saved for food and clothes for the young boy hiding behind her bright-colored skirt.

The last thing Rorren wanted was another run-in with the gangster.

The audacity of robbing someone in broad daylight rankled every fiber in him.

Rorren glanced at the clock above the mirror and wrinkled his brow. Maybe it was time for a standoff.

Hevcar lifted his hand, reflected in the mirror, intending to strike the woman after taking her money.

Rorren crossed the street in three strides and caught the wrist of the Rodilian in midair.

They stood suspended together for an instant, locking hostile gazes.

"You do have a death wish?"

Hevcar clung onto the wrist of the Sandorian woman.

"Let her go."

Hevcar sneered, pulling his arm from Rorren's grasp.

"Let her go and return her money."

Rorren tossed some moss in Hevcar's face, making his scales go white with rage.

The gangster let go of the woman and she ushered her child to a safe corner of the food court. Hevcar pulled a rod out of the sheath fastened to his armor and flicked his wrist. Spikes emerged down the metal to the hand grip.

The onlookers vacated tables so fast chairs tipped over. Wetting his lips with a grin, Rorren drew the compressed staff from his belt. He copied the Rodilian and his diamond-tipped spear appeared with one flick.

"You just had to do this the hard way," Rorren said.

Hevcar unstrapped the satchel of stolen goods from his shoulder, letting it fall to the ground.

"A soldier of the Galactic Order thinks he can take me down?" Hevcar asked, shaking his greasy head.

"Easily."

"I'm going to kill you and take your money," Hevcar said.

"That the best threat you got? You wouldn't have enough to blow your nose if your brains were gunpowder."

This time, a growl accompanied the sneer. Rorren missed this kind of action and that worried him. Twirling his staff, he circled Hevcar. A crowd gathered and Rorren heard onlookers shouting bets about the outcome.

The odds were against him. Just how he liked it.

Taking Hevcar wouldn't be easy, but Rorren was confident. It was the three Rocbull henchmen in the crowd that worried him. They'd come after him if he bested their boss.

The clang of weapons sent echoes of battle through the marketplace alleyways, drawing more spectators. Two hundred pounds of anger hurled toward Rorren, overpowering him at first and winning a strike to his shoulder. Grunting at the pain of the spike embedded in his flesh, Rorren pushed off the attack.

He sidestepped the lunging Hevcar and slapped his staff across Hevcar's obliques, giving back some painful blows. The action triggered a new luster in his enemy's eyes and Rorren dodged more of Hevcar's superhuman assault. Landing a strike on Hevcar's knee sent him down, exposing his chin for Rorren to hit again with the staff.

The ruffian fell flat on his back.

Rorren leaned on his staff and peered down at the mass before him.

"Tell me, what else is nasty, smelly, and you avoid when it's lying in the street?" He asked, drawing laughter from the crowd.

The marauder flung a handful of sand into Rorren's face. The grains blinded him and he endured a few powerful hits to the stomach before doubling over. His eyes stung, but he caught Hevcar's boot before it made contact with his head. Swinging his staff at the marauder's other leg, he sent the desert scum to the dirt again.

Caw! Caw! Caw!

Rorren's vision cleared in time to see his raven swooping toward the loot bag.

Every time.

"You're fouling me up again," Rorren said as he regained his balance. The raven scooped a jeweled pendant and soared into the suns.

Hevcar lost interest in the battle with Rorren, grabbed the loot bag, and re-sheathed his weapon.

"I feast on bird tonight," he said and his Rocbull gangsters glowered in agreement.

"The only thing you'll be eating is crow."

Ignoring his pun, the four Aklaren barreled into the crowd. They piled into a motor cruiser and the hovercraft lifted into the sky after Angel. There was no way Rorren could catch them in the lethargic sandcrawler.

He scanned the area and his muscles buzzed with adrenaline. Another cruiser was parked outside one of the market shops, and Rorren slipped all the money he had on him into the hand of its nearby owner before he jumped into the pilot seat.

Flying up into the sky, Rorren questioned his wisdom. Here he was doing the thing he loved—chasing bad guys—right out in the open for the first time in years.

The raven veered right and the Aklaren gang followed. They fired at her.

Swinging the cruiser after them, Rorren threw himself into a hard right turn and the force threatened to fling him from the pilot seat.

His coat flapped against the turbulence and he pulled the collar over his scars.

Below him, grains of sand swirled, but under the barrage of gunfire, the raven didn't seem to be able to call on the sand to help her as she had before.

Every so often, the pendant in her talons reflected bouts of sunlight like a beacon for friend and foe.

The marauders followed the bird straight into the badlands. Crossing over the border of the Blood River sent a prick of uneasiness across Rorren's skin. He never liked this part of Desandor. The seedier population camped in the red rocks and the place smelled of dark magic.

"I've heard of winging it, Angel, but this is ridiculous."

Revving the engine, Rorren closed the gap between the two cruisers. The tops of twisted rock formations grew between them, separating him from victory.

He matched speed as best he could, taking every swerve faster, trying to close the distance. He swerved again, assuring himself that should he crash into a rock, it would be quick, painless, and better than falling to an agonizing death in the Blood River.

Rorren couldn't shake the feeling that his raven's deadly interest in Hevcar's jewels lifted them higher for a reason.

He spotted a gap in the rocks, and reacted to opportunity without hesitation.

He strained and twisted the wheel to the right, digging his knee into the dashboard.

By the time he realized the two ships were on a collision path, he was committed to the maneuver.

For an endless instant, he floated forward, the bow of his ship aimed at the Aklaren, gravity preventing him from hitting the deck to avoid the onslaught of gunfire.

Just before impact, he jumped out of the ship in desperation, his hands clawing at the rock for any hold.

An undertow of wind fought against him, tearing his fingers over loose pebbles until he managed to find an inlet. His body grazed to a halt against the hot surface.

The explosion from the motor cruiser forced him to pull against the rock, clinging tight to avoid impact with falling debris.

When the heat and raining metal stopped, he used all his power to swing his leg over the ledge and forced himself to a standing position.

He scanned through the forest of rock columns until he spotted Hevcar dangling like a sack of sandfruit from a cliff about twenty feet away.

The bird landed just above him and mocked Hevcar with triumphant cawing. Talons scratched at the pendant, popping loose the jewel in a flash of emerald.

So greedy was her fixation with the treasure that she didn't see Hevcar pull a gun from his boot.

"Move!" Rorren shouted.

Her beak twisted, but she lingered too long. Hevcar opened fire.

Ricocheting bullets hit the rock column behind the bird, showering the two of them with boulders that grew in size. Hevcar did not stop his assault.

The raven's screams sobered Rorren out of his fixed state. A stray shot hit her and the entire rock column gave way.

The Aklaren and the raven tumbled together, but the heavier of the two reached the Blood River first.

As the raven fell, something strange happened.

Rorren, climbing down, was torn between watching the scene and focusing on survival.

About twenty feet above the river of red sand, the raven's black feathers doubled, then tripled in size.

A sick heat fermented in Rorren's stomach.

The now large feathers hit the sand, splattering mud just as Rorren reached the bottom of the cliff.

His muscles throbbed like he'd been climbing for hours. The strain made his movements sluggish and frustratingly slow as he struggled to the edge of the quicksand.

The Blood River swallowed the feathers like a starved beast, earning its name not because of its color but because of its appetite.

Rorren scanned for a way across, and discovered a trail of boulders clogging the river at intervals. Taking his time so he didn't stumble in, he jumped from one to the next. He could hear the sloshing of sand as it ran beneath him, hiding unknown lost wonders in its depths.

The barest hint of feathers flashed before him, sinking deeper into the river. He crashed to his knees, balancing over the boulder, then to his stomach, face down, mouth submerged in sand. Rorren tucked tighter to the rock and extended his arm. The pulling current threatened to take him under. He refused to quit. *Son, words contradict, but deeds testify.*

Unknown objects slithered past his fingers and his body slipped from the rock, stopped only by the power of his thighs squeezing over the stone. His head dipped beneath the sand, but his fingers locked onto something heavy.

Yanking and tugging with all his strength, he pried more of it loose by sheer force. His head came up above the sand and he swallowed gulps of air. He heaved. The river fought to hold its prey, but Rorren fought harder, willing to risk his life for the cursed animal.

The raven appeared out of the sand. He found a better hold by latching onto something soft and fleshy.

Arms.

With legs propped against the boulder, he increased the pressure. The body came loose with a snap that sent Rorren stumbling backward. He landed next to the lifeless form and caught his breath before he had the clarity to take in the sight before him.

The body was wrapped in a cape of black feathers. Mud and grime covered every inch of the her. Tendrils of hair were matted across her face, concealing her features.

Peeling away the cape, Rorren discovered a bodice of sleek silver armor. His senses went into an intensified and unsettling state of alertness—like in the war before battle when his palms turned sweaty and he could feel the beat of his heart in his throat.

Scorth armor.

Hearing, smell, and taste lurched into overdrive when he saw the enemy. Tensed fingers brushed the hair from her face.

She looked human, like all Scorth, but there was no denying what she was. The pitch-dark hair and fair skin were unmistakable. Her clothes reeked of it. Even nearly dead, her figure screamed of her arrogant belief that Scorth should rule over everything in the universe.

Rorren rescued a Scorth witch.

Draping elbows over knees, he pondered the situation.

To be in the presence of one of them again, far removed from battle, invited a surreal shiver. Dread flowed through his body at the same maddening pace as the turgid sand river surrounding them.

He watched her chest move with the shallow intake of each breath.

Ah, ginger. Still alive.

He could throw her back, no one would know, and it would be a favor to the universe.

Blood oozed from the gunshot wound across her torso. If he walked away, she would die.

What did he care?

But, hot beans, he did care and he knew why. Cursing the suns silently, he remembered the old warrior from his past saying he'd recognize the moment. Saving the witch was the favor he could do—the last thing—to honor his promise to that forgotten woman from his past.

Looking across the desert, he found the remains of the cruisers smoldering on the side of a far cliff.

Saving her meant carrying her to the spaceport—a grueling three sectors, if not more.

He sat on the boulder, arms resting on knees and mouth dry. Forcing his eyes to the woman's face, he studied with more scrutiny.

Beautiful.

Scorth were always beautiful, but this one was more so than was typical. Somehow, it made her more dangerous. More rank with evil.

"This is for you, Lady Layeyre," he said with a glance at the clouds.

He scooped the limp body up in his arms.

"This makes us even."

CHAPTER 5

R ORREN ENDURED A QUIET agony hauling so much dead weight across the dunes. He climbed upward, straining, and then surveyed the minimal distance he'd covered. Determined to conquer the desert without dehydrating or dropping the bleeding body in his arms he pressed on. The skyline of the spaceport came into view. He stepped toward it erratically. Sweat poured down his face, stinging his eyes.

The sand became finer and denser the closer he got to the shop tents on the city's outskirts. His feet sank deeper into the sand with every step, causing him to grunt against the suction as he lifted them free.

Thirst was an ache convulsing through his body. He dropped the witch onto the hot sand, heard a muffled groan from her lips, but her lashes didn't flutter open.

He stretched his vertebra, heard a crack, and wiped the moisture from his forehead. Scanning the skyline, he honed in on a wooden structure that looked ready to tumble over.

He hoisted the woman over his shoulder with a new goal in sight. His torso and arms ached and he couldn't carry her cradled like a baby anymore. She gasped when her wound hit his shoulder, but he didn't feel guilty enough to change her position.

He stumbled up to the door of the run-down medical station. Glancing inside, he wouldn't have trusted a sunwart he liked to the butchers that owned it. He was dealing with a Scorth witch. Good thing she was worse than vermin.

The nurse came out, bare hands covered in what he hoped wasn't blood. She looked at him and the body over his shoulder with a flat, heavy glance.

"How much can you pay?"

Her indifference didn't faze him.

"Case of sandfruit, but it'll have to be an I.O.U."

The nurse went inside and slammed the door. Rorren set the witch down and waited. He thought they had no deal, but the sour-faced nurse reappeared with a man in a stained lab coat.

Doctor Sawbones, as Rorren named him, was an angular man with a thin mustache. He snagged the Scorth witch by the arms and dragged her inside, the nurse peeling the expensive armor from her body. Rorren followed behind, picking up the pieces and piling them in a corner beside the bed they plopped the witch on.

"Come back in an hour."

"Will she live?"

The nurse snorted, handing the doctor tools from a medical cart. Both ignored Rorren so he left.

He traversed the market to get the sandcrawler, wondering where Brawn might be, when he came across a line draped with various garments.

The witch would need something to wear. He traded an hour worth of labor for the cheapest gown they had and all the water he could drink, then hurried to the sandcrawler he left parked at the church.

On his return to the medical station, he spotted Brawn chasing some sunwarts down an alley.

Reunited, Rorren and his pet arrived at the medical station. Doctor Sawbones greeted them with a frown and lectured Rorren about returning with the promised fruit. The nurse snapped the garment from Rorren's fingers and told him to wait.

Rorren bent, scratching Brawn's ears, and decided the witch must be alive. They wheeled her unconscious body out and the nurse shoved gauze and bandages into Rorren's chest.

Brawn sniffed the Scorth witch with his tail wagging.

"Re-dress it twice a day," the nurse said, "if it shows signs of infection, make her take this." She shoved a bottle into his hands.

She went into the shack, the door slamming behind her.

A few hours later, they were home.

Rorren watched the farmhouse come into view with a heaving sigh of relief.

The day left him wrecked.

Rorren laid the witch out on his bed.

As ordered by Nurse Grump, he re-bandaged her wound. Surprised him to find a neat row of stitches across her muscular abdomen. He decided not to judge doctors by the condition of their rundown buildings next time.

Satisfied with the cleaning, he pulled the sheet over her. She looked too pale.

He wondered if the morning would bring her death. Not sure how to process such an outcome, Rorren left the room and returned to the sandcrawler.

Her armor and fine linen rested in the hauling bed, caked with sand and slime from the river.

Rorren retrieved the stiff gown with a grunt and went to the wash basin behind the house. He threw his muddied trench coat in with it.

Cursing as he worked, he scrubbed the Scorth attire until it returned to its natural glory. Years had passed since he touched material as soft and delicate. Even the worst mud could not ruin the black feathers of the elaborate Scorth cape. His tattered coat looked pitiful next to such grander.

The suns disappeared behind the dunes as Rorren took the clean laundry inside. He laid the witch's ornate costume over a chair in the bedroom. If she lived, come morning, he suspected she might take her clothes and disappear without a word. That was the best-case scenario.

Rorren made up the couch in the den. A pillow and his favorite blanket were all he required to tumble into sleep. He was exhausted.

He woke the next day to find she was still alive. And the next. She fought for her life for the following week.

Rorren managed to help her eat some broth in her delirium and make a few trips to the toilet. Opening for just an instant, he caught a glimpse of her blue eyes, the rarest color for a Scorth. They were dull and lifeless. She wasn't going to make it.

He left her alone only once in those first weeks to deliver the promised sandfruit to the doctor.

The raven opened her eyes. The paint on the ceiling crashed over her in vivid streaks, almost like a dream. Or nightmare. She blinked. Her vision cleared. The strangeness of the familiar surroundings made her gasp. She moved with heavy wings. More oxygen filled her lungs than she was used to. The first full gulp she had tasted in years.

Rays of sunlight warmed her skin.

Skin.

Tears stung her eyes.

She dreamed of freedom for decades. The years faded into a foggy cloud of memory. Planet after planet. Thieves and gangsters. Cages and forests. Cruel masters, wizards, and galactic tyrants. Of them all, the human sand farmer from Desandor set her free.

Struggling upright, the wound above her right hip sent a jetting pain along her nerve endings. She cried out. She despised her weakness but savored the pain. Real pain. The sound of her voice pleased her.

Could she speak?

Could she stand?

Thoughts came only with great effort.

Falling onto the soft pillow, she waited for the throbbing to subside. Her fingers traveled her restored flesh to the bandages.

Across the room, she spotted her clothes—her feathered cape and armor hanging on a chair.

She tried to remember.

A pastel blue dress covered her body.

Blurred memories of a brutal doctor and a hospital came.

For that experience, she was glad the raven form dulled her senses. The assault on them now overwhelmed her. The sunlight hurt.

Every morning after chores, Rorren re-entered his home feeling like he was doing something indecent—or at least unwise.

The first time he made the mistake of entering the private sanctum of a Scorth witch, he'd nearly lost an eye. *Knock first, son*, his father advised after calming the visiting diplomat all those years ago. At the time, Rorren considered it an affront to his pride to be scolded by the man he revered in front of a stranger.

The following years had taught him how dangerous it could be to disturb a Scorth woman, so he tip-toed inside the front door.

He had poked his head into the dreary bedroom enough times over the last few days that the way she slept—ramrod straight on her back—was etched permanently in his mind. This morning, what he saw was shocking.

The witch had propped herself against the pillow, sheets strewn up her torso, gown dotted with small blood spots.

He reached out to knock, but that seemed pointless since her blue eyes were already on him, piercing through him like he wore no clothes.

Wearing his coat around the house just wasn't practical and she raked her eyes over the exposed scars on his neck.

She tried to lift herself upright but slipped against the pillow.

Approaching the bedside—lesser men wouldn't have dared—a giddiness overcame Rorren's terror.

Oh, was he ever going to enjoy this.

"Those drumsticks not working for ya?"

Long lashes dropped over her eyes. Rorren could tell he infuriated her.

Yes, this was turning out better than he imagined.

"Here, let me."

Touching her shoulder with a gentle hand, he guided her into a sitting position.

He doubted any human had ever touched her.

She was prickly as a barbwire fence, even without her armor. She probably frightened small children when she wore it.

Tucking in the pillow behind her, he held in a chuckle.

Part of him worried she might wake in the middle of the night and murder him while he slept. That fear passed now that he saw how weak she was.

Her chest lifted in heavy wallows like the labored breathing of an enraged Rocbull.

"You must have been a cold turkey for a long time."

Expelling a lengthy sigh, the Scorth witch faced him.

At the military academy he learned a little about his enemy. Scorth culture. Scorth rituals. Scorth war tactics. Scientists estimated that Scorth aged the equivalent of one year for every four human years.

Rorren thought his raven looked close to his age, thirty-five, which made her one-hundred-forty years old. She was not young, but middle age was still likely five decades away. He had known Scorth as old as two hundred. Rumors had it some lived to be well over three hundred.

He dropped his hand from her shoulder and she balanced upright.

"There. A new roosting spot for you."

She was *his* raven, he kept thinking, *his friend*. Except Scorth were greedy. Dangerous. Evil.

She probably thought him weak for showing her compassion. She didn't know he was a murderer. He might be more compassionate if he kicked her out.

He cleared his throat.

"I'm getting breakfast. You want to join me?"

Those dark lashes seemed like black molasses from her soul that had bubbled up and spilled out. Looking up at him from under them, he saw thoughts racing inside her head.

Scorth women wore their hair coiled and high, but after her many days in bed, the raven's hair was a wilderness. Rorren grinned. He had never seen a Scorth woman, so—what was the word? Messy? Comical?

He extended his hand.

Vulnerable.

"Come on then. Stand up. You can cook for me."

She glared with all the malice of her kind.

Never argue with a woman, his father warned him. *You lose more by winning*.

"Let's get a few things straight about our odd predicament."

She rested her hands on the sheets with her palms flat, fingers lacking the dexterity to grip.

"Scorth aren't ravens. They're a bunch of vultures. Never met one I could stand."

The weight of his own words crushed him with guilt. Saying them with so much passion helped him hide the lie in them. Of all the humans on the four Cardinal Worlds, he was among a handful who knew the true worth of a Scorth.

She inhaled, looking weary.

"You're only here now because you saved my crop. I owed you."

Another lie. Rorren angled his body toward the bedroom door.

"As soon as you can walk out of here, I expect you to."

The woman pushed herself off the bed, standing up in a rage despite her condition. She wobbled two steps and her legs gave out. She hit the floor with a cry of pain, then propped herself up on her hands, clenching that lovely jaw.

Rorren hated to see anyone crawling like a wounded animal, even his worst enemy. He bent and she growled at him when his hand touched her shoulder.

"Now you sound like Brawn."

Despite her objections, he helped her to the bed, careful not to disturb her injury. He could almost taste the anger emanating from her being.

Ignoring it, he plopped on the bed beside her. She rolled over, away from him.

"How did you get cursed like that, anyway?"

Silence.

"Kencat got your tongue? Or are you afraid all you can do is talk birdy to me?"

She peered over her shoulder with her lips parted. Rorren half expected some curse to come at him from behind those perfect teeth.

"You need to eat something."

Rorren prevented his grin from appearing and folded his arms.

"You need to eat and you know you can't without my help."

He discovered that cooking up some grub was almost enjoyable when done with morbid delight.

Returning to the bedroom with a bowl of hot cereal, Rorren sat beside her and scooped up a spoonful.

Life couldn't get any better than witnessing her utter humiliation.

"Come on, Angel. You will never fly the nest unless you regain your strength."

The sheets stirred, but stalagmites in the eastern caves formed faster. The Scorth witch finally sat up, nostrils flaring.

Rorren held the spoon in front of her mouth, relishing the sheer absurdity of it. Would she really eat from his hand? He wouldn't believe it until he saw it.

She hesitated.

He waited, with the spoon hovering just beyond her mouth.

The nearness of his fingers to her teeth sobered him. He could lose one.

Her mouth opened and she took the food, chewing as if she only vaguely remembered how. She swallowed like it hurt.

"The food is im-peck-able, but no, I'm not going to chew it first if that's how you've been taking it."

Those striking eyes sent daggers at him and he laughed outright. He hadn't laughed in a long time.

CHAPTER 6

I N THE BARN, ALONG each side of the sandcrawler, piles of random junk had accumulated over the years—things Rorren thought he might use one day.

He tossed away the tarp, coughing at the sand and dust he stirred. Satisfied after locating an old wooden chair and two broken end tables, he ended his scavenger hunt.

He tore the legs from the chair and then dismantled the end tables until he was left with two large metal rings. He hammered and measured, using his teeth to store nails that he used at various intervals.

Once finished, he gained some distance and looked at his masterpiece.

It wasn't pretty, but his Scorth guest's new mobile chair was functional. Best throne she would get in the wasteland, other than the latrine.

With hinges creaking, Rorren proudly wheeled the chair into the bedroom.

The witch looked from the chair to him and back again.

No anger or disgust there.

Surprising.

"You want to try it?"

The witch perked against the pillows. When Rorren neared to help her into the chair, she did not flinch. Maybe he had tamed the feral she-cat. He stepped back when she was settled, prepared if she was tempted to claw his face.

Waiting for a beat to ensure his safety, he pushed her into the main living area.

They arrived and no one lost an eye.

Rorren moved her to the edge of the kitchen table where her plate awaited. He dished up a meager breakfast for each of them.

He seated himself on the opposite side of the table, pretending not to watch her as she stared at the fork.

"Give it a try."

She paused, hesitating, before snaking her hand across the table. After three failures, she gave up her attempt to grasp the handle.

A strange, inexplicable impulse overcame Rorren, prompting him into danger. He took the fork, her delicate white digits, and matched the two as if they were always meant to be.

He let go in a hurry. Burying his head in his meal, he cursed Lady Layeyre for making him reach out like that.

The witch stabbed at the food in awkward jerks until catching a single fleck of food between the prongs. With total concentration, she lifted the fork to her often-sneering lips. She slid the food into her mouth, chewed, and swallowed hard.

"At this rate, you'll be done by midnight."

That provoked another sneer, but her eyes told Rorren a different story. Unlike most Scorth he encountered there was something humble about her, maybe due to her predicament. He suspected she had never been as destitute or dependent in all the years of her long life.

"We are going on a little trip today."

Her body went rigid.

"Don't get your chickadee in a twist. It's to visit friends."

She watched him with her fingers wrapped around the utensil as if she'd achieved the most extraordinary feat among all the men and Scorth in the galaxy.

"My neighbors. The old widow and her grandson."

No objection. After eating the last bites off his plate, Rorren went to the sink.

"It's my weekly visit, and you need a bath. You stink worse than Brawn."

Her eyes pierced his head.

"You know I'm right. Would you rather I washed you?" Rorren asked, lifting his brow.

The Scorth stabbed the fork into the table.

He wasn't sure whether her strength or sudden dexterity surprised him most.

"Didn't think so."

Brawn came in through the side door and trotted to the table, nestling his head under the witch's elbow. She left the fork wedged in the table and took the kencat's head between her hands. He purred.

Brawn was Rorren's protector, but clearly, he had fallen under the witch's spell.

Most Scorth were incapable of the affection that she showed to the beast. Thinking about how to cultivate that trait left Rorren grumpy. He pushed the implications far from his thoughts—but ignoring Lady Layeyre's last wish was not so easily achieved.

He pulled the fork out of the table and glared.

"A Scorth witch on Desandor. Whatever you were doing out here, it can't be good."

The sandcrawler treaded the dunes like a caterpillar inching its way across a branch. What took only a few minutes in a motor cruiser, the sandcrawler could do in an hour. Brawn slept in the hauling bed, undisturbed by the gentle bouncing. The raven woman kept her eyes forward, silent across from Rorren in the passenger seat.

Her presence upended his routine.

"I've lived here since the war ended eight years ago," he said.

Rorren saw the grandson on the covered deck, sweeping futilely at the endless sand. The widow appeared, framed by the front door, somehow knowing he was about to arrive.

Rorren lifted his chin toward the house.

"She's been here all her life. Your people killed her children."

The witch cast her glance to her lap.

"Her grandson is all she has left."

Her fingers gripped the handle of the passenger door, concern in her treacherous eyes.

"Don't worry. Metra is a good woman. She'll help you."

The Scorth witch did not look convinced.

Rorren parked the crawler. He turned to her and said, "Wait here," as if she had a choice with her limited physical abilities.

Greeting his neighbors, Rorren found them both preoccupied with studying the woman in the passenger seat. Metra couldn't see her well, but Rorren suspected her inner eyes were glancing deep into the soul of the Scorth. Apparently, what she found delighted her enough to welcome in the evilest soul in the galaxy as if she were kin.

"Poor little birdie," she said. She reached for Jon, but the teenager's jaw gaped open so wide Rorren expected he might choke on blowing dust.

"Holy ginger! The raven is a Scorth witch? Did you know they could shapeshift?"

Jon's unabashed enthusiasm bounded toward Rorren like a runaway freight train.

"She needs your help," Rorren said.

He thought Metra might tell him *I don't help murderers*. That wasn't true. Time and again, Metra came to his aid.

"She saved my crop," he said, but he suspected she already knew.

Metra's black shawl fell to the crooks of her arms as she traversed the front steps. Moving sideways, balancing on Jon, her aged body shifted from one leg to the other over each rung.

Shuffling up to the sandcrawler and reaching it after an eternity, Metra peered into the window. The Scorth witch, frozen in her seat, kept her gaze on the horizon.

Moving up the porch and away from the clash of the two women, Rorren stood beside Jon. The kid had the broom in his hand, holding it like a soldier's staff, and Rorren envied him.

"You got a mess o'hair there, little birdie."

Metra opened the door and waved the witch out.

"You come inside and we'll get you cleaned up."

Somehow, the widow took hold of the witch, the two women balancing each other as they climbed the stairs together.

Rorren gave them space.

The kid fluttered around them like a newly hatched grubmite.

"You're a Scorth witch? Can you make soldiers from stone? I've only heard legends of the Obsedei armies."

Rorren steered Jon by the neck, directing him to help unpack supplies. The widow and the raven disappeared into the house.

"You need to keep your mouth shut," Rorren said, tossing a crate of sandfruit at Jon harder than necessary.

Catching it, Jon stumbled and almost dropped it. The kid carried the carte with no acknowledgment between them of just how generous the offering was. Rorren preferred it that way.

"Why? Aren't you curious? What if she can make a menti blade—"

"Just shut up."

The stars in the kid's eyes kept dancing, so Rorren kept shoving supplies at him.

"You speak of things that bring death, war, and blood," Rorren said, "You don't know anything about them. Don't encourage her to remember."

Jon's youthful face tightened, but Rorren refused to let it rankle him. He slammed the tailgate shut and Brawn grunted at being disturbed from his nap.

"Metra says you were a great General in the Galactic Order like your father. How come you hide it? Why do you hide your tattoo?"

"It's not—"

"I know, I know. It's not a tattoo. What is it then?"

Not answering sent Jon marching up the stairs in a tantrum and the door slammed behind him.

Reminding himself that the kid knew nothing of the galaxy beyond the borders of his grandmother's farm, Rorren cooled the hot liquid of his temper.

A noisy breath cleared his lungs, but his stride was heavy as he entered the house.

The witch sat in a chair at the table. The sound of running water from the bathroom filled the small living area.

The widow had a stone-carved tub for bathing, which Rorren remembered because of the ordeal of bringing it out to her. It was a luxury for such a remote area. He'd been happy to do it.

Jon sat beside the witch, fidgeted, and slid his chair closer. Rorren watched from just inside the door with arms folded as he glowered. The kid's leg twitched under the table and his eyes were embarrassingly glued to the beautiful Scorth woman.

The witch's lithe fingers rested on her lips and hid a mirth-filled smile that enraged Rorren. She knew she had power over the teenager.

"They say Scorth ladies are the prettiest in the galaxy." The boy stammered. "You are very pretty, even if you're probably an old lady. You don't look old, though."

The witch tilted her head, exposing her neck a bare fraction. Jon had no idea what she was doing.

"What are you? About a hundred?"

Rorren snorted loud enough to make his presence known.

"One forty if she's a day," he said.

Fingers left her lips and brushed at the air in his direction, waving him away.

"Don't you go making a ruckus again," he warned just as the widow returned to the room.

She had several garments draped over her arm.

"You need more than one dress. I know these aren't like you're used to, but we are simple folk."

The widow spread three dresses across the table. The witch ran her fingers over one of them and wrinkled her nose.

"I see. Not good enough for Little Miss Birdie?" The widow asked, stooping with hands on her hips, expression slack.

Turning down the generous offering was beyond insulting.

Maybe Rorren shouldn't have brought her.

The witch grabbed the widow's arm.

Rorren drew the staff from his belt. The boy jumped up beside his grandma, chair skidding across the room.

The witch let go and lifted her hands in surrender.

Rorren realized she hadn't meant to attack. Relaxing, he retracted the staff but kept it at the ready as a precaution.

"What's she doing?" The boy asked, hovering close to the widow.

Rorren watched the witch's gaze wander the house and land on the dresser in Metra's bedroom—the spot missing the vase the raven had destroyed.

"She doesn't want charity. She wants to trade," Rorren said.

The widow squeezed Jon's arm, speaking to him but keeping her eyes on the witch.

"Where's Nanna's vase?"

"It's still in the bucket. I haven't made much progress," Jon said.

"Go fetch the pieces."

Jon hesitated.

Metra mashed her lips at him in that old lady way that reminded Rorren of home.

"You want to see Scorth magic? Then, go," Metra said.

The kid obeyed and returned a few anxious moments later with the bucket.

The bucket was set on the table and then the three stood static, pinning all attention on the witch.

The raven woman closed her eyes and breathed so deeply that Rorren understood where all her bluster came from.

A secret breeze stirred her hair.

No way she could do it without a Scorth Pod.

If she could—

The bucket shook—just a jiggle or two but then the shards of glass began floating upward one by one. The pieces came together, sealed by flashes of white fire until one complete vase landed on the table.

"Holy ginger!" Jon ran a hand through his hair. "How did you do that?"

Twitching her lips, Metra didn't look at Rorren. They didn't have to look at each other to know what the other was thinking.

"Mic Rorren, help me turn off the water," she said.

He knew she didn't need help.

Following her with solemn steps, Rorren ignored the gaze of the Scorth and ended up in the bathroom.

He bent over the glazed stone tub and looked into a pool of crystal-clear water. He cranked the squeaky valve closed.

"You are thinking of letting her go without doing what you know needs to be done?" Metra asked as Rorren wiped his wet hands on the bathroom towel.

He kept his back to her.

"I can't."

The widow reached up and put her hand on Rorren's shoulder, then, turning his chin to face her, she smiled. Her eyes were more vibrant than he'd ever seen them.

"Both of you have a choice to make. Oh, I know, you make your own destiny, Mic Rorren. That is true, but nothing risked, nothing gained."

"Now you sound like my father."

The widow pulled the shawl up over her shoulders.

"You see her for what she is. Scorth are evil, though she is stunning, charming even. She may have helped you, but you know better than any of us what Scorth are capable of. Especially one with her power. Best to get rid of her. Wash your hands of it, yes?"

Rorren never forgot the war. He saw in his mind the old Scorth witch who wielded the power of the Fire-Scar Warriors. Lady Layeyre saved his life and won the war against her own people. This new Scorth woman might lead him again down that familiar path of heartache and death.

"Yes."

The widow sighed. She dipped her fingers in the water to check the temperature.

"I will do all I can for her. And I know you will make the harder choice because I believe in you. Many of us do, General."

Rorren clenched his jaw and squeezed her hand before he left her alone.

While the raven got a bath, Rorren and the kid fixed a hole in the roof caused by the last sandstorm with the materials Rorren had purchased. The two of them cleaned out the stables and checked the water level in the moisture tank before returning to the house.

The suns were gone, but the sky blazed with purple and orange streaks painted by the exhaust from distant starships.

Colors splashed across the living room when they entered, breathing new life into the drab farmhouse.

The witch and the widow stared at each other from across the table, the former now in a state of cleanliness. Her wild hair, thick and intimidating as the style of her people, fell over her shoulders, untangled and shining.

One of the old dresses the widow offered hung from her slender frame, too large at the waist and too small at the shoulders. Where the witch's armor flattered her figure, the dress had the opposite effect.

Despite the clothes, her eyes were bright as if they, too, had been scrubbed clean.

"Least I can tolerate your smell now. We should go," Rorren said.

The witch glared and the widow nodded.

"Can you walk or should I get the chair?"

"She's tired. She's had an eventful day. I think fixing the vase took it out of her," Metra said.

Rorren started for the wheelchair, but the witch's movements stopped him. With one hand, she pushed herself up from the table. She wobbled on her feet, lifting her chin toward him.

"Stubborn," Metra and Rorren said in unison.

With one arm wrapped around her waist—and fear of it being snapped off—Rorren steadied the witch on the way to the front door. They reached the sand at the bottom of the porch stairs and the Scorth stopped.

Rorren tugged on her, but she wouldn't budge.

The witch pushed on his shoulder, forcing them both to turn around. The kid and his grandmother stood next to each other on the deck, watching in anticipation.

"Thank you." The weak rasp barely carried up to the recipient.

The widow recovered from the shock first.

"You're welcome, little birdie. Don't be a stranger."

Rorren gave a nonchalant wave as he pulled out of the drive. Darkness engulfed the sky within ten minutes of their departure. The Scorth dozed off on the ride home. Just as well. Gave Rorren time for thinking.

The witch found her tongue and her feet on the same day.

Watching the dunes roll by like bubbling marshmallows under the moonlight cleared Rorren's head. He had many questions for the Scorth witch and now she had the voice to answer them.

CHAPTER 7

THE SMELL OF FOOD filled the house, driving home the reality of circumstances Rorren didn't understand. A woman slept under his roof, yet he fixed the meals, did double laundry and made an effort to keep the house clean. The toast popped up. He snatched it and slammed on the butter hard enough to tear a hole.

Annoyed, he carried the two plates over the table. The moment he set them down, the witch appeared in the bedroom doorway.

"You would get up just in time to eat," he mumbled.

Mornings on the farm were busy for him; all the while, she slept comfortably in his bed.

He missed his bed.

She stumbled to the table half asleep, her leg faltered and she reached for balance. Her hand hit Rorren's plate, dumping eggs all over the floor.

She looked up, wide-eyed, like she expected to be slapped.

What a harsh world she must have come from.

He let out a long, low breath, just managing to keep it from turning into a growl.

He fetched the walking staff from the corner, his shoulders tensing more from annoyance than anger.

"I made this for you. It should help."

Genuine surprise on the face of a Scorth somehow made him forget all his exposed scars and the trench coat hanging in the closet.

She took the stick and hobbled around the kitchen. Rorren couldn't decide if the staff made her look like a typical Desandor farm woman or a galactic Queen.

The witch placed the staff against the side of the table, sat, and ate her still-in-tact meal.

"You can thank the widow, but not me?"

Ignoring him, she shoveled in the food with a shocking lack of grace. Rorren retrieved the broom and cleaned away the mess.

"Just tell me one thing. How long?"

She paused, causing him to look up from the floor. She swallowed.

"You have an unsettling amount of bird puns." The rasp was still raw and grating, but her returning voice held a soft elegance.

"And yet you're the one that's quackers."

Rorren brushed the ruined breakfast into the waste basket and turned, expecting to see her roll those baby-blues in disgust. Instead, her jaw jutted, and he remembered most Scorth had no sense of humor.

"How long," he asked again.

"Seventy."

"Seventy...years? Are those like dog years?"

He succeeded in getting another evil glare and he took a satisfied bite of toast.

"Human years," she snapped.

Seventy years ago, his parents hadn't been born. Scorth aging unnerved many people, even the hardest of his soldiers. The youthful face across from Rorren surrounded a mind a hundred years older. A mind that spent a lifetime as a bird.

"At what point are you categorized as bird-brained?"

"I am smarter than any living human."

"Brave of you to say with your hair like that." Rorren shoved another piece of bread into the toaster. "I have to travel to the far tower. I'm taking the crawler so it will be all day. I plan to have lunch while I'm out there. I'd invite you, but I know you'd just make it," he knew he was pushing his luck but annoying her was delightful, "hawkward."

Using the staff, the witch lifted to her feet.

"I grow tired of you and your pathetic dwelling. A change of scenery is welcome." She knocked into him on her way out of the kitchen, her dirty dish left on the table.

"You know, for a moment there, I almost forgot you were Scorth."

✦

Rorren dangled from the harness forty feet above the sand. Replacing the wind-damaged panels on the tower's outer shell wouldn't have been such an ordeal, but the soft bursts of laughter from below distracted him.

Scorth laughter.

He didn't remember they could laugh.

Below him, the witch lounged beneath a canopy he'd set up, feet propped on an empty sandfruit crate and cold drink in her hand.

The antics of the kencat seemed to amuse her.

Brawn was showing off and loving the attention.

Rorren roasted in the blazing suns. He took off his hat and dabbed his face with his shirt.

"Glad you're enjoying yourselves," he shouted.

He leaned in the harness, hoping to see if the witch reacted. Too far, one way. His body tipped out of the leather, but Rorren rebalanced, the split-second reaction saving him from a disastrous drop. With his hand on the side of the tower, he pushed himself upright.

Finished with the panel, he released the line and slid until he landed just beyond the canopy.

Maybe he was showing off a little bit too.

The witch, sipping her drink, did not stir from her reclined position. Her posture reminded him of a Scorth painting his mother once showed him. A regal Scorth woman sprawled over a throne as mine slaves served her fruit on a golden platter.

Rorren retreated into the shade of the canopy. Sitting on a crate beside her, he took a long gulp from the canteen. Trickles of water ran down his neck and cooled him.

Brawn plopped down next to him and set his head on his crossed paws as if he knew what Rorren was thinking.

"Not talking to you, traitor," he said to his pet.

Brawn snorted.

The witch removed her feet from the crate, her body shooting upward.

"Do not worry, kitlush. I will leave as soon as I am able."

The abrupt comment made Rorren turn over his shoulder. Thanks to his mother's knowledge of Scorth, he knew what *kitlush* meant. It was not a compliment.

"I have a name. Mic Rorren. This is Brawn."

The Scorth dropped her dark lashes like a mask. She did that a lot. It seemed the only physical sign of emotion she knew.

"I know your names."

Rorren twisted the lid on the canteen and tilted his hat up so he could see her better.

"You got a name? Should I keep calling you a witch? Angel is definitely out."

She opened her mouth but must have reconsidered her comment. She paused and then relaxed a little against the chair.

"I am Vesta."

"Popular name for a Scorth witch, at least, during the war years."

Mic Rorren readjusted his hat, thinking he liked it better when she fought with him.

"Do you know about the war? You were a raven for all of it," he said.

Vesta reached for the staff but did not stand up.

"I know your people slaughtered mine."

He found in her no closed fists or defensive sneer, no physical gesture to match his indignation. Her coolness would not be allowed to outdo him despite the fact he lost both parents during the war. That made him anything but calm.

"Slaughtered? That's interesting, considering the Scorth planned to take over the universe and enslave everyone."

The witch put her fingers to her brow.

"Must we argue this?"

Rorren rubbed Brawn between the ears.

"Nothing to argue. Humans won. Peace was restored," he said.

"Was it? You carry a relic from the war. The scars of the relheer."

The Scorth word off her tongue churned his stomach.

Relheer. It meant *remaining host*.

Regretting going without his coat today, Rorren left her in the shade and gathered his tools. He tossed each one into the crate with more force than necessary, relishing the noise and hoping it prevented her from getting too comfortable.

He carried the box to the sandcrawler, standing there momentarily in seething hatred. A kind of alarm went off in his head when he was ready for the next round and he returned to the canopy.

Her Scorth eyes were closed and her head was in repose.

"Scorth never do anything for others. Why did you save my crop?"

Her eyes remained closed, her body motionless. Rorren thought maybe she was asleep.

"You guessed why. I was bird-brained. I did not know what I was doing."

A blatant lie. Rorren was getting as clairvoyant as Metra. Rorren looked toward the rocks beyond the edge of the crop.

"I'm going to rustle up lunch. Want to come?"

She opened her eyes and followed his gaze toward the cliffs. She lifted one arched brow but said nothing.

Trailing after Rorren seconds later, she used the staff to navigate the sand, still unsteady on her feet. They reached hard ground and boulders of various sizes. Rorren overturned rocks in search of lunch.

"I do not eat insects," Vesta said.

"Why? Are they kin?"

Focusing on the small clumps of green clustered in the shadows allowed him to ignore the glare he knew followed him.

"You could help. I'm looking for desert moss. When cooked over a fire, it's considered a delicacy."

She sighed in an overt performance that might have been comical if it hadn't annoyed him so much.

"If I must."

With one wave of her hand all rocks in the immediate area lifted.

She was getting stronger.

More dangerous.

A few of the floating rocks were sizable.

He pretended it was normal for a single Scorth to wield such power without using a Scorth pod.

He suspected she was pretending, too.

Rorren spotted the desired plant tucked in a corner near a large boulder. He ducked beneath the hovering rocks and retrieved enough for both of them. He retracted, but not quickly enough. A rock landed on his big toe.

"Hey!" He hopped a few steps on one foot, waiting for the sting to subside.

"For the insect comment."

She walked away and Rorren could half imagine her feathered cape swinging behind her.

Tamed raven no more.

They returned to the shade of the canopy and Rorren cooked the moss. The witch ate several helpings.

"On my planet, the women do the cooking." He wondered if she knew enough about human culture to spot his half-truth.

Vesta dabbed her mouth with her napkin.

"Cooking is for peasants."

No, cooking is for arrogant Scorth women, he thought. *Suitable for teaching them humility and gratitude.*

"Why are you not on your home planet?" she asked.

Rorren stared into the smoke of the doused fire. He didn't answer.

"Desandor is hardly the place to make your fortune," she said.

"And that's all you care about. Wealth, diamonds."

The witch set her plate down, wisps of shadow gliding over her nose and brow.

"To be honest, kitlush, I know not what I care about anymore."

"You certainly stole plenty of jewels while you were a raven."

"That was instinct."

"Or true nature. Kencats don't change their stripes."

She glanced at the tower.

"Get to work or we shall never return home."

He hoisted his tool belt over his shoulder and crossed out of the cool shade into the sunlight.

She said *home*.

CHAPTER 8

RORREN WOKE LYING ON his stomach with the sheet tangled around his ankles and the vague sound of shouting invading his dreams. A restlessness in his legs plagued him when he slept on the couch, and tonight, the thunder of a distant storm made it worse.

He rolled onto his side.

Not a storm, pounding at the front door.

The sheets snagged around his feet and he tumbled off the couch. He rubbed his sore neck on the way to the door. He swung it open while grumbling at the disturbance.

The shock of what was on the other side cured his headache.

"What in the blazes happened to you?"

Jon smelled of smoke. Dark streaks of soot smeared his chin and forehead.

"Aklaren attacked the moisture hub. On fire," he said between breaths. Jon tucked his head to his knees and his hands rested on his legs while he sucked in gulps of air.

"Come in. Take a rest." Rorren swung the door wide and the kid lurched in, grabbing Rorren by the shirt.

"Still on fire! Grams said you'd help. We have to get back there."

Rorren unlatched the kid from his body and went to work, pulling on his trench coat and his boots. Not a split second of hesitation in him. He hated being as predictable as Metra foresaw.

When he looked up, he found moonlight pouring in from the window, kissing the elegant curves of a Scorth woman.

"You're coming?" Rorren asked.

"I grow tired of—"

"My pathetic dwelling, I know."

A flicker of something in her gaze made him think it was more than that—almost like she wanted to help.

A cloud of smoke billowed into the sky, looming over the dunes as they reached the moisture hub.

Rorren considered the hub an ingenious Sandorian invention. Steel beams supported a tank the size of a small starship, suspending it over the sand—an octopus with hundreds of tentacle hose lines connecting to ports all around the valley.

Rorren's farm had its own moisture machine, but most homesteads, like Metra's, were fed from the central hub.

Arriving in chaos, Rorren jumped out of the sandcrawler into blasting heat from flames that engulfed one of the oxygen pods.

"Watch out," he yelled just before an explosion rocked the ground, raining debris around them.

He pushed the witch clear of danger and crouched beside her, using the crawler to shield them from splinters, stones, and an unwelcome shiver. Obsedei warriors landed the same way.

The roar of the fire gave way to the sound of jumbled voices. In the heart of the commotion, Rorren saw Sandorians scrambling to save the other oxygen tanks from the ever-spreading fire, their long legs floating over even the most pliable sand. Most Sandorians stood at least seven feet tall, but their bodies were slender and agile.

Three-fingered hands drew water from the hub reserves, passing buckets in a production line doomed to fail. Once the fire reached the main tank, all hope of stopping total destruction would be lost.

A robust Sandorian broke from the line, soot-stained boots leaving a trail in the sand as he approached them. Rorren knew him by name, though he doubted the opposite was true.

Tribe Chief Yan-hara's neck was twice the length of a human neck and covered by leathery skin, protecting him from the harsh suns of Desandor. His thin muscles defied gravity as they supported his rectangular head, which he twisted away from the fire. Dark but kind eyes rested in deep pockets above high, narrow cheekbones, reflecting flames and acts of courage.

Between the two high points on opposite sides of his head usually rested a colorful cap that signified his status as the Tribe Chief. The cap was missing, most likely a casualty of the fire.

"We cannot get the water to the flames fast enough," Tribe Chief Yan-hara said. Two long twigs of skin dangled from each side of his chin—a trait belonging only to Sandorian males.

Yan-hara took in a breath of smoky air through the holes just above his lipless mouth.

"Do my orbs deceive me? Rorren-sun, have you brought Scorth into our tribe?"

Not only did the Tribe Chief know him, but apparently, Mic Rorren ranked highly enough to earn a Sandorian name.

Yan-hara's words stilled the passing of buckets of water. The witch became the new focal point of fear. Her presence consumed all attention until the crackle of the forgotten fire became the lone sound in the night.

Keeping close to Rorren's side, the witch leaned on her staff. He guessed this was not her first time staring into the face of a hostile horde.

"No time. We need to stop the fire," Rorren said.

"Banish her!" someone said.

"She will kill us!"

"She started the fire!"

Yan-hara silenced his tribe by lifting his three-fingered hand.

"Your plan, Rorren-sun?"

He studied the terrain and the structure, rubbing his chin, and didn't look at the witch. The choice left him looking at the Sandorians, which was worse. The hope in those alien faces descended on him with a physical weight. He was supposed to be as dried up as the rolling sands around them and dried-up hearts don't swell with compassion.

"I need three of your men to help me cut through the tank."

"And forsake the water?" Yan-hara asked.

"We can repair the tank, but if we lose the hub, that's the end of it."

Yan-hara's lipless mouth formed a line and his head moved in a show of Sandorian gratitude.

"Clear your other men out of the way. Go!" Rorren, waiting until Yan-hara glided away over the dunes to carry out his duty, turned to the witch.

"You need to lift the tank above the fire."

Vesta straightened, knuckles white around the staff.

"Why should I help these peasants?"

"Don't ask stupid questions. Just do it."

"They will still hate me."

"Yes, but you might stop hating yourself if you do some good for a change."

Either he was a fool about to spontaneously combust under the heat of her glare, or he was about to save the water source for the entire valley. Her emotionless expression lingered a beat longer than expected.

"Unless you don't think you can do it," he said. That drew a sneer and a huff.

"You shall tremble at my power."

"Impress me half as much as you do yourself and that will suffice."

Rorren ignored her blustering and sprinted across the dunes to join four Sandorians at the ladder. The narrow metal rungs led high into the air, making the climb to the top of his towers seem like a small sunwart hill.

He climbed, pumping his legs until they ached, fingers burning on the hot metal.

Three Sandorians, one of them the Chief Yan-hara, reached for him, pulling him to the top of the moisture tank. Another explosion rumbled beneath them and the tank dipped sideways. Rorren lost his grip on the ladder, slid across the sleek metal, and snagged the ladder on the other side. He dangled by one hand, waiting until the motion subsided, and then climbed up.

Yan-hara tossed him a fire torch. The four of them tethered themselves off, readying to repel down the side of the tank with the torches.

"Now or never, gentlemen," Rorren said and received nods from all but the Tribe Chief.

"What if the Scorth fails us?" Yan-hara yelled.

What makes trust trust is placing it without having a reason.

Hearing his father's voice in his head, Rorren doubled his resolve.

In a few more minutes, the flames would reach the heart of the hub, rendering the question moot. Rorren propped his legs against the tank, wrapping his hand around the tether as the sand gathered beneath them.

The witch summoned her power across the dunes, standing against the framework of the planet's two moons. She gripped the staff with one hand, the other extending toward the tank. Wind from the fire tossed her hair wildly around her head.

"We're going to find out," Rorren yelled.

The sand underneath the tank bubbled, swirling until Rorren and the hub lifted into the air. Metal groaned as it twisted and bent with the movement. The sand reached up like a finger and funneled them forward, the tank floating into position over the fire.

"Now!"

Rorren and the three Sandorians repelled down. The rope burned Rorren's hand as he plummeted, but he focused on the torch. He used the laser-flame to cut a gash in the side of the tank. Water burst from the hole, blasting him in the face and chest.

The other three cut similar gashes and a steady stream of water drizzled over the fire.

Rorren saw the Sandorians unhook their tethers and roll into the sand. There was not enough stream to douse the fire.

Rorren kicked at the hull, not releasing his tether, pounding against gravity until the metal caved and a wide fissure opened.

He swung out of the way just before an enormous wave of water crashed over the blaze.

Steam and smoke blurred his vision. Through holes in the plume, he saw Vesta collapse to the ground. The sand that lifted the tank dissolved, leaving Rorren and the tank suspended.

The tether snapped. Wind hurled by his head as the ground raced toward him. He ducked and rolled; his shoulder hit the sand first, sending him somersaulting downward.

Left over water from the fire washed him across the giant dune.

Sand clogged his mouth. He coughed, spit out the mud, and then rolled to his stomach to see the damage.

Cheers sounded in the distance.

Smoke engulfed the hub but the fire was gone. The water tank was half buried in the sand, its open wounds glistening in the moonlight.

Rorren stood, brushed himself off and flicked his collar into place before he started toward the group.

Jon greeted him with a bear hug and a slap on the back. Rorren had forgotten what it was like to have friends.

Vesta stood just behind him, hanging onto the staff like it was the only thing keeping her upright.

"Rorren-sun's plan worked. We must now repair the damage the Scorth caused," Yan-hara said.

Vesta glared at the Tribe Chief's skull.

"The marauders caused the damage," Rorren said.

Defending the Scorth, again. His mother would be proud.

"We need the Galactic Order to come here and—" Jon started.

"Silence, vah." The witch's raised voice made Jon go pale. Rorren knew she used the Scorth word for *child* to intimidate them all. Everyone recoiled.

"My tribe is uneasy with the Scorth. Take her away, Rorren-sun," Yan-hara said.

"You need not ask, dune-dweller," Vesta lifted her chin, "I gladly take leave of you."

No words were spoken between Rorren and the witch as they drove to the farm.

Rorren used the silence to star-gaze and think.

In the morning, he would ask Vesta to leave even though part of him regretted dashing Metra's hopes. Promise to Lady Layeyre or not, having a Scorth witch on Desandor was more dangerous for his neighbors than the Aklaren gangs. The Tribe Chief was right. It was time Rorren sent the witch home to Ragora, where she belonged.

CHAPTER 9

The Royal Palace
Ragora
136 years ago

THE LITTLE GIRL HOPPED from stone to stone under the cover of vines said to be the greenest in the universe. The crystal water in the stream, dawdling as it floated over ancient pebbles, mesmerized her. Vesta followed it until it met with the other inlets peppered in the jungle beyond the palace. She waited—breath held—anticipating something magnificent or dreadful around the next bend.

A voice carried on the warm breeze. Her mother's call. The girl stopped dead, still in the middle of the brook. Her foot slipped into the water. It was warm but she shivered.

Peering through the vines, she saw waves washing up along the sandy beach that flanked the southern wall of the castle.

The stones of the palace were tinted white, a hue that matched the feathers of the birds that circled overhead. Unlike the birds, those stone walls made her feel trapped.

She inhaled the salt in the air and basked in the presence of the ancient trees of Ragora as they swayed to greet her. She imagined living in the arms of the jungle. Endless possibilities danced in her child imagination. Nothing seemed impossible. The future was brighter than the reflection of the sun off the water.

But imagination was impractical.

That is what her mother would say.

The call came again. This time colder, scolding.

The young princess shook the water from her shoe and hurried to the castle. Her foot sloshed along the cobblestone in the courtyard. Worried about what her mother would say about the wet garment, she almost walked past the rows of grownups standing at odds.

Her mother—the Queen—and a group of the royal guard were on one side; her grandmother and a group of poorly dressed Scorth on the other.

The kind old face caused the girl to swell with joy. She hadn't seen her grandmother since the day the Queen forbade unapproved visitors to the castle.

She ran into the open arms of the old Scorth woman, almost like being in the arms of the jungle except warmer. The Queen's scowl was so powerful it caused Vesta to shrink from her grandmother. She retreated to the side of her mother's royal robes, biting her bottom lip.

"You promised," her grandmother said. The Queen visibly swallowed. Grandmother was tall for a Scorth. Vesta might have thought the old one was still pretty if her clothes were nicer, but the bad clothes didn't explain the fear she sensed in her mother.

"And if I keep my promise, you will leave?"

Vesta winced. No one ever disobeyed her mother.

"I will leave and deny the dying wish of my son but it will be on your head, Talie."

Vesta knew they were fighting over her, but she didn't know why.

Even the soothing sound of the nearby waves could not ease her.

Her mother's hand gripped her shoulder. Clenched. It hurt.

Her grandmother frowned.

"We banish traitors in my court. We always have," her mother said.

Not for the first time, Vesta wondered about her father's death and her mother's reaction to it. He had been gone for a year and she missed him.

The Queen's hand left her shoulder.

Her grandmother walked from the courtyard toward a sizeable moss-covered tree at the jungle's edge. It was her favorite tree to play under with her grandmother. A vine hung down and, years ago, her grandmother had attached some wood to it, making a perfect swing.

Patches of light through the leaves splashed over her grandmother's ugly clothes.

"Come here, Vesta."

The girl looked up at her mother. The cold stare froze Vesta in place.

"Go, then, vah," the Queen said with disgust.

Her legs loosed up and she skipped a few steps until she reached the tree. Her grandmother took her by the hand. Vesta liked to hold her grandmother's hand. None of the other adults ever let her touch them. She knew they didn't want to be touched, but her grandmother was different.

Instead of going to the swing, her grandmother led her down the sandy beach to a large, flat rock. Vesta climbed up on the rock and her grandmother sat beside her.

Vesta wondered what fascinated her grandmother about the water, so she sat and imitated her gaze. She saw a few birds and a starship in the sky.

"I must leave Ragora."

Vesta laced her tiny fingers together to keep them from trembling. Something bad had happened or might happen. She wasn't sure which.

"Why, granda?"

Her grandmother took her eyes from the ocean. She wrapped her arm around Vesta. No one else made her feel so warm and happy.

"I love you, my little angel, and I wish you to come with me."

Vesta pressed her lips together.

"Can Edda come too?"

Her grandmother took in such a deep breath that Vesta wondered where all of the air went.

"No, angel. She wants to stay here."

Vesta looked into her grandmother's kind face.

"This has to do with those bad people. The ones that do not dress right."

"The bad people? Is that what your Edda calls them?"

Vesta nodded. She knew it would upset her grandmother, but Vesta could not lie to grandmother Vahza, even though her mother said lying was sometimes necessary.

"They are not bad. They are different from other Scorth because they…" Her grandmother removed her arm and bent low. Vesta memorized her every move. She knew her grandmother spoke important words even though she didn't understand them.

"We believe in different things than your Edda. She said you may choose. By law, she cannot deny the last wish of your father. She will allow you to come with me. I want nothing more than to have you with me."

Vesta bit her lower lip.

"Can we come visit Edda?"

"No, Vesta. I am afraid we could never come back."

Vesta scrunched her nose. She did not understand why her mother and grandmother could not get along. She did not understand what happened to her father. It was painful to think about.

Tears brimmed. She wished she was older so she would know more about the adults. She looked at the palace and then up to her grandmother.

"I like my bedroom and I do not want to wear the ugly clothes."

"You would have to give up these things. It would be hard."

Vesta squeezed her fingers together until her knuckles went white.

"If I do not go, will I see you again?"

Vesta saw tears in her grandmother's eyes. The girl looked around, afraid someone else would see the emotion and think less of grandmother Vahza.

"No, angel. You will never see me again."

Vesta unfolded her clasped hands. She wasn't supposed to say it but she loved her grandmother. The thought of never seeing her again was too hard to think about.

"Come. We must go back now."

Grandmother Vahza stood, extending her hand one last time. Vesta slipped her hand into hers. They walked along the beach together. The memory of that final walk burned into Vesta's mind forever. The smell of the salt in the air, the cry of the birds in the distance, and the bright green of the summer jungle vines all carried a sense of the ordinary in an extraordinary moment.

They reached the courtyard. Queen Talie lifted her crowned head. The guards surrounding her stood at attention.

The Scorth dressed in the ugly clothes fell silent, huddling together near the castle entrance.

"Well, naset?" Her mother's demand made Vesta freeze. She lost her voice.

"There is no question, Talie. She is your daughter," Vahza said.

Even before her grandmother let go, the loss echoed through Vesta. The path to her mother stretched before her, narrow, hollow, and rough. When she turned around, she watched her grandmother through bleary eyes. The tall Scorth bent down.

"If you remember nothing of me, remember this: there is no treasure greater than the soul of a living being." She put her index finger under Vesta's chin. "I will never forget you."

Vesta's mother waved her hand.

"Enough! No more filling her head with nonsense. Depart immediately before I change my mind and sentence you traitors to the mines."

When the Queen spoke of the mines, tone consumed with anger, Vesta saw even her most loyal guards shiver. Vesta shivered the most. She hated it when her mother was angry but admired the Queen's strength.

The only genuinely fearless person in the wake of Talie's answer was Vahza. The old woman removed her necklace and latched it around Vesta.

"This was your father's. Guard it well."

Something inside Vesta attached itself to that necklace—to treasures like it—because that seemed to be the only thing capable of easing the turmoil inside.

Vahza straightened and when she faced Vesta's mother, Talie trembled.

"Be kind to her. Love her."

Talie sneered.

Her grandmother and the ugly Scorth lifted the hoods of their hideous robes and disappeared beyond the castle walls.

Vesta did not try to stop the tears.

Her fingers gripped the narrow crystal of the necklace. She knew it well. Her father wore it often.

Through her tears, she saw the shadow of her mother's figure appear over her.

"Have you forgotten your heritage, naset?"

Stiffening, Vesta dropped her fingers from the necklace.

"We have no use for tears."

She wiped away the wet from her face and showed her mother.

"That is better."

Talie led the way into the palace. Vesta followed, hurrying to keep up.

"You made the right choice. With Vahza, you would be nothing."

Vesta watched the ground as she walked. The end of her mother's cape was swift over the cobblestone, picking up tiny flecks of dust.

"Here with me, the universe will be ours."

Vesta looked up at the regal figure before her.

"Yes, Edda."

<hr />

Desandor
Present Day

Rorren found her shoving her feather cape into a tote she stole from one of the piles in the barn.

With her tresses pulled into a benign bun, he might have mistaken the Scorth witch for a human, except there was no taming her air of superiority. Even the dingy rag draping her shoulders and hiding her lithe figure could not conceal her massive ego.

He'd spent the morning developing a tactic to kick her out, but looking at her now, next to the sandcrawler and ready to depart, a pang of regret hit him.

"What's this all about?" Rorren asked with arms folded.

The witch zipped the bag closed.

"We must leave now if I am to catch a ship off this planet."

"You have no money."

She hoisted the bag over her shoulder and said, "I will find some."

"You mean, steal some."

"Does it matter?"

Rorren lifted a storage crate from the stack inside the barn, pretending to be more interested in it than her.

"To those you steal from."

Rorren ignored her scoff and pulled another crate from the pile. In the last few weeks, he readied the crates for harvest by washing them off and carting them to the harvesting machine.

"Do not fret, kitlush. I shall steal from someone who deserves it. A Rodilian, perhaps."

The angry clanging of the crates fit his mood.

"Of course, you would never consider there might be another way."

No, he told himself, *no, no, no. Don't do it.*

She drew up her staff, transforming it from a walking stick into a symbol of authority.

"For Scorth, there is only one way," she said.

Running a hand over his chin, Rorren looked out the barn door, thinking he'd have better luck talking to a boulder in the desert.

"Scorth never use their power in circles less than eight. What you did at the hub, the control you had. I've only seen that once before. In a Fire-Scar Warrior."

Rorren braced against the darkness filling her face. Her anger manifested in every pore of her porcelain skin and flaring nostrils.

"The Aux Katan were traitors to my people long before the war."

He remained calm, letting her wild rage burn out.

"How did you do it? Without others to help you?" he asked.

Her mouth pressed into a straight line, cheeks indrawn. Rorren recognized the expression. Those who lived through starvation or some other horrific ordeal carried that look just like a scar.

"I was desperate. You saw the natives. You would have killed me if I did nothing."

"We don't kill for no reason. That's a Scorth trait."

"Drive me to the spaceport, human. Arguing is a pointless pastime of your people."

Resting his hand on the chain metal around the track wheels of the sandcrawler, Rorren tried to be as casual as possible when broaching a forbidden subject.

"You could return to the galaxy. Get yourself stuck as a bird for another seventy years."

Vesta averted her attention, picking at her nails.

"Or," his voice lowered with his inner voice screaming: *YOU WILL REGRET IT*! "You could stay here and learn to control and develop your power."

"And what?" She reacted too quickly. Too passionately. She stood taller, stretching her body but still shorter than Rorren. "Even if I possessed that kind of control, which I do not, and you found some ancient master to teach me the ways of the Fire-Scar Warriors, the last thing I would ever want is to be counted among them. I hate them more than I hate kitlush humans."

"But not as much as you hate yourself."

"Stop saying that!"

"Why? Because it's true?"

For a moment, Rorren thought the desert might be conspiring to prepare a way for this illicit partnership. The anger, the ego, and self-loathing of the Scorth witch, whether she admitted it or not, snuffed out that flicker of potential.

Letting go of the crazy idea, Rorren climbed into the sandcrawler. He turned the engine key as if it weighed as much as the vessel itself.

Vesta bent and said her goodbyes to a clearly upset Brawn. Rorren interrupted them with the horn. She glared at him and sneered but left the whimpering animal and took her place in the passenger seat.

The silence must have become unbearable for the Scorth because she broke it about a sector from the house.

"Your harvesting machine, you will never get it working in time."

Rorren kept his eyes on the endless sand and the stark road ahead.

"That's my problem."

Another sector passed in silence.

"Do you truly know an ancient master? I thought they were all dead."

"I know someone who has the tool used by a master."

Vesta's eyes raked him over.

"No." The ridicule in her tone twisted his gut. "I do not believe you knew an Aux Katan master."

"I fought alongside one in the war for over a year."

"A traitor."

"Maybe in your eyes. To us, she was—"

"She?"

Rorren found mischief dancing across her face.

"A lover? You are full of surprises," she said.

"She was two hundred and ten. That's way too old for me."

"Perhaps it is. Still, I would not put it past a traitor to take up with your kind."

Rorren glanced up to the sky, spotting a lone ship in the upper atmosphere making its way into the unknown universe—steadily pressing forward against gravity. The sight inspired him for the first time in years.

"The point is, I could show you. That is if you stopped sucking like a black hole in the center of your own universe."

The Scorth went still. For a few fleeting moments, Rorren thought she might take up his offer.

"It is best if I leave. And you suck more."

A bit of mirth from the Scorth. He found no reason to argue, too bad, because she was just getting interesting. They reached the spaceport without further discussion.

They walked through the merchant streets. Vesta assumed a position at least two strides ahead of him. Ships rumbled overhead and Rorren recognized the logo on their hulls—four blue planets surrounded by four rings and dotted with stars. The Galactic Order had arrived on Desandor.

The news was a gut punch and a blessing.

Uniformed soldiers bearing the same logo on their upper sleeves mixed with the villagers and local traders.

Lifting the hood of her cloak, Vesta covered her hair.

"Is the Galactic Order usually this predominant?" she asked.

"No."

They stopped side by side, watching their reflections in the towering glass of the spaceport entrance.

"Goodbye, Mic Rorren."

He thought about extending his hand.

"Don't steal too much."

She inclined her head and then blended into the crowd. After a few steps, she turned, glancing over her shoulder at him. Passengers darted around Vesta's motionless figure on their way to endless places in the galaxy.

Her stillness surprised him. There, in her remarkable eyes, was that regret? A large cargo wagon blocked his view. Once the wagon passed, she was gone.

Rorren focused on his grumbling stomach. He had skipped breakfast.

CHAPTER 10

BEYOND THE MERCHANT TENTS, Rorren found a throng of people gathered in front of a raised platform in the square. Their cheering drew him in.

Jon, the widow Metra's grandson, was among them.

"What's the occasion?" Rorren asked.

"The Order is here recruiting."

Rorren already pitied Metra because Jon was barely containing his excitement.

"Look," the kid said, pointing to the stage.

The woman wasn't beautiful, but such was her charm that no one seemed able to look away. In her face, Rorren made out the sharp blending of the delicate and the robust. Astride a pointed nose, he found an arresting pair of eyes and a bone structure punctuated by a square jaw. Her sun-bleached hair hung at short angles beside her cheeks, cutting a startling knife line across her youthful skin.

She was not tall, but her frame was solid and emanated a physicality that Rorren appreciated. The uniform didn't hurt either. She was the first woman he had seen on Desandor that piqued his interest.

A few years working the land could make her just about what he wanted in a wife. Deep and forthright, even her voice challenged the elements as it carried above the crowd.

Besides that, he knew exactly who she was.

"I'm gonna sign up."

Rorren put his hand on the boy's shoulder.

"Think of your grandmother."

Jon pulled away from Rorren.

"I am. The Order is here to stop the marauders and I will help them."

The woman on stage directed interested parties to sign up at a table across the square—her encouragement drawing a line like moths to a flame.

She made eye contact with Rorren. He lowered his head in appreciation of her persuasive words. With closing sentiments that drew more cheers, she stepped off the stage.

Rorren was surprised to find her making a hard line toward them.

"She's coming over here." Jon spat on his hand and used it to slick his hair. He straightened his shirt and puffed up his chest.

"New recruits?" she asked.

Rorren liked her confidence and the intelligent sparkle in her eyes.

"I am. Thank you for coming out here, ma'am. Makes joining easier for us," Jon said.

"Of course. We need the tough, handsome boys from Desandor." Her flattery seemed distinctly at odds with her well-groomed uniform and demure smile.

Face going flush, Jon grinned from ear to ear.

"I'm signing up now." He left them for the booth. The galactic agent turned her enticing smile on Rorren. He didn't hate it.

"And what about you?"

"Your line doesn't work on me."

Her smile never faltered.

"I see. Already a disillusioned soldier." She clasped her hands behind her as they walked, falling into a harmonious synchronization at his side.

"If I had to guess, I'd say you are the infamous General Rorren. Turns out the rumors of you hiding out on some washed-up old planet are true."

"I didn't catch your name," Rorren said, though he didn't need to ask.

"Galactic Agent Sevet Neece. The Premier speaks highly of you. Not every day does he send a fleet to the sticks to help an old friend. But then, your exploits are legendary, aren't they?" She craned her neck to see the scars beneath the collar of his coat as he scrutinized the string of metals on her uniform. *An old legend of the Galactic Order meets the new one*, he thought sarcastically.

"He sent me to convince you to return to us," Sevet said.

"Not likely."

"I can be very persuasive."

Rorren met her glance, half tempted to tell her that murderers don't belong in the company of heroes. They stopped.

"I believe it."

Her dimple deepened, but her lashes didn't flutter as he imagined Vesta's would have.

"The Premier must find that a useful talent," Rorren said.

Her shoulders tensed a fraction, just enough that he noticed.

"Yes, well..." She did not look at him. "He's angry with me. That's why I was selected to visit your little wasteland."

"It never was wise to get on TK's bad side."

She glanced at him, her thin eyebrows slanted nearly as severely as her hair.

"You call him TK?"

"Childhood nickname."

"I'll remember that."

The communicator box on the left shoulder of her uniform chirped.

"Agent Neece. Please report to space dock ten. We have a problem with implementation."

"Amateurs," she said. She touched the box, all business except for one annoyed glance. "On my way."

Agent Neece changed directions. Rorren continued to walk next to her.

"Implementation?"

"The mission here is twofold, General."

Twinging at the title, Rorren found they were headed straight through the vendor tents toward the enormous gateway of the dock.

"Desandor Dock is notorious for harboring criminals and galactic fugitives. They attract the bounty hunters and Aklaren gangs soon follow. For some time, we've needed to get control of the situation. We are installing soldiers at the dock and more identification readers. Now, no one can board a vessel without our knowing. We only had them up and running since this morning and already the brig of my ship is full of the worst in the galaxy."

"You said twofold. What's the other?" Rorren asked.

Agent Neece stopped before the open entrance of the spaceport.

Shattered shouting from inside the building interrupted them and two uniformed men emerged holding the arms of a woman who struggled for freedom. They pushed her to her knees at the feet of Agent Neece. A familiar sneer turned up at them.

"This woman has no papers. We were about to scan her when the system crashed."

Rorren dug in his heels, communicating with Vesta as subtly as possible. She caught on.

"There you are," Vesta said, pulling free and planting herself beside him. "Would you explain to these gentlemen that I only wanted to see inside the port? I had no intention of going anywhere."

Agent Neece retrieved a scanner from one of the soldiers.

"She's with you, General Rorren?"

While Rorren weighed how best to answer, Vesta said, "General? You know each other?"

She gripped his arm possessively and glared at Sevet. Rorren sensed a hatred between the two women palpable enough to make the breeze tremble between them.

He wanted to brush off the fingers clinging to his sleeve, but she might be in serious trouble if he did.

Scorth. Master manipulators.

"Yes, she's with me. My farmhand."

Neece frowned. Vesta glared at Rorren. He wounded her pride. Good.

"Next time bring your papers, even for a look around."

Agent Neece turned and ordered her soldiers to return to work.

"It was nice to meet you." Rorren managed to get a nod from the Agent.

"I'll be in touch," she said, then vanished beyond the glass doors.

Vesta's brow lifted with curiosity, but Rorren didn't bother to explain on the way to the crawler.

They rode in silence for three sectors.

"You shorted out the readers, didn't you?" he asked.

"Why do they need readers out here? Galactic Order and their control issues. No less evil than the Scorth attempt to enslave the universe."

Squeezing the steering wheel helped Rorren manage his temper.

"You didn't want them to scan you. Why?"

"I thought I could exit this planet quietly, re-group, and buy forged papers. Skip the scanning process altogether."

"You have been out of touch for seventy years. You wouldn't have made it far. Most docks scan everyone now, papers or not."

"You are joking." Vesta exhaled and shifted her gaze out the window. "Then, kitlush, it appears I am stuck here."

———

Rorren did not sleep or dress in the morning. He sat on the couch with one thing clear in his mind. He vowed to settle it.

"Where is breakfast?" the witch demanded. She pushed the bedroom door open and stood there, hair piled high and hubris on her lips.

"From now on, you cook for me. You do the laundry. You wash the dishes. You keep the house in order. It's woman's work."

She grinned, a throaty chuckle parting her lips, wrenching from him a profound disappointment.

"Never."

"I want my bed back as well."

Wide shafts of sunlight poured in through the window, flooding the room with warmth but not enough to counter the chill of Vesta's stare.

"I dislike charity," she said, sauntering into the light. "You can have the bed. As payment for my board, I will help you on the farm. Housework is for peasants, and you, kitlush, are a peasant."

He rose from the couch, cursing their new pact because he knew it would bite him later.

"The harvester has some issues." He sounded more eager than he wanted.

The harvester required the power of smooth beads no larger than acorns to function. A year ago, the harvester vomited the beads from its stack. Rorren rubbed his thigh where the marble had struck him and burned through his clothes. Dangerous little things, mined from the Diamond Moon of Ragora, were nearly impossible to retrieve by hand—even more impossible to funnel into the harvester. It was the second-worst chore on the farm he could give her.

"You can help me with that to earn your keep."

The threat of the grueling work didn't seem to faze her.

Rorren pulled on a shirt and the fabric irritated his skin.

"But first things first. We will be driving out to sector twelve in one hour. You can find your own breakfast."

CHAPTER 11

Vesta took slow steps over the sand, leaning on the staff, eyes filled with a brightness lacking in her gait.

"Are you ill?"

She hadn't let him near her injury in weeks, leaving him to wonder if it had healed.

"I like the staff. It is a compensation in the absence of my armor."

Whether it was a lie or not, he couldn't tell.

With a single thrust, he sliced a shovel into the ground.

"Dig."

"Why?"

"You'll know when you get there."

Anticipating what it would be like to see a Scorth witch attempt manual labor, Rorren joined her next to the little waving pendant that marked the silo. He listened to Vesta's shovel scrape the grain.

He heard something else.

Fabric ripping.

She tore the dress to free her movements and exposed her porcelain skin to the thigh. Rorren pretended not to notice.

"I hope the widow does not mind. I can see you do not."

The flash of arrogance in her grin made Rorren aggressively scoop a shovel full of sand.

"I'll find you some better work clothes tomorrow," he said.

He listened rather than looked and heard her toss another shovel full of sand over her shoulder.

"On Ragora, even among my people, I was considered exceptionally beautiful. As was my edda and granda. An exquisiteness of body and mind is a family trait."

"Looks like humility isn't."

"I feel sorry for the women of your race. Like your agent girlfriend. She could never be beautiful like Scorth."

Rorren stopped digging and wiped his forehead, though he hadn't drawn up a sweat yet.

"She's not my girlfriend."

Her grating but rhythmic laboring continued. Rorren discovered her hole was already twice as deep as his.

"You wish she were," Vesta said.

"At least she's not afraid of an ID scanner. Tell me again why you don't want them to scan you?"

Her digging stopped. Rorren used the interval to connect their efforts into one hole, pumping his muscles and not resting for air.

"You are not going to drop this, are you?" she asked, leaning on the shovel.

Plunging the shovel in faster gave him raw satisfaction, so he worked his calves and arms until they ached. A refreshing sweat formed on his brow.

"After I," Vesta paused, "left Ragora, before I lost a talisman to transform, I spent many years doing *things*. I made enemies."

"By things, you mean stealing, plundering, and killing."

"Not killing. I am no murderer like soldiers of the Galactic Order."

Like a hot knife through butter, his father had said, except her words went through his heart.

Balancing with one boot on the heel of the shovel, precarious and erect, Vesta stood with a somber wind at her back. His body resisted his commands, muscles pounding, her beauty threatening to collapse his resolve to hate her.

The skin of her face tightened over sharp cheekbones.

"To have qualms about killing." Vesta shoved the metal into the ground, scowling. "Edda would not be pleased."

Her arms flexed as she shoveled, her body filled with a darkness that reminded Rorren of death and war.

"Is that why you left?" he asked.

The trance or whatever prompted her to share vanished in the stronger breezes.

"Agent Neece was giving your regards to the Premier. The Premier of your human Cardinal Worlds?"

Rorren tossed the sand slower and with more precision.

"I'm not part of that anymore."

She paused, sand lodged in her hair and stuck to her flawless skin. Her stillness tempted Rorren to sneak a glance.

"Are you part of any world, Mic Rorren, but your own? A, what did you call it," she asked, grinning, "sucking black hole."

"Shut up and dig."

Working to the sounds of shovels and falling sand, Rorren let mid-day heat seep into his bones. On the slopes, dark splotches of water-soaked clumps mixed with the lighter sand, turning each mound into a design worthy of a kencat hide. He rubbed shoulders with Vesta as walls of sand rose around them.

Metal clanged on metal.

"I hit something," Vesta said.

Dropping his shovel, he climbed up, striding over pliable grains on his way to the satchel he left behind, not as graceful as a Sandorian but just as fast.

He retrieved it and glanced into the hole to find her holding her injured side.

Rorren jumped into the hole and brushed the sand from the cover of the blown console. Vesta copied his actions, exposing the round latch of the bulkhead, a sight Rorren hadn't seen in a decade.

"Lightening blew the panels last year. Digging out the silos is the only way to get to the main interface. The sand changes so much; it's no easy feat."

Rorren retrieved the new circuit panel from the satchel. He tossed away the charred one and slipped the new one into place. The silo hummed to life, echoing into an endless abyss.

"How does it work?"

"The circuit generates a harmonic field. It's like a magnet, strong enough to pull the fruit through miles of sand. Plus, it only attracts the fruit when it's ripe. Ingenious invention when it works."

"Crude at best. Why did you let the lightning strike? This manual labor could have been avoided."

Rorren grunted, lifting from his kneeling position and feeling the effects of digging.

"You don't say? I just thought I'd torture you with an epic mess to clean up."

Vesta dropped her hand from her injured torso.

"You are good at creating messes, kitlush."

He climbed out of the hole and offered his hand. Taking it with a huff, Vesta climbed up next to him. They stood together briefly as he surveyed the remaining work.

"One down."

Small flags marked each silo, six in total, flapping in the distance beyond the scope of the naked eye.

"There must be an easier way." She pulled her hand away from his.

Rorren brushed the sand from his clothes, pretending he didn't notice the warmth of her skin on his.

"If there were, everyone would grow sandfruit."

He handed Vesta the shovel. In silence, they went to work.

They uncovered four of the six silos. Starting on the fifth, Rorren spotted dark clouds dropping jealously through the heavens, reclaiming the land for Mother Nature.

Rorren tapped Vesta's shoulder, drawing her attention from the work.

"Sandstorm is coming. We need to go."

To save their work, they hauled over metal sheeting and Rorren directed Vesta with the placement. Vesta clutched her side and lost her grip. The metal landed on Rorren, bruising his shin. He cursed, but the sandstorm swallowed the sound.

They climbed out of the pit and Rorren raced to the sandcrawler. He switched on the lightning shield to prevent another blowout. Vesta climbed into the vehicle next to him.

"No time. We need to take cover. Go for the caves. They're not far."

She glared at him, perhaps because her side was hurting or his orders annoyed her. Neither her mood nor injury concerned him more than the storm.

Her lack of urgency in the race for the caves put them in a dangerous situation.

Sand rose, forming a wall around them and whipping them on a hot, beating wind. Dust engulfed all visibility.

"Vesta?"

She couldn't be more than four paces away but he couldn't see her. His hands groped through the dust, mouth parched, anticipating the touch of solid cave walls.

Fur.

A tail.

"Brawn, find her."

The kencat snorted and vanished.

Rorren crouched to the ground, waiting and listening. The howling storm disoriented him. He knew they were at the mercy of the elements and dependent on the instincts of the native animal.

Brawn knew where he was. His loyal pet would return, though Rorren doubted it would be in time for them to make the caves.

He hadn't been this worried about a woman since Lady Layeyre boarded a starship to Cardinal World Delta.

A distant noise came on the roaring wind.

"Slow down, you smelly oaf!"

Seeing blurs of shadows and movement, Rorren reached out and gripped a clump of fur, finding his hands not the only ones there.

"Take us to the caves," he shouted. Brawn lurched forward, pulling them against the wind.

His powerful body withstood the onslaught and Rorren used him as a steel rod. They clung to him as he led them across the plains.

The dark outline of the cave appeared, beckoning them from across the tortured dunes. Brawn did not stop until they were safely out of the storm.

Inside the quiet cave, Rorren's ears still howled with the effects of the wind.

He groped along the side of the wall until he found the lamp stored among the other supplies.

With the flick of a match, lamplight flooded the area. Vesta sat on a rock near the entrance, one hand resting on Brawn, the other clutching her side.

"Storms can last a few minutes or a few days."

Brawn dropped to his hunches, watching the sand through the cave opening and whining.

"Go play," Rorren said.

The kencat darted in a flash of fur. Vesta's hand remained in the air with no Brawn underneath.

"He likes it?"

Rorren set the lamp down and rummaged through the supplies.

"It's what he lives for."

Rorren retrieved the medical kit and sat next to Vesta.

"What is that?"

He opened the lid and pulled out gauze and disinfectant.

"You overdid it today."

"I am fine."

He moved her hand away from her side.

"Then you won't mind if I take a look."

Inhaling a sharp breath, she batted his hand away and snatched the gauze and medical kit.

"I can do it myself."

She retreated to a secluded recess behind a boulder.

Rorren muttered to himself, "Scorth."

He drew up to the perch Brawn had taken, mesmerized by the raging storm like his pet. Cracks of light appeared between squalls of sand, white beams suspended in the air that vanished into dark clouds swept by the wind.

He chewed on a piece of straw he found in the cave and rolled his shoulders, releasing the tension of a hard day's work.

The slap of the medical kit next to his foot startled him.

What the Scorth lacked in subtlety, they made up for in rudeness.

"How bad is it?"

"I have known worse injuries. It will heal in time."

"Not if you keep working like you did today."

"I told you I despise charity."

"Not as much as it despises you, I'm sure," he smiled at her, straw still between his lips. Long lashes dipped and he knew he was on thin ice.

A lonely structure appeared in the distance, bathed in red and oranges from sunlight and dust.

"A strange formation," she said.

Rorren leaned against the rock, wondering if he should go there.

"A sandstorm castle."

Vesta tilted her head to the side like Brawn sometimes did. Her curiosity was palpable, so Rorren got comfortable. He reclined against the flat rock, arm dangling, and crossed his ankles one over the other.

"There is a legend they tell on Desandor about sandstorm castles. Ever heard it?"

The Scorth witch made an exhibition out of sitting on the rock across from him. She tucked her legs underneath her and went so ramrod straight he thought she winced at the strain it put on her wound.

"Stories of primitive civilizations do not interest me."

He was getting good at spotting her lies.

"There was a prince from the North. He loved a princess from the South. She became his universe, but the Sandorian tribes were at war."

"Typical."

"You want to hear this or not?"

"You may continue," she said with a hand gliding through the air as if he needed her permission.

"To stop the marriage, the princess' father hired a wizard to hide the princess away forever."

Rorren inclined his head toward the cave opening.

"He placed the princess in the castle that only appears during the fiercest sandstorms," he said with the straw between his lips. "The prince rode into the heart of many storms in search of his lost love."

Vesta brushed the dust from the torn dress and wrinkled her nose.

"Of course, he saved her and all ended well," she said.

"He found the remains of the castle. A shell of sand that still exists on Desandor after a storm. The legend is open-ended. Whether he found her or not is up to the imagination of children."

Vesta turned, almost wistful, as she looked into the storm.

"Do you think he found her?"

He pondered for a moment, then tossed away the straw.

"If I had to answer now, I'd say he's still looking."

The slight upturn of her perfect lips betrayed her amusement.

"What do you think?" he asked.

A shroud of mischief shadowed her face.

"I think the princess was a weakling. She should have over-thrown her father, enslaved the wizard, and conquered both kingdoms."

Rorren shook his head.

"You're hopeless."

With instincts as mystic as Metra's, Rorren sensed the sandstorm would last through the night. He rummaged up a few dusty blankets from the supply box and offered one to Vesta.

"You cannot be serious?"

When she refused to take it, he tossed it at her. She caught it and a puff of dust that made her cough.

"We're stuck until the storm is over."

"I do not sleep on rocks."

Rorren laid out his blanket, bunching a second into a makeshift pillow.

"Go out there if you want. Good luck surviving."

On the blanket, Rorren twisted and turned until he found a comfortable position. He closed his eyes.

"Some prince you turned out to be."

"You want to waste the night and the rest of eternity looking for sand-storm castles? See ya."

Rorren rolled over on his side.

The blasted woman would be foolish enough to face the storm alone. Cursing on the inside, Rorren waited until she was safely asleep before letting himself drift off.

No one had assigned her to him. She wasn't one of his soldiers, which made taking responsibility for her all the more obnoxious.

He woke in the dead of night and found her body cupping around a small boulder, shoulders shivering in the cool air.

Considering his subsequent actions, he allowed his caution to surrender to boldness. Despite all he knew about Scorth, he picked up his blanket and settled beside hers.

There was no ventilation in the cave for a fire, so body heat would have to do.

He woke the following day to find her snuggling against him. Her head rested on his shoulder and one lean arm draped snugly across his chest.

Rorren opened his eyes.

Grinned.

She was going to be so pissed.

He dipped his chin until it touched the top of her head.

Enjoying the warmth of her flesh and the fresh smell left behind by the sandstorm, he went to sleep. The howling wind disappeared, replaced by the click of desert insects.

Something wet and rough slid over his face. Brawn licked him, then lapped his tongue over the witch.

Her dark lashes flew open. Jolting upright, she pushed off Rorren's chest.

With her other hand, she pushed the kencat away.

She stumbled to her feet, using every curse word in her native tongue, from kitlush to aux rand.

What Rorren wouldn't have given for a holo-recorder. Hot beans, she was mad.

"Stay away from me! Both of you!" she hissed from as far away from him as the cave allowed.

Rorren propped up on his elbow.

"You were cold. I swear I only moved over for warmth."

An invisible wind blew in and her hair lifted like it had in the moonlight at the moisture hub. The sight sobered Rorren and he held up both hands.

"I swear."

Tense seconds passed as Rorren waited for the coming attack. The wind disappeared and the cave went still. Brawn watched the interaction with his head tilted to one side.

"Keep your distance unless you have a death wish." Vesta tossed the blanket at his head.

"Pretty strong reaction for something so innocent," he told the kencat.

"Excuse me?"

Rorren kept his attention on Brawn.

"I'm just saying, being a raven for so long must have been lonely."

"All Scorth are alone. It is how we live."

Vesta moved to the mouth of the cave.

Rorren blinked into the morning sunshine, watching its rays ignite dark tendrils of Scorth hair and bathe fair skin in fire. She had been right about her exceptional beauty, as unappealing as her bragging was.

Rorren stretched and joined her at the opening. Brawn ran past them and out into the sunlight.

"There are your sandstorm castles," she said.

The kencat weaved through tall structures of sand left behind by the storm. Some looked like castle watchtowers, others like palace walls. Dotting the land to the horizon, they created the illusion of a miniature kingdom hiding within the dunes.

"They will all be gone by afternoon. Back to dust like they never happened," Rorren said, careful not to touch her on his way out of the cave.

CHAPTER 12

R ORREN OPENED THE FRONT door just as the sun vanished behind a cloud, leaving the world in a colorless shadow that shrouded Agent Sevet Neece.

A green sheen fell over her platinum hair, and the face that had been so appealing only a week ago wilted into something manufactured.

Rorren's attraction to her re-emerged as the sun returned, pouring a new glow over the slender body before him.

"Is this a bad time?" Her lips were inviting.

Rorren blocked the door, dug his fingers into the wood frame and glanced over his shoulder.

"Come in," he said. His mind was ten steps ahead of Sevet and out of the house, praying Vesta would stay occupied in the barn.

Rorren led Agent Neece into the kitchen.

He pulled out a chair and gestured for her to sit. She eyed it, then strolled around the room as if it were her command center—hands clasped behind her, tall black boots noiseless as she performed an inspection.

"I feel like I'm back at the academy."

"Old habit," she said, "I like to get my bearings in new places."

Her intensity suggested something more urgent, like hunting the shadows for unseen enemies. The same way he used to search for Scorth enemies.

"Would you like a cold drink?" he asked.

Neece inclined her head and Rorren poured them both a glass. She sat across from him and he marveled that the agent's legs could bend. She landed ramrod straight with her hand around the glass and her elbow at a ninety-degree angle. The pose mimicked sociability as if only an imitation.

Maybe she was just nervous. Rorren knew he was.

Silence overtook them. Neece stared, maintaining her awkward façade, and Rorren grasped for anything to break the tension.

"So... Did Jon get off to the academy alright?"

"Eager as they come."

They both took a sip.

"Still think Desandor is a wasteland?"

"My month of penance on this God-forsaken planet is nearly over."

Her arm remained at that ninety-degree angle.

"And you? Ready to return to a life of service and excitement?"

"Is that what you call it?"

Teasing her did not lighten the mood. Her presence, unnerving but intoxicating, cast a spell over Rorren. A mere snap of her fingers and he'd obey her every command.

"I have a message for you. From Premier Krave. Delivering it was the secondary purpose of my mission." She removed the communication box from the left shoulder of her uniform.

"Would you like to see it?" she asked, but whether he answered yes or no, he suspected she would do precisely as planned.

Not waiting for his response, she took liberties and set the box in the middle of the kitchen table. The holo-projector lit up the kitchen in shades of white and blue.

A familiar face emerged from the pixels. Up the slender nose from a winning smile, Tagion's striking eyes dazzled. White teeth complimented a bone structure so perfect the man could have passed for Scorth.

"I should do the proper thing and greet you as retired General Mic Rorren, but I think I'll shock Sevet and call you Mic Stick."

Rorren laughed. Even the burden of the Premiership of the Galactic Order of Cardinal Worlds couldn't dampen the humor of Tagion Krave.

"Sevet knows about my nickname, thanks to you. Payback is only fair, Stick."

Sevet shrank into the shadows and her presence changed from all-consuming to a faint outline against the wall.

"But listen, General, we are doing amazing things here. Why don't you come and join us? There is still a spot for you as head of the Delta Army or in the cabinet if you prefer."

Rorren folded his arms, chest lifting, remembering the old days. Even as Tagion climbed the political ladder, he never forgot Rorren—that lost friend serving in the trenches. Seemed he still hadn't.

"You're a legend around here, you know. The soldier who survived. I know you're probably shaking your head at me."

Rorren tilted the chair, its front legs a half inch off the ground, glad he wasn't entirely predictable.

"I'll leave you alone. Before I go, what do you think of Sevet? She is amazing. My right hand. I couldn't do this without her, so don't you go getting funny ideas."

Sevet peered cautiously through the holo-projection and her face grew as hollow as the projection itself.

"Really, Mic. It would be good to see you again. Don't be a stranger too long. The Order could use you."

The transmission ended. Agent Neece retrieved the communication box and, after reattaching it to her uniform, clasped her hands behind her.

"Good ol' TK," Rorren said.

"He is a beloved Premier."

"He has his critics," Rorren said. He took another sip from the glass.

Neece prowled the length of the table, moving until she reached the front door. Rorren followed.

"Why do I get the impression you're one of them?" she asked.

"Nobody is perfect. TK's biggest flaw is that he thinks he is."

"You won't leave Desandor?"

The idea sent a wave of prickles up the scars on his neck.

"Jon and I will be glad when you've cleaned out the marauder camp."

Agent Neece chuckled, lips parting over white teeth.

"I told you our mission here is two-fold. Installing readers and delivering this message. The Order has no interest in the plight of a few farmers."

Rorren paused, trying to shake the sting of that truth.

"You're going to take off without lifting a finger?"

With her gloved finger, Neece traced the seams on the collar of his coat.

"You're a big, strong ruffian. I'm sure you can handle it."

"You could stay and do the right thing. These people need you."

"Un-tempting as that is," she began, "I'm afraid I have more pressing problems to address."

"Running the Galactic Order as the Premier's lady?"

Her darkening scowl indicated he might be onto something.

"I'd settle for an admiralship."

She opened the door and Rorren stepped onto the porch behind her.

"Something tells me you'll get it."

With confidence radiating from her, Rorren saw she didn't need him telling her what she was capable of.

"You could come with me. We could explore," Sevet lowered her eyes, then looked up, "things."

A woman hadn't come on to him in so long he half didn't believe it was happening now. "Need to bring my crop in soon," he said.

She smirked, this time placing a gloved hand on his chest.

"For a moment, I thought you might say that bizarre, ugly little woman was keeping you here."

Hoping Sevet didn't see, Rorren glanced at the barn, half expecting Vesta to fly out in full Scorth armor.

"She's my farmhand. I told you she—"

"Good. Then she won't mind if I do this."

Reaching behind his head, Neece pulled him down, lips meeting his in a passionate kiss.

When she finally let go, she strutted down the stairs and called to him.

"If you ever find yourself on a Cardinal World, look me up."

Rorren leaned against the weathered wood of the porch post, imagining his father saying *never get involved with a woman who commands an army.*

Sevet disappeared into the sleek military cruiser, started the engine and sped away. Rorren turned, coming face to face with Vesta, her dark figure framed against blazing sand.

"What?" he asked, seeing for the first time the wisdom of her hundred and forty years in her youthful face.

"If evil exists in the Galactic Order, it begins with her."

"Jealousy is an ugly trait," he said, though he found no jealousy in her expression.

No anger or amusement clouded her eyes. Her solemnity baffled Rorren.

"Sometimes we can sense the future. Did you know that? Sevet Neece," Vesta said and gestured to the lingering trail of dust in the distance, "is not good."

Meeting her gaze for gaze, Rorren steeled his body against the breeze.

"I trust a woman who has dedicated her life to protecting the universe more than a Scorth witch with a past so shady she's afraid of an ID scanner."

Vesta's dark lashes dropped, a shield that failed to hide her disgust.

"Fool."

She walked away.

"What happened to kitlush?" he shouted after her.

Vesta's spoiled, alluring mouth uttered not one word to Rorren for three days, so he was surprised when she slithered into the cab next to him.

With the suns plummeting soundlessly into a sea of sand, they traveled west, and Rorren mused over the growing connection between the Scorth witch and the widow.

He dropped the sun visor in the sandcrawler, blocking the shine from the medallions in the western sky.

Vesta dropped her visor rapidly and with scorn but the action didn't fool him. She wanted to see his favorite neighbor or she wouldn't be there.

Loneliness had a way of chipping at invisible walls.

Against the shades of gold, he watched a little black box expand on the horizon until the widow's farmhouse filled the windshield.

Stepping out of the cab, he heard the front gate creak and his stomach did a little flip. He liked this part—watching the two women pretend not to be happy to see each other, ignoring each other until everyone was seated at the small kitchen table and cold drinks began molting.

While Metra was assembling her latest culinary delight in the kitchen, Vesta scanned the room—alert and on edge.

"Something is…"

The breaking of the three-day silence caused Rorren to take a celebratory sip, but Vesta glowered.

He chalked it up to Scorth stubbornness and her discomfort with making a friend of the widow.

The gritty taste of powder-thin sand soaked the air like it always did before a sandstorm and not even his drink washed it away. Never a good omen.

After serving them a slew of baked goods, Metra's aged bones creaked with the chair as she sat. She drew in a labored breath, her chest puffing.

"Got another holo-message from my boy. He's taken to military life. He has a dream to see this place restored."

She looked pointedly at Rorren, aiming at him a message he didn't want to comprehend. How long had it been since he uttered the truth about his scars? Too long. Not long enough.

Metra dropped her eyes to the velvet-covered box on the table. Glancing at it periodically since they arrived, Metra succeeded in making it Rorren's focal point.

"Had an argument?" Metra asked while Rorren kept staring at the box. "I remember my newlywed days."

"I do not see what that has to do with anything," Vesta said.

Metra reached for the box.

"Mic Rorren has spent years looking for a good woman to share his life with."

His father used to say *trouble will invite itself in, but you don't have to feed it beans*. Avoiding Vesta's gaze, he sank into a nice shadowy corner.

"I hope it's easier for Jon," Metra said.

"He'll come back to you," Rorren replied, grateful for a chance to change the subject.

"Your culture is too sentimental," Vesta added.

"Perhaps so, but I was thinking..."

Metra clutched the box to her chest. The somber reverberation of her hands drew Rorren and Vesta closer.

"You must be missing home. I don't care how un-sentimental you think you are. Maybe this will help."

She opened the case and presented her encrusted, azure stone necklace to the witch.

Rorren expected greedy talons to snatch it. Instead, he saw Vesta go still except for a quiver in her shoulders.

Metra removed the pear-shaped pendant from the box and her blemished hand extended toward Rorren.

"Mic Rorren, you put it on her. My arthritis."

The Scorth didn't protest. Rorren gave in to the charade, angry breaths marking his steps as he came up behind Vesta. Still no objection. Her irritation with him wasn't stronger than her lust for treasure.

Brushing her hair out of the way, he relished the pleasant smell. The strands were softer than he expected and he wondered if she had stolen some expensive shampoo at the market.

"There," Metra said, "it was meant to be worn by someone so lovely as you."

The women blinked at each other, Metra drawing a rare smile of humility from the witch.

"It is beautiful, but I will not take your—"

That was the last thing Rorren heard before his body rocketed across the room. He hit the wall and stone and timber fell on top of him.

He didn't know how long he was out, but when he came to, his ears were ringing like they always did during the war after heavy artillery fire from the enemy.

A painless throb shot up his leg and side until it reached the base of his skull with a brilliant burning. He tried to push up to a sitting position. Something heavy pressed down on him and constricted his lungs. Or was that the smoke?

He tasted blood and coughed—forced himself upward. The heavy object had a sharp edge that wedged up against his ribs. He groaned through the pain. Pushing his leg muscles beyond their capability, the ache of exertion pulsed through his body.

He kept pushing and the debris gave way. Rorren crawled on top, sucking in breaths of air still heavy with smoke. Shapes danced in the distance, blurred by the lingering pain and the waves of hot air from a dozen small fires surrounding him.

Rorren glimpsed a half dozen shadows under the moonlight, moving through channels between the smoke and fire. Each inky form bent and dug through the rubble. He heard them laugh and cajole each other until one of them called over the others.

Rorren climbed to his feet, movements tender and sluggish. Exposed nails punctured his skin, leaving a trail of bleeding wounds across his body.

He recognized the three-spiked symbol on the armor of one of the figures and adrenaline surged through him.

He neared the source of the shouting and saw Hevcar Duronilan bring his cleated boot down on Vesta's arm. She was trapped under the broad side of a crushed wall, but that didn't stop her from cursing him.

"This is the raven Scorth?" Hevcar asked. The Rocbull marauders around him nodded. Rorren recognized several of them from the crash by the Blood River.

Inhaling a silent breath, he slipped behind the still-standing corner post of the farmhouse.

The brutal reality of what lay in store made him pause. Even on a good day in the war, he would be reluctant to take on so many—unless he had the power of the Fire-Scar.

He looked at Vesta and frowned.

She struggled under Hevcar's boot but didn't cry out.

The Aklaren leader bent, gloating over her and she spit in his face. His scaled hand latched around her throat.

"I should kill you, witch. Return the favor of what you nearly did to me."

Rorren readied to make his move while Hevcar was distracted, but a distant moan drew his attention.

Metra.

A limp hand twitched about twenty paces away. The rest of the widow lay buried beneath smoking rubble. He'd be exposed if he charged for her.

Rorren didn't hesitate.

He tossed away splintered wood and shingles, not stopping until he uncovered her. He had no time to take in the sight of her broken body. Something hard slammed into his skull. He fell face first against the splintered wood, then rolled onto his back.

The marauders surrounded him, biceps flexing as they clutched various pain-inducing weapons, including a Galactic Order staff.

Lifting to his elbow, Rorren watched Hevcar drag Vesta over to them. He shoved her violently to her knees beside Metra.

"You got the old one killed. We're almost even for the loss of my best pilot."

Soot covered the pale cheek of the Scorth. Her hand reached for Metra's and the widow made contact.

Metra touched the necklace, smiling, and then she was gone.

Something dislodged inside Rorren. A molten core of rage that smoldered with fire a thousand times more potent than the ones around him. He squeezed his eyes shut, giving in to his desire for revenge.

Testing his body's readiness for the inevitable fight, he leaned against the uneven debris.

"Ah," Hevcar said. "This will do." He ripped the necklace from the Scorth's chest and examined it in the moonlight.

"I was going to kill you, but I think I'll take this and leave you with the knowledge you were too weak and pitiful to stop me."

The hair on Rorren's arms tingled as a rush of strange wind passed over. He knew that wind. He'd smelled that electric charge many times before the appearance of a Fire-Scar Warrior.

He heard Vesta say, "I will kill all of you."

Her hand was still clutching Metra's. A wild hatred clouded her eyes—desolate and fierce.

In the ways of the Fire-Scar, she was an adolescent. The weight of her wrath crushed any inner calm she possessed.

He knew before she did that her power would fail her.

Grabbing a sturdy splinter, Rorren rammed headlong into the nearest Rocbull.

He stabbed the splinter into the gangster's thigh and pulled the diamond-tipped staff from his hands. Rorren charged into battle.

He spun the spear around him, knocking away the blows from two boulder-sized fists.

A sword came hurling at him, but he used the staff to block the blow. Thanking the Maker that the G.O. spared no expense in weapons construction, he readied for the next attack.

Rorren reared, allowing him leverage to stab the oncoming marauder in the arm with the staff.

He glanced over his shoulder at Vesta. She tried to call her power, but the sand did not obey her command. Hevcar struck her across the face and the blow sent her tumbling next to Metra.

"Get up!" Rorren yelled.

To have any chance at all, he needed her.

Turning his attention to his battle, he disarmed the marauder with a gun. Another gun fired at Rorren, but he reacted with a sidestep. The shot missed him and landed square in the chest of the first Rocbull. A dozen more Aklaren appeared, pouring out of the smoke and moonlight.

"Get up!" Rorren shouted.

Vesta obeyed, rising to her feet with confidence.

She lunged for Hevcar but the coward sprinted for a motor cruiser. A Rocbull three times Vesta's size blocked her from her pursuit, swinging a menacing ax.

Rorren took a blow to the jaw as punishment for watching her instead of dealing with his attackers.

The witch had some combat skills, as most Scorth did, but it was clear to Rorren that she came from a pampered background.

Heaving the ax over his head, the marauder tried to strike her, but Vesta scrambled out of the way. The blade struck a piece of the farmhouse foundation and the Rocbull worked to pull it free. Vesta picked up a piece of the burning wood and charged forward, bashing his skull with it. The blow only made him growl. He unstuck the ax blade and stalked after her.

Rorren's Rocbull attacker abandoned their fight for the safety of Hevcar's motorcade. Rorren raced over debris and jumped between Vesta and the ax swinger.

He sized up the eight-foot beast and cursed Vesta for choosing to tangle with the biggest and ugliest. The marauder's blade clashed with Rorren's staff, but the weapon forged by the finest in the Galactic Order remained unbroken.

The force knocked Rorren flat. He scrambled away from slicing swings.

"Concentrate!" Rorren said, rolling to dodge another attack.

"I cannot control it."

Rorren jumped onto the Rocbull's back, clutching the staff under the monster's thick neck. He squeezed the creature's air supply but the leathered skin was too thick.

"You can. Focus. Calm your rage and embrace peace."

"This is no time for humor," she said.

"You have to be calm to call the power."

The marauder slammed Rorren into the remains of the kitchen wall. The blow flattened his lungs and he gasped. He lost his grip on the staff and fell to the ground.

The marauder kept swinging and Rorren's leg, still bleeding, gave out when he scrambled forward. He watched the final strike coming at him and a dozen regrets flashed before him. His mother's face. His father.

A two-foot boulder bounced off the Rocbull's skull and landed beside Rorren.

The ax fell, followed by a thunk as the massive bulk dropped.

Vesta lowered her hand, gathered her strength, and ran to Rorren. She knelt beside him. Her fingers nearly touched his arm, but an engine revved and captured her attention.

Rorren rose to his feet in time to see Hevcar and the other Aklaren speeding away.

"Come back here. You loset kay aux whiff!" Vesta yelled.

Rorren touched her shoulder, but she pulled away and went to Metra's side.

Bending with tenderness, the witch picked up the limp hand and pulled it to her chest, filling the space where the necklace had been.

"I will kill them all. I swear it." Vesta said. Her body shivered with anger and the blackest magic.

Rorren had seen Scorth evil before—saw it every time he looked at his scars. He smelled it on her. He knew his raven was in danger of choosing a path worse than death.

CHAPTER 13

En route to the Advent

Ragora

131 years ago

VESTA WASN'T HUNGRY FOR breakfast during the flight aboard the Royal Transport. She sat across from her mother, poking at her food with listless enthusiasm.

Segments of merchant houses passed across the window, nestled between the dark green jungle and winding rivers.

Vesta gave up on food and went to the glass, stretching on her tiptoes to get a better view.

She saw the faint outline of towers and the stunning buildings around the harbor. The white shores of the sea blended with the sails of Ragora's famous fishing ships.

Vesta loved the harbor but her mother rarely allowed her to venture there. A tingle of disappointment further upset her stomach as the transport carried them in the opposite direction.

"Finish your meal." No command of her mother was ever to be ignored.

Vesta brushed the wrinkles from her royal gown, hoping that looking more presentable would please the Queen.

The fabric of her dress was of the same quality but no one wore the royal robes like her mother. The indigo gown, embroidered around the bodice with black Scorth designs, seemed almost mathematically precise clinging to the body of Queen Talie. A velvet robe covered her shoulders, and, as if her status as ruler of all was not clear, the edge of the robe was laced with jewels mined from the Diamond Moon of Ragora.

It wasn't just the gown. The way the Queen sat and ate and moved made everyone obey her. Regal, spine straight but always slanting, as if she held a wave of physical violence from bursting out.

Vesta sulked to the table and forced herself to swallow a mouthful.

"Edda, why can I not wear the royal jewels for the Advent?"

One glance from the Queen could make anyone feel stupid.

"When you have earned your place in the royal court, you shall have such a gown."

"I am part of the royal clan. I have earned it."

"To be born of noble blood is no guarantee of its continuance. You will learn, naset, unless you rise above all Scorth and make the decision others will not, our clan will no longer control the planet. The other clans will always be there, looking for an opportunity to seize the crown and destroy all I have built."

Vesta mulled the words but they went down just about as poorly as breakfast. A queasy feeling bubbled in Vesta's stomach when she saw the black towers of the boarding Academy. The transport descended and tiny specs of people came into view. She saw families standing on the dock, all with children Vesta's age. Every single one tensed and stilled when the Royal Transport landed.

Glancing at her mother, Vesta was desperate for reassurance even though she knew there would be none.

They exited the transport with all the traditions of the ages. Guards lined the platform from the ship to the docking bay entrance. Her mother marched down the ramp as if she owned all of Ragora, which, in actuality, she did.

Skipping a step to keep up, Vesta kept her head down. She hoped by ignoring the gawking stares from other students and their parents, they would disappear. Watching her mother's robe trailing over the polished platform, Vesta wished to carry herself with the same power.

Near the entrance stood a Scorth man so old his hair had turned completely white. He blocked their path and terrified Vesta. She reached for her mother's hand and the action received a death glare.

"My beautiful Queen, welcome to the Advent."

He bowed, hands clinging to his sides. As he lifted, his eyes fell on Vesta.

"And this must be the young princess."

Talie's fingernails dug into Vesta's shoulder and pushed her so close she could smell his overpowering cologne.

"Yes, Intendent. In the top clan, I have no doubt."

The Academy Head pressed his thin lips together.

"We shall see."

Turning, he addressed the small crowd that had gathered.

"This is what the Advent is all about. You will prove yourselves on the Spires of Knowledge where it will be determined which of the four Academy clans suits you best."

One boy called out from behind them: "No one wants to be in Lorn Clan!"

Several new students let out a peal of nervous laughter that settled Vesta by a fraction.

The Intendent escorted the Queen through the busy docking center. Ships landed on numerous platforms beyond the glass walls of the building, while inside, a flurry of activities pulled Vesta's attention in multiple directions.

Older Academy students sat in chairs that looked uncomfortable, hunched over books. Some browsed the fine cloth and hand-crafted weapons for sale in the gift shop. They walked by a restaurant where a marriage barter was taking place. Vesta lost her spot behind her mother, fascinated by the arguing parties.

She leaned over the railing surrounding the high-top tables and bit her lip. The groom used his family's political standing to secure more from the bank of jewels the bride's family had lined across the table.

The negotiations stopped when they saw the Queen. Vesta frowned as they all bowed, annoyed the proceedings ceased.

Talie's voice ripped Vesta away from the Scorth custom. Not that there was much to see now, anyway.

She focused again on the Queen's robes, not looking up even when they boarded the motor cruiser.

Passing beneath them, the trimmed landscape of the outer grounds of the Academy seemed sterile and barren, far from the lush jungle she loved.

The Academy appeared. Vesta had seen pictures of the vine-covered walls and stone dormitories, but the pictures never induced the anxious flutter that overtook her now.

The ship rounded the towers of the Great Hall, revealing covered bleachers that rose into the air around the Spires of Knowledge. Slowing, the transport entered the tunnel beneath the bleachers and Vesta's heartbeat sped up.

The Academy Head ushered Vesta out. Everyone was surprised when the Queen followed.

She looked at them and said, "I wish a moment with my daughter."

Rare was it for the Queen to explain herself. Even more so, to call Vesta *daughter* instead of *naset*, the Scorth word for girl-child.

Squeezing Vesta's arm, Talie took her to a secluded corner near the moss-covered wall of the arena. The moss smelled like the jungle and Vesta inhaled until she went lightheaded. She needed to hold onto that smell.

Talie bent to Vesta's level. Had Vesta ever looked into her mother's eyes like this? She could not remember a time.

"You will make me proud."

It was an order.

Swallowing, Vesta nodded. Her eyes fell to the ground rather than face the stone gaze of the Queen.

"You must rank highest in the Advent for the sake of our legacy."

Another order. Thinking of the consequences of disobeying made Vesta bite her bottom lip.

Talie took Vesta's face between her hands, nails digging into her skin.

"I fear your granda's influence will cause you to fail."

Vesta raised her chin, seeking approval in her mother's expression.

"I will not fail, Edda."

Dropping her arms to her sides, Talie straightened until her figure blocked the sun and left Vesta shivering in her shadow.

"You must win, no matter the cost. Suppress the instincts Vahza awoke in you. Remember what I have taught you. Be clever. Be cunning. Be willing to do what others fear to try. Crush them and win."

Vesta welcomed the rush of adrenaline coursing through her twelve-year-old frame.

"I will make you proud." She meant it with every fiber in her. She'd given up her granda for this and was determined to make that sacrifice meaningful.

Talie absently waved her hand through the air.

"Go and see that you do."

Her mother boarded the cruiser and vanished. In the emptiness of her departure, Vesta stumbled, limbs numb, into the ranks of the other new inductees.

They all meshed together, shoving and laughing, nervous and excited. Vesta had never been one of them, just another face in the mob, a commoner.

A pudgy Scorth boy plowed into the pack and broke through to the wings, where everyone was clamoring to get a view of the arena. They squeezed Vesta out. Tripping backward, she tore her uniform and scraped her arm.

With a surprising amount of strength, soft, delicate fingers lifted her to her feet. Vesta gawked, jaw hanging, at such a brazen gesture. How dare someone touch her!

"Are you okay?"

For a Scorth, the girl was not only not pretty, but she was as common as common got. Her clothes were not the highest quality and her hair, *that hair*! Vesta shoved her away. The girl smiled.

"Luha Zyne. Nice to meet you." She offered her hand like some propertyless kitlush.

Going rigid, Vesta gave her best impression of her mother.

"I am Vesta, daughter of the Queen."

Luha glanced over her shoulder, brow wrinkling. She put her hand on Vesta's arm and pulled her back into line.

"I would not announce that. They will be meaner to you if they know."

Vesta tore her arm away from the impertinent peasant.

"My edda will not be pleased with your behavior. She will punish you if you do not leave me alone."

The girl did not obey.

"I just wanted to make a friend."

Vesta's upper lip curled in disgust as her mother's often did. Vesta shoved into the crowd of students to distance herself from the weakling.

Vesta could not see the arena over the taller pupils. An adult stepped up on a platform with a pencil tucked behind his ear and a clipboard between his hands.

"Each of you will be divided into groups. You will ascend the spires with your group once the Advent has begun."

Once the Scorth man left the platform, organized chaos ensued. Vesta found herself corralled into a group and ushered into one of the waiting rooms. She was with a group of twelve others. One of them was Luha Zyne. The girl looked at Vesta but Vesta avoided her glance.

The man with the clipboard entered the room and took down all their names. When Vesta announced who she was, the pudgy Scorth boy shoved her and pointed.

"You? The daughter of Queen Talie? You look too scrawny."

The other students laughed, all but Luha. Vesta sat up straighter, receiving an I-told-you-so look from her would-be friend.

The man with the clipboard touched the com device in his ear.

"You are group eleven. I will be back for you as soon as your turn has arrived. We are all eager to see who is strongest among you."

He closed the door and the room went silent. Vesta thought she might have to endure more teasing, but the other students must have been as nervous as she was.

The next few minutes would decide their fates for the next eight years.

Which clan Vesta ended up in meant everything.

The Lorn Clan was the worst. It was unthinkable to associate with anyone in Lorn Clan, let alone become one of them. Students of all backgrounds ended up in Lorn for being weak, uncompetitive, and valuing hard work above class standing.

Largess Clan was the second worst of the bunch. The unrefined, middle-class drones. Her mother would probably disown her for landing in Largess. Vesta knew for sure Luha Zyne would end up there.

Vesta vowed to earn her place in the Lucre Clan. Only one percent of the Advent inductees ended up in the Lucre. The clan was reserved for royalty, the elite, and where her mother expected her to be. If Vesta ended up in Vulgus Clan, her mother would not be happy, but she could live with it.

Luha moved from her chair in the corner and plopped into the empty one next to Vesta.

"My older brother is a student here. He is in Vulgus Clan. He and my parents will be watching, but they are protesting against the Advent."

Surprised by the admission about the brother and raking over the girl's appearance again, Vesta considered giving Luha another chance.

"Then your parents are traitors."

Vesta hoped her insult would entice the girl to leave. Luha scooted closer.

"They knew your granda before she left."

The air left Vesta's lungs, like being punched in the chest.

"Edda says Vahza was a traitor, too."

Luha looked up at the ceiling, her lips pressed together as if deciding whether to continue. Vesta hoped she would be quiet.

"My parent say that the Queen wanted to banish Vahza and her clan to the diamond mines but she dared not."

Vesta hated herself for hanging on the girl's every word.

"Why not?"

"Because your granda has a power that no one understands. The Queen was afraid to fight her clan."

"I do not believe you."

Luha puckered her lips, shrugged, and continued.

"My parents decided not to go into the stars with your granda's clan. They love Ragora. They want to fight for it."

Everything Queen Talie told Vesta came true at that moment. The other clans were after the throne. Her family's rule might end unless Vesta proved herself on the spires. Luha's story, whether true or not, cemented Vesta's resolve to win the Advent.

"Then your parents really are traitors and they should go to the diamond mines forever."

It was a low blow, unworthy of the daughter of the Queen, and Vesta knew it. Rather than watching tears well up in Luha's eyes, Vesta stood and crossed the room. She did not want to be seen in the company of a crybaby traitor to the crown.

The door opened.

"Group seven, you are on deck. Follow me."

All twelve students lined up, with the pudgy boy pushing Vesta to the end of the line. She shoved back, vowing to get her revenge on the spires. The Academy teacher scolded them. They were directed into a narrow corridor, passing by burning torches in decorative slots along the wall.

Muffled sounds came through the stone walls, cheering and chants from the audience above them. Occasionally, there would be a scream. Probably someone's mother, Vesta thought. Not her mother. Never her mother.

Emerging onto a platform several stories up, Vesta shielded her eyes from the blare of sun and sea blue sky. Squinting, she saw them—the Spires of Knowledge. The polished black towers formed a forest of varying obelisks lifting higher and higher.

Her stomach tingled with excitement and dread. The spires intimidated her in a way they hadn't in the textbooks. Each narrow tube widened at the top to form a pedestal, an uncomfortably tiny platform to land on.

Spotting the royal box in the highest corner of the highest bleacher, Vesta couldn't see her mother, but she sensed her eyes. Watching her. Not cheering her on but ordering her success.

"You know how the Advent works, but if you have been living with the reclusive clans of the jungle, let me explain." The teacher extended his hand toward the nearest spires. "You must climb the spires to the top where treasure awaits you. Whoever claims the most valuable treasure will be rewarded with membership in the Vulgus Clan. Show extraordinary skill in doing this, and you may be offered entry into Lucre clan."

The students all reacted to the name of the most elite group at the Academy.

"Medics are standing by. Be warned that deathshade has been known to grow on the columns and in the swamps below. If you do fall, try not to fall into a patch."

Students chuckled at the teacher's joke. Not Vesta. Her focus was honed to the spot where the treasure was waiting.

"The fire signal will alert you when to begin." The teacher left the platform, his presence replaced by a voice from a loudspeaker.

"Welcome, group seven." The announcer read the names of every member of the group. The crowd settled into silence when he said Vesta's name. Tensing her body, Vesta planned to win their applause, no matter what.

She found Luha standing poised beside her, ready to run.

"Good luck."

Vesta sneered.

"I do not need luck."

Twelve black ravens dropped from the clouds, flying in a v-formation. They dove toward the arena and spread their wings in unison. Each hovered over one of the spires. A flash of light drew applause from the crowd as the ravens turned into Scorth warriors.

"Wow!" Luha said. "They must all have a transformation stone. I never saw a transformation before."

Vesta hated to think she looked as wide-eyed and impressed as Luha, but she was. The warriors placed various valuables at the top of the spires and Vesta bent low. With her heart pounding in her ears, she watched the warriors change into ravens and fly away.

A blast of fire erupted across the arena from a cannon and the pudgy boy shot into action, spire wobbling as he jumped onto it. Vesta observed before she acted, noting the spires teetered sideways when students landed. The pudgy boy held on, but two others fell, splashing into the water below.

Vesta climbed cautiously onto the first spire and saw Luha do the same on the spire to her left. Each time Vesta launched to a higher platform, her breakfast bounced to her throat.

From ledge to ledge, the threat of deathshade below, her senses sharpened into a clarity of vision. She willed herself to win. Not even the challenge of landing on a moving surface could deter her from her goal.

She heard the crowd cheer and looked ahead to see the boy make an impressive landing up to the next level. At this rate, he would win.

Hissing with determination, Vesta sprang up behind him, feeling pressured when she heard the crowd cheering for her.

She knew they would cheer.

Relishing it, she sank her teeth into her people's hopes like a fresh piece of tresacoi.

Luha jumped behind her but she came up short. Her fingers struggled to find a hold. She slid toward a nasty patch of deathshade, latching onto the edge of the pedestal with just enough strength to stop her fall.

Two paths appeared before Vesta. Her granda's kind face filled her mind. *Help your friend.* It overpowered the other voice, the one telling her to win no matter the cost.

Without thinking, Vesta jumped to the spire next to her, landed painfully, and rolled to avoid a patch of deathshade. She clipped her arm on a sharp rock but kept sliding until she reached the edge.

Locking her fingers around Luha, she pulled her to safety seconds before the girl lost her grip.

Luha landed beside her, out of breath.

"I knew it," Luha whispered. "I knew you were like your granda."

The audience went silent. Vesta looked up to the box where her mother sat, but she was too far away to hear the Academy Intendent lean over to the Queen and say, "Looks like your daughter has earned her way into the Lorn Clan."

Vesta could not see the daggers in the Queen's eyes or the fingers that clutched around the Intendent's throat. She didn't hear her mother's murderous tone.

"Never! My daughter will never belong to that clan!"

Vesta only saw the Queen rise to her feet and stand motionless over multitudes of her subjects. It was a warning.

Vesta knew she must win. Her life depended on it.

Reflections from the jewels above consumed Vesta. Luha no longer existed. Pumping her legs until they ached, Vesta ignored the pain as she climbed higher and faster than anyone else.

The boy got there first.

Vesta launched herself off the last spire and slammed into him. A thin ringing from the impact left her dizzy until the boy violently shoved her away. She tasted blood. It sharpened her senses. Pulling on his arm before he retrieved one of the gems, she anticipated his reaction. He swung at her, but she bent sideways and he missed.

With a growl, teeth bared, he charged at her, but he had more strength than cleverness. Vesta sidestepped and he went barreling over the edge.

Relieved, she turned to take a gem but found Luha there first.

"We can share it."

Luha took two of the gems, offering one of them to Vesta.

The audience went so motionless Vesta forgot they were there. A flood of anger rushed her senses, making her hands shake. She wiped her mouth and knew her mother was watching.

"We can both be in Vulgus Clan." Luha's face was bright.

Whether Vesta wanted or needed a friend didn't matter.

"No."

Vesta took both jewels and pushed Luha off the platform. The girl's boots disappeared over the ledge where the pudgy boy was pulling himself up.

"The crown will not be shared," she yelled to the audience.

Vesta held up both jewels for her mother.

"I give you the future Queen of Ragora." Talie's voice carried through the arena. Wild applause and cheering followed. They dared not react any other way.

Soaking in the moment, Vesta ignored the twinge of guilt. The emptiness of losing a friend threatened to overpower her.

Vesta saw the Queen beaming with pride. It was the first time she ever saw her mother smile like that.

Vesta smiled, too.

Desandor

Present Day

There weren't many flowers in the desert but Vesta obtained some at the market. A neat row of bright petals lined the coffin. Metra's Sandorian friends marveled at Vesta's choice. The flowers she selected were an old-fashioned species that Metra secretly loved.

There were no tears in her eyes, but Rorren knew what it meant to the witch, this last thing she could do for the widow. As the speakers celebrated Metra's life, Vesta stood so still she left Rorren wondering if she had turned to stone.

The gathering was small but the size did not reflect the abundance of love. Jon had taken a special leave from the military academy to attend. Though Rorren spent sleepless nights up to the funeral, standing there now, he was satisfied they had done right by the widow.

After saying their goodbyes, Rorren and Vesta traveled by sandcrawler to the farm. Halfway there, Vesta said, "I wish to visit the place it happened."

Remorse and sorrow were too near for him to refuse anything.

He turned into the shadow of the suns, traveling in silence until they arrived.

The embers from what was left of the house and barn still smoked.

Vesta left the sandcrawler and he gave her some time to herself before he sought her out.

Stepping over the charred foundation, Rorren found her crouching by the bath. The famous stone tub still sparkled beneath the soot.

Vesta ran her hand over the rim, her fingers picking up the loose ash and revealing the white marble beneath.

"They could not destroy this."

Holding his hat, Rorren studied the hair that fell over her shoulders and hid her face.

Vesta's hand formed a fist and she stood.

"Teach me, farmer. Teach me so I may punish them for this wrong."

The desire for revenge was not uncommon in Scorth, but her acknowledgment that right and wrong existed was.

"Killing them won't make you feel better."

A lesson he learned the hard way.

"Yes, it will," Vesta said, attention glued to the spot where Metra had died. "They must pay for what they have done. If I had control, this would not have happened. If I had the power of the Fire-Scar, she would not be dead."

He said the same thing once about his father.

Rorren put his hat on and the brim shaded his face from the afternoon rays.

"Or we might all be dead. Besides, it doesn't work like that. You can't become Fire-Scar with revenge in your heart."

"Will you teach me?"

Folding his arms, Rorren considered his faith in his abilities and hers. She was not now capable of harnessing such power for good, but through time and with training, Rorren had to believe she could be.

If not, he risked creating a monster worse than he was. It was a risk Metra encouraged him to take.

"If you swear to do exactly what I say," he said, pointing a finger at her. She nodded.

"And you don't question my methods," he continued.

Another nod.

"And, if you succeed, we talk to the other homesteaders before you do anything crazy. The last thing I want is more innocent people getting hurt."

"I agree to these terms, Mic Rorren."

Shaking his head and sighing, he looked toward the horizon.

"I better not regret this."

"You will," Vesta said and grinned wickedly. "But you are eager for this. I can see it in your eyes."

"I need you to understand why I respect the Fire-Scar Warriors."

"The Aux Katan are traitors," Vesta said.

Rorren frowned, already regretting the long and treacherous days ahead.

CHAPTER 14

BENEATH A SKY AS blue as the eyes of the Scorth witch, Rorren gazed over his farm. The reflection of the sky skipped across the tops of dunes and engulfed the world in a cerulean dream.

"I am ready."

Vesta's armor had been polished and clung to her trim body without hindering her natural agility. The pitch-black feathers of her cape left snake trails in the sand as she moved.

Weaving up into a sharp collar that flattered her neck, the fabric dared any man, woman, or child to cross her.

Vesta swept across the sand with one hand clutching the edge of her cape, the other around the wooden staff he carved.

Sizing her up, Rorren found her doing the same to him.

"Fire-Scar Warriors don't dress like that," he said.

She twirled her cape and regarded him with a conscious coolness.

"This one does."

Rorren stuck his tongue under his bottom lip and kicked at the sand with his boot.

"Uh-huh. You're a long way from that yet."

"Then get on with it."

Rorren took a step to the side, revealing the presence of a thick, round rock in the middle of the sand.

"Sit."

Distrust flooding her features, she surveyed the rock as if it might turn Obsedei and attack her.

She moved with deliberate slowness, leaving Rorren no room to misunderstand that she hated taking orders from him.

"There is only one lesson a Fire-Scar Warrior must learn before wielding a menti blade."

"Enlighten me, kitlush," she said. She landed on the stone as if it were the throne of her desert kingdom. The cape flared behind her, also instinctively knowing how to act like a spoiled brat.

Rorren paced before her, focusing on the lesson and not his impudent student.

"I can't tell you what it is. You have to learn it for yourself."

"I despise riddles. Besides, I am sure I already know it," Vesta replied.

Rorren stopped, propped a leg on the boulder, and bent over her.

"The first thing you must accept if we are doing this is that you know nothing. When I want your opinion, I will give it to you."

Her mouth tightened, her lashes blinking with hostility.

Rorren continued before she sent a boulder flying at his head.

"Your task today and for the next and the next, is to come to this spot and sit."

She stabbed the staff into the sand, exhaling.

"And do what?"

"Just sit."

"I do not see how sitting on a rock in the middle of nowhere is supposed to do anything."

No breeze unsettled the dunes and the pleasant air welcomed deep thoughts from the cloudless heavens. Spotting the path of a starship in the upper atmosphere, Rorren followed its trajectory until it vanished into the stars.

"Find peace in the world around you," he said, feeling like a hypocrite. "The sky, the sand. Taste the scent in the air. Notice what you've never noticed before."

"And I must stay awake?" Vesta asked with a yawn. "I am to do this day after day for how long?"

Rorren latched his hands behind him, the leather of his trench coat tightening at the seams.

"Until you've learned."

"Learned what?"

"It's not something words can explain."

Vesta's mouth curved into a grimace.

"You sound just like the Scorth traitors. Always with the puzzles. Never accomplishing anything."

He left her there, surprised to find she stayed for the rest of the afternoon.

And the next day.

And the next.

A week passed.

One afternoon, he entered the house and found her pacing around the kitchen table.

"This is a waste of time."

Rorren took off his hat and plopped into the chair.

"Is it?" he asked. He unlaced his boots with his peripherals on Vesta.

Vesta wore the simple blue dress the widow had given her. She gave up on the heavy armor and sweltering cape sometime during the week.

"I want to go after the marauders, not gaze off into the sky for pointless afternoons."

Rorren set his boots by the door. He knew if he left them in the middle of the floor, Vesta would scold him.

"It is a necessary step."

"I quit."

Rorren ran a hand across his chin and analyzed her posture.

"We can take a short break from it. Tomorrow, we will try something new."

"It better not be boring."

***

She joined him in the barn without hesitation or regret. Her actions made him feel guilty. Here he was, hoarding up the best parts of himself while she went all in every time.

Despite acting annoyed by his orders, her raw determination gave him a glimpse of who she might be, separate from the baggage and the scars.

He didn't let her see that part of him. He stood like a statue, holding his Galactic Order staff in one hand and a rusted sword in the other.

"What is this?" she asked, tying a knot in the modified shirt she raided from his closet. Even with the baggy clothes, she was still undeniably female.

And undeniably Scorth.

Rorren tossed the blade into the air and she quickly snatched it.

"If you are going to use a menti blade, you must first be able to use a sword."

"I already know how to—"

He glared at her.

"At least this is less boring," she muttered.

"I assume you had the basic combat training of a woman in upper-class Scorth society?" he asked, snooping for information about her past and hoping it went unnoticed.

The coldness in her stance came with a warning. She lifted the blade a bit more expertly than Rorren expected.

"Sparring with colleagues and fighting in battle are two very different things," he said.

"For all your flaws, kitlush, you are a skilled warrior. I wish to learn."

He gestured for her to strike. She came at him, swinging. Her passion startled him but made her vulnerable. In one move, he knocked the sword from her grip with his staff.

"You fight wild when you need to fight smart."

Picking up the blade, she charged again but with more control. This time, metal clanged on metal three times before Rorren disarmed her. She landed on her back and he pointed the spear under her chin.

"You fight as if we are equally matched. You are strong but almost all your opponents will be stronger."

Batting the spear away, Vesta scrambled to her feet. Her spirit reminded him of a time when he used to care. A humbling and painful memory.

"You must use your opponent's strength against him. You must fight with your mind."

Twirling the staff around pleased him. He hadn't forgotten how to show off with it.

"I should just use a veer rifle and be done with it," she said.

He brought the staff to his chest, stilling his body.

"Again," he said. "This time, watch for weaknesses in my approach."

When she attacked, Rorren purposefully left his right side exposed. Vesta took advantage, bringing the rusted blade up to his rib cage, stopping just before making contact.

"Good. We will practice every morning before chores. Then, you will go to the rock."

"I would rather help you with the farm," she said, pressing the blade to his side.

"You can help me by doing what I say."

Vesta did not look convinced but she did as he said.

Weeks followed and her skills with a sword improved.

Her affection for patience did not.

Dusk blanketed the farm and Rorren worried when Vesta missed dinner. Her stomach had a knack for sensing when he set out a meal. She was conveniently never around for the preparation of said meal. When the stars came out with no sign of her, he went searching. The last place he thought to look was the rock.

That is where she sat. Hair bathed in moonlight; eyes closed.

They opened as he tromped up the dune.

"Today, I determined to sit here until I learned what you think I need to, but," she said, "I have failed."

Rorren gazed up at the stars, a million blinking lights caught in a web of swirling nebula and black molasses. Inhaling the crisp, cool air rejuvenated him. He lived for nights like this.

"You continue to try. That is not failing."

"There is a beauty in the desert. A calm. I mistook it for a tedious repetition of sand," Vesta said.

"Maybe you haven't failed after all," Rorren replied, touching her shoulder.

"Then, I may discontinue this task?"

He squeezed, then let go.

"No."

As he walked away, he counted how many new Scorth curse words he learned in the last weeks.

CHAPTER 15

A FINE SHEEN OF sand coated the farmstead overnight, requiring Rorren to sweep off the sandcrawler before he ventured onto the worn road. Daily chores waited.

His muscles groaned as he climbed into the cab. Morning sparring sessions woke more than just a fighting spirit in the Scorth witch, as his backside discovered when he sat down.

Vesta sat erect in the passenger seat and heaved the door closed.

"What are you—"

"Today, I wish to help with the farm."

Rorren frowned as he adjusted the rear-view mirror.

"It's not on the schedule."

"It will be a test for me."

Intrigued by the words, Rorren slammed his door closed, giving her a glance and a grunt.

The engine rumbled to life and he drove until they reached the metal bowl and stack of the harvesting machine.

In the last weeks, he managed to pick up a couple hundred metallic orbs. The amount was insufficient to make the machine function, but the dangerous and grueling process required time and effort.

He climbed out of the cab, muscles tender, and guided his steps to the empty crates. He loaded them into the harvesting machine in slots along the conveyor belt. Each crate he placed was like an unspoken promise to himself. He would not lose the crop this year. The vow had buried itself into the recesses of his soul since Metra's death.

Vesta helped him place the crates, working with him until the sun was high overhead. He guzzled half his canteen, pretending not to watch her from the corner of his eye. She leaned against a crate, focused on the broken equipment and scattered beads. His old faded shirt and slacks anchored her to the shifting sands like the boulder she visited in the middle of the desert. Sunlight brushed her face, illuminating something he thought could be immovable resolve or inner evil.

A familiar tingle crept up his skin.

Holding out the canteen, he offered his water, but she ignored him as some invisible force pulled her to the edge of the circular pit.

"You have made little headway."

Rorren screwed the lid on.

"Hard work, the Maker, and a miracle will help me get it done," he said. He hoped in rather than believed his words.

"We must make our own miracles."

Ye of little faith. That was one of his father's favorites and too raw for Rorren to utter.

A warm burst of air circled them and lifted her hair and oversized sleeves into the air.

The smell of magic that tingled his senses made Rorren wonder if murderers like him could turn demons into angels.

A dozen tiny orbs vibrated, sand peeling away in waves, and beads began jumping from their nests.

The beads lifted in tandem with Vesta's hands and Rorren hitched his breath, waiting for a miracle.

The metallic orbs hovered together in a circle, catching the light at different angles and painting a kaleidoscope of colors over the sand.

The wind died and the beads dropped like rain.

They bounced out of the harvester and across the sand.

Rorren sprinted and crashed into Vesta, knocking her out of the path of the dangerous, flesh-burning droplets.

"Aux rand kitlush!" she shouted.

He decided she was generalizing and didn't mean him when she said feces-brained idiot-human in her native tongue.

Ignoring the spasm of overexcited muscles, he stood and brushed himself off.

"Why was I able to succeed at the moisture hub and not now?" That low, throaty snarl made him think twice before moving closer to her.

She glared at him, searching his face for the answer.

He calmed his breathing and waited until she copied his action. She unleashed her tension with a growl. The electric energy in the air evaporated and the smell of evil dissipated.

"You just changed from the raven. Your mind was clear. Turmoil from your past did not weigh you down. You were after something more."

"More," she hissed, "An engineered concept to make slaves of us all."

Rorren picked up a handful of sand. He let the grains trickle between his fingers.

"It is if you're seeking the wrong kind of treasure."

"All you have *more* of is riddles. To hold in the mind the power to manipulate every orb is impossible," she said.

Opening his hand, Rorren returned all the sand to the ground.

"A closed mind makes everything impossible."

In the dead of night, Rorren rummaged for a snack, light from the icebox creating shadows in the kitchen. Now that the witch was here, his humble dwelling swirled with secrets. He tasted them in the chalky air and not even the sandfruit sandwich could soothe his palate.

He wolfed the bread down while flipping through wrinkled old pages. By studying the writings in candlelight, he conserved power for the farm towers. Funds ran thin and his power bill kept climbing. Besides, darkness concealed the mark of the relheer better than his coat.

"You are up late," Vesta said. She moved to the table in nothing but his oversized shirt.

"So are you," he replied, closing the war-ravaged book.

"Your couch is not comfortable."

Rorren moved to blow out the candle but Vesta pulled it away.

"What is that?"

Rather than fight the inevitable, he yielded, letting her get a good look at the piece of forbidden Scorth history.

"A gift from a friend."

The candlelight flickered across her face. There was a cold but luxurious fragility about how she looked at the book—as if its mere existence degraded her.

"Which is?" she asked, following his movements as he traced the outline of the worn lettering.

"Kira Tahu. A text of the Aux Katan."

"The dirt farmer likes to read banned books. Shocking," she said.

Rorren pulled the candle to the middle of the table, light touching a round object behind a velvet cloth.

"If you think that's something, wait till you see this."

He reached out and slipped the cloth from a sleek ball about the size of his fist. Vesta was visibly startled, but to her credit, she didn't gasp. Many would have.

"How? Where?"

The breathless whisper made him bold.

"You're not the only one with secrets."

Her attention left him to stare at the churning of violent gases inside the clear encasement. The orb's radiance dwarfed the candlelight with flashes of purple and white.

Vesta draped one arm over her chair.

"The squeaky soldier boy has a dark side."

"It was also a gift," he said.

"A solstal is a rare treasure in the galaxy now. Worth a fortune."

"And dangerous in the hands of the black-market crowd," Rorren said but was thinking, *dangerous in anyone's hands.*

"These were gifts from your Aux Katan woman?"

"She told me I would have occasion to use it. I didn't believe her."

With one graceful movement, he tossed the blanket over the solstal. He'd never touched it in all the years it had been his. He imagined how ice-cold the glass might be or maybe he would feel the pulse of the fire it contained.

His head spun, no longer worried about Vesta as he watched her return to the couch, wondering why he ever let a Scorth in his house.

Rorren performed his morning routine with the same grind and empty hope he had every morning.

Staggering out into the desert, part of him screamed that something was wrong. No heat or dust in the desert air touched his skin. He caught no whiffs of black magic.

His limbs burdened him—hard to control—but his entire body was loose as if some puppet master loomed above him, pulling his strings.

He resisted the idea of going into the heart of the farm, yet some invisible force pulled him there.

Moving with heavy steps up the dune, he fell into the shadow of an enormous ship that overhung the expanse.

The buzz pulsing up his body sounded like it was coming from deep underground, but his head told him it was from the ship.

Fear swallowed him and he squeezed his eyes shut, refusing to look over that next dune.

The fear was unspecific, yet part of his subconscious knew where it came from.

Dust filled his mouth, thick as cotton, and his hands grasped at clumps of sand until he reached the top of the dune.

His chest tightened when he saw them—two silhouettes against the horizon. One was tall and lean, the other shorter with long hair.

His parents. Mom and Dad.

His vision blurred and then nothing existed but the elegant, sleek lines of the Scorth warship.

Smoke from the engine stained the sky in black splotches. The massive vessel turned and its pointed wings spread across the desert like a circling vulture.

As the ship dropped altitude, Rorren tried to scream.

Run.

Neither silhouette moved.

Rorren skipped down the dune, half tumbling over, but didn't slow his pace. He screamed louder, sprinting with all the power in his capable legs, struggling to breathe. Bile surged up his throat as he watched the ship crash into the ground. In a wave of sand and smoke, they were gone.

The ship tore a hole in his farm. He sunk to his knees, his fear replaced with rage.

Precious fruit was strewn around him—shells cracked open and oozing like bleeding soldiers on the battlefield.

The Scorth ship landed and the enemy poured from the wreckage into the safety of his land.

Every atom in his body went electric with hatred for every one of them.

They took everything.

He found his mother on the edge of the dune, cradling the body of his dead father.

"This is your fault. You did this! Murderer," his mother screamed.

A sunwart tugged on his arm but he shoved it away. Scorth warriors descended on them. He couldn't let them take his mother. He rose to his feet, spinning his Galactic Order staff, digging in his heels and ready to fight.

"Let go, Mic Rorren!"

The world tilted on its axis. The cool glass slipped from his hand. He blinked twice and waited for the double vision to clear, realizing Vesta had pried the solstal from his fingers.

He was no longer in the middle of the farm.

The kitchen lay still and silent, lit by the flickering candle.

The solstal rolled across the table. Vesta caught it before it hit the ground. She wrapped it tightly inside the blanket.

"It's never done that before," Rorren said.

"You are tired. You should never touch it when your mind is not awake."

"You shouldn't touch it at all," he growled. He meant to say, *of course, you're right*, but his pride was bruised for being so foolish.

"It tried to take you. What did you see?" Vesta asked.

"What I fear. What holds me back," Rorren replied. He rose from the table with tremors still rippling through his body.

"Not even you can conquer the solstal, how will I?" she asked, but she had no idea who he really was.

The answer stared at Rorren from the book.

"Tomorrow, we go into town. I will show you how."

Her mouth twitched with the hint of a grin.

"You won't like it," he added.

"I never like anything you make me do."

She got up from the table and disappeared into the den.

CHAPTER 16

Royal Academy
Ragora
131 years ago

VESTA WATCHED WITH FASCINATION as the miniature pyramid unfolded. Elaborate traps and levers became visible—on display for the class to study.

In the center of the toy model was a shining gold coin.

"Now, your turn. The challenge. Let us see which of you shall give up your most prized treasure," the instructor said.

Vesta tensed. Some of the players were clever. Luha's older brother, Norn, especially. Vesta was glad he wasn't in her age group.

"Begin."

Vesta worked on her miniature Rishka as hard as anyone, but since she was the hero of the Spires of Knowledge, she had a lot to prove and a reputation to maintain.

The weak students lost quickly.

Vesta understood the intricacies of the mines, false floors, ticking bombs, and invisible blades. There was no challenge in destroying them.

Beating them until they were sniveling crybabies was fun.

All of them were nothing.

Vesta split her attention between the game board before her and Luha. Amassing as much treasure as Vesta, Luha seemed to be enjoying herself. Vesta itched to play her nemesis and crush her dreams.

The Intendent said Luha was lucky because she survived the deathshade and Lorn Clan welcomed her.

Even the thought of Lorn Clan made Vesta's nose wrinkle as if they smelled. Aux whiffs, for sure.

The deathshade healed across Luha's face in a disgusting yellow crust. Some of Vesta's peers started calling Luha "crusty." Silly Luha pretended it was a compliment.

One boy inched close to beating Vesta's Rishka. Vesta rubbed her neck, feeling the bare skin where her father's pendant usually hung.

She didn't win easily this time, but she won.

Another crybaby beaten.

Only two of them left now.

Vesta strutted to the front of the class and sat across the table from Luha. She soaked in the admiration of her fellow students with the nonexistent humility of the daughter of the Queen.

Luha's Rishka was small, but once Vesta started playing, it only took her a moment to become lost in a maze of ingenious traps.

The aux whiff had a knack.

She was clever.

Vesta could almost admire her if she hadn't hated her so much.

A single, uniform gasp erupted from the class and Vesta looked, her heart sinking when she saw the necklace. Her most prized treasure, the one granda gave her, dangled from the fingers of her nemesis.

Lunging out of her chair, Vesta flung herself across the room, and slammed Luha's Rishka into the classroom wall. It shattered it into pieces.

That landed Vesta in detention.

She didn't care.

She'd rather stay in detention forever than face her clan or her mother.

The defeat of the Queen's daughter spread across the entire Academy by the time lunch arrived. Instead of eating at her table, her throne in the lunchroom, she scuttled like a coward to the outskirts of the gardens.

Her food tasted bland. She chewed, sighing, and watched the starships overhead, destined for better places in the universe. Longing to be aboard one of them and leave Ragora forever, she thought, *the universe will be mine*. Her mother said that a lot.

She pictured her mother's face and the pulsing anger when she found out.

Vesta pushed the sandwich away and cupped her rolling stomach.

"Vesta?"

The timid voice came from around a vine-covered tree at the jungle's edge. Luha appeared.

"What do you want?" Vesta spat out the words as if they tasted as nasty as her lunch.

Luha walked up to her and hesitated for a long time. Vesta audibly sighed.

The Lorn Clan girl took Vesta's hand and deposited something inside. The necklace.

Some kind of trick?

The girl beamed so bright it made Vesta nauseous.

"I accidentally beat your Rishka. You can have your necklace back. It belongs to you."

"Pathetic," Vesta said. She should have thrown the necklace at her. Her arms would not obey the command. She clutched the jewel tighter. "This is what I would have expected from someone in the Lorn Clan."

Luha's face clouded over and her shoulders slumped as she walked away.

"Wait." Vesta caught up to her.

"I refuse to be in debt to you. When we are old and know how to transform, I will let you use my father's jewel for one flight." Vesta said, holding up a finger. "One time only. Then we will be even."

Luha's face twisted in a strange grimace and then Vesta realized she was trying hard to suppress a smile. She failed. Her head nodded with an exuberance Vesta envied.

"Can I eat lunch with you?"

Vesta shook her head.

Luha hurried up and said, "No one will see us out here."

Vesta looked around. After satisfying herself that Luha was right, she gave in. Luha joined her under the tree and unwrapped her lunch.

Vesta took another bite of her sandwich. It tasted better than it had a moment ago. Luha talked more than anyone she ever met.

Desandor

Present Day

Fear kept Mic Rorren from explaining why he couldn't overcome the solstal. He hated himself for it. If she knew what he'd done, she would never trust him enough to complete her journey and become Aux Katan. He wanted that for her.

He walked beside Vesta, dragging his feet through the marketplace, keeping his elbows tight to his body and not relaxing even as they started to unload the crates.

The Sandorian, Ferin-Ray, the brother-in-law of the Tribe Chief, was a trader Rorren had come to rely on over the years.

Rorren batted away flying feathers and took the chicken crates from Ferin-Ray's three-fingered hand as the Sandorian unloaded his transport trailer.

It was butcher time, which meant more crates for Rorren, provided he helped with the process.

Little shops rose around them, stacked one against another in a world filled with a thousand humanoid creatures. Under the strain of emptying the crates and then loading them into the sandcrawler, Rorren found a tentative peace. The tremble of his muscles left him tired. Too tired to think or care about the bustling world around him or the solstal.

Simple work gave him purpose and focus and emptied everything inside him. Emptiness was preferable to feeling.

"When do I learn how to conquer the solstal?"

Vesta interrupted his reverie, jerking him into painful reality. She wore a tattered old cloak and brown cargo pants. The white feathers lodged in her hair made her stance of shrieking impatience look ridiculous.

Ferin-Ray watched them and Rorren flipped up the collar of his trench coat. He had been out in public more since finding the raven, but acclimating to people again was difficult.

"This is it. Just doing hard work," Rorren said, wiping his forehead. They were down to the last of the crates.

"You are lying."

She was good at spotting his lies. Rorren waited until Ferin-Ray took two handfuls of chickens inside the butcher shop, and, pulling Vesta aside, he lowered his voice.

"You have to seek the greatest treasure in the universe."

She blinked at him, waiting for more.

"And that is?"

"I can't tell you. You have to learn for yourself."

Stacking two more empty crates into the sandcrawler, he didn't look at her, but he knew those cold eyes followed him.

"It is love, is it not? Scorth do not believe in love."

Ferin-Ray returned and pried open another crate as Rorren held it steady.

"I do not believe in love," she continued, "another construct of human frailty."

Ferin-Ray pulled out another chicken, waiving his hand to divert feathers from his mouth.

"Is your Scorth witch a philosopher?" the Sandorian asked, conversation seeming to amuse him.

Annoyed, Rorren glanced up at the clock tower in the square, wondering how much longer the torture might last.

"She's not mine," Rorren said. She never could be. No woman could.

"You are hiding something, kitlush. What is it?" Vesta asked.

"Doesn't matter," he said. He took the last crate as Ferin-Ray went inside the shop. "All that matters is figuring out how to complete your training if you want to stop the Aklaren."

"The greatest treasure," she mused, "No one is better at seeking treasure than I."

He closed the tailgate of the sandcrawler with more force than he meant to.

"Go to it then."

Lifting her chin, Vesta glanced around the market. She took a deep breath, closed her eyes and focused her breathing.

"Filter out all the noise and commotion," Rorren said, "open your mind to possibilities. Let it come to you. Ask yourself, what is the greatest treasure here in the marketplace?"

"I would," she mumbled, "if you shut up and let me concentrate."

Moving to the middle of the square, she allowed people to bump into her, passing on their way to many destinations.

Vesta opened her eyes and her gaze drifted to a group of Sandorian children a few shops away. They were kicking around a leather ball. One of them stopped and, whispering to another, pointed at Vesta.

Vesta fidgeted under the gawking eyes and returned to Rorren's side. Her actions struck a chord in him. He felt the same discomfort when people saw his scars. Most kids knew stories of the Scorth war but he doubted they had ever seen a real Scorth witch.

Rorren leaned against the sandcrawler, plucked a piece of straw from a crack in the tailgate and slipped it between his lips.

"Go talk to them. Let them see you're not going to eat them. That is, unless you are."

Something was drawing her to those kids. Rorren sensed it.

"Go on. We'll finish up here."

She glared, hesitating.

"Think of it as part of your training," he said.

Vesta flung out the dingy cloak as if it were her feathered cape.

"I despise children."

Rorren watched her approach them, glad she left the spikes home.

These last months, she had grown into a legitimate person. She was still an infant in some ways, still learning, but as Vesta stepped further into the fray, he saw real courage.

The children were shy and skittish. A brave boy marched to Vesta and stopped, large eyes peering up at her. The witch squirmed. The insecurity of her movements was at odds with everything else about her.

"My ma says you are an Orth witch."

Vesta bent to one knee. The Scorth kneeling to a child drew more attention than just Rorren's. Her straightforward actions erased any doubt Rorren still held about her becoming Aux Katan.

"It is pronounced Scorth, little vah, and yes, I am."

By the time Rorren and Ferrin-Ray finished the work and joined her, Vesta managed to make friends.

The children gathered in a half circle around the witch, watching an unusual performance. In the center of a circle, Vesta commanded grains of sand into various shapes, including into a likeness of Brawn. The sand became a miniature version of the sandcrawler and drew a round of adolescent cheers. The crawler crashed into a dune, swirling up sand and tickling the children.

When they laughed, Vesta glanced up at Rorren, beaming.

Her beauty in that moment seeped into his blood.

"Rorren-sun tamed the Scorth," Ferin-Ray said, "we could not see it but you could. The greatest treasure in the universe is the soul of a living being."

The simple Sandorian farmer knew a truth that eluded kings, premiers, scholars, and mystics. It was not the first time Rorren's neighbors humbled him.

Vesta looked so pleased with herself that Rorren didn't have the heart to tell her what following the path of Aux Katan would cost her. Pain and death or worse. In his case, murder.

"Are you magical?" one of the Sandorian children asked, squeezing the leather ball. They were cute little things with their large eyes and lipless mouths.

"Scorth do have certain abilities," Vesta said.

"Can your 'bilities find Lanta-Bree?"

"Who is Lanta-Bree?"

Ferin-Ray put his fingers on Vesta's arm, bending to whisper.

"She has gone missing. Others have, too, Scorth-Vesta. We know not where."

Rorren perked up. Did Vesta just earn herself a Sandorian name?

"She is my friend," the little Sandorian added.

Lashes falling halfway, Vesta set her gaze and tensed her shoulders.

"I know where she is," Vesta said. She dashed into the crowd.

Ferin-Ray stood there, bewildered.

Rorren spat out the straw and cursed. She was going to get herself killed in pursuit of the greatest treasure. He wasn't about to let that happen.

CHAPTER 17

R ORREN TRACKED VESTA TO the far edge of the east port, where the storage containers butted up against the space dock, casting shadows the size of starships. Over the years, Rorren had seen enough of Desandor to know he didn't want to know what unimaginable secrets slept in those shadows.

Vesta moved upward in darkness, head tilting in a way that made Rorren think she was listening for something. They climbed higher and he tasted the rocket fuel in the air.

Vesta stopped between the dueling shade of two titanic shipping containers. Rorren neared her, slowing his steps, waiting for his eyes to adjust. Her head tipped near the metal slat, dark lashes half closed.

"This is dangerous," he said, hunching close to her. These were the kind of shadows that made him feel like whispering.

"Listen," she said.

Faint and far away, the muffled sounds inside the container grew louder. At last, Vesta tapped into her power, but Rorren hated that what she discovered was sinister.

He didn't want to hear the sniffling. Only one kind of creature made sounds like that.

Vesta pressed through the darkness to the rusted edge of the container, stopping just shy of the light that illuminated the port side of a starship.

Below them on deck, Sandorians in uniform marched in patterns.

"Ten to one, they won't let us in on their nasty little secrets without a fight." He touched her arm and she didn't pull away.

"We have to get inside," Vesta said.

Rorren gripped the collar of his trench coat while he considered their options. He was done with being at the forefront of a battle—some were better fought from the shadows anyway.

"Why?" he asked. Vesta's arm tensed under his grip.

"This is what I am to learn, is it not?"

"You care about some kids you've never even met enough to risk your life?" He liked testing her resolve.

Her dark lashes fell before they lifted, revealing a bright determination.

"I care about finding Lanta-Bree. I promised."

Rorren licked his bottom lip to keep it from drying out in the heat and hid a smile.

"Then, go do what you must."

With a nod, she pulled the old rusted sword from the sheath behind her. She took a step toward the light and turned over her shoulder.

"Are you coming?" she asked.

There are other ways to fight. Both Lady Layeyre and his father taught him that.

"I'll watch your six."

She tilted her head, brow squeezing.

"It's a military spaceflight term. It means I'll protect you from unseen dangers while you focus on—"

Ah, ginger. He did it again—promising to protect people, knowing he would just murder them.

He swallowed the taste of bitterness and watched her dive into a platoon of Sandorian soldiers.

They circled her and Vesta discarded her disguise to a round of gasps. Even in her plain clothes, without armor or traditional hairstyle, the Sandorian soldiers trembled. They recovered, shock prods fizzing with electricity between three-fingered hands.

The captain took a step toward her.

Tiny grains of sand lifted into the air and pelted the metal containers. Some of the sand patted Rorren like the kiss of little raindrops.

A crackle of electricity came in staccato bursts as the guards charged the Scorth witch. Vesta swung the rusted blade, aglow with newfound life, same as the bright clothes of the Scorth witch, Lady Layeyre, deep in the trenches of war.

Rorren gripped the cool metal of the container, breathing hard. Phosphorus streaks of light emerged from the battle and he shrank into the shadows.

There was movement behind him. A guard crouched in the darkness just around the corner, veer rifle aimed at Vesta.

Rorren used the darkness to his advantage. Scrambling forward, he punched the Sandorian in one candid knock-out blow.

He picked up the weapon, recognizing the branding on the grip—four blue planets surrounded by rings and dotted with stars.

"The Galactic Order is supplying the Sandorian guard?"

The symbol fed his curiosity but he didn't have time to dwell on it. He took out two more guards with his staff, spun, and clocked a third on the chin.

The screech of metal sliding against metal echoed from Vesta's fight in a deafening hail of sound.

Rorren rushed forward, slipping the electronic key card from the belt of one of the downed guards and hurried over to the side of the container. Fumbling with the security lock, he managed to snap open the container latches. Sandorians, primarily women and children, poured out of the container, looking malnourished and covering light-sensitive eyes.

Rorren melted into the shadows, hidden away so that the first person they saw, their savior, was a Scorth witch battling to free them.

A victorious Scorth witch.

And like that, Vesta was surrounded by a group of tattered Sandorians, all worshiping her with tears and gratitude.

He could see it but he wanted to ignore it. How happy Vesta's newborn self-worth made him. How much closer it brought her to becoming a Fire-Scar Warrior. He kept to the shadows but her eyes found him.

"My six has been watched proficiently," she said.

Chuckling to himself, he shoved his hands into coat pockets.

"Yes, it has."

Dangling from the ladder in the vibrant moonlight, Rorren savored the crystal shine of the stars against the black sky of the desert. The moons of Desandor appeared in layered bubbles, the massive moon blocking out part of the smaller. His legs cramped with tension, straining as he repeatedly traveled the rungs. The soles of his feet stung and his lungs burned as time worked against him.

The sandfruit was ready.

His face had been bronzed by the sun. His shirt clung to his torso in damp patches but he forgot all that.

Opportunity remained for a fleeting instant once the fruit ripened.

Moonlight made the black beads glisten in the sand like a million tiny land mines, impossible to navigate. Impossible to clean up.

Even if he worked through the night, the chances of placing enough beads into the funnel to save even half the crop were as fleeting as the harvesting window.

No matter how little progress he made, he had to turn on the machine at dawn. He would pull the fruit from the silos by hand if it failed to ignite, though he doubted he could harvest more than a couple hundred crates. Enough to get him by for the year but not enough to feed his neighbors or put the profits to good use. Unacceptable.

Despite the prospect of failure, he relished the work. He didn't mind the exhaustion; it made him sleep well at night. The way the ache of his muscles blocked out memories of his parents.

The first rays of the suns opened over the horizon like an awakening eyelid.

Rorren dropped one last bead inside the funnel—watched it swirling out of sight, heard it plunk into the machine's guts.

He crawled down the ladder until he felt sand warm and soft under his feet.

Sinking steps carried him to the control panel. His hand lingered over the switch and sending up a despairing prayer, he readied to turn it on.

Soft fingers touched his.

"Wait."

Vesta passed him on her way to the machine's outer wall. He followed her trail in the sand—two footprints and a hole from her walking stick.

She stood, cape catching the wind, armor reflecting purple highlights from the sunrise. The rusted metal glared at her, insulting the grand marble halls and luxurious jungles she likely came from.

He found a dark satisfaction in watching her go against her nature, cursing at himself for hoping she would succeed and not just for the sake of his farm. He wanted to see her wield a menti blade.

As he watched beads lift into the air, he longed for days he knew would never return. Days when life was measured by a single goal—keeping his family and the universe safe.

Her slender fingers stretched before her, her brow tightening in concentration as more beads jumped into the air. A large conglomeration hovered above the machine, pulling a growl from Vesta each time a bead dropped out of formation.

Under the shadow of the strange floating mass, Rorren saw Vesta wrestling with it. She, the fisherman, with a line too weak and catch too large to reel in.

The exhaustion melted from his body, replaced by a fascination with the angry swarm of beads writhing toward the funnel.

Vesta wobbled. He moved beside her, steadying her with his hand on her shoulders.

He knew too well the toll failure took on one's soul.

"I believe in you," he said.

The beads dripped into the funnel, one by one at first, then more and more until the downpour was like pictures of the incredible waterfalls on Ragora he'd seen as a child.

The black shadow over the sand evaporated as the last bead fell. All went silent.

Rorren still had his hands on her shoulders.

She turned, chin lifting.

"Simple."

Her hubris broke the momentary connection between them.

"Turn on the machine, kitlush. We must begin the harvest."

"Yes, ma'am." Tipping his hat at her, he slammed his hand on the power button.

Engines vibrated the sand, sending a hum through the ground that shot up through Rorren's boots.

The conveyor belt rotated with a lurch, the gears grinding and gaining speed. A few beads inside the machine bounced free and Rorren used his arm to shield his face from flying debris.

A puff of dust swallowed him as the machine cleared its throat and roared to life.

Then he heard it. A sound that hadn't met his ears in an age.

The tumble of freshly harvested sandfruit.

The machine washed away the sand, peeled the hard-outer shell, and wrapped the soft core in a transparent casing. The finished product exited the spinning conveyer, rolling gently down the canals where it was deposited into a crate.

Rorren floated to the crate like he'd just been awakened from a dream.

He retrieved a single fruit, removed the casing, and took a bite. Juice trickled down his chin.

"Perfect."

He held out the fruit to Vesta. She approached, not reaching for the sample.

"Have you ever tried it?" he asked, wiping away juices.

"Of course I have. I spent years in space."

"Never like this. Something about reaping the fruit of your own labor makes it all the sweeter."

Vesta's jaw went slack but she took the fruit from his hand. She took a bite from the other side and though she did not show it, Rorren knew she savored the taste.

"I think you just saved my farm."

"A menial task for one as great as I," she said. She shoved the fruit into Rorren's hand.

"Most people just say, you're welcome."

CHAPTER 18

R ORREN LINGERED UNDER THE canopy of an old military tarp, seeking the reds of sunrise as they splashed across the wooden columns of the Sandorian church. For a brief moment, Vesta stood beside him, saying nothing, arms wrapped around a crate full of sandfruit.

Straw from the roof quivered over the empty pews. Without the natives, it was nothing more than a lonely building. Rorren didn't know why but the church upset him.

Working together, he and Vesta unloaded the impressive harvest. He should have been grateful and rejoicing that he brought in the crop of his dreams. Fetching a price that would sustain him and his friends for at least another three seasons made him a local legend.

All his efforts had been rewarded but it wasn't enough.

The wind billowing through the empty Sandorian pillars created a hollow sickness inside him.

Shadows in the alleyways visibly set Vesta on edge and watching her hide behind the sandcrawler didn't improve his mood. Two civilian space travelers emerged. Nothing to worry about. Not Galactic Order troops or Sandorian ones, which Vesta now spent all her time avoiding.

When she reappeared, he said, "I know the Premier. Maybe we could get your name cleared."

Her dark lashes dropped, failing to veil the intensity of her stare.

"I wish to use the solstal now."

Rorren took the straw from his mouth.

"You're not ready. Not even close." He wasn't in the habit of flat-out lying, but that church, the harvest, and being in town in all the commotion made him not himself.

Before she could respond, Yan-hara, the Sandorian Tribe Chief, padded over to them.

"We are pleased for your harvest, Rorren-sun. The Aklaren raided many of our crops but your generosity has made up for it."

Gratitude, not blame, filled those large, dark orbs, but sadness unexpectedly punched Rorren in the gut.

"The Aklaren must be destroyed," Vesta said. Shadows engulfed half her face.

"It is curious that so much ill befalls our lands," Yan-hara replied with his wise head hanging low.

"More than the marauders?" Rorren asked, suspecting the answer.

His chin dipped in response and the tendrils of Yan-hara's skin touched his chest.

"You have loved ones that have been taken like the children," Vesta said.

Suspecting Vesta already had, Rorren also vowed to get to the bottom of the mystery.

"We are not warriors, nor do we wish to be, but one cannot hide in the sand while evil overtakes." Yan-hara didn't look at Rorren as he spoke but the words still cut like a blade.

"You have earned your place here, Rorren-sun. May the spirit bless."

The Tribe Chief disappeared into the market.

"We go after the marauders. Tonight," Vesta said. There would be no arguing with her but Rorren didn't want to. His crop came in and he achieved all his goals, but his churning insides cracked, as dry and dusty as the old Sandorian church.

If he murdered a few Aklaren or allowed her to, Desandor would be better for it. Justifying the breaking of his age-old promise came too easy.

The Palace
Ragora
131 years ago

The slap was crisp and exacting. Vesta's cheek burned but the humiliation was worse than the sting. The delicate hand of the Queen always hurt more than Vesta thought it should.

"That was for your pathetic attempt at a Rishka."

A second slap stunned Vesta.

"And that is for taking back what you lost. That is the coward's way, naset. I am ashamed of you."

Talie moved away without ceremony, lifting her elaborate gown above her ankles as she ascended the throne.

The tingle in Vesta's cheeks tempted her to fight. Suppressing it, she latched her hands behind her. Her knuckles went white under the strain. She would not upset her mother more by crying. She wasn't like her classmates.

Talie perched her slender body between two enormous armrests, both cut from a single piece of quartz, aqua-green with swirls of yellow fire. The Queen leaned to one side, elbow planted and chin resting on her palm. A deliberate pose deliberately planned. She always sat that way. It terrified everyone.

"What punishment is worthy of your mistake?"

An inferno of raging words threatened to spill out of Vesta, so she dared not speak.

"I am busy and have little time for your foolish escapades."

"Maybe," Vesta stammered.

"Speak up. Are you a girl or a grubmite?"

"I should be in Lorn Clan?"

Talie blinked. Vesta had never seen her mother look so surprised.

"Do you wish me to look a fool? Do you want your shame to fall on me? This punishment is meant for you alone."

No longer seeing her mother or the Queen, Vesta saw only her executioner.

"I... I am sorry, Edda."

Talie dropped her hand from her chin, marring her refined features with a grimace of disgust.

"Apologies are worthless and they show weakness." Talie drew herself up from the chair, her posture the image of perfection. She moved to the window behind the throne. Her slender fingers pushed open the drape. Light from outside bathed her face and elaborate hair. Vesta thought her mother was the most beautiful Scorth woman that ever lived.

"Never apologize, naset."

Talie let go of the drape.

"I suppose I must devise a fitting punishment. You will stay at the palace tonight and return to the Academy tomorrow."

Spending the night at home did not seem like a punishment but she didn't tell her mother that.

Talie waved her hand.

"Leave my sight."

Obeying, Vesta marched until her mother couldn't see her and then dashed up the stairs to her old room. She opened the door and found one chair and a bed.

Empty shelves. Vesta's clothes, toys, and everything she grew up with were gone. She sat on the bed, wondering if this happened to all Scorth who turned twelve or if it was part of her punishment. Falling into her pillow, she refused anyone the satisfaction of her tears.

Hours later a knocking woke her up. She wiped the stains from her cheeks. One of her mother's royal guards entered.

"The Queen requests your presence."

Given what happened Vesta did not expect a dinner invitation. She pulled on a robe, hood swaying behind her as she followed the guard. The hood was her protection against peasants when traveling the streets but today it served as security to hide from her mother's cold stare. She didn't dare use it but it helped knowing it was there.

Instead of taking her into the throne room, the guard led Vesta up the stairs to the observation balcony. He moved a chair to the railing and Vesta sat, teetering forward to see the proceedings below.

Queen Talie was poised, gaze cast over the Royal Sentencing Chamber, the precious stones of her scarlet gown beating against the light like tiny wings. Her hair was coiled, knotted, and half concealed by a tiara with the royal crest in the center.

Covert glances came from those standing before the Queen. Vesta watched them as they studied the marbled hall and its occupants. The pages and servants, the royal guard of Ragora all alert beneath a violent mural that depicted the ancient defeat of the Aux Katan.

There was a father and mother. A boy older than Vesta and a girl, clinging to her mother's unfashionable skirts. A girl with a familiar face.

"Luha," Vesta whispered, glancing up to see if she had attracted the guard's attention. She writhed in the chair, wanting to fade into the rafters.

"The Zyne family." Talie's voice had exquisite control. It chided and welcomed.

The father avoided her gaze but not out of fright. No, he seemed angry.

"What am I to do with you?" Talie asked, brushing her fingers over the arm of her throne. "Your daughter makes a spectacle of mine. You encourage rebellion among my followers. You defy our ancient customs and protest the Advent, one of our most sacred rights. One might ask why—"

"For starters, encouraging children to maim each other for wealth is wrong."

No one interrupted the Queen. Ever. Vesta winced. Either Luha's father was an idiot or he had a death wish.

Chortling, Talie cooed, "Ah, yes."

The Queen shifted her posture, causing Luha's mother to splay her arm over her daughter's body.

"Poor little urchin, sentenced to Lorn Clan and, of course, the deathshade. Tragic. Would have been such a lovely face." Talie's thin, high tone hinted at enough false pity to make Vesta shake with concern for them all.

"Is there some reason you brought us here?" the father asked, his wife squeezing his shoulder and sending him a furious glance.

"I am afraid so. I have found you all guilty of the charges laid out. Your punishment," Talie said with a glance up to the gallery, "life in the mines on Parkell."

Talie strode up the steps, twirling as she had in the annual palace parade, and resumed her perch on the throne.

The guards abandoned their stations and surrounded the Zyne family.

"Say it, you coward. Say what you fear. Your daughter is not like you. Luha got through to her. Vahza is more Queen than you will ever be. We will live to see you fall."

He momentarily reduced the Queen to a stupefied, glaring fool, but when she recovered she flew at them.

Vesta gripped the rails, paralyzed by fear.

Talie's gown flared behind her as she descended the stairs. Her fist clipped the man's jaw, splitting his lip.

"You will only live to see the horror of the mines."

Talie yelled up to the balcony.

"Naset!"

An invisible force made Vesta stand. Her legs were jelly but her terror kept her upright.

"What do you think of this punishment? Is it too harsh, or shall I kill them all where they stand?"

Vesta hated seeing her friend trembling behind her mother's skirts.

"It is fitting, Edda," Vesta said, though she ached with guilt.

The voice didn't sound like it belonged to her. The question that grew inside her at that moment lingered year after year. If she had gone with granda the sentencing might not have happened.

Talie's triumphant gaze should have made Vesta feel proud. She was again her mother's favorite. Yes, it was satisfying but also empty.

"Take them away," Talie said. The guards marched the Zyne family out of the throne room.

"Come down here, Vesta," Talie ordered.

"No!"

Vesta pushed the guard out of her way, racing across the balcony before his paws could grab her.

"Should I go after her?" Vesta heard the guard ask the Queen.

"She will not go far. She is truly mine now."

The icy words of her mother followed after her, a curse never to be undone.

She ran through the palace halls, clutching the jewel around her neck.

She tore the necklace from her body as she intercepted the company of troops.

Shoving it into Luha's hand, the girl grabbed it before the guards could pull them apart.

"Someday, you can transform and use this to leave the diamond mines," Vesta said.

A sweaty officer tossed Vesta over his shoulder. She watched Luha's lips move, too far away to hear. In her memory, the words became *goodbye, my friend*.

CHAPTER 19

Desandor

Present Day

T HEY CAMPED WITHOUT A fire on the edge of the badlands. Tomorrow they would enter the canyon where Rorren crashed the motor cruiser and pulled Vesta from the Blood River.

In the darkness, Vesta's face fell into a blur of shadows. Resting against a flat rock, Rorren propped his head on his arm. The stars mingled with lights from late starship flights off Desandor. It was hard to tell the difference between the lights except for an almost imperceptible movement.

"Why?" he asked.

The question went unanswered. Rorren shifted to see if Vesta was asleep. "Why, what?"

Rorren picked out a few constellations he learned at the academy, ignoring how far from home he was.

"Why did you stay here? Despite the Galactic Order troops, you could have hopped a starship out of here if you wanted."

No answer.

Rorren saw the outline of Vesta's frame, spine straight, stance vigilant, facing the badlands.

"Must be a tough way to grow up," Rorren said, "Not ever receiving kindness, even from those who are supposed to love you."

"You believe you understand Scorth because you spent time in your human academy studying us before you slaughtered us? You know nothing."

Dropping his arm, Rorren sat upright.

"Then set me straight."

He bit on some straw clipped from a nearby weed and waited. One thing the desert taught him was patience.

"Backstabbing murderer that she was, I knew my mother would never forsake me."

So, Vesta lived with a murderer before. Made a kind of sense to him but he ignored that tidbit.

"Was?"

Rorren fought a deep and growing irritation with himself. Keeping a respectable distance from her became more complicated by the day. She seldom spoke of her past. His fondness for her compounded when she did, tricking him into breaking more promises.

"My parents both died in the war," he said.

In the eight years since moving to the desert planet, he had not mentioned his parents to anyone, not even Metra.

"My father was murdered long before the war began," Vesta said, sounding tired and far away.

He swallowed, throat dry and sand grains uncomfortably scraping his skin.

"I'm sorry."

"Why should you be? It does not affect you."

Rorren's mother once said *great men aren't easy to love but they have the greatest love in the world.*

He nibbled at the straw.

"To lose your parents that way must have been hard," Rorren said.

"My mother was not murdered. She long outlived my father." The swiftness and sharpness of her reply encouraged Rorren to share more of his pain.

"My dad was a General. Galactic Order Delta Corp. He," Rorren spit out the straw, "*died* late in the war. I fought in his place after that. Tried to keep up his legacy."

And failed.

"You must have been a young soldier for a human."

Wishing he hadn't discarded the straw, he ran his fingers across the sand, grateful the darkness hid everything.

"They forced me to partner with the Fire-Scar Warriors. The Scorth traitors. It was like bringing the enemy right into our midst."

"What did young Mic Rorren do?" she asked, tone soothing.

"I followed orders. I always followed orders."

Vesta's dark silhouette fell deeper into shadow.

"To earn the respect of a parent requires difficult concessions," she said.

He tasted despair and bitterness floating on a pleasant breeze from her lips to his.

"After time and battle, the Fire-Scar leader made us all love her." Rorren dug his feet in the sand, resting his forearms on his knees. "Her fiercest critic ended up falling *in love* with her."

"But that was not you?" Vesta asked, too quickly for his liking.

"No, not me. The woman was two hundred and ten years old, but that didn't stop the gruffest old soldier in my command from talking about marriage like a bridezilla."

Vesta's visage, motionless and quiet against the horizon, changed the feel of the desert for him. What was once dry and empty was now profound and elusive.

"What about you? Any arranged marriages in your past?"

Rorren brushed the sand from his hands and adjusted his hat.

"No."

He waited with breath held, hoping for more on the topic.

"I never found a political ally trustworthy enough for that," she said.

"You never loved anyone?"

"You humans and that word. Love. You obsess over it," she hissed.

He heard the sweep of her cape over the sand.

"I do not believe there is such a thing as love," she continued. "It is an invention of the Galactic Order to convince people they are happy, to make them slaves."

Once weighed by despair, her shoulders now squared themselves into that confident arrogance he found appealing and maddening.

"Then I hope I'm around to meet the Scorth who proves you wrong about that," Rorren said. Despite her protests, he could see some nobleman changing her opinions about love. Saddened him a bit that he wouldn't be the one.

"If I have not found it in a hundred and forty—a hundred and thirty-five years, then it does not exist." Her chin lifted, creating a flash of moonlight in her eyes when she looked at him.

"What about you, Mic Rorren? Shall a human woman ever turn you into a bridezilla?"

"I'm married to my farm."

Placing his hat over his face, he nestled his neck against the high collar of his trench coat, folded his arms, and waited for sleep. Instead, he got memories. The strongest was the gleam on Lady Layeyre's face as she foretold of him finding love.

———

Nobody ever hiked across the badlands but footing was easier to find there than on the dunes. The flat surface was a baking tin for any poor creature caught in the afternoon heat, as Rorren and Vesta discovered.

The cracks deepened the closer they came to the Blood River. Towers of red rock rose in columns, offering a sliver of shade only enough to be maddening for any traveler seeking relief from the heat.

Rorren ignored the blisters on his feet and imagined Vesta must be in even more pain, though she said nothing.

When they reached the Blood River, Rorren followed the winding path of sand sludge until they found debris from broken motor cruisers. He bent and picked up a piece of metal left after the Aklaren pillaged what they could.

"The crop has brought in enough for you to buy another vessel," Vesta said.

Rorren sat on his haunches with his back to her. Nodding, he looked across the river to the cliff where he had last seen the raven.

He didn't want a motor cruiser. He preferred the sandcrawler. He chose to be that sludge of sand rolling downstream in no hurry to be anywhere. Vesta pushed him into feeling things he didn't want to feel. He deliberately slowed the pace despite his mind racing with plans to deal with what lay ahead.

There was one sight on Desandor he wished to see again. Reaching the base of a slope, Rorren waved Vesta over. He anticipated her awe once the landscape filled her blue eyes.

He reached the summit, finding the view still took his breath away. Vesta climbed up beside him.

"Why have you stopped?" she asked, then looked. "Oh."

Mountainous trees lifted out of the desert and touched the starless heavens. Around the rotting roots, bright red, yellow and orange moss spread across the valley floor.

"They say Desandor was not unlike Ragora once. With forests so ancient, even the air could make you wise," he said.

Rorren jogged down the hill to the path through the dead forest and waited for Vesta.

"What happened?" she asked, steadying herself on the staff.

Rorren offered his hand. Refusing, she stumbled over the rocks and Rorren caught her by the waist. They locked gazes and he pretended he didn't want to kiss her.

"Thousands of years ago, everything died. No one knows what happened," Rorren said. He let go of her and proceeded forward.

They reached one of the tree stumps and Rorren, craning to see higher, imagined the summit covered in snow.

"Everything, including the people?" Vesta asked.

"Let's just say the natives aren't native. Who knows what civilizations lived here before the Sandorians."

They kept to the edge of the stump for at least a mile and reached another impressive sight. The stone ruin lay on its side with only one eye and half the mouth visible above the sand. Its face was not human, Sandorian, or Scorth. The scale of the head left Rorren wondering how enormous the statue was. It was impossible to tell from the exposed piece but Rorren envisioned it towering the giant trees.

Studying the face, Vesta put her hand on one of the bricks in the enormous mouth.

"Perhaps a foreshadowing of the fate of my planet," she said, tracing the masonry with her fingers.

"Why would you say that?"

"Do you not know what happened to Ragora after the war?" She didn't wait for his response. "Of course you do not. The Galactic Order ignores us now that we are no longer a threat."

Skipping a few steps to catch up to her, he asked, "How do you know? You were a raven."

"Do you not think I tried to go home? I needed a talisman to change but that road led nowhere good."

"Tell me."

"Maybe later. Right now let us keep our focus clear."

They moved across sponge moss and sage until the suns set behind them. Inky cliffs appeared in the distance and something else. Rorren spotted a light flickering between narrow passages.

The marauder camp.

The hard ground morphed into a springboard, propelling them forward. They climbed to the top of a cliff and peered over the crest.

The marauders camped near a vast barn with pillaged goods spilling beyond the sliding doors. Beyond the barn small fires littered the cracked landscape, each flame surrounded by three or four Aklaren gangsters. Vesta pointed and following her finger, Rorren observed several beasts of burden tied to a fallen tree branch and three or four motor cruisers.

"After we destroy them, you shall have one," Vesta said. Her greed rankled.

"What's the plan?" he asked, "go in there and kill them all?"

He took some comfort in the guilty look on her face.

"Do you have a better idea?"

"Maybe."

There was no need to be a murderer when shrewd thinking meant less chance of dying.

CHAPTER 20

RORREN FACED THE ENEMY, remembering the thrill—odds against him. Sand prickled his skin as it swirled around him.

"Hey, stinkworms," he shouted.

Four Aklaren unsheathed weapons. Their blades glistened under the glow of the campfire.

"Looking for this?"

Rorren held up a jeweled goblet he had swiped from their pregnant storehouse.

Sneers and growling answered him. He retreated one step at a time, slowing his movements, swallowing when he lured out more Aklaren than anticipated.

They oozed from behind the storehouse and over dunes blackened by the starless sky.

"You have a death wish, aux rand?" the closest marauder asked.

Grinning, Rorren said, "No, but looking at your face is making me reconsider."

Pleased to find he drew another growl, Rorren sobered when about a dozen more marauders appeared from the shadows. No use doubting his plan now.

He twirled his Galactic Order staff just to give them a tease of who they were dealing with. That momentary hesitation in their approach gave him another chill of excitement. Nothing matched rushing into battle, taking down bad guys and fighting for a cause.

"I'm going to gut you myself," the lead marauder said. Rorren squinted through the darkness but his eyes couldn't pinpoint Hevcar.

The silhouettes piled up, shadow stacked against shadow.

He took a few steps and hit the cloaking button on his wrist com. The stolen motor cruiser appeared behind him. He heard gasping.

"Hate to tell you, but your breath is doing that already."

They opened fire, barraging him in waves of bullets.

Rorren tossed the goblet in the seat and jumped over the edge of the motor cruiser. He ducked and avoided the bullet that shattered the windshield, then stomped on the power pedal.

The engine roared. Sand pelted Rorren's face without the protection of the forward shield. He increased speed.

Smooth dunes gave way to a canyon clogged with massive boulders, each wedged into steep cliffsides.

A beep from the console drew his attention. He knew what that small, red flashing meant. Rorren slammed the brakes. The goblet he stole flew out of the passenger seat and rolled across the sand. Leaving it, Rorren jumped from the cruiser to the edge of a boulder. He glanced behind, finding hordes of Aklaren on his heels. They'd chase him now whether or not they recovered their treasure.

Climbing with incredible speed and intensity, Rorren raced up the nearly impassable cliff face. He was considering whether he had miscalculated the location of the drop zone when the clink of metal disrupted his thoughts. Boots scraped against stone.

Rorren paused about halfway up, seeing the ground below become deceptively small. The dots climbing upward appeared to move like weightless insects instead of half-ton Rocbulls.

Rorren tripped up the slope, scrambling on all fours, adrenaline revving. He kept his eyes ahead. The marauders were close enough that he could hear them muttering and the clink of armor each time they jumped to a new boulder.

The closer they got, the slimmer his chances of reaching the crest. Dread and excitement fermented in his gut and he loved it.

Stooping at the top of the cliff, he faced the oncoming doom. A whiff of the breath he joked about preceded the arrival of his attackers.

A fist flew at him. He grinned, pulled away, and vanished.

The loose pebbles and sand carried him down the cliff faster than he could control. He kept upright until about halfway when his ankle caught on a rock, sending him sprawling on his backside.

A searing flash of pain pulled a grunt from his lips. He rolled over and recovered some of the air knocked from his lungs. Pushing to all fours, he found he had landed right where he expected, surrounded on three sides by boulder-lined cliffs. There was only one way out.

A dust cloud formed around two dozen Aklaren gangsters as they slid down the hill, stinging his eyes when it reached him. Rorren coughed and the enemy emerged from the haze. The canyon trapped them all. Rorren vs two dozen gangsters. He's seen worse odds.

He glanced up, finding the sky clear and crisp. He saw no demon storm nor smelled black magic.

Vesta kept out of sight but Rorren searched for her anyway. Amazed by how implicitly he trusted her, he thought it unfortunate she didn't trust him the same way.

Large, craterous nostrils flared. An entire unit of angry Aklaren forced him against the canyon wall.

The leader, not Hevcar to Rorren's irritation, panted, wiping the dust from his face as he glowered.

"I'm going to enjoy ripping you apart."

Excitement overpowered Rorren's better judgment.

"That's the problem with you dunderheads. You're all talk. I don't know what magic makes you that delusional but it really works."

Rorren didn't wait for a response. He pressed the ignition button on the box strapped to his belt.

Explosions shot up from the tops of the cliffs, rocking the immense boulders and tearing them free.

The marauders scrambled, proceeding pebbles showering them like bullets. A dozen legs jetted across the canyon toward the single opening.

Rorren didn't move. A boulder twice his size rolled straight for him. Even if he tried to run, it would be too late. It was all up to the witch now.

The boulder flew over Rorren's head just before impact and landed near the fleeing gangsters.

Rocbulls skidded over pebbles, some falling to the ground, some knocking over the others.

A boulder left its natural path, flying across the canyon.

Rorren brushed himself off as he watched the cage form. Boulder after boulder piled into place, creating prison walls capped by a final stone about the size of the farmhouse.

When the rumbling stopped, Vesta appeared at his side.

"Next time, you get to be the bait," Rorren said.

Ignoring him, she prowled around the prison. Rorren could see the whites of angry eyes through the cracks between boulders. Fingers and arms reached through pocket-size crevices, but there was no way out.

Their reign on Desandor was over. Rorren thought of Jon and Metra.

"This is what you call justice?" Vesta asked.

Rorren pulled a small metal object from his belt. He hurled it at the prison wall and the object stuck. A small blue light began flashing.

"The Order will pick them up in a few hours. It will be a nice haul for some lonely outer rim patrol."

She leaned on her staff and Rorren could see the fight had drained her energy.

"I know you, Scorth witch," the lead marauder hissed through the crack, spit wetting the stone.

"Hevcar recognized you as the witch who betrayed Zarog long ago."

"Zarog was responsible for his own prison just as you are for yours," Vesta replied.

The tension drained from her face and perhaps crushing memories weakened her legs. Rorren caught her mind fall and then guided her away from the angry Aklaren.

"Come on, we have Sandorian treasure to salvage before the Order claims it."

As he helped her out of the canyon, he made a mental note to search for Zarog in the archives when they got home. It was the most concrete thing he'd learned about her past since they met. Discovering the fact from an Aklaren gangster made his nose itch but he tasted no black magic in the air.

They walked away from the canyon in silence. Without the threat of marauders, Rorren stoked one of their fires. He cooked some sponge moss and offered a plate to Vesta.

He ate in silence.

"Are we going to talk about what happened back there?" he asked, setting his empty plate aside.

Vesta sat on an old tree stump across from Rorren, gazing into the fire, food untouched.

"You say they will spend time in a Galactic Order prison. I suppose the widow would be satisfied with that."

"She would but I meant about you knowing an Aklaren marauder. Zarog?"

Her expression was impenetrable and her soul-piercing eyes landed on him.

"You were different out there, Mic Rorren. Like you belonged there but did not wish to."

Rorren poked at the fire with a stick.

"Nice try. You're not getting out of your turn at being bait that easy. You didn't answer my question."

"And you didn't answer mine."

"Technically, yours wasn't a question," he said.

Sponge moss hit him on the side of the head.

"Hey!"

Vesta inclined her head with a smirk and retreated to the darkness.

CHAPTER 21

THE SAFETY OF NIGHT vanished, exposing them to overhead suns that burned like smoldering embers.

Vesta joined him midway to dawn. She had recovered enough to assist him, and they loaded two cruisers and hover trailers with enough pillaged goods to last the Sandorians for months.

Morning arrived, bringing with it an urgency to depart. Rorren knew the Galactic Order wouldn't be far behind the suns and wanted to be long gone by then.

Vesta slipped behind the wheel of one of the cruisers and Rorren leaned over her.

"Do you know how to drive one of these?"

She gripped the steering cog like an amateur.

"How hard could it be?"

The cruiser lurched forward, showering Rorren with sand and fumes and rocking the massive supply trailer.

Rorren coughed, removed his hat and brushed grains from his hair. He glared at her.

A grin tugged at the corner of her mouth and the Scorth witch laughed outright. A throaty cackle, not unpleasant, with a hint of rust like it hadn't been used in a long time.

"I do beg pardon. The controls are more sensitive than I presumed."

She looked so humble and ridiculous sitting there, apologizing, that he laughed despite himself.

"It's true. You do *exhaust* me."

She rolled her eyes, still bright with mirth.

"Do not start with the puns again."

"They don't *fuel* your amusement?"

She tilted her head, smirking, and pressed on the pedal again. The cruiser pulled forward slowly, grinding in increments until the hover trailer jolted forward.

Rorren climbed into the second cruiser and followed her, watching her comedic attempts to navigate out of the badlands.

They weren't far when he saw Galactic Order patrol ships passing overhead, low enough to the ground to hear the rumble of massive engines.

That familiar sound bolstered him. They were probably arresting the Aklaren, making Desandor safer for the natives. It had been a while since he rested easy, but he did now, knowing his friends were safe.

The cruiser bounced over a rough patch and brought him to his senses. Hevcar was still out there. Rorren hunched over the steering wheel, annoyed the Aklaren leader eluded them.

Against the oxidized horizon boxes piled together in various colors that comprised the Sandorian village.

As she entered the small village square, Vesta's massive supply trailer drew a crowd. When she stepped out, the Sandorian wives pushed their children behind them.

Rorren climbed out, recognizing one of the Sandorian boys from the market. The kid came forward against his mother's advice. He studied the goods on the trailer and tossed his lanky arms around Vesta's waist. She looked over at Rorren in surprise. She let the kid hug her momentarily, then gently pried him loose.

"Bless you, Rorren-sun," Tribe Chief Yan-hara said, coming up behind Rorren. A three-fingered hand rested on Rorren's shoulder.

"Bless you, Scorth-Vesta," he said.

Rorren wondered if Vesta knew what a compliment it was to receive a Sandorian name.

He and Vesta unloaded the stolen goods, returning them to their owners and giving away perhaps more barbules than had been stolen. As the swarm of grateful natives engulfed them, he saw faces made alike by gratitude. Rorren never understood how people with so little always managed to be so content. It warmed him from the inside to witness it and he suspected it also warmed Vesta.

"Come, you take nourishment with me," Yan-hara said. He led them away from the crowds.

The hut of the Tribe Chief was modest. Three rooms opened onto a patio where intricately woven hammocks hung. Most Sandorians slept outside save for during sandstorms which is why each hut also came with an in-ground bunker.

"My life-compeer made those," Yan-hara said. He gestured toward the hammocks. "She was admired for her skill."

"Was?" Vesta asked.

Rorren reached across the table, warning Vesta off the sensitive subject with a glance.

Yan-hara bowed his head almost like a prayer. A younger Sandorian appeared from out of the shadows of the bunker. Rorren recognized him.

He helped protect the moisture hub. He was a respected warrior within the clan and the Tribe Chief's oldest son.

"She lives still but Father will not try to find her or our Ben-hara."

"Now is not the time Dusen. Go, help with the supplies."

Dusen-hara made a fist, took a deep breath, and left the hut.

"He does not understand the dangers of what he asks. He would risk the extinction of our people, but how can I? Even for my compeer or youngest son."

Vesta seemed on the brink of jumping forward, volunteering them both. In setting her on the path of the Fire-Scar, Rorren feared he may have created a crusading monster.

"We must find another way," Yan-hara said. "Will the Aklaren return for their goods?"

"The Aklaren are in the custody of the Galactic Order. They will not bother you again," Rorren said. Vesta impatiently tapped her boot.

"All but Hevcar," she hissed.

The Tribe Chief looked between Vesta and Rorren.

"You are a powerful force, Scorth-Vesta and Rorren-sun. We have not much but anything you ask, we will give."

Vesta opened her mouth but Rorren cut her off.

"We just want to unload this stuff and go home for a nap. Your gratitude is more than enough," Rorren said, glaring at Vesta.

He left the tent but Vesta stayed behind. Rorren hoped she wasn't begging for some pillaged goods to stoke her coffers.

Either that or she was saying, let's rush in like aux rand kitlush fools. Kick butt and take names. Ask questions later.

That was a terrible plan and not Rorren's style. His father taught him that one watched, observed, and reasoned before charging in.

As he drove her home, Rorren formulated a wiser means of helping Yan-hara find his missing family. To begin with, finding out who took them and why. His thoughts went to Hevcar. He now suspected the whiff of dark magic he smelled had nothing to do with Vesta.

Rorren woke to the smell of breakfast. He showered, dressed, and, feeling somewhat alive, sat at the kitchen table. He saw her empty plate—no food left for him—but found no sign of the woman. After searching the house, his efforts turned up empty.

Venturing outside, he stood beneath wide cracks in the clouds, morning sunlight swimming over to the farmhouse, bathing the old wood in a warm patina.

He discovered Vesta sitting on the swinging porch bench.

Her feather cloak draped her shoulders, parting in the center to reveal the polished silver armor clinging to her body.

One of her hands rested on Brawn's head.

Next to her, on the porch table, a piece of velvet cloth covered a round object.

The solstal.

He passed in front of her and sought the comfort of his favorite chair, needing suddenly to be surrounded by the familiar.

"You're going to go through with it then?"

Her fingers stroked Brawn's ears and the kencat purred.

"It is time."

"You might not survive. Some don't," Rorren said. He pinned his focus to the horizon to avoid her gaze.

"I will return with a menti blade or I will not return."

Leaning forward, she cupped Brawn's face between her hands.

"It will just be the two of you again. Look out for the kitlush, my friend. He is not the brightest."

She sent a sly glance over her shoulder. Rorren tried to smile but nothing came. Vesta slipped the solstal into the supply bag and strapped it across her torso. She picked up the staff and started down the stairs.

Rorren hesitated, cursing inside, and then followed her.

"I don't know what fate led you here but I'm glad it did," he said.

"I am loath to admit it but you have been a good teacher," she replied.

"Even though I'm not too bright?"

Vesta's beauty sent a few shivers of pleasure down his neck.

"You already knew, didn't you? The greatest treasure," he said.

"The soul of a living being," she replied and the inexplicable sadness in her shoulders darkened his mood.

"Do you believe it enough to convince the solstal?" he asked, searching her expression for answers he couldn't find.

She tightened her grip on the staff.

"We shall see."

A barrage of emotions ran through him. A few months ago, he couldn't wait to see the last of Vesta. Now, he dreaded the reality he might never see her again.

Leaning forward, he aimed to kiss her.

I murdered him, Mom.

The memory jolted him and he pulled back. Curious eyes stared up at him—the opposite of his mother's that day. His mother's eyes, stern and cold with agreement, still haunted him.

He murdered his father. His mother did not deny it. No one could deny it. This was his curse and his burden. No power in the universe could ever change it. Not even the beautiful Scorth witch who wanted to be Aux Katan.

"It is not like you to doubt your course," Vesta said.

Rorren pretended not to see her disappointment.

"All I can do is wish you luck." He sounded as cold and stern as his mother. He extended his hand. Her brow wrinkled but she took it.

"Goodbye, Mic Rorren."

He watched her walk away, Brawn sitting at his side. The kencat looked up with questions in his tiger eyes. Rorren knelt next to him and scratched his furry chin.

"Our raven will come back. When she does, you'll see the most amazing weapon in the universe."

THE CRUSADE

CHAPTER 22

Desandor

Present Day

THE VASTNESS OF THE wasteland lay before Vesta, punctuated by the rolling of tumbleweeds.

She pressed forward and absorbed the familiar desolation of it all. A similar despair rooted itself inside her long ago.

She walked until her feet numbed. Every step grew heavier by the weight of the solstal buried deep in the pouch at her side.

Despair melted into the heat of the rising suns, blurring the lines between them.

A pleasant wind drew her to the south and she followed its pull. Over the last few weeks, she had become a nomad of the desert, searching for something elusive like in the story of the prince and the sandstorm castles.

Her legs and mind burned as she climbed a steep dune. She did not understand the human fondness for allegory. It was an ineffective way to communicate leading to confusion and chaos.

Loose sand caved under her boots, requiring more strength to navigate.

Despite her disdain for the fanciful, she thought of Mic Rorren's story on her way up the incline.

Strange sounds rose from the valley, a rhythmic crackling muffled by scraping as if something heavy were being pulled across the sand.

She didn't know why, but she dropped to all fours and hurried her pace. She hoped her thudding pulse meant the time to use the solstal had arrived.

Heat, isolation, and thirst made her weary, but taking in the sight over the ridge diminished her physical discomfort.

In the valley, strange dunes decorated in a swirling pattern too elaborate to be made by the wind moved. The sand fell away, revealing a mammoth shell.

Her childhood flooded to her—nights of sneaking into the dense jungles of Ragora in search of the elusive gantis.

Looking at one now sent a thrill through her. She watched its giant head curving with majesty as it chewed on a patch of scrubby cacti.

It turned, munching and studying her, its head coming so close the breath from one of its nostrils misted her skin. For something so massive to have such stealth surprised her, but these creatures were not often spotted for a reason.

They were enormous, some the size of a Scorth starship. There were so many of them. An entire herd freckled the landscape.

The Galactic Order said gentle giants were extinct—that galactic expansion had wiped out their numbers. Even then, Vesta sensed the lie. A ploy to restrict access to star systems the Galactic Order wanted for itself.

She stretched out her hand and the beast moved near, allowing her to touch the plated scales of its square head.

The gantis looked like the cacti they ate. Leathered, green skin ran down to stumped hooves extending from under the hard shell.

Its small yellow eye focused on her, soul connecting to hers. She smelled its fear.

"What is it?"

The oversized turtle pulled away from her and called to its herd. A low horn-like sound followed by a rumble that shifted the ground. Vesta lost her balance but not her curiosity.

With a tight grip on the staff, she chased them. By the time she climbed into the valley, the gantis had vanished. They seemed to have a kind of magic about them that rose from the same pool of power as the Aux Katan.

Large footprints left divots in the sand, which made navigating the path of the gantis difficult. Vesta rested on her walking staff, panting, annoyed that she could not catch them.

Lightning struck the horizon with veins emboldened by the pitch-dark storm clouds around them. The ground rumbled again, and, for a moment, Vesta thought the herd had returned. Thunder flooded the atmosphere, energy from the solstal tingling her skin.

Now, of all moments.

Vesta stabbed her staff into the sand and retrieved the crystalline ball from the pouch.

The storm dominated the sky in varying degrees of darkness. Grit and dust as fine as gossamer powder assaulted her skin. Before long, pebbles struck her armor, clinking as they bounced off.

The wind enfolded her with an odd intimacy, bringing her past and present nearer.

The velvet cover of the solstal blew free and Vesta gasped as a flame of dark purple engulfed the orb.

A shadow appeared in the rising sandstorm—a looming, blurred silhouette undisturbed by the chaos. Fear constricted Vesta's spine as she recognized the figure that emerged.

A queen stood before her, dressed in the armor of the royal Scorth house. A distorted vision of herself as the Queen.

Looking down her torso, Vesta found herself dressed in the rags of the widow's old dress.

"You cannot vanquish me," the Queen screamed in Vesta's voice.

Vesta growled at the vision, hating the idea of being caught in a riddle.

"I have lived too long and conquered too many foes," the Queen said, drawing a sword with a glistening silver blade. She placed it under Vesta's chin. "Look how strong you have made me. I shall give the galaxy the Queen it cries for."

A strange, electric cloud overtook them, sending shivers of panic through Vesta. She lifted her staff into the air, deflecting the rain of stone that spewed from the sky.

The clouds swallowed the Queen's shape, her voice growing as large and threatening as her shadow.

"You do not understand the power. You cannot yet fathom what you are."

"What I do understand," Vesta replied, fighting off the deadly stone drops, "is the human phrase feeding one's ego."

The shards of the Obsedei fell with a heinous ire, landing in the sand where Vesta knew they would grow.

"But I do not think the humans meant it so literally," Vesta said. She hoped her humor was an affront to the Queen.

A sharp stone tore the skin of her cheek and another lodged in her thigh. She relished the anger the pain triggered. She refused to scream as she pulled out the shard.

A hand struck her and nails dug into her scalp. The Queen flung her across the sand by the hair.

The Queen clomped forward, letting the sword drag behind her as if so confident in her victory that she need not defend herself. With one hand on her hip, she rested the sword across her shoulder.

Her smirk faded as Vesta found the strength to rise—clutching Rorren's handmade staff between her hands like a lifeline. She wiped the blood from her cheek.

The evil on her face staring back at her was sobering. Vesta watched a grimace of silent doubt crack the mirrored reflection.

"I will never stop. I will never die," the Queen said.

"No, what you will never do is stop babbling."

The storm roared, a deadly mix of lightning and wind, and the Obsedei cracked from the stones. Warriors grew into bodies the size of Rocbulls, each sprouting three obsidian arms on either side.

"It is too late for you," the Queen said. She gathered her minions to her, blades swinging from magically animated rock.

"Just as it was too late when granda left you."

Vesta's staff shattered, victim to dark magic.

"Now kneel. Kneel to your Queen and your destiny. The universe shall be ours. Make Edda proud."

Her leg throbbed but Vesta refused to kneel. No pain or despair could make her bow to the evil before her.

The Vision Queen and her Obsedei warriors lifted two dozen swords over Vesta—all poised to deliver a final blow.

Scorth War
Cardinal World Delta
10 years ago

The Scorth attack started the same way it always did. Like a nightmare. Except Rorren could wake up from a nightmare when it became unbearable. It had been amassing for months—growing and overtaking—and now the burden of leadership left nothing for him but a malignant dread of defeat.

A Field General of the Delta Army on the brink of losing and his one chance, his hope, alive in the Fire-Scar Warriors standing at his side. His enemy. Now his ally. Traitors to their own people. He hadn't slept for weeks. The scars on his neck were raw, still burning.

Rorren took on the weight of exhaustion among his troops, battered and longing for home, as they watched the rocks pour from the heavens. Fear was blatant in the bravest eyes as the arrowheads tore through clouds in acrobatic feats until rooftops, buildings, and streets were covered in spikes.

Thousands of evil seeds were planted in the heart of the Cardinal World.

Spotlights from the garrison tanks combed across the area, making the stones glisten as if alive.

They *were* alive.

Once the obsidian rain ended, the air went stale. Arriving at the moment just before the battle, Rorren was unprepared for what he saw next.

"Steady."

The first lieutenant honed the light with shaking hands as he searched for signs of movement. Rorren glanced over the line of soldiers, finding muscles strained and tense gazes, each soul clinging to their weapons.

The Fire-Scar Warriors contrasted Rorren's garrison.

The strangers stood motionless, the breeze moving their long, plain robes as if the cloth adorned statues. Not dressed in ornate regalia like their Scorth brothers on the opposite side of the battlefield.

He wondered when their leader would draw her menti blade. Rorren had never seen a Fire-Scar Warrior in action. There were the pictures in textbooks and rumors from the battlefield, but he hadn't believed them.

The cracking of the alien stone tested the nerve of his men. Arms and legs sprouted from the black rock like roots from a tree. Silicon amulets turned into hands gripping swords laced with spikes.

The Scorth put fantastic effort into the details of the armor, the six arms, and each weapon wielded by the Obsedei warriors, but they forgot the face. Crude slits marked the eyes, each concealing a hot red glow. No ears, nose or mouth. Rorren knew better. Braver men than his had fled in the path of such monsters.

The troop would not flee because of Rorren—because he wore the mark of the relheer.

It took twelve of Rorren's top soldiers to stop one Obsedei warrior. Once they succeeded in destroying the Scorth avatar, the victory was empty. The real enemy sat tucked away, safe in a control pod far from the battle.

Rorren shouted orders and soldiers readied their staffs. Guns and veer rifles were useless against the Obsedei. The diamond tip of the staff was the only material capable of cutting through the stone.

Row after row of Obsedei materialized, marching toward them with rumbling precision. Rorren stood at the head of the battle, time suspended as the enemy approached. The world around him slowed. Liquid rain hit rock and steel, hissing up steam that mixed with the labored breathing of his soldiers. He sensed them gripping the metal of their spears between cold fingers.

The old Scorth woman, robes unaffected by the rain, stepped out of line. Rorren ordered her to return to her post.

She disobeyed and a sword appeared in her hands. Particles in the air swirled together, solidifying into a blade unlike any Rorren had seen before. The tint of the metal reminded him of a mountain lake he visited with his father as a child. The water was so clear it was like looking into a mirror.

Rorren watched the reflection of the world around them in the blade of the Scorth sword.

With both hands wrapped around its handle, swinging, she cut through the onslaught.

Three Obsedei warriors fell.

She struck again, dropping two more monsters.

Streaks of flame burned in midair along the path of her sword strikes.

Fire scars.

The flames burned themselves out in seconds, but the memory of seeing it for the first time in the hands of Lady Layeyre would be with Rorren forever.

CHAPTER 23

Desandor

Present Day

"G RANDA IS THE ONE I wanted to make proud," Vesta said as the blade of the Vision Queen hurled toward her.

She braced for pain but something warmed her palm.

The Queen vanished and the storm broke.

Stars overhead cast a pale light and Vesta's leg stopped throbbing. Her cheek healed as if the cut had never been there.

Opening her hand, she found grains of sand still blazing with the flame of the solstal.

While she examined the tiny flecks, they cooled into dark kernels. This was the beginning. The solstal went dark, creating a deceptive hole in the sand. Vesta funneled the special kernels into a small draw-string pouch and retrieved the solstal.

A strange glow appeared against midnight blue, floating in the air like tendrils from a jellyfish. It was beautiful and—as she studied it—familiar. As a raven, she had followed this strange light to Desandor.

Her instinct then was to trust it. Reason now prevented such blind faith.

The light strands faded into smoke emerging from the hull of a damaged spacecraft. Swallowed in the starless sky, Vesta couldn't make out the insignia on the ship before it crashed beyond the distant sands.

Instead of resting, she packed her supplies and started toward the fallen craft.

The peculiar, almost lethal vision that overtook her moments ago had been vanquished. As Vesta's steady footfalls sunk into the sand, she knew the war was not over. Her stomach roiled, the familiar scent of the desert bringing her no comfort. Walking through the night helped.

Vesta reached the crash site just as the suns cracked over the horizon. The orange of sunrise reminded her of a sapphire necklace she'd once stolen. Her mouth watered at the thought of holding that sparkling gemstone again.

Below the horizon line, a spacecraft lay under a smoldering cloud of ash.

A gash peeled away the hull, exposing the cargo hold and distorting the ship's insignia. Four ringed planets.

Galactic Order.

She crouched, alarmed, but saw no movement below. The site seemed abandoned.

She hoisted her supply bag and stabbed the ground with her staff. Soldiers could fend for themselves.

A shriek tore across the desert.

The ear-piercing scream left her shaking.

Vesta knew what it was even though she never heard it before.

The gantis she befriended called for help.

She climbed to the top of a nearby dune, peered over the edge and encountered a battle from the ancient age. Her shelled gantis swung its spiked tail at the slightly larger gantis, a horned beast with a snout like a lizard.

When the spikes lodged in the torso of the lizard, it snarled, exposing razor teeth. Drool fell from its lips and drenched one of the scrambling soldiers below. The lizard gantis lifted to its hind legs, talons raking across the giant turtle's shell. The creature screamed again.

Vesta recognized the gash marks—slashes the same as those that tore the hull of the crashed ship.

She decided to stop the fight but hesitated, knowing she could not carry out her plan without hurting the soldiers. *Aux rand kitlush* soldiers.

When she reached the bottom of the dune, she tossed aside her staff and supply bag.

She darted toward the soldiers, dodging the feet of the dueling giants and straining her muscles.

As she sprinted, she watched the fight happening above her. Diving forward in time to escape a drool bath, she bumped into a soldier and pushed him into the path of slime.

She caught a flash of his armband before drool covered it up—the rank of a Commander.

"Get out of the way!" one soldier yelled.

Shots scattered through the air, but they only enraged both animals.

Another shot flew by her head and Vesta turned, glaring at the culprit.

"Scorth! It's a Scorth attack!"

She marched to the kitlush boy and pulled the gun from his grip. He was too petrified to stop her.

Another soldier came to his aid. He aimed his gun at her but did not fire.

"Vesta?"

She knew his face.

"Jon."

He lowered the gun.

"You are out of the academy already?"

He shook his head.

"This was a training mission. My first. The cage onboard wasn't strong enough to hold it." He yelled over the sound of dueling beasts.

"I can contain it but your battalion must fall back," Vesta said.

"I'm in charge here." The drool-covered Commander sloshed up to them, scrunched nose looking more petulant than intimidating.

Life or death hung in the balance and the Commander wanted to quibble over power. Typical human.

"Tell them!" Vesta ordered Jon.

"I can vouch for her. Trust her, Commander."

The Commander frowned but gave her an arrogant nod. He cared enough about his troop to risk trusting her, which she respected.

"You don't leave my sights, witch. Understand?" he asked, aiming his weapon at her head.

And there went her respect.

Rather than acknowledge the Commander, Vesta turned to the battle between the two gantis. The soldiers scrambled clear and Vesta focused her mind. Sand from the neighboring dune swirled and took shape.

The Vision Queen appeared there, sword drawn, blocking Vesta's attempts to control the particles.

Vesta fought the darkness, the temptation to show the Commander who possessed the real power threatening to distract her from her mission.

She extended her hand, crossing the barrier into an unknown magic.

Particles of black sand stirred as her mind reached deeper, picking each grain with purpose.

Vesta plunged into a well where a profound power slumbered, and the Vision Queen fought her for control.

Vesta won and stood in the shadow of the sand creature she conjured. Its wings beat up into the air, sending sand into the path of the dueling animals, momentarily confusing them.

The shelled gantis retreated, licking its wounds, but the lizard gantis from the ship shrieked, and pursued its injured prey.

"Not today," Vesta said, commanding her flying dragon into battle.

The monsters locked horns, talons thrashing. She straining the limits of her new ground well of power, and sensed her creature losing the battle.

"Drive it back to the ship," Jon yelled.

Complying, Vesta guided the gantis toward the damaged ship. She maneuvered the beast around the soldiers who worked to reseal the hull. With cables and pulleys, they heaved a metal welder to the gashes, awaiting the arrival of the gantis.

The sand dragon flew higher, swooping through the air, driving the lizard into the cage but taking a devastating thrashing to its wing. Vesta grabbed her arm, falling to her knees in pain. Her control slipped and the sand dragon crumbled.

The Galactic Order had likely taken the lizard from its home world against its will. Vesta did not want to kill it, but she didn't have the strength to force it into the cage.

A shelled body appeared from beyond the dune, bringing with him a dozen others. With their square heads, they rammed the lizard toward the torn opening in the ship's hull. The lizard recoiled, but pushing past the pain, Vesta used the last of her sand dragon to protect the herd. Three more blows and the lizard retreated through the gash in the cargo hold.

The soldiers turned on the welder and a beam of light struck the ship, sealing the creature inside.

Cries of the trapped monster echoed on the hollow wind.

Behind her, the rumble of the escaping gantis herd faded away.

Vesta retrieved her staff and supply bag, hoping to leave.

"You're Scorth. We have to bring you in," the Drool-Commander said, again pointing his gun at her.

"She saved our lives, Commander. Let her go," Jon said.

"Quiet cadet!"

A shadow blocked out the suns, interrupting the argument. The military vessel landed ten meters away, mounding up a trench of sand around its base. The fight took more out of Vesta than she realized. Fatigue prevented her from a hasty escape.

"They must have received our distress signal," one soldier yelled above the roar of the engines.

A plank extended from the underbelly of the command ship and Vesta watched two companies of soldiers file onto the sand.

The impact of a well-muscled elbow to her obliques caught her by surprise and sent her sprawling.

She outstretched her arms to soften her fall and the solstal escaped its confines.

The stiff end of a Galactic Order staff struck her back and she curled in pain.

She watched the orb roll through blurred vision, stopping just short of polished, military-grade boots. Glaring at the solstal as if the strength of her displeasure could regain its loyalty, Vesta reached for it.

A white cloth fluttered into view and fell across the orb.

With a curse, Vesta pushed to her knees. She looked up, recognizing the face before her.

"General Rorren's bizarre farm maid is Scorth, after all."

Sevet Neece's thin lips curved at their sharp corners.

The Drool-Commander bent and sucker-punched Vesta across the jaw. She doubled over. Out of the corner of her eye, she saw Sevet raise a hand.

Surprising. The kindness made Vesta uneasy.

Sevet Neece had secrets. Dark ones. Vesta could smell them.

Vesta doubted she could take on so many trained soldiers, even in top form. Conjuring the elements was one thing, but only a menti blade could aid her in close hand-to-hand combat.

Unless she wanted to kill everyone. She did not want that.

"Enough, Commander. She just saved your life," Sevet scolded, then turned to the man on her right. "Scan her."

The soldier lifted a rectangular piece of metal.

Vesta closed her eyes until she heard the scanner spark and fizz. The soldier cursed and dropped the malfunctioning machine.

Someone handed him another.

The more power Vesta used, the harder it became to hold onto consciousness. He brought the scanner to her face; light warmed her skin and the machine beeped.

Sevet hovered near the soldier's shoulder, peering at the screen.

Vesta filled her mind with static. Judging by Sevet's scowl and the soldier's wince, that static also scrambled the read-out.

With jaw clenched, Sevet crossed the distance between them and yanked Vesta's head by the roots of her hair.

"Scorth tricks won't save you from justice," she hissed.

"Should I try again?" the soldier asked.

Sevet let go of Vesta with enough force to send her to the ground again.

"No time. Besides, the trade agreement obligates us to let the Sandorians have the witch first."

Vesta lifted her head, seething. Her well of hatred for the icy-blond human woman had no bottom.

"But Agent Neece—"

Sevet held up her hand once again. *She demands total loyalty from her men,* Vesta thought. A vision came to her, perhaps brought on by the lingering influence of the solstal. The Cardinal Premier, Tagion Krave. Based on the way Sevet looked at him, at some ceremony with spotlights and dress uniforms, he was the one Sevet wanted loyalty from. After fixing a medal on Sevet, he flirted with another woman. Vesta saw he was a man far from loyal.

Sevet scowled at Vesta as if she knew Vesta had been shown one of her secrets.

"There is a power in you I will have," she whispered.

The Agent picked up the object under the cloth.

"You know solstals are outlawed. What were you doing with it out here?"

Vesta took pleasure in Sevet's frustration.

"Keep your secrets then, Scorth. Take her away."

The hands of several Galactic Order soldiers pulled her to her feet and cuffed her in metal chains. She met Jon's eyes, but she could see that if he helped her, he would only make both of their situations worse.

Sevet slipped the solstal into a cargo bin and Vesta followed its path up the ramp of the command ship until it vanished into the gray bowels.

"Unhand me, kitlush," Vesta ordered the men. In response, she was tossed—instead of guided—into the bed of a military cargo sandcrawler. She slid across the slick interior and her back slammed into a supply crate.

She heard muffled voices and then part of the cloth covering flipped open. In the glare, Vesta saw the outline of a figure, but the light stung her eyes.

"We are taking you to the Sandorian Citadel. Charges will be brought by the Sandorians, but after they are done with you, you're mine."

The voice belonged to Sevet. Cursing in her native tongue, Vesta hoped the insult had the impact she wanted.

In the shadow beneath the blaring sunlight, Sevet smiled.

"The natives are... primitive. I'd prepare myself if I were you."

The flap closed. Sevet Neece and the light vanished.

Concentrating, Vesta tried but failed to unlock the chains and conjure the power to escape the cargo transport.

Propping herself against the crate, she found a comfortable spot and let exhaustion overtake her.

CHAPTER 24

Scorth War
Cardinal World Delta
Battalion Station 8
12 years ago

RORREN PILOTED THE SMALL ship to the military port on the front lines. The Scorth witch, Lady Layeyre, had sense enough to remain aft rather than assuming a seat next to him in the cockpit.

She sat in silence among a half dozen Scorth devils. They did not look like the Scorth Rorren fought in battle. Their clothes were simple, plain, but clean. The men had buzzed haircuts, not the sleek locks of most Scorth males. The women wore their hair almost as short. Without the impressive coil of hair, Rorren almost did not recognize them as Scorth females.

Lady Layerye was the oldest of them. She looked in her early fifties by human standards—probably meant she was over two hundred years old. Rorren shook off the creepiness of that fact.

He prepped his soldiers for the witch's arrival, but until they saw her, he knew their assurances of acceptance were hollow.

His munitions expert, a gruff man named Freyde, who used to be a steel smith, presented the biggest obstacle to integrating Lady Layeyre and her warriors. Most soldiers considered the Scorth the enemy, but Freyde's hatred of them went beyond common prejudice. Freyde's personal goal and vendetta was to wipe out all traces of Scorth evil for the galaxy's sake.

They docked at the spaceport as Rorren looked out the cockpit window to see the leaders of his battalion lined up inside the terminal. All of them stood at attention. All but Freyde. He had one leg on top of a cargo chest, bending over it with his elbow on his knee and a thick cigar between his lips. The other soldiers were clean-shaven. The women had their hair pulled into tight buns. Freyde sported a harsh line of whiskers on his chin. His hair spiked up from his head as if not combed in weeks.

Despite the lack of concern for protocol, Freyde was not a discipline problem. The other soldiers trusted him with their lives. Rorren trusted him on the battlefield, but Freyde was not socially acceptable and the chances were good that he would make a scene when the witch arrived.

Rorren shut off the power to the ship, reprimanding himself for not finding a polite way to ask Freyde not to be present.

No delaying the inevitable.

Rorren left the cockpit and joined the Scorth witch at the exit ramp.

"You are anxious about the reaction of your soldiers." Her voice, an enticing, husky coo, held an undeniable strength. Rorren approached, trying to use his height to intimidate her. She stood nearly six feet, giving him only three inches on her.

"Most will behave. One might..." He hesitated. The serene expression on her face remained undisturbed.

"I just hope you're not offended easily."

"I am prepared," she said.

Rorren frowned, nodded, and opened the hatch leading to the terminal. He walked side by side with her down the endless ramp. How she walked made Rorren feel like an escort at some red carpet event. She carried an innate elegance Rorren recognized from the royalty and foreign ambassadors that sometimes dined with his parents.

He tried not to think about his father.

"You are curious, Mic Rorren, yet you do not ask questions."

"Just trying not to be rude."

He lied rather than open the floodgates. The witch said nothing more and they entered the terminal.

Captain Cantona squared her shoulders, petite frame conspicuous stacked against the men behind her. She watched the witch out of her peripheral vision, the streak of white in her eyebrow as dazzling as the cunning she displayed in battle.

Zak 'Racer' Joren, a newly promoted first lieutenant and pilot, outright gawked. He lost a finger in recent battle, but his bandaged hand moved to rest on the butt of his veer rifle.

"This is Lady Layeyre," Rorren said.

She made eye contact with each one of them.

"Hello."

Freyde waited at the end of the lineup. Taking the cigar from his lips, he strutted toward them. Rorren stiffened, moving before the witch to protect her from what he knew would be an unpleasant encounter. Her hand on his arm stopped him.

Rorren was surprised by her touch. Most Scorth avoided physical contact like the galactic plague.

Freyde got up in her face, blowing cigar smoke at her. Rorren clenched a fist and forced himself to let the scene play out.

"You think you're one of us?" Freyde looked her up and down. "You're nothing but an old hag, shoved down our throats by the idiots at G.O. Command."

"You're out of line, soldier!" Rorren barked. He intended to discipline Freyde further but again, the Scorth witch lifted her hand.

She met Freyde's eyes. Freyde maintained the gaze but the gruff soldier turned away after a few moments. He put the cigar between his lips, retreating to the corner. Rorren's brow wrinkled as Lady Layeyre addressed the battalion.

"You harbor much hatred for my people. Deservedly so. All that I ask is a chance to earn your trust. Your respect."

The witch glided down the line, dragging her long robes behind her. The way she moved somehow infused the air with serenity.

"Never gonna happen," Freyde muttered from the corner.

The Scorth witch waited for a beat and continued.

"How you feel about the Scorth, about me, is secondary to winning the war. If we can agree on that, then we have already made a start."

"We can agree on that, ma'am," Captain Cantona said. Racer nodded, adjusting his red headband with his uninjured hand.

"This is Lady Layeyre," Rorren said again with emphasis. He glanced down the lineup. "I only want to hear her addressed respectfully. Any name-calling," he moved his eyes to Freyde, "is cause for immediate dismissal."

Freyde folded his arms.

"I'll call her what I think she is."

Rorren started for the man but the Scorth witch's eyes asked him not to.

"There will be a briefing at fourteen hundred hours. Dismissed."

Rorren heard murmuring as the company leaders filed out of the port terminal. Navigating the ins and outs of assuming his father's command was tricky enough without the presence of the enemy. Failure haunted him. Freyde was the easiest target so Rorren blamed him.

"Do not be hard on them or yourself," Lady Layeyre said. "You have a compassionate heart. It is why I chose you."

For the first time, Rorren saw the Scorth in her. Her arrogance—thinking that she had chosen him like some all-knowing God. There was only one God and He wasn't a Scorth witch.

Exhaling, Rorren resigned himself to a long, ugly war at home and on the battlefield.

Desandor
Present Day

Vesta's body ached when she came to. Touching her forehead caused a tender cut above her eyebrow to sting. She could not remember sustaining that injury.

Before she completed a full physical assessment, grabby hands were tugging at her, pulling her into the light, and kicking sand into her face when she hit the ground.

Growling, she looked up at the culprits.

"Go on, witch. Do something about it," the Drool Commander said.

The other soldiers laughed. Jon tried to intercede but they pushed the cadet aside.

Vesta forced her vengeful tendencies into check. Circumstances tempted her. The Queen still lived inside her. There was strength in that darkness and tapping into it was easy.

Sevet Neece rounded the side of the cargo sandcrawler, glanced at Vesta on the ground, and then looked up at the Commander. With kencat reflexes, she kneed the Commander in the groin. He dropped beside Vesta, groaning.

"It's so hard to find good help these days," Sevet said. The other soldiers went gaunt with fear. No one dared look at Vesta funny from that moment on.

A grudging respect for Sevet formed inside Vesta but generated even more suspicions. Beware a kind gesture done in malice.

Sevet lifted Vesta to her feet, her soldiers flanking each side of them. Sevet spoke to one of them, her voice low.

"Take her to the Chairman. After the sentence is decided, bring what is left of her to the lab." Sevet grabbed his uniform lapel, eying Vesta like food. "Tell the Chairman there better be something left."

Agent Neece parted ways with them and the soldiers escorted Vesta into a large domed building.

The structure stood alone against vast desert-scapes, the spaceport barely an inkblot on the horizon. Vesta lost her bearings during transport and pondered how far the structure was from the familiar marketplaces.

As they led her inside, a moment of childish wonder overtook her. Under the pale golden ceiling, planes of masonry spread in geometric patterns down enormous pillars. The tapestries were even more colorful and exquisite than those she'd seen in the quaint Sandorian church.

Realizing this is what they called the Citadel, Vesta observed various transaction centers and headship meeting rooms.

Beyond the swirling textiles, enormous statues of armored Sandorians overhung every entrance and exit point in the building, a warning for intruders and escapees alike. At the center of the dome, two oval glasses a least a meter wide kept time by filtering vats of sand down a narrow tube that connected them.

The soldiers pushed Vesta into a line of all kinds of humanoid species. A native woman walked along the row, handing out thin paper squares. She was dressed in fine dark linen, attire far different than Vesta had seen the nomadic tribe people wear.

One of the soldiers took the ticket from her and then directed Vesta to another corridor.

They came to another line and Vesta endured a longer wait.

She scanned the area for natives she might recognize, but drew hateful glances from strangers. No friend appeared who might fetch Mic Rorren and clear her of the mess she was in.

Worse, waves of bitter hatred kept washing over her.

Around another pillar, the line shortened and the guards moved her inside the grand hall.

Seats loomed above them in a half-crescent, surrounding the circular room. Vesta suspected the well-fed bodies scattered among them belonged to Sandorian diplomats.

Across the far end of the hall, she found a throne much too gauche compared to Ragora's royal seat.

Atop the throne sat an equally unappealing figure. Most natives Vesta had seen till now were tall and slender. The Chairman had a girth wide enough to fill the large lounger and then some. Like the diplomats spying above, the tentacles of skin from the sides of the Chairman's chin did not dangle like Yan-hara's but rested on the bulk of his stomach.

Vesta studied the proceedings, watching native peasants and alien merchants take turns kneeling, addressing the Chairman, and receiving an answer from the magnate. An emaciated Sandorian next to the Chairman clicked keys on a com pad, dismissing the petitioners whether or not they were satisfied with the outcome.

A pang hit her as a Sandorian family exited, tears streaming from the faces of the children.

Vesta cursed Mic Rorren for getting her into such a situation. She fought the soldiers as they brought her forward.

They forced her to her knees and warned her not to speak. The actions triggered a boiling rage inside Vesta.

If she were stronger—

Something in her stomach stirred. No, not her stomach. Movement in the pouch on her belt.

A pouch full of magic sand that had been given to her by the solstal.

"What is this? Scorth on Desandor?" the Chairman asked, shifting his weight. Ripples of skin visible beneath his robes squeezed together as he leaned forward.

"Chairman, this witch was caught in the wastelands with a solstal." Drool Commander seemed pleased with himself.

Vesta snarled, drawing the attention of the other petitioners. She glared at them.

"The Galactic Order will let us sentence her?" the Chairman asked.

As he whispered to his emaciated assistant, Vesta sensed the tension between the Chairman and Galactic Order soldier. Her curiosity went into overdrive.

"Because of your—" Drool Commander searched for the word, "hospitality, we will honor our promise to let Sandorian law pre-empt the Galactic Order. We will take the remains."

Her mouth watered as she thought about showing them her power. She could rid Drool Commander of that smug grin and trim some girth from the Chairman.

Pushing those thoughts aside, Vesta did what Rorren taught her. She focused on sensing the needs of others. She closed her eyes. The clerk standing next to the Chairman had an ill child at home. The alien in line behind her needed to petition the Chairman for a permit to build a new moisture hub.

The Chairman sank against the throne, massive movement breaking Vesta's concentration.

"Scorth are not welcome here. The people shall decide. Take her to the prison cell. She will stand trial in the pit at dawn," the Chairman ordered.

The tall Sandorian next to the Chairman bent nearer.

"My liege, rumors have reached my ears from the outlaying tribe people. Perhaps this is the Scorth witch who has befriended them."

The Chairman's thick three-fingered hand waved in the air.

"Nonsense. There is no such thing as friendly Scorth. Remove her from my sight."

Soldiers shoved Vesta out one of the exits, through the shadow of the Sandorian statues, onto a conveyor belt.

Etched stone walls gave way to glass windows, and the sunlight glittering off flecks of golden sand weaved into rows that made up the pews of an outdoor colosseum below. The suns beat down on her, hot, and then gone again, hidden behind the walls.

They forced her off the conveyor into the darkest depths, then down a series of elevators until the air became rancid and moist.

Marching her along a plank, Vesta couldn't see the occupants of the barred cells lining the walls. More catwalks and railings connected a gap between the plank and the cells, dangling over a drop so deep that Vesta saw no bottom.

Overhead, about thirty meters up, she could see a small opening and distant sunlight fighting to break through.

They moved to a lift, nothing more than a wooden pallet with a lever manned by an oversized Rocbull.

"Never had a Scorth prisoner before." The operator's voice was as rough and solid as his body.

"She is to stand trial at dawn. Pit number eight. Don't let her escape," Drool Commander said.

The operator growled and the Commander hurried away, leaving Vesta alone with the brute.

The Rocbull pulled the lever in a circular motion and the lift dropped them into the endless pit.

Vesta squinted to see the figures inside the cells. Sandorian women and children. Not warriors or dregs.

Descending four or five more stories, the operator pulled the crank and locked the lift into place.

He grunted toward the catwalk and pushed Vesta off the lift. They moved along a plank to a row of barred cell doors. Plucking a vast set of keys from his belt, he located the one he wanted and opened the door.

A loud metal whine echoed around them as the Rocbull shoved Vesta inside. He slammed the bars behind her.

"Don't get any funny ideas. We can give rations or take them away," the Rocbull snarled.

Vesta waited until he was gone, then turned to the darkness, eyes landing on two figures huddled together in the corner of the cell. A Sandorian female clutched her young one close.

"I will not hurt you," Vesta said, "When my strength is back, we shall escape."

"Can she escape? I thought no one could," the child whispered.

"Who knows what a Scorth witch can do," the woman said. Her accusing gaze was full of fear. "There is no way to leave this place unless by order of the Chairman."

Vesta rubbed her aching oblique muscles and examined the room.

"There is always a way."

"My people are good sand farmers. They are good moisture hub builders and they are good prison makers," the Sandorian said.

Vesta approached them and the female pushed her son behind her. Their fear was annoying and Vesta cursed some more.

"The aux rand did say he has never had a Scorth prisoner. Tell me, native, why are you here? You and your loset do not look dangerous to me."

Before the female could answer, Vesta heard something akin to the rushing of a distant faucet. It grew louder, the sound suctioning up from individual cells until it reached Vesta in a chorus of unintelligible mumbling.

"Quiet you!" the Rocbull yelled, banging on the metal railings. The clang echoed through the cells but the odd voices did not stop.

The Sandorian mother released her hold on the boy and directed him to the corner of the cell furthest from Vesta. The female then moved to the bars, head tilting peculiarly, listening. "The Elder has heard you are here. He has a message for you," she said.

Vesta was not prone to paranoia, but the way the simple Sandorian looked at her and the timbre as she spoke sent a sweeping cold through Vesta's armor.

"The Elder?"

The chorus of sounds ebbed in swells and the native female held a finger to her lipless mouth. Vesta tuned her ears but nothing she heard made any sense. The operator obviously did not understand either. He shouted another warning before the voices died down.

"He says you've lost something. A spheroid that the soldiers took. Something you need to become..." She turned to Vesta. "I cannot translate. The words are dirty and rags?"

Vesta approached with as much patience as she could summon. The Sandorian jerked away from her and reached out her three-fingered hand. Her son raced to her.

"Who is this Elder? How are you translating? I do not understand."

The female took a moment as if rallying her courage and Vesta drummed her fingers.

"They keep the men in a different section of the arena. The Elder has been here for many years. He has come closer to escape than any. He created 'the whispers' so families could communicate."

The whispers came again. Vesta studied the native as she listened to the message.

"You do that one more time and I start limiting rations for the young ones!" the operator screamed above them.

The sounds stopped.

Vesta flung out her cape, finding skepticism a valuable shield against her unease.

"And? Speak, woman, what more has this wizard to say?"

The Sandorian rubbed her son's arm, looking at Vesta cautiously.

"He says your granda told him you would come. He almost gave up hope. He is ill. He thought he would die before her words were fulfilled."

The primitive Sandorian would not know the Scorth word for grandmother and it added a chilling legitimacy to the message.

"I do not believe you or the Elder," Vesta lied. "How could my granda know I would be here on a remote planet in the middle of nowhere years after her death?"

"I do not know the ways of the Scorth but I do know the Elder. He never lies."

Vesta swept across the room, not caring if she alarmed her cellmates, and sat on the edge of the single cot. She coughed when dust from the mattress caught in her nose and glared at the Sandorian.

"What does this Elder want me to do?"

"I cannot ask now. We must wait until nightfall," the Sandorian said.

Vesta grunted, thinking the small boy looked frightened enough to scale the walls to escape her. Ignoring them, she paced the length of the cell for what seemed like days. Going from the open plains of Desandor to a cell no larger than Mic Rorren's kitchen made her claustrophobic.

She tried to sleep, to recover her strength, but the message from the Elder, mixed with the dank smell of sweat and rot, upset her senses.

She had not sensed her granda this close in years. Maybe Vahza had not lied to her the day they said their goodbyes. Maybe Vahza was still with her, just as she promised.

Fearing the loss of her sanity if she dwelt on the subject, Vesta rose from the cot and grabbed the bars. She rattled them loud enough to wake the sleeping Sandorian woman and child.

The female consoled her son and Vesta watched him drift back to sleep.

"Scorth witch," the female said.

Vesta moved toward her, not caring if she scared her witless.

"Please, I do not ask for me but my son. I want him to know a life outside these walls."

The plea triggered a flash of memory—not a memory of the past but a future memory. Prisoners escaping. The image passed in an instant.

"Will you take him when you escape?" the Sandorian asked.

"You would trust me, a Scorth witch, with your loset?"

"Even for the chance of his freedom, yes, I would."

Vesta looked the native female directly in the eyes and then sat next to her.

"Why are you here? Why did they take you?" Vesta asked.

The native lifted one of her bony elbows and pointed to an emblem on her torn garment. It was a Sandorian tribe symbol and it looked familiar.

"My compeer and I farmed the land in peace. We sometimes saw the gantis. They are the soul of Desandor."

Sensing the truth of her words, Vesta encouraged her to continue.

"There is evil in the sands. Experimenting on the beasts. Harnessing their power. Anyone who suspects is thrown in here. My compeer and the tribe warriors tried to find the secret camp. We were all punished for it."

"What is this evil?" Vesta asked.

The Sandorian shook her head.

"I do not know. No good will come to Desandor for it. The Chairman turns a blind eye."

"What is your name, female?" Vesta asked.

The native blinked, hesitating, and then lifted her head.

"Reen-hara."

The wife of the Tribe-Chief Yan-hara. Rorren's friend.

Vesta put her fingers over the three fingers of the native still clutched to her son.

The female tried to pull away but Vesta held her tightly.

"I promise you, Reen-hara, I will not only help your son but also see to it that every unjustly imprisoned person in this hellhole goes free."

Reen-hara's other hand covered Vesta's. Squeezed. The Sandorian was not afraid anymore. A splash of warmth sprung from Vesta's chest, filling her with hope.

"You may be lying, Scorth witch, but it is the best lie I have heard in years."

Reen-hara slipped her son from her lap and then moved to the cell bars. The native female rolled her lanky shoulders and whispered in a tongue Vesta could not understand. Whispers echoed down the hallways and up the walls of the prison.

When all went silent, Reen-hara returned.

"I have asked the Elder what he wants of you."

Vesta gestured to the boy.

"He would rest easier there."

Reen-hara bowed to Vesta then lifted her son onto the dusty old mattress.

Vesta paced the length of the cell as they waited for the answer. They did not have to wait long.

The chorus started low, then swelled as the voices drew nearer.

Waiting for Reen-hara to speak, Vesta paced faster.

"He wants what your granda wanted. He says they took your magic orb to..." Reen-hara stopped.

"Where?" Vesta asked.

"To the place I spoke of in the desert. The secret place. The one no one returns from."

Vesta stopped pacing and folded her arms.

"I see. If Mic Rorren were here, he would say, ah, ginger, though I am not sure what it means."

"Rorren-sun? You know Rorren-sun?"

The whispers came once again. Reen-hara's excitedly bobbing head stopped to listen.

"The Elder asks a favor of you."

"I have come this far. I might as well plunge prodigally in," Vesta said, tone dripping with sarcasm.

"Your trial is set for dawn in sandpit number eight. He will be in another pit with a message he wants you to deliver. He asks if you will find him before you escape?"

Vesta jutted her bottom jaw, considering. The Elder might be setting a trap for her. The Galactic Order might be behind the messages and attempting to foil her chances at escape.

She thought of her kind, wise granda.

"Tell him, yes, I will."

CHAPTER 25

Military Academy
Cardinal World Delta
20 years ago

RORREN HURRIED TO SCORTH culture class with the same excitement his peers displayed on the way to combat training, flight school, or command tactics. War, after all, was almost upon them and all desired to learn how to destroy the enemy.

Rorren's interest ran deeper for a reason closer to his heart.

The class was taught by the foremost expert in the field. A female professor who bravely lived among the Scorth for a time before the war. A scholar who had been granted limited access by the Scorth government at a time the war still seemed preventable. Students called her their favorite. Faculty called her a worthy rival. Critics called her a meddler.

Rorren called her mom.

Every day, Rorren anticipated hearing the stories his mom never shared when he was a child. He was only seven when she left them to live among the Scorth. It was a dark period in an otherwise happy childhood, in which his father was always moody and the house was in chaos. The first time he ever heard his parents argue came on the heels of her selection for the diplomatic mission.

Attending Scorth culture class gave Rorren answers about the enemy and his childhood. A semester he could spend understanding why his mother jeopardized her marriage and put them all through hell.

His parents' relationship was strong now and the past seemed like a distant nightmare.

Rorren sometimes thought his family alone carried the weight of running the entire Galactic Order, his father being Field General of the Delta Army Corp.

"What's mummy got in store for us today, MicStick?"

Rorren slid into the seat next to Tagion Krave, a mischievous, strong-jawed kid who distracted Rorren while his mom was off fraternizing with the Scorth. They'd been friends ever since.

Tagion's girlfriend leaned in.

"I can't take any more talk about how Scorth females can give birth up to age one hundred and eighty. It's terrifying to think how easily their population could overrun the galaxy."

Rorren reminded them that his mother taught facts and did not give in to the fearmongering by some in the ranks of the academy.

"Honestly, I'm waiting for the lecture on Scorth mating habits," Tagion said. He laughed and ribbed Rorren with his elbow. Tagion's girlfriend pushed his shoulder.

"You would be!"

As soon as Professor Rorren entered the room, all talking ceased. They still had a few moments before class started. Straightening in his chair, Rorren was proud that his mom could command a classroom just by walking into it.

She took off her glasses and hooked them to the pocket of her purple dress. The color sometimes got her called eccentric.

He knew she had a busy day because a few strands of her chestnut hair were free of the bun and frizzing up by her ears on both sides. She distributed her notes in a row across her desk and bent over them. She was so focused that Rorren saw her shoulder wince when the starting bell chimed through the lecture hall.

Fiddling with her glasses, Professor Rorren removed them from the dress and held them in the hand on her right hip.

"We are going to do something a little different today."

Some students snickered, some looked worried, but everyone moved to the edge of their seats. Rorren's mom had a reputation for being unpredictable and entertaining.

"Mic, you don't mind helping me for a moment? Come down here, please."

Tagion lifted his eyebrow. Rorren forced himself from the seat and walked to the stage with pained steps. To the guillotine. Great.

"This is my son."

The class laughed. Professor Rorren put her other hand on the desk and struck a pose.

"How many times in your life have I told you I love you?"

The class laughed again with a few *isn't-that-sweet oohs* and *awes*. Rorren pushed aside a flush of embarrassment. Every fifteen-year-old's nightmare. Glaring at his mom did no good. She kept her eyes on the rows of students that cascaded upward. Secretly, he liked the attention.

"I don't know."

She chewed on her lip and he knew that meant he was about to get in trouble unless he played along.

"Come on, sweetie, give me a number."

A few more chuckles.

Rorren gritted his teeth. It was getting to the point where he'd admit anything just to get off stage and end the torture.

"Like, a lot. Probably, maybe once a day, just about every day of my life," he admitted, jamming his hands into his academy uniform pockets. He was definitely going to kill her later.

She nodded.

"Except when you were on Ragora and we couldn't get a message through," he added.

That made the class go quiet. Everyone feared Ragora—even the name.

His mom shot him an annoyed glance. Rorren thought it a fair dig for the agony she was putting him through. She walked across the stage, arms outstretched like some grand lady of the theater.

"And how many times would you say I hugged you that you can remember?"

"Awe, MicStick, your mommy wuvs you," Tagion said.

Tagion had no fear.

Rorren did not answer so he could make a face at Tagion.

"Mic?" She drew his attention, looking at him with her professor gaze. He hated that.

"I don't know, also a lot. Do you have a point with this?"

She paced across the stage.

"And how many times has your father hugged you?"

"Probably the same amount, maybe a little less because he was on duty."

Professor Rorren nodded again. She lifted one hand in the air but the other still rested on her hip, glasses between fingers.

"What about aunts, uncles, grandparents and friends? Have they hugged you and expressed that they care about you?"

"Yes, mother." He forced the words through clenched teeth.

The professor stood next to him. She put her hand on his shoulder. He wondered what she was up to because she usually didn't make a fool of herself.

"I want you all to think about the times in your life you've received affection from your loved ones."

His mom did not remove her hand. Rorren detested that he was stuck on stage until she released him.

"Now imagine your life without that touch or those words. Not even a smile. Ever. From anyone."

With her gaze landing on student after student, she let the idea settle.

"This is your life if you are Scorth. You've never heard a word of love. There isn't even a word for love in the Scorth language. You've never been hugged or comforted. If you have, you were likely punished and shunned by society."

A charged silence filled the lecture hall. Her statement impacted harder than her gentle hand on his shoulder.

"I love you, son. Now, go sit down. Thank you for putting up with me."

Rorren tried not to grin. He looked at his classmates.

Why the blazes not?

Turning, he took his mom's petite frame into his arms for a hug.

The class made cooing sounds. Rorren heard his mom laugh.

"Yes, thank you, Mic. You may let go now."

He obeyed and when he returned to his seat, Tagion slapped his shoulder.

"That was adorable, man," Tagion mocked.

Rorren punched his shoulder.

"Shut up, TK."

"But seriously, you'll get hot booty calls after that little display. Girls like that crap."

Sandorian Prison Block 14

Desandor

Present Day

Vesta woke up colliding with something hard.

"Time for judgment," a Galactic Order soldier said. They pressed her against the bars and locked chains around her wrists.

Vesta heard Reen-hara's boy calling her name as the guards forced her toward the lift. He somehow slipped past security and Vesta suddenly found his skinny arms latched around her waist.

Despite the yelling soldiers, the boy held tight.

Reen-hara met Vesta's gaze and her lipless mouth trembled.

"I will keep my promise, vah," Vesta said. She gently pried the boy from her. He might have smiled but the soldiers shoved him into the cell.

Reen-hara nodded to Vesta as she caught her son in her arms. The trust of the natives meant something to Vesta just like Mic Rorren's did.

Odd.

It was a monstrous betrayal of her Scorth upbringing to crave trust. She took relief in the unnatural sounds around her. In the damp, rotting smell. In the absence of light.

The ruffians manhandled her out of the cell and up the lift. Throwing a fit—kicking, biting, and railing against them—brought a satisfied smirk to her lips. She made nothing easy for them.

When they entered the arena, Vesta tried shielding her eyes from the light, but her chained wrists restricted movement. She snarled, delighted when one of the soldiers stumbled off balance in fear.

The curtain of sunlight sparkled over the stone colosseum, revealing rows of people high in the stands. Some were Sandorian, but the majority looked to be the less desirable part of society from the spaceport. Many Aklaren.

This was not the first arena she'd been in but certainly the crudest.

Cheap stone walls rose around the arena floor, made of rusted bricks that wound together in a maze, reminding her of the palace hedges. They pushed her through a gauntlet of screaming observers and rows of pits. Each hole dipped into the ground inside the maze like a lonely teardrop.

Long wooden planks were propped against the walls, probably for maintenance when the pits were empty.

Vesta didn't have long to dwell on the single method of escape.

The soldiers caught her by surprise, hitting the small of her back. She fell from the wall and into the sandpit.

She gasped and heard the distant murmur of the crowd swimming above her.

With her hands still chained, she struggled to find her footing.

A horde of shouting aliens and natives lined the stone walls above.

"This Scorth was found in the desert with contraband. She also freed criminals bound for this prison. How do you judge her?"

A stone struck her across the shoulder before the dust cleared.

"Guilty!" someone shouted.

Two more stones hit her; they stung, but it wasn't the worst part of the experience. She rolled out of the way of a third, but guilt found her anyway. She should pay for more things than the jeering crowd knew about and that turned her into an easy target.

The silhouette of the Vision Queen moved through the crowd as a smoky darkness that encircled the aliens, prompting a slew of shouts.

"Pathetic waste of Scorth flesh!" The Queen mouthed the words as the stranger said them. He hurled a stone and Vesta stepped forward, letting it hit her. She had no way to atone. Compassion and forgiveness were foreign concepts. Darkness consumed her, clouding her mind.

The crowd booed.

The Queen helped another alien fling a rock, moving through them until her dark shadow encompassed the haphazard jury. Her shadow stirred them into a frenzy.

Stones showered Vesta, bringing new voices of self-doubt into her mind.

You are the witch they all think you are.

Granda would laugh to see what a pathetic creature you have become.

And the worst of all, *you mean nothing to Mic Rorren.*

Exposing her body further, Vesta challenged her attackers with a glare. Another stone struck her and she fell to her knees. One good blow to her head would end it.

The fog of the Queen began to melt, no match for the blaze that roared from overhead light. At first, Vesta thought she was seeing some natural phenomenon of Desandor. Under the waves of light, the darkness wiggled into little black coils, draining power from the shrieking Vision Queen. The light formed a wall around Vesta, this new vision protecting her from the old.

The gray robe of a new figure glittered as it descended, cutting through the darkness. Vesta knew who it was before the blurred image came into focus.

Her granda.

Her hope. Her light.

Vahza hovered over the Vision Queen, her brightness reducing evil to a trembling, thrashing mound of dust.

Propping her shoulder against the pit, Vesta forced herself upright, ignoring the sting of rocks and bruises on her body.

Her granda's light warmed her and filled her with strength unlike any she'd known.

Another thought filled her mind, growing stronger and brighter until it shone like the robes of her granda.

Do not accept defeat.

She pushed away from the wall into the onslaught of stone.

She confidently moved to the center of the pit and her endurance made the crowd falter.

Sand and rock swirled around her, bubbling beneath her until it lifted her into the air.

She rose, winds bringing her level with the aliens on the wall. The chains on her wrists cracked and shattered when she pulled against them.

When her arms broke free, her attackers dropped their stones. Some turned away in shame. Others gaped, jaws slack.

The shadow of the Queen flared up for an alarming instant. Out of it emerged Sevet Neece.

Fearless. Strong. Smiling.

Unaffected by the light.

"This Scorth witch is powerful," she said as her soldiers encircled the pit wall. Sevet aimed her laser sight at Vesta. More guns lifted until a half dozen red dots floated over Vesta's chest.

"I do not wish to hurt your men," Vesta said.

Sevet Neece tightened her grip on her weapon.

"Hold your ground," she ordered.

"But please," Vesta taunted, "give me an excuse to hurt you."

The agent did not drop her smile.

"Galactic Law binds me. I must order my guards to stop you," Sevet replied. The pleasure on her lips unsettled Vesta.

She acted as if goading Vesta into action was the means to an end.

Staring each other down, the women reached an impasse that engulfed Desandor.

"Open fire!"

Sevet took the first shot.

The winds that suspended Vesta in the air broke under the barrage of bullets. She managed to control her fall and landed on the wall.

Vesta conjured a sandstorm to cover her escape.

She sprinted, passing sandpits and prisoners, picking up as many planks as possible. She lowered them into the pits and shouted to those trapped to join her.

She did not know what the Elder looked like.

Soldiers continued firing as people scattered in all directions. Amid the ricocheting bullets, she shouted for the Elder. One of the native males she freed took her by the hand and led her to a sandpit deep in the center of the arena. Far from the escape gait, the opposite direction she wanted to go.

They slid down the plank. The Sandorian brought her to a group of prisoners huddled around a figure that lay bleeding and broken from the judgment of stone.

Vesta, lamenting the compounding distance to freedom, snapped to attention when the Sandorian pointed and said, "that is the Elder."

CHAPTER 26

Military Academy
Cardinal World Delta
20 Years ago

PROFESSOR RORREN GUIDED THE class into a circular room and Mic Rorren followed at a safe distance. He wanted to stay far away from his mother to avoid drawing attention to himself but not so far away as it would look like he was avoiding her.

She chatted with several students, answering questions and delighting them as the room filled.

Desk consoles formed individual compartments along two crescent-shaped aisles. Tagion sat in the center of the classroom with Mic Rorren beside him. Mic Rorren noticed Tagion's current girlfriend on the opposite side. Tagion's ex-girlfriend ended up in the far corner of the room.

Rorren's mom clicked her fingers over the console keyboard, dimming the lights.

"Romantic date, Professor," Tagion said and got a laugh from the class. Rorren was proud of his mother for not flinching at the disturbance.

Above them, in the center of the room, holographic star charts descended in a splash of dazzling light. Mic Rorren's mother scrolled through the charts and Rorren recognized Cardinal World Alpha and the Tallum Nebula. The projection flashed through several star systems and landed on the forbidden planet, Ragora.

"I would hope you all recognize this planet after a semester in my class."

A lot of heads nodded accompanied by nervous chuckling.

The holographic images stunned Rorren. The planet was as appealing as described in textbooks, with spectacular jungles, beaches, and water formations. Rorren imagined the white shores, rich soil, and dense salty smells. Paradise spoiled by the inhabitants.

A hologram of a new planet appeared, dwarfing Ragora, at least four times the size and more shimmery. Rorren heard a few gasps and glanced at his friend with a grin. The holographic light glistened across Tagion's face, absorbing into his skin and leaving behind a pale silver glow.

"Is that?" Tagion started.

Professor Rorren, clicking the remote to zoom in, came around the console.

"Parkell. The Diamond Moon of Ragora as seen from space, though no human has been near enough to know how accurate this representation is."

A hand shot up.

"Is it true what they say about the slave mines? Are the Scorth really so savage they send the poor and disobedient to work there?" a student asked.

This time, Rorren fell into the blinding holo-light, trying to soak up as much as possible. These were questions he wanted to ask his mother for years.

"When I was Ambassador to Ragora, I dared not broach that subject. But I heard whispers."

The whole class fell under her spell, silence deafening.

"From what little we know, the diamond moon is a place one doesn't return from. It is a dreary life of hard labor and eventual death. I gathered it was more like a prison colony, but the Scorth only showed me what they wanted me to see."

Tagion raised his hand.

"Did you see any of the jewels mined there? Rumor is they contain magic."

Professor Rorren's lips curved, forming a half smile.

"Magic? Really, Mr. Krave, next you'll be telling me you believe in the Aux Katan."

The class laughed. Tagion folded his arms, lips pouting, and sunk into the seat. Mic Rorren liked seeing Tagion put in his place, but he was annoyed his mother dodged the question.

Hooking her reading glasses on the top edge of her blouse, Professor Rorren stepped through the hologram, one hand on her hip.

"They say there are three great power sources in the universe. One, you know. The minerals mined from the Tallum Nebula that power most of our modern worlds. The second. The power the ancients used, the brute force of the giant beasts that still roam the outer planets in our galaxy."

"And third is the power of the Scorth? The fire sword?" Tagion asked. Professor Rorren walked over to him.

"Yes, Mr. Krave. And if you interrupt again, you can forget dinner next time Mic invites you over."

The class laughed and Tagion, smiling wickedly, said, "You wouldn't do that, Professor. I'm like your other son."

The professor wrinkled her nose.

"Yes, the troublemaker."

More laughter.

"Who can tell me something about Scorth power?" Rorren's mom asked.

One student answered, "It's telepathy."

Another said, "Science can't explain it."

Professor Rorren inclined her head as she patrolled the room.

"You are both right and wrong. The Scorth can telepathically link with each other, allowing them to tap into this unexplainable power. It is a mystery, especially given humans and Scorth are genetically identical."

Returning to the console, the professor pressed more buttons. The holograms of the planets vanished, replaced by a strange oval object covered in moss, slime, and vines.

"This is a Scorth pod, one of the few pictures ever taken. The pod protects the Scorth while their minds are linked together."

Top secret. Classified. Wondering if General Rorren permitted his mother to show them an actual pod, Mic Rorren wished he could take the image home and study it. Hot beans! It was probably already at home, password-protected and stuffed in the family safe.

"Science might not know everything about this power, but we have learned it's elemental. The Scorth never engage an enemy in space. They have dominion over rock, tree, and soil, so that is where they prefer to fight."

Resisting the urge at first but giving in, Rorren raised his hand. His mother paused before she called on him.

"Yes, Mic?"

"So, if the Scorth link together to get this power, then are Fire-Scar Warriors only a legend?"

Professor Rorren unhooked her glasses from her blouse and addressed the class.

"One too many comic books, son. He's referring to what the Scorth call the Aux Katan. The Fire-Scar Warriors. From all I saw on Ragora, these warriors don't exist."

The professor clicked the remote and a holographic sketch of a male Scorth warrior appeared. Rorren had seen the picture before. It was how all the Cardinal Worlds imagined Fire-Scar Warriors. Men in heavily armored body suits, gripping long blades and spikes adorning every surface.

"However," Professor Rorren said. She captured the whole class under her spell. "The idea that an individual Scorth could call on this power is intriguing. What that would look like, we have yet to see."

The hologram disappeared and lights flickered on.

"What do you think? Are the Aux Katan real?" she asked.

Tagion interrupted again.

"If war comes, Professor, I guess we might find out."

In Professor Rorren's darkening countenance, Rorren saw war was no longer an if. It made the idea of a Scorth so powerful he wouldn't need a pod even more frightening.

The Citadel Pits
Desandor
Present Day

The Elder was human. Patches of gray peppered his hair and a scar ran the length of his square jaw, probably earned in war. She could tell by the eyes, sitting beneath his thick, heavy brows, that this man had seen things.

Weak fingers pulled a cigar from somewhere inside the rags he wore.

Lips curving up, he placed the cigar between them.

"Been saving it for a special occasion," he said, "you qualify. Special. Just like your granda."

Vesta knelt by his side, ignoring the Sandorians as they searched among them for a match.

"How did you know her?"

"In the war. Name's Freyde."

A strange electric impulse burned through her nerve endings, but she did not understand its meaning.

"Nothing is a coincidence," Freyde said. He reached into his pocket and produced from it a small rectangular circuit. He coughed and Vesta saw the pale hue of his skin infected with a plague that doomed him long before the stones took their toll.

"After she died, I came here to deliver a message to a friend. I didn't get far. Take it."

Freyde wrapped Vesta's fingers around the object, squeezed and let go.

The raging storm, dependent on Vesta's concentration, waned with her focus. The veil shielding them from danger collapsed and the hum of marching footfalls shook the walls in ominous beats.

Mic Rorren would use some colorful but inefficient idioms. *Shooting fish in a barrel. Sitting ducks.*

"We must go," she said.

Vesta latched his arm around her shoulders and took on the brunt of his weight. They staggered toward the plank. Sandorian prisoners, helping each other out of the pit, turned their attention to her. They moved to assist, but Freyde sank to the ground and Vesta's hope sank with him.

"No!" she said, "we need you. I do not know who this is for. I have so many questions."

He grinned, cigar between his lips, and his eyes twinkled.

Vesta clenched her fists to prevent herself from violently ripping him off the ground.

"There is only one thing you need to know. Your granda loved you and believed in you. Don't be afraid to believe in yourself," Freyde said. His hand wormed its way over hers. "Find the solstal. Become Aux Katan. Make her visions come true."

He wasn't looking at Vesta but at something beyond her right shoulder. His eyes glazed over like he was hallucinating.

Glancing over her shoulder, Vesta saw the outline of a woman appear from particles of sand. Sparks of light churned within the storm, familiar strands of jellyfish tentacles filled in the details. They brought to life the curve of a smile—the kind eyes.

Her granda.

Confusion set in. Vesta couldn't tell if this was real or a vision from the solstal, but the brutality of it threatened to pull tears from her.

"She's been guiding you for a long time," Freyde said, propping himself against the pit wall, "but today she's here for me."

Vesta and the Sandorians slammed against the wall, using it as shelter from the showers of bullets from above.

They were trapped.

Vesta prepared for the sting of a ricocheting bullet and closed her eyes just as a flash of strange light cut through the air.

Bullets crumbled into dead slugs and dropped like pebbles. The particles of sand glowing inside Vahza's menti blade stopped them.

Vesta led the prisoners up the plank, convinced the vision was real. With her granda slashing and Vesta sending windfalls, they tore the soldiers from their perches.

Feet soared over heads as the soldiers fell into the adjacent pit. Vesta charged upward, leading all to escape. One remained behind.

Vahza stayed in the pit with the human.

"Go!" the Elder shouted.

Vesta watched his human hand touch the sand grains of Vahza's hand and the storm swallowed them up.

Vesta hesitated, putting them all in danger as the ground trembled beneath the march of another wave of troops.

When the particles swirled away, both figures were gone.

Emptiness welled in Vesta as it had the day she parted with her granda. An insatiable desire to steal something shiny, to fill that hole, carried her up the plank and into the arena maze.

There was no treasure here. Vesta settled for revenge on the soldiers.

She picked up more Sandorians on her way to freedom and tore through the maze as if she owned it.

With no way to open the gate from the inside, Vesta climbed. The Sandorians followed.

She ripped her feathered cape coming down the other side, cursed, and landed on all fours.

A boot kicked her stomach.

She curled up, gasping. The second blow from the blunt end of a Galactic Order staff damaged her armor and the Elder's message came tumbling free.

Rorren's training flooded her mind. Combined with her temper, the poor kitlush humans stood no chance. Dodging the next blow, Vesta happily kicked the soldier's legs out from under him. Another soldier appeared from out of the sandstorm, firing on her. She rolled and savagely disarmed him with a round-house kick and an upper cut.

With the battle stealing her attention, the winds from the storm she conjured died around them, exposing them to another bombardment of bullets.

In search of the message chip, Vesta dug in the sand until the Sandorians pulled her away from the amassing troops.

She growled, standing half a dune away from the arena, watching Sevet appear behind the massive prison gate.

If not for the natives restraining her, hands on her arms, Vesta would have returned for the message. Soldiers buzzed across the landscape after them, swarming like angry grubmites.

Bullets tarnished the sand near Vesta's boots and she conjured another rageful storm.

Before allowing the storm to cover their escape, Vesta looked over her shoulder to see Sevet bend and pluck the computer chip from the ground.

"Ah, ginger," Vesta said. She wished for just one fair battle with Sevet.

Vesta's sandstorm ensured neither the Sandorian military nor Galactic Order soldiers could follow them.

She parted ways with her fellow prisoners once she led them safely to the space hub. She turned her attention to the horizon, finding the arena had become just another dune in the distance.

She committed herself to that dune and her promise to Reen-hara and her son. She would return for them all.

Her cape flared as she traversed the sand. Each step brought her closer to the moment she would convince Mic Rorren to join her.

CHAPTER 27

Scorth War

Cardinal World Delta

10 years ago

B LASTS FROM THE ROCKET cannons, crashing on them in intervals like the erratic breathing of a dragon with a belly of fire, brought swirls of grey dust up from war-torn terrain. Groans and curses from his troops resonated as Rorren and Freyde carried wounded men away from the battlefield.

A blast knocked them off course and Rorren scrambled to the top of the wounded soldier, protecting him from a shower of pebbles. He looked up and saw Freyde shielding the other man, grinning, a cigar between his teeth.

"Heck of a party you've discovered, General. It's a real blast."

Hoisting an arm over his shoulder, Rorren picked up the injured man. They dodged more gunfire, and Rorren turned, ensuring Freyde was close on his heels. Rorren wondered if his troops followed him into danger because they trusted him or because of the mark of the relheer. By surviving, he unintentionally gave everyone hope—a heavier burden than bearing his soldiers to safety.

They jumped into the cover of the trench, escaping the explosion of the next bomb. Rorren braced for the impact while calling for medical assistance. He looked down the line at his men and women, all scorched by flame and coated in mud and grease. Every hour or so, a brave fool would try his luck on the battlefield, only to return broken if he survived. Rorren and Freyde went with them all day, bringing back the ones they could.

The soldier beside Rorren adjusted his dented armor, a gash in his arm bleeding red down the once bright metal. The wound didn't stop him from helping other injured to the infirmary.

They were battered and exhausted, but the brightness in their eyes was undeniable.

Rorren knew why.

One among them stood out.

She walked the trenches with a calming gait and bent to offer water to the wounded from what might have been a golden challis instead of a chipped bucket.

Her gown drew attention.

The first time Rorren saw her dressed like that, he asked why she wore her pajamas to war. The old Scorth warrior laughed. So did the humans.

Until that moment, Rorren had not thought Scorth capable of laughter. Neither had his men, Freyde especially.

"This is the traditional garment of the learned," she explained to them.

What she never explained was its magic.

By some miracle, the gray fabric still sparkled as it had that first day, even after weeks in the heat and mud. Rorren studied her now, feeling guilty for his pajama comment. The fact her elegant clothing stayed free of the stains of war became a symbol for his soldiers—another symbol of hope like the scars on his neck. Day after day, he saw them eagerly scanning the front lines for a glimpse of the she-demon in the sparkling robes.

She visited each soldier in turn, soothing with words or a gentle touch to a cheek. When she reached him, Rorren saw beyond the sparkle to her exhaustion.

A soldier tumbled over the trench, landing between them. He took a few deep breaths, hands holding his knees. Blood covered the side of his face. He took the water from Lady Layeyre.

"No disrespect, General, but we are getting killed out there. You should have let Lady Layeyre fight today."

Freyde stood close to the Scorth witch as if he had been assigned as her personal bodyguard.

Lady Layeyre acknowledged the wounded man, respectfully nodding, and then she moved to allow the medical staff through.

"She can't fight every day," Rorren said.

Lady Layeyre glanced at Rorren's scars and then at the trail of injured behind her, all with new resolve and courage in their souls.

"There are other ways to fight," she said. She conjured her menti blade and charged into battle.

Desandor
Present Day

Vesta spent the night in the desert shivering under her feathered cape. She was in a foul mood since losing her provisions and the solstal. The night air permeated her dented armor and costly fabric with a hint of frost.

She dreamed of curling up next to Brawn and the warm fireplace of Mic Rorren's farmhouse. Vesta abandoned her fitful sleep before sunrise, eager to see the tattered old roof and sun-scorched barn again.

The suns dangled halfway up the azure sky by the time the house came into view. Vesta's feet throbbed, her stomach churned with hunger, and her calf muscles screamed for relief from walking in the sand.

She reached the fence post at the edge of the property, leaning on it for support, chuckling and groaning.

She was home.

Movement from the porch caught her attention.

Brawn bounded off the stairs, sprinted across the yard, and jumped onto her. He licked her face, disgusting her, and they fell to the ground in a tangle.

She relished the feel of her fingers through his soft fur.

The front door creaked, the familiar sound sending a wave of delight through Vesta. Peering around the kencat, she spotted Mic Rorren on the porch. He stopped at the edge of the stairs, folding arms across his broad chest, lips and jaw locked in a scowl.

"You're late."

She forced herself to her feet and walked beside Brawn, pumping her weary legs to the house. Her temper flared with each step, realizing she needed this place. A real home. How dare he challenge everything she knew about life.

Rorren's arms pulled her into a tight embrace.

The force of his hold alarmed her. She went momentarily languid. Her Scorth instincts told her to push him away. Show no weakness. Reject a comforting touch.

But, oh, it felt good.

"Is this what they call embracing your mistakes?" she asked, surprising herself by preparing to hug him in five, four, three, two...

He let go of her and—to her annoyance—turned his head so she couldn't see his face.

"You were worried?"

Rorren stuck his tongue against his cheek and rubbed Brawn's head.

"Nah, Brawn and I know troublemakers always come back to haunt us."

Exhaustion prevented her from a witty reply. Vesta took his arm, leaning on him as he helped her inside, only half conscious of what she was doing.

Rorren placed her at the kitchen table. He piled some food on a plate and set it before her. A bribe to pry loose the questions he didn't ask.

He sat in the chair across the table and waited, studying her.

She forgot how aggravating he was.

"Agent Neece took the solstal. I need it to complete the training or I will not be strong enough," she blurted.

Unburdened by the facts, she reached for the utensil and attacked the food. It tasted better than she remembered. She savored each mouthful.

"Strong enough for what?"

"I saw Jon and thousands of Sandorian families. Prisoners at the Citadel. The Chairman has amassed half the planet in his dungeons."

Vesta watched a silent resolve form around the creases of his mouth. She found no trace of fear in the cold oceans of his eyes. His stature, soul and strength slapped her with their intensity. Her wish to be near him disgusted her. Developing it instead into a convulsion of protest and resistance, she soothed it away. The kitlush might pass for handsome on Ragora if given the proper attire and posture, though his features would always be too rough.

"We have to approach this delicately," he said.

A strand of hair fell over his face as he rubbed the alien swirls on his neck.

"If they knew what you had survived, Mic Rorren, they would follow you."

Light from the suns reached the table's edge, casting half his torso in shadow. She did not understand why he was ashamed of the scars. Few Scorth, let alone humans, survived what he had and they wore the markings with pride.

"We can't just barge in there without a plan."

"Why not?" Vesta asked, spreading her fingers as if pushing against an invisible wall between them. "You taught me to sense the needs of others. Even from this distance, I hear the people calling for help. Should I deny them?"

Rorren stretched in the chair and Vesta found the informality of it as offensive as its intimacy.

"My job was to teach you how to become a Fire-Scar Warrior, not to get you killed. We have no army and I only fight if there is a chance I can win."

The markings, she thought, were a kind of prison for him, the same way her desire for treasure had trapped her. Every day, even as a raven, she awoke with a singular goal: *steal it all*. That lust took her freedom the same way the scars of war were taking Mic Rorren's.

He changed her. A cold, concise anger chilled her from the inside out. It was his fault she now spent each day struggling against the compulsions that once controlled her.

He had the power to change her while remaining obstinate to change himself. The dark irony of it infuriated her. Clutching her feathered cape, she swept across the room.

"Be a coward then. I will not be. I crave something more than jewels. A chance to fulfill the dreams of my granda."

"I'm not a coward. I'm a General and I know how to win wars. Sit down!"

She swallowed, more thrilled than annoyed by his raised voice. Maybe he was awakening.

"Fine, General. Then, win this one for your friends."

Inching close to him, she placed her hand on the back of his chair. One movement was all she needed to reach out and touch him. She bent to his ear.

"I leave at dawn with or without you," she said.

She kept her word the following day. Twilight blurred the lines between the dunes beyond the barn as she readied herself for the unknown journey into secret realms.

A shadow fell over her fingers as she finished lacing up her boot.

The end of a staff dislodged the sand near her boot. Looking up its sleek, polished line, she found an intricate design at the top, knotted wood coiled around a worthless green gemstone.

"It looks Scorth," she said and reached for it.

Mic Rorren withdrew it by tapping twice on the handle. The rod collapsed into a square about the size and thickness of a belt buckle, just like a Galactic Order weapon.

"Try not to lose this one," he said, tossing it to her.

She latched the square to her armor, movements smooth and calm, opposite of her mind. She held her breath, hitching on a faint glimmer of hope.

He leaned against the sandcrawler and gnawed on a piece of straw.

"I think you must join me to ensure I do not lose this staff you clearly spent many hours making," she said.

He plucked the straw from his mouth with a relaxed energy she envied.

"I was bored. Nothing better to do."

That was a lie.

He stepped sideways, revealing the presence of two resaurs, bags on each side of the saddles bulging with supplies. Vesta had not seen the four-legged pack animal in seven decades.

"Now the question is, do Scorth rabble-rousers know how to ride?"

Vesta flung out her cape and grinned.

CHAPTER 28

THE RESAUR JERKED AWAY from Vesta, beak snapping at her, cloven hoofs stomping the sand dangerously close to her boots. She snarled at the beast. The shine of its silver coat, changing colors in the sunlight, looked better than it smelled. No animal, save Brawn, had ever endeared itself to Vesta. The reeking creature before her was no exception.

"You sure there is a secret base somewhere in those sands?" Rorren asked.

His hands moved absently over the saddle straps. The resaur purred under his touch and a surge of jealousy irked Vesta.

"It is where Sevet took the solstal," Vesta said. She hoisted herself up on the beast and pulled the reigns as it attempted to spin her off.

"I'll believe it when I see it," he said.

Once Vesta gained control of her smelly humpback, she aimed it toward the Galactic Order crash site.

"You will see," she said. She coaxed the resaur with a click and it finally obeyed.

They reached the crash site near dusk, but Vesta found someone had erased the signs of battle. With Rorren's assistance, she plotted a course following the ship's trajectory.

The deeper the beasts pressed into the wild deserts of Desandor, the more skittish they became. Vesta cursed at them, annoyed she let the animal's paranoia affect her.

The resaurs could reach places the sandcrawler could not, from narrow canyon passages to seep sand inclines, though Vesta's backside preferred the plush seats of the vehicle.

A blemish appeared on the horizon at noon on their seventh day of wandering the sands. Even from a distance, Vesta knew what it was. A sickening, measured tension started to build in the recesses of her mind.

When Rorren guided his resaur into the sharp lines of the building's shadow, the scope of the threat left Vesta reeling.

Rorren wiped the sweat from his forehead and Vesta focused on his movements rather than face what lay ahead.

The well-muscled contours of his arms and neck glistened as he drank from his canteen. He tucked it away and leaned forward in the saddle, shirt pulling tight over his chest.

"Never knew Sandorians built pyramids. Or maybe this is from the civilization before, like the ruins in the badlands."

Massive stones interlocked, sealing themselves against intruders with some unnatural force. A silent whisper of death sent swirls of sand into the air.

"No. This structure is something else."

As the tapered walls seemed to awe Rorren, Vesta fought her fear.

"What?" he asked.

"We should move on," she said. She guided the resaur again to the path.

At the first dune, Vesta pulled her heel out of the resaur's hide and reduced speed to keep from drawing unwanted attention from Mic Rorren.

There were no signs of habitation this far out. Vesta sank into the wasteland, desolate and peaceful, and found comfort in it.

Rorren took them straight up the valley between boulders, nothing to guide them but the rough trajectory of a ship that never reached its destination.

The land flattened, then curved into rolling sands.

On the horizon the same structure reappeared.

The pyramid had four triangular walls of glistening masonry, though the others cast one of the walls in shadow.

Vesta kicked in her heels and sped past the building, resaur clucking over the dunes, throwing her against the saddle as it galloped.

She left the dunes and entered the rocks once more. The canyon fell away behind them and they were there again at the base of the monument.

There was no wind. The peaks of the dunes around them stood static.

"Three identical pyramids? Are these some ritual landmarks?" Rorren asked.

Vesta climbed off the resaur, leaving it squawking after her as she approached the building.

Sand drifted across her boots, carrying that whisper she heard before, a diminutive noise within her, enough to unsettle her stomach.

"This is the same structure," she said.

"What?"

Rorren dismounted loudly enough to disturb the silent landscape and her thoughts. His shadow loomed beside her but she did not look at him.

A flash came barreling across her mind. Scorth warriors with twisted, bony faces, screaming as death came—a warning to retreat.

"Vesta?"

"It is not a pyramid."

"Incomplete solstal training is said to cause hallucinations," Rorren said in jest, perhaps, but he wasn't wrong.

Vesta drew her feathered cape over the sand and strode to the invisible entrance at the center of the nearest side. Stones towered above her at least a hundred meters high.

"This is where the Galactic Order has established their secret base," she said.

Rorren slanted his hat, squinted into the sky and then to her.

"So, we're suddenly a secret base expert now, are we?" he asked.

Habitually irritating human. Not cute in any way. At all.

"This is a Rishka. Designed to protect Scorth treasure from outsiders. How the Galactic Order has obtained this technology, I do not know."

"Never heard of it. I'm sure the Order hasn't either. Maybe the Fire-Scar Warriors—"

She growled and swiveled her cape over the sand.

"This is an ancient weapon of my people. To build a Rishka, one needs the collective power of a Scorth pod. This one is not the work of a Fire-Scar Warrior," she said.

Rorren lifted his hands; she hoped in surrender.

"Let me guess. To get to the mystery base, we have to go in there."

She nodded.

"Ah, ginger." Rorren rolled up his sleeve and revealed an appealing bicep. "So, how do you get inside? Open sesame?"

The pyramid rumbled and pebbles bounced over the stone until the walls began moving. The jigsaw arranged itself, cranking and grinding, forming into an elaborate gateway. Marbled columns lined each side of the gold-plated archway, deceptively inviting.

"Can't believe that worked," Mic Rorren said, running a hand through his hair. He started for the entrance but Vesta sent a burst of wind and sand at him. The blast hit him hard and he tumbled over.

"What in blue blazes, Vesta!?"

"To enter a Rishka as it beckons means death. Only a handful of warriors have ever come out alive and those who do survive are often too crippled or maimed to enjoy the spoils."

Rorren got up, brushing the sand from his clothes with more patting and slapping than she thought necessary.

"Give up, then? Go home. Game over?" he asked.

The west wall called to her. She drew near enough to touch the hot, flat surface.

"If this is like my mother's Rishka there will be an alternate entrance."

Each stone possessed unique markings, dazzling enough to get lost in. Disorientation clouded Vesta's thinking as she traced the outlines.

Then—from the cracks—a scream.

Snapping her fingers from the keystone, she glanced over. Mic Rorren adjusted his hat forward, then to the side. Oblivious. Like always. The kitlush.

Her lips formed a circle and she blew the dust away from the stone. She pressed two round inlets in the design. Her heart thumped up to her throat. It had been a long time since she sought treasure like this.

A slab of rock rumbled away, revealing a new passageway far from the grand entrance.

Mic Rorren frowned, looked into the tunnel and then looked to Vesta.

"Narrow abyss of death versus golden entrance of delight? You really know how to pick 'em."

"Get in," she ordered.

The human swaggered up to the wall and leaned against the stone. He adjusted his hat.

"Ladies first."

"I will go last. I will need to save you as you vet out the traps."

"You know," he said as he climbed inside, "you think you're all sexy when you're acting like the queen of the galaxy, but it's very, very..."

Vesta tossed her cape over her shoulder and followed him inside, ignoring the half-pleasant, maddening sensation his words provoked.

"I find humans often make insolent comments to hide their fear."

"And Scorth get cranky."

Vesta followed him down the corridor with the light from the narrow entrance guiding them. They both stilled at the sound of cracking gears. The light reached only a few steps beyond the entrance, making Vesta grateful for the distraction his juvenile insults afforded.

Over her shoulder, Vesta saw the slab roll again, sealing them inside, shrouding them in darkness.

"Is that supposed to happen?" he asked.

The kitlush stopped right in front of her. She splayed her fingers against Rorren's back and pushed.

"Go." It was an order—one he did not obey.

"I can't."

His breathing was calm. Steady. It reassured Vesta there was no immediate danger.

"Explain."

She heard noises like the trickling of water over stones.

"The tunnel is too narrow up ahead. We have to turn sideways."

"Then do so," Vesta said, trying to keep her temper in check.

"I think I can go now, but there is something warm and kind of round. What is that?"

His fingers roamed her body. She growled, but, in truth, she did not mind that much.

"That is me, kitlush. You are turned around."

Rorren's hand dropped.

"Ah, ginger. That was an honest mistake, I swear," he said.

"It is the Rishka. It is constantly changing. Deceiving. Now move!"

They traveled beyond the narrow passage, the lack of light constricting around her almost like a physical sensation. Once the walls stopped pressing in, Vesta slowed her breathing.

"I thought you said this was the easy way in," Rorren said.

"Easy, no. Less dangerous, perhaps."

The clicking sound grew louder, and above them, a small beam of light from cracks in the stone allowed her to see.

"Mic Rorren, wait."

Her warning came too late. A blade dropped from the ceiling. Its sharp edges reflected the infinitesimal light as it hurled at them.

Scorth War

Cardinal World Alpha

10 years ago

Rorren left the warmth of the campfire and traversed through lines of moonlight and forest shadows in search of her. Peeling further from his small band of troops, he kicked little dark balls of fallen pine cones, soft laughter fading as the pines grew taller.

He reached a small cove with a rock in the center, where he found the Scorth witch sitting, legs folded beneath her, stripes of soft light making her gown sparkle.

The pines guarded her jealously, swaying in the breeze like a warning to intruders.

Her hands rested on her knees with her palms aiming upward.

Despite her age, Rorren thought she was beautiful. Not only in her physical appearance but deep in her soul.

"You seek me for counsel, Mic Rorren?"

Rorren stepped out of the shadows, crunching over a dry branch.

"You meditate more than anyone I've ever seen."

She opened her eyes and angled her head toward the full moon.

"I find that sitting on a rock in the middle of nowhere builds inner strength. I must stay in tune with the elements. With my soul," she said. Her eyes landed on him. "With yours."

"I've seen you do amazing things but you can't know anyone's soul."

Her spine remained ramrod straight.

"In the dregs of war and hollows of peace, I have come to know all of you. I see your desires. Your fears."

Rorren sat on a fallen tree shaft across from her. The spreading stars in the black of night turned silver and then white, as mystical as the witch.

"Racer wants to win the war to return home to his fiancé. Cantona believes in justice. She wants to conquer my people for freedom's sake," she said.

Rorren glanced over his shoulder to the slope where firelight flashed between the pines and silhouettes of his soldiers.

"What about Freyde?"

The Scorth lifted her severe eyebrow.

"Interesting human. His ego could perhaps eclipse the Diamond Moon of Ragora."

Rorren laughed.

"Scorth with a sense of humor. You are unique."

Lady Layeyre bowed her head, eyes closing for a brief instant. The serenity in her soul emanated through the air like a physical presence, soothing

Rorren's war-frayed nerves. The knots in his neck untangled. He took in a breath of pure oxygen for the first time in weeks.

"But you're right," Rorren said. "Freyde would claim the entire Diamond Moon for the Order and think he was entitled to ninety percent of the profits."

The Scorth made a humming sound.

"But that is not what he wants," she said.

Rorren focused on a lonely star hanging far from the others, a spot of red in the darkness.

"No? What is the old scoundrel after?"

"To my surprise, me."

"That must be another joke. Freyde hates Scorth."

Lady Layeyre turned the full force of her gaze on him. He understood the honor she gave him, letting him into her confidence.

"It does explain why he acts like a sunwart's ass around you," Rorren said. "Do you like him? Scorth, human love is controversial, even if you are on our side."

Her eyes seemed to pierce into Rorren's soul.

"He is young and I have already known three great loves in my lifetime."

Rorren rested his elbows on his knees.

"Come on, Lady Layeyre. There's always room for one more," he said with a wink.

He liked to tease her. She took it well for a Scorth.

"You are a romantic," she said.

The Scorth lifted from the rock and moved into a stripe of light cast by the glowing moon.

"That is the desire of your soul. You wish to find a good woman. To create a life like the one you had as a child. Loving parents. A safe home.

Lasting hope. You deny yourself these things because of the scars on your neck. Why?"

"Hardly time to think about that with war raging."

The Scorth basked in the moonlight, rays pouring over her like some healing salve.

"You will find her. You will lose her, but you will be content."

"They say you can see the future. I never believed it, but I never believed in Fire-Scar Warriors either."

The forest suddenly became empty and hollow, echoing silence to answer his doubts. Rorren glanced toward camp.

"What about Freyde? Your future predict you will marry him or will I have to deal with a love-sick soldier for the rest of the war?"

"The war will consume all that I am. That is what I know."

Shaking his head, Rorren went into leadership mode. He never let any of his troops talk like that and she was not exempt.

"You're paranoid. You're the best fighter among us. Don't lose hope."

"It is not lost hope. It is fact. I have made peace with it."

"How can you be so cavalier about it?" he asked.

"Because of you."

Rorren hated mystic talk.

"My one regret will be made whole because of you. Our fates are entwined. This vision brings me peace," she said.

"I don't get you or any of the Scorth. Not the evil ones, not the ones that fight with us," he said. He started back to camp. The Scorth called after him.

"Then, I will teach you, although it is a lesson you already live."

He let the words linger in the air behind him. He marched toward the firelight, pushing a branch out of the way and finding no reason to learn the ways of a Fire-Scar Warrior. He couldn't become one.

CHAPTER 29

Desandor
Present Day

A LARMS RANG IN HER skull, screaming *get out now.*
Do not think.
Act.

In unison, dropping down, bruising elbows and knees on the stone floor, Vesta and Mic Rorren both came shy of losing their heads.

Icy points of light reflected off long, sharp spikes that appeared out of the wall in clinging spurts, all reaping closer—locking them in.

"If Ragora is this charming, I can't imagine why you left," Rorren said.

Despite the heat, Vesta shivered, eyes desperate to see anything in the darkness that might save them. The answer hit her with a painful brilliance—the shine off the odd marble tile wedged between the rough stones on the floor.

She met Rorren in the middle of the compacted space, backs touching, nowhere else to go.

"Can't you whip up some wind or something?"

"The Rishka negates Scorth power."

"Now she tells me."

A nasty spike cut the fabric of her cape and rattled forward, intent on slicing flesh.

"Vesta?" He sounded worried. Not worried enough for her to act. "Get us out of here."

"I can think of one thing, but it is—"

"Do it!"

She cursed and slammed her foot hard on the marbled tile.

Rorren wrapped his hand around a spike prodding his neck, but when the wall adjacent opened, he jammed inside and pulled Vesta with him.

They tumbled downward and sand broke Vesta's fall. She blinked and adjusted to the light. A small square room trapped them in.

"We are now off the less dangerous path."

Rorren, only a grateful shadow across amber beams of dust, tilted his head.

"How bad could it be?"

He just had to say it and the Rishka accepted the challenge. Grates appeared on the floor, sound deafening as a cascading waterfall of sand funneled between the rifts.

The Rishka was primed now and groaning through its death cycle, and Vesta, impatient with its games, jumped over gaps in the beams toward a wall of geometric markings.

The complex puzzle of Scorth symbols and colors demanded her attention, so she failed to notice when the beams began rolling into the wall. Something latched onto her. At first, she thought the metallic liquid churning in the pool beneath them somehow reached up with an icy finger.

Rorren's hands steadied her, restoring her balance enough she could step along the beams as they retracted into the wall.

"Is it a hobby on Ragora to think of hideous ways to kill people?" Rorren asked, hugging the wall and balancing on what remained of the beam beneath him.

Vesta stretched her arm up, standing on her tiptoes, and strained to touch the symbols. Her calf muscles ached as she tapped in sequence. She lunged for the last symbol, tearing her shoulder nearly out of the socket.

"Every Rishka has its secrets," she said. She cranked the two pegs in the wall to the left and held her breath. She waited, jaw locked.

The beams ceased retracting, leaving just enough length against the wall for one decent foothold.

"Now what?" Rorren asked, flattening himself against the wall.

"Get ready," she said.

With nothing but a gaping hole beneath them, Vesta looked up and located a thick piece of cable—the inner workings of the Rishka.

She jumped and the thick wire slapped her in the face. The sting made her curse just as her hands seized the cord. The rough alloy cut her fingers, but squeezing, she held through the pain, tight enough to stop her downward slide.

After a dizzying spin, stomach churning, she scanned for Mic Rorren.

She found him dangling about a half yard away, flexing as he gripped another cable. He lost his hat and his hair was a mess. That large, muscular frame twisting around the thin piece of rigging might have been comical in less dire circumstances.

"Much fun as I'm having," he deadpanned, "please tell me you know how to get us out of here."

She glanced up to the intermittent sparkle of light.

"Climb."

For the first ten yards, all went well, except for the trickle of blood weaving down Vesta's wrists.

A boulder about the size of a kencat dropped from the ceiling. With a desperate swing, Vesta's head dodged the boulder but it clipped her shoulder, jarring her fingers from their hold.

The wind rushed by her for a terrifying instant, but she caught hold again, abs straining as she pulled herself up. She heard Mic Rorren calling but when she turned, she saw him swinging out of the way of another boulder.

The higher they climbed, the faster the stones fell.

"Now I know what it feels like to be a piece of sandfruit in the harvester," Rorren said. His human need for small talk in perilous situations aggravated her.

"Only a fool would attempt to reach the top." She dodged another boulder, watching him from her peripherals. "Good thing I travel with a fool."

"Why, Vesta," Rorren said as he reached one hand over the other, making significant strides to the tunnel of light, "are you saying you're glad I'm along for the ride?"

"Fools have their uses."

She grinned to herself, pretending it was because the hole in the top of the pyramid was only a meter away—nothing to do with having him by her side.

With hands swelling and throbbing, she fought the pain. The stones rolled through an ancient funnel system, landing on a plank with hideous clunking sounds before dropping.

The onslaught made climbing any higher impossible.

Vesta gasped for air and her hold slipped. Maddening specks of sand and sweat stung her eyes, but she couldn't wipe them away.

Near the stones on the closest wall, she spotted a rusted lever. She didn't try to swing because her arms couldn't take it.

"Push me."

Rorren was close enough now to reach out and touch, light from above bathing his face in gold.

He obeyed with a frown, grabbing her cable and rocking her sideways. She kicked at the rod, missing on the first swing. Dodging another boulder, she kicked again. Once. Twice. She snarled, hitting the metal with the pad of her foot on the fifth try. Leather snagged and tore.

The plank above them retracted and stopped the downpour of the boulders.

"Loset kay aux whiff!"

"Did you just say, son of a dirty crap smeller?" Rorren asked, wasting no time climbing beyond the tangle of funnels. She followed, straining, aching, and trying not to show it.

"These are my favorite boots," she said. A warm blast of air hit her calf where the leather had split.

Rorren swung from the cable to the ledge at the top of the pyramid and landed with a puff of dust. He reached out, grabbed Vesta's cable and pulled. Her fingers gave out. Her muscles spasmed and turned to jelly. She fell into Rorren's outstretched arms—a pleasant way to arrive. After an awkward beat, he set her feet on the ground. With a feather-light touch, he turned her palms upward to find oozing cuts and blisters.

"That looks bad."

"No time."

She brushed past him and pushed her head up through the opening at the tip of the triangle.

"Up and out," he said. He bumped Vesta's shoulder as he climbed.

"Up, yes, but this is not the exit. It is the next test of the Rishka."

The outside wall descended at an angle, the wide edge kissing the sand at the bottom, the surface so hot under the suns of Desandor sweat beaded on Vesta's skin.

Her vision stretched to the horizon from the high vantage point. Thunder boomed through her body in disruptive waves.

No.

Not thunder.

The roar of a starship swooping over them with so much force they both ducked. Vesta followed its trajectory beyond the sea of sand, where it sank into the rocky cliffs in the distance.

Smoke billowed from stacks of angular buildings wedged between black peaks, looking much to her Scorth eyes like a fortress. The lightning storm and the smoke from the factory mingled interchangeably.

"We found the camp," she said.

Rorren hoisted himself up onto the stones.

"Let's get down there."

Heat visibly hemorrhaged around him, but Vesta's blood froze cold.

"Wait."

Squeezing his arm, hard bicep under her fingers, she stopped him from a deadly mistake.

"Is that concern I see?"

"If I lost you, I would have no one to set off the traps."

"There's that legendary Scorth charm."

She vanished down into the hole, searching for a smaller-sized boulder. She found one, ignored the pain in her shoulder and hoisted it up through the narrow opening.

Rorren stood beside her and the two of them watched the stone roll down the building, slow at first, then gaining speed.

The first one shot out so fast Vesta saw only a blur of teeth.

The boulder bounced away, narrowly escaping the chop, chop of mechanical jaws.

Another one sprouted out of the wall, revealing its snake-like body. Scales of metal alloy coated the hull, giving it an unnatural shine.

It missed the target. The third snake crushed the stone in its jaws. Smaller pebbles bounced but were swallowed up by a dozen more machines.

"That is strange," Vesta said.

"Really? Cause I was thinking killer death worms are perfectly normal."

"Sometimes Rishkas are infested with parasites found on Ragora, but those creatures are mechanical."

Rorren removed a small rectangular box from his belt. He pressed it and his diamond-tipped staff appeared. The weapon made him look like the soldier he was. He lurched into action. She liked him in action.

"One way to find out."

He gamboled out of the opening, testing his footing. Everywhere he stepped, a deadly set of teeth emerged seconds later. With enough speed to avoid losing a leg, Rorren jumped into the opening and thrust the staff through the air.

He jabbed hard forward, spearing one of the creatures through its cylindrical skull. The machine screeched and twisted, body coiling, as it attempted to escape into its burrow. Sparks showered them, but Rorren never lost his grip on the staff. Vesta saw his muscles flexing as he held on. The electric force powering the worm sputtered and smoked until nothing remained but the smell of burning grease.

"Looks like you're right," he said.

"I am always right," she said, flinging her hair over her shoulder.

Rorren pulled his staff free and used his shirt to wipe the oil from it, staining the fabric in a way that reminded Vesta of blood. The weapon retracted and Rorren reattached it to his belt.

"What do you think? The Galactic Order working with some renegade Scorth sect?"

Vesta crouched out of the heat and back into the Rishka.

"It is hard for me to believe any Scorth sect, traitor or otherwise, would give up the secrets of the Rishka," she said.

"And it's hard for me to believe the Order would come up with something like this without Scorth help," Rorren replied, leaning against the wall.

Feeling the consequences of the last few hours, the bruises covering her arms and legs throbbed. Puncture wounds from the metal cables speckled her hands. The bleeding stopped, but the skin around each contusion was red and swollen.

No injury surpassed the arresting pain in her shoulder, courtesy of one of the falling boulders.

Lifting to her feet, she scavenged over more Scorth markings until she found one that opened yet another secret passage within the Rishka.

Rorren followed her into the tunnel and another narrow stone path with a steep downward slope. She rolled her shoulder as she walked but lost the battle to drive the raw soreness from the muscle.

With every step, she relied increasingly on the markings to guide their path. Tunnels shot off in multiple directions, creating a maze in which one could get lost for centuries.

Her internal map told her they were about halfway down the Rishka. Her fingers ran along the wall, skin burning with pain, in search of the vital markings that would guide them out of the maze.

Hunger gnawed at her.

Her muscles demanded a reprieve, but her instincts overrode physical needs. They had to get out. Soon.

The nature of the tunnel changed. Light returned, flooding the room, and the slope evened into an almost pleasant walking path.

Fresh drafts of air found them and lifted her spirits. Being near an exit gave her a sense of accomplishment. They conquered the Rishka. She and the kitlush. Not bad for a pathetic team of misfits.

Coming at them in all glory, broad daylight appeared beyond the opening of a stone archway.

Sprawled between danger and freedom was a square room, fifteen feet in each direction, and the chilling wail of a fast-moving breeze.

CHAPTER 30

"Let me guess. I should go first?" Mic Rorren spoke for the first time in minutes and the sound comforted her.

"I must admit you have ideas that are not altogether intolerable."

As he mused on that, he stared at her with those piercing eyes.

"Don't overdo the compliments. I might get the wrong idea."

Unable to bring herself to put him at risk, Vesta coaxed him to stillness and examined the room.

"I am not familiar with this trap."

Rorren grabbed her shoulders and pulled her against his chest. A small dart swished through the air.

She heard the woosh as it passed, narrowly missing her ear. The pellet struck the wall on the other side.

She scanned the room, hunting for the source and finding a thousand half-inch incursions freckling both sides of the passageway. The tips of more darts were visible from inside the holes in the walls.

"Look," Rorren said. He let go of her shoulders. She followed his gaze beyond the gantlet of arrows, where a control panel beckoned to them, daring them to try.

"How do we get over there?" he asked.

Vesta scanned the walls for more markings or clues.

She found nothing.

"Every room has a key. We must find this one."

Rorren went to the opposite wall and copied her movements, touching each glyph.

"The stones themselves have a pattern. The pattern will lead us to the key," she said.

"Unless whoever built this decided to forego Scorth logic," he added.

She continued searching until a grating screech of gears descended on them.

"I think I found something," Rorren said.

The floor gave out and he plummeted from her sight. Vesta ran and her cape flared behind. She dropped hard to her knees, bruising them at the pit's edge. Too late to stop metal grating from barring over the top of the chamber.

"Are you injured?"

Rorren rose to his feet, hand rubbing his neck.

"Only my pride."

"Nothing vital then."

"Guess I found the wrong pattern."

"I will find the way out."

The sound of water tumbling through canals should have been welcome, but this was a Rishka, so instead, it knotted Vesta's muscles. A row of holes popped open at Rorren's feet. Liquid streams shot out in white-capped splashes, soaking Rorren up to the ankles.

"You know, I'm really beginning to hate this place," he said.

Vesta shook the tension from her body, then jerked upright. She raced over the stones and flung her hands over the walls. The markings were gone, leaving her to reason that the panel at the end of the corridor was the only way of opening the grate.

"Anytime, Vesta," Rorren called from below.

Sounds of splashing water disappeared, which meant the spouts were already submerged. Vesta had experienced plenty of fear and homesickness in her lifetime. This new kind of worry slammed into her, scrambling her senses, preventing her from thinking clearly about anything but the danger Mic Rorren was in.

Inside one of the stones, she found a round glass peg. Instinct told her not to press it. Desperation made her.

Pulleys groaned and the grate lowered, still barring Rorren's escape and now cutting away the time he had left as the grate dropped toward the waterline.

"Tell me you didn't just do that," he said.

Pounding her fist against the stone, she relished the sting in her tender fingers.

"It was not intended."

She peered through the small squares in the grate, but Rorren was far away and unreachable.

"There might be some trigger inside the cage to help you escape," she said.

Rorren nodded, took a deep breath and disappeared beneath the water. While he was under, Vesta found it hard to breathe. She dug her nails into her cape, realizing how much it sucked to care about someone. No wonder her mother forbade it.

She heard splashing and an intake of breath. Water dripped from his hair and skin as he looked up at her, jaw locked. Defeat seemed inevitable.

A powerful anger boiled inside her and escaped her lips in a growl. Wild determination guided her hands over the ground, desperate for anything to release the trap.

Her fingers nudged a loose brick in the floor. She removed the square from her belt, extended the staff and chiseled at the mortar.

She pulled the brick free and pounded it repeatedly over the metal bars. Dents appeared in the bars as Vesta hammered. Not enough to break them free.

With a furious hiss, she tossed the brick aside and wrapped her hands around the steel. She pulled left, then right. No good. She pounded the Scorth markings, succumbing to hopes of triggering some secret switch.

The water level rose high enough that Rorren floated up. He reached through the bars and grabbed her hands.

"Vesta, look at me."

She couldn't. Not until she blinked away her anger.

His body was submerged entirely. He kicked his legs, keeping his head just above water.

"If I don't get out of here—"

"You will."

His fingers touched her face.

"If I don't, you find the solstal. Make your menti blade and lead the Sandorians to freedom. You have greatness in you. I've seen it before."

Vesta avoided his eyes, but turning her head caused his hand to fall away from her face. She heard his breath grow short and panicked as water reached the grate.

"Hope is not lost yet," she said.

His mouth and nose found a last air pocket through the narrow square in the grate.

Inhaling one last time, his hands fell away from the bars and water swallowed him.

Vesta rocked to the balls of her feet, a tense moment before she exploded into action.

The breeze at the end of the tunnel caught her hair, whipping it around her face. Fresh light and wind from the outside came with particles not tainted by the Rishka. Maybe enough to give her a chance.

He was worth the risk.

Vesta lifted the coiled staff and marched straight down the corridor as a stab of exhilaration sharpened her reflexes.

Darts came at her in waves. She twirled the staff and a weightless tingling sensation buzzed through her each time she successfully deflected a round of projectiles.

She protected her flesh but darts ripped holes in her cape. Feathers floated in the air, propelling her forward with new anger. She ignored the nagging sense of danger—honed her focus on the rhythmic swing of her staff and the lever just beyond.

The darts came in thick waves, blocking almost all light from the other side.

The vision of the Queen appeared. Her cruel laughter rang through the chamber in Vesta's voice.

A hallucination, care of her incomplete training as Rorren had warned. The Vision Queen waved her hand and the darts flew faster and harder. With arms aching under the strain, Vesta fought through the onslaught.

Near the control panel, the darts gave out. Vesta's mouth watered at the thought of success.

The Queen flung a final projectile from the shadows and Vesta reacted, bringing the staff upward.

She blocked the blow and the projectile ricocheted. The dart stabbed her left eye.

She dropped the staff, exceptional pain shooting through the nerves in her cheek and neck.

Blindness followed and the feel of liquid oozing down her cheek.

Not blood.

It only took her a moment to recognize what it was.

Deathshade.

Groping along the floor, she reached the wall. Heightened alertness overtook her other senses and she fumbled over different components on the control panel. Teetering and spinning in a world of darkness, Vesta forced her way to the lever and pushed.

A blast of sound filled her ears: a moving pulley, the echo of an unlatching grate. She waited, fighting a migraine that pounded the base of her skull.

Silence.

The dart, throbbing in her eye, needed to be removed, but her arms were too weak to reach for it.

Sinking against the wall, thoughts of Mic Rorren lost forever somehow caused all the physical pain to melt into violent despair.

She heard gasping—the gurgle of water.

Coughing.

"Mic Rorren?"

Someone approached. Warmth emanated from the body close to hers and a hand squeezed her knee.

"You can't get rid of me that easily."

Despite the pain it caused, she laughed. Relief came first, then the pain flooded her.

"What did you do?" he asked.

"You must remove the shard."

"Let's get out of here first."

His arms encircled her and began to lift. She resisted.

"Listen to me," she said. Her hands flailed until she caught a piece of Rorren's shirt. She pulled him beside her on the floor.

"The darts are laced with deathshade—a plant from my home world crippling to my people. If you remove it now, there is a chance I will not be permanently blind."

Unable to see if Rorren was worried, irritated, or indifferent, his silence made her restless.

Fabric ripped. Steady breathing tickled Vesta's skin. Rorren's face was close. He tore out the dart. The pressure in her eye vanished and then came searing pain.

She cried out, doubling over, but his arms caught her.

Wet fabric pressed against her eye where the dart had been.

"Now," Vesta said. She pushed his hand away and held the fabric with her own. "Clean out the wound. The poison must not take root."

She heard steps sloshing down the corridor. The lever must have turned off the darts.

She waited alone in darkness.

When he returned, he cradled her head down onto his leg, tilting her injured eye to the ceiling.

He removed the cloth and a stream of water hit the wound. Vesta inhaled, digging nails into Rorren's shoulder as she forced herself not to scream.

More water washed across the wound and then Rorren dabbed at her eye and cheekbone with the wet cloth.

"I think I got it all," he said.

Vesta blinked, sending another wave of agony through her skull. The hole in her eye would soon fill and harden, as all deathshade wounds did. The touch of the poison to Scorth flesh, even with its removal, always formed a golden scab. She remembered it happening to a childhood friend.

Vesta could not see and a pit settled in her stomach.

Rorren lifted her by the arm.

"I've had enough of this place. How about we get out?"

Vesta let him lead her forward.

They had not traveled far when Vesta heard the clicking of the weights and pulleys once again.

Rorren stopped and his solid body tensed beneath her touch.

"What is it?"

Metal scraped against stone.

"Nothing to worry about."

Rorren slipped her against the wall. A high-pitched scream worsened her headache.

Not an animal or human sound.

Mechanical.

She counted by sound. One worm. Then two. Three. Five.

"Don't move," Rorren said.

The clang of metal and chop of teeth fused into a tangle of noise around her.

CHAPTER 31

VESTA HEARD EVERY SOUND of battle, struggling to gauge the passage of time as a slew of lightning-fast clanks ebbed and surged. Shrieking animal ferocity stung her ears.

A brutal rumble tingled her toes as something fell. Then another. She lost count.

She stopped breathing, hoping Mic Rorren was not among the fallen.

Trembling in the unknown intensified the stinging in her eye.

"Mic Rorren?"

Metal dropped on metal.

The human grunted.

"Bunch of tin cans," he said, familiar drawl holding her like an embrace. "Shoddy workmanship from the Rishka builders if you ask me."

With her staff for balance, Vesta worked her way up to a standing position.

She waited for his touch to find her. She refused to reach out to him. That was not the Scorth way.

"Careful where you step."

He guided her over what she assumed were corpses of mechanical parasites—the scent of oil and burnt rubber stained the air. Warm rays from the sun heated her skin. The fresh smells rejuvenated her body and spirit as she breathed in.

Her feet left the cold stone of the Rishka, sinking into the generous sand of the desert. Dark vibrations of the pyramid shrank behind her, morphing into a low-decibel hum that faded away.

"There is a ridge up ahead. We'll camp under it for the night," Rorren said.

She forced herself over the dunes. Fatigue and her wound left every muscle aching. After an eternity, Rorren settled her on the ground. She rested against a hill, relishing the sensation of warm sand on her back.

"I'll find some food."

In his absence, the silence was blaring.

The suns bathed her skin with sweltering heat. Not being able to see them was odd. Claustrophobic.

She wrapped up in her torn cape and pulled her knees to her chest, trying not to think about a future without sight.

Poison still coursed through her veins—an intruder that made her shiver.

Exhaustion pacified her enough for sleep.

She awoke to the smell of steaming desert moss and meat. The scent transported her to her first experiences with Rorren. The rock she let fall on his foot as he searched for the delicacy.

Pulling herself upright, a half-dazed smile on her lips, she blinked and opened her eyes.

Blurred flashes of light and dark assaulted her vision.

"How long until your sight returns?"

Vesta peeled the cape from her torso, realizing Mic Rorren had bandaged her hands.

"If it returns, it will be soon."

"Here."

Rorren's fingers guided hers to a flat stone. She prodded it until she found a clump of meat. Her stomach gargled as she brought it to her lips.

The warm, soft food went down without trouble.

"You cooked with a fire?" she asked, worried about spies.

"I was careful. You can only see the base if you go through the Rishka, right? I doubt they care about natives in the hills."

Too tired to confirm, Vesta ate in silence. She chewed, slow and rhythmic, trying not to let depression over her condition spoil her appetite.

"Thank you for saving my life, by the way," he said.

"Which time?" she asked.

"You're welcome for saving yours."

Vesta curled up under the ridge and the temperature dropped. She guessed that meant the suns had set.

She wondered if Rorren was looking up at the stars. Where they twinkling or overcast by clouds?

"I never learned about Rishkas at the academy. My mother was the foremost scholar on Scorth culture, but I don't think even she knew about them."

Vesta wrapped her arms around her, grateful for a conversation to keep her from bleak reflections.

"Your mother was a scholar?"

She could hear Rorren shift, perhaps stretching his long torso across the sand.

"She was the smartest person I knew. My parents nearly split up when she was made Ambassador to Ragora just before the war broke."

"You had me believe your mother was some sort of primitive slave of the kitchen," Vesta said.

"My attempt to coax you into cooking for me and cleaning up the farm."

Vesta scooped a handful of sand and tossed it in his direction.

"Hey!"

Her aim must have been on target because she heard him brushing off.

"Obviously, it didn't work," he said.

There was a motion to the conversation and neither of them could stop it. Sitting stationary, Vesta pondered whether or not to interfere with destiny.

"Tagion Krave was my best friend at the academy," Rorren said. Precise, sure of himself, no emotion in his tone. He did not fool her. It was a revelation. Guilt for hiding a few secrets of her own pestered her conscience.

"He always pushed the limits. Can I believe he's experimenting with Scorth technology? Maybe. If he is, he has good reason."

The comradery between them had become more comfortable, no doubt aided by living through the same disasters and a mutual desire to know the secrets of the galaxy.

"He learned of Scorth as you did?" Vesta asked.

"Yes, but he was more interested in Scorth mating rituals at the time."

She imagined Rorren lifting his eyebrows.

"Your wise edda did not know of Scorth mating rituals?"

"Not really," he said.

Perking against the sand, Vesta found herself eager to enlighten him.

"It is because the Scorth have no courtship rituals. We do not believe in that as you humans do."

Stinging pain shot through her eye, but the conversation provided ample distraction.

"There are no romantic dinners," she said. "No awkward meeting of the parents. No first kiss and other such things I have heard happen among humans. Scorth marry for political and monetary gain.

"My parents had an arranged marriage. Almost all Scorth marriages are arranged but not sight unseen. The more beautiful a Scorth man or woman is, the better political asset they are. Often, one presents a contract or formal agreement to the other."

"Then how do you get baby Scorth?" he asked, his voice confirming he hadn't fallen asleep. "Where did little Vesta come from? Did the magical ravens bring her?"

Her eye hurt but not enough to take away the pleasure of further educating him.

"Scorth children are rare. One in twenty Scorth alliances produces offspring."

Rorren chuckled—an empty, hollow sound.

Curious.

"Why do you laugh?"

"The Galactic Order feared a Scorth population explosion. We knew Scorth women could have babies well into their hundreds. We thought that meant you'd multiply like home-world bush-tails. We'd have no chance of stopping a galactic takeover."

Picking up subtleties of human sentiment even with the use of her eyes was a challenge, but Vesta recognized silly kitlush hoopla when she heard it.

Resisting the urge to mock him, she wondered if any Scorth War Ovokars knew of the human fear. During the war years—time she spent as a raven—she paid little attention to the political concerns of the human clan.

"Why do you think there are so few Scorth children born?" he asked.

"I know what you would say," she snapped with more snarl and passion than she intended. "Romantic love is missing. That obsession again."

"Your words, not mine," replied the kitlush, infuriating smugness in his tone.

A brief silence ensued.

"My parents had it," Rorren blurted. His words carried a weightiness that saddened her.

"If Agent Neece is at the base, perhaps you can woo her with your delusions of love."

"Hot beans! I feel sorry for the Scorth man who takes you on. The green-eyed monster of jealousy."

Vesta shuffled over the sand but stopped when she bumped into his shoulder.

"I am not jealous. I simply think Agent Neece incapable of love in the way you wish."

"You have no idea what I wish."

"If you mean to imply, Mic Rorren, that you wish for a romantic relationship with me, that is utterly absurd. Neither your people nor mine would ever accept us as an alliance."

"I didn't mean to imply that, but it's obviously on your mind."

"You are absurd," she hissed, "Only the Sandorians are present in my thoughts."

"If you free the prisoners, you'll have more of their respect and gratitude," he said and redeemed himself by half.

Despite the casual delivery, his words sent an intense adrenaline rush through her system. She hated that his whims of teasing and talk had so much power over her.

"It is we who shall free the prisoners. Why will you take no credit for your courage?"

Rorren was silent for a long time. When he finally spoke, she could tell he had fallen into a reclined position.

"I'm no hero," he said.

She pulled her cape over her, turned away from him, and closed her eyes. No different from having them open.

Shivering beneath the fabric, she pretended not to hope for a miracle. She found no point in thinking about the Sandorians or Mic Rorren. None of it would matter if she could not see in the morning. Fitful spurts of sleep brought her no relief.

———

With her heart thudding in dull beats, Vesta forced herself to open her eyes.

Her mind registered a bright, unbearable light.

She blinked through billowing pain.

Swirling vortexes of color.

Turbulent flashes.

The smell of breakfast. The crackle of fire.

"Well?" Mic Rorren must have stood ten paces away.

She sat up and there came a crushing blur of motion, shadows of dunes and rocks. The landscape came into focus.

The vision restored in her right eye was some consolation for the partial loss of the left. Her left eye distinguished colors and shapes, but the deathshade sap clouded the details.

Still, malignant forces had not left her blind. She permitted herself to think about a joyful breakdown, never with any intention of acting on the emotion. She glided across the sand, as giddy as Scorth ever got.

"What happened to your face?" she asked.

Rorren ran a hand over his chin.

"I haven't been able to shave the last few days."

"Scorth men do not have facial hair. This is not natural."

"You like it."

She didn't but treasured everything she saw. The blue of the sky. Harsh rays of triple suns. Vast wasteland and sparse spikes of cacti sweltering in the heat.

"If you didn't scare small children before," Rorren said as he handed her a knife from his belt. In the reflection of the blade, she examined the damage. One perfect eye, accented by her long eyelashes, the other covered by a golden scab with a narrow split in the center, allowing a glimpse of her pupil.

"Brawn will like it. Makes you look like kin."

She pushed away the metal.

"It suggests I am a fool to let the Rishka best me. I told you no one ever escapes undamaged."

Rorren reattached the knife to his belt.

"I did."

"I can remedy that," she said. Her usual bite affected Rorren little, if at all. She lost her edge, the threatening reputation Scorth prided themselves on as diminished as her marred beauty.

Rorren bent and caught a section of her cape between his fingers.

"This thing was full of holes yesterday, " he said.

Vesta followed his gaze, discovering her cape looked as though the master weavers had just finished with it.

She examined her boots. The tear in the leather was gone. Her face might be hideous now, but at least her clothes were respectable.

"In the middle of battle, when all the rest of us were covered in mud and rain, the Fire-Scar Warriors looked like they had just stepped out of a Cardinal World beauty parlor. I never could figure it out."

Vesta snapped the cape out of his hands.

"A side effect of being Aux Katan."

Rorren brushed her cheek, admiring, then pulled away with an abrupt jolt.

"As if your people weren't beautiful enough," he grumbled.

Beautiful. Even with her damaged eye. Vesta wanted to laugh loud enough for her mother to hear in her resting place far below.

"The solstal is nearby. I can sense it. Enough of your nonsense."

Vesta stumbled over a steep dune, clinging to her staff as a lifeline. She used it instead of Rorren's offered hand, navigating the rolling sand, grateful for any excuse to avoid his touch lest he recant again like she had the plague.

By late afternoon, the nature of the landscape changed. Sand hardened into rocky cliffs of black granite. The suns vanished behind storm clouds, flat terrain growing smaller and farther between.

Jagged mountains appeared and cut the skyline with inky silhouettes as smoke and storm clouds bathed the harsh climate in unnatural darkness.

They reached the edge of a cliff and wind blasted Vesta's hair.

A locomotive engine shot out of a tunnel beneath them with vibrations so violent that Rorren and Vesta clung onto each other for support.

Boxcars poured onto tracks, one after another, latched together, riding on wheels that rattled over the steel rails. Each rectangle came mightier than the last. Some were big enough to store entire starships, others the size of the crates that enslaved inquisitive Sandorians.

The engine lights vanished around a curve, but steam from its exhaust carried above the distant cliffs toward a looming fortress. Two thousand feet high with ominous towers and stacks of pumping smog, the structure surged over flickering rows of track and scattered barracks.

"Wonder what's in those?" Rorren asked, shouting over the rumble of the train.

Vesta followed his gaze to a row of silos bubbling up from the ground about a half-mile from the main fortress.

"This is what taking over the universe looks like," she said.

They stood silent, gazes locked. Neither of them spoke. They both knew what had to happen next.

"We only get one chance at this," he said.

She watched his body stretch like a slingshot about to release.

He jumped before she could stop him.

The kitlush.

Rorren landed on his feet atop the train car, momentum forcing him to drop and roll. He tumbled across the metal panels and over the edge. Vesta readied to take drastic action, but she saw him clinging to a margin of metal running along the side of the car as his legs dangled over rapidly passing terrain.

Setting her concern aside like it never happened, Vesta conjured the wind. Rocks beneath her feet moaned as they obeyed her, forming an elegant staircase that descended to the rushing train.

Cape flying behind her, she carried herself down to the last step.

The bottom step detached from the stairs and sped forward until it matched the train's speed.

She stepped off the rock onto the moving cart. Simple. With lips curved in a smirk, she sent the stones away.

Rorren glared at her as he climbed up to join her.

"You can do that? You could have saved me a brush with death."

"You seemed in a hurry to show off. I felt I should not interfere."

He rubbed his arm.

"Oh, please, next time, interfere."

Playing with the kitlush was awfully fun.

The train turned a corner, speeding toward the enormous fortress. Rorren crouched and pressed his ear to the metal.

"Animals," he said.

Her instincts sensed he was right.

"How did you—?"

"The smell."

She inhaled and rank odors filled her nose. Large animals, perhaps gantis, and not well cared for.

A change in the sound of rushing wind drew her attention to a tunnel straight through the black heart of the fortress.

"Get down," Rorren yelled, sliding across the boxcar. His hands grabbed her. They dropped into the gap between cars, Vesta banging her elbow on a metal slat just before the tunnel engulfed them.

Vesta lost her footing. Rails and wheels came hurling at her until something caught onto her.

Rorren pulled her up, his arms wrapped around her waist. Her hands landed on his chest. Neither of them moved as a blanket of darkness consumed everything.

CHAPTER 32

THE TRAIN CLANKED INTO light, emerging into a hanger of such magnitude even Vesta marveled. Ten Desandor space hubs could easily fit inside, leaving room still for the giant orb chandeliers, numerous spaceships, and endless rows of cargo containers.

Men and women crossed the tarmac, some in organized platoons, others chasing stray trolleys or working machinery, all wearing unmistakable uniforms. Galactic Order.

Grasping all the sights with her single eye was impossible. Vesta growled when the train entered another tunnel. Fluorescent fixtures streaked past them, rushing with a halogen glow and vanishing.

They broke free into a sweltering heat, shielded on all sides by glass windows. Vesta had grown used to Desandor's desert suns but this heat was different. More tempered. Artificial.

Beyond the windows lay an assembly space overrun with hundreds of titanium basins ten meters in height, each containing various concoctions of molten stone. Encircling the reservoirs, Vesta took in the sight of a complex harnessing system. Thick straps of leather were attached to five or six gantis. Mammoth legs quivered under the snap of the overlord's whip, and the motion churned the boiling soups with pure animal force.

Some of the gantis were from the shelled herd, but Vesta recognized one in particular. A lizard, mouth filled with fangs, drool trickling from its lips as it obeyed its master.

Hard laughter resonated from below, snapping Vesta's attention to Rorren. He hadn't heard it.

"That's metal from the Tallum Nebula. It has many industrial uses. Hulls of starships and the metal stack of the harvesting machine," he said.

The train rounded the assembly room, entered another corridor and reduced speed.

"What are they up to?" Rorren asked, adjusting the collar of his trench coat.

The train decelerated in increments, passing one shadowed platform after another, the wheels squealing over rails.

"The next stop is ours," Rorren said. If he meant he wanted to jump, Vesta didn't understand why he didn't just say as much.

She moved with him to the edge of the boxcar and leaned forward, feet pressing against the metal grating. The timing would have to be perfect, or else.

"We'll be flatter than a flapjack if we miss."

Humans and their similes, she thought with a smirk.

The platform grew, dominating Vesta's shrinking world as the moment neared.

Ten seconds to the platform and her fingers twitched.

Five seconds. An expectant gasp escaped Vesta's lips.

She sailed through the air, propelling herself with gusto. Her shoulder hit first and crackled, then she rolled over and over, bruising her knees and hands before skidding to a stop.

On her first attempt to get up, a wave of nausea rocked her off balance. She shook it off and Rorren lifted her by the arm. His voice swam to her, asking if she was damaged.

"I am fine."

He put a hand to his head, wincing from his injuries.

"Any landing you can walk away from."

Dim light from the single lamp did not reach beyond the platform but gave enough for her to spot a series of stairs and tunnels lining the walls in either direction.

She heard the laughter again. A mocking, cruel laughter that belonged to the Vision Queen.

"What is it?"

She closed her eyes, ignoring Rorren.

"It's the solstal. You're seeing things," he guessed.

A sudden, unexpected tremor of anger took control of her.

"I see things no human can fathom."

"Sounds interesting. Maybe you should charge admission."

The suffocating ignorance of his stance—languid and loose, brow skewed—was intolerable.

"Maybe you should stop hiding behind that coat of yours," she said, baiting him for a reaction. She spotted no clenched fist or strained jaw. He was always so collected, so in control. His tranquility was an insult to her.

"Never said I was perfect."

"You do not say anything."

"Sometimes you don't have to. Listening is best anyway."

"Then listen to me. Sevet Neece is a liar and evil lurks here."

The hallucination scraped against her as cold as icy fingers along her skin. Something sinister pulled her toward the tracks and the darkness on the other side.

"That might be so but you're not yourself. We need to get you out of here."

"Maybe I am who I should be for the first time," she replied.

Vesta stood, immovable, vision blurred and phantasms flooding her mind.

"Do you know what happened to Ragora after we lost the war?" she asked.

His image fell away into a cloud of darkness.

"I went home to find a talisman. What I found was a planet in despair."

Vesta inched toward the tracks, strings from the invisible force drawing her in.

"Most of the men died in battle. The women were made poor by galactic sanctions against us. The children were orphaned and worse. Our great cities had toppled. The most mercenary of us overran the royal palace. My mother. Dead. And then the humans came."

She turned away from Rorren and saw the image of the Queen standing beyond the tracks, grinning wickedly.

"I'm sorry about your planet. That's what happens in war. No one came out of it unscathed. Not the Scorth, not the humans."

"Yes, Mic Rorren, we all have scars," she said with a huff because he understood nothing. "But sometimes they are to be embraced."

She sprinted across the tracks and reached the void on the other side. She heard Mic Rorren shout her name—far away and filled with concern.

She aimed herself at the endless pit and jumped.

———————

Vesta breathed in the emptiness, tasting air sour from engine exhaust and chemicals. The wind hammered against her face as a deceptively placid pool of darkness spread beneath her. Disoriented, without a guide or compass, she dropped deeper. The descent became tedious with no landmarks to gauge the passing minutes.

Pressure fizzled around her body as she commanded the elements to slow her fall. Judging the distance wrong, she slammed onto sleek metal and slid, sucked into the faint light below.

Welded paneling turned into jagged rock. She rolled at the mercy of gravity and landed in a field of small pebbles.

Her vision swam and shallow breathing made her dizzy. Her functional eye grasped details in the shadows.

Cold and unearthly light saturated the cavern. Vesta moved under stalactites toward the source. She touched the glowing walls. The phosphorescent alga living on pockets of limestone coated her fingers.

There were carvings in the stones, half faces like miniatures of the ancient statues she and Rorren discovered in the badlands. Swallowing her uneasiness, she pressed on, boots crunching over pebbles. Stone turned to skeletal bone. She entered some ancient burial ground.

Twenty yards ahead, a speck of hollow light anchored her in time and space. Both the forces of good and evil seemed to be driving her to it.

The light grew and with its development came a change in the structure. The stone carvings gave way to a wall of manufactured titanium, hinting at a secondary fortress deep below the manufacturing plant.

A white beacon of light overhung an elaborate keypad—craftsmanship care of the Galactic Order. The pad guarded the entrance of a massive sealed door. She found no human way to enter without the code.

Vesta tossed her hair over her shoulder. Good thing she wasn't human.

She closed her eyes, calling on the elements around her.

A scream came first and then shrieking voices from behind the steel door.

An irrational fear seized her, urging her to recoil from what horrors lay ahead. She persevered through it, and, shaking, she focused her power.

Elemental stone conformed to her will, twisting the ruble into two hideous but functional hands.

Giant fingers clawed at the door seal, found a hold and forced it apart. A crack appeared, then a hole large enough for Vesta to squeeze an arm through.

The strain weakened her.

She rammed her torso into the passage, tumbling out the other side as the stone crumbled into a million pebbles.

The door sealed itself behind her and trapped her in a well-lit room filled with strange equipment. Sensing the solstal was near, Vesta sprung upright with renewed energy. She prowled over tiled floors, monitors glowing along the far wall above a console of flashing lights and keyboards.

She heard laughter.

A door closed.

She chased after the sound.

Out of the room, she threaded her way along more corridors, passing rooms filled with lab tables and beakers. The echoing laughter lured her into a corridor between giant machines. Gears and bolts reared from the shadows.

Stopping beneath a serrated hole, she looked up into a room howling with the screams of ghosts. The metal seemed to quiver under the force of the powerful cries.

She pulled a crate beneath the hatch and waited until the sound of approaching footsteps faded. Were they real or in her head? She didn't know anymore.

On her tiptoes, she opened the latch and pulled herself inside, tearing one of the bandages on her hand.

A sign on the wall read, *Lab 17*.

Large, cylindrical vessels crowded the room, paralyzing her with fear.

Inside, organic material floated in translucent slime. A piece of an arm. A pair of eyes wrenched from their sockets. Someone's liver with a bite taken out of it.

Vesta's stomach churned as she pivoted toward the exit, stumbling over chairs and banging into the walls in desperation to escape.

She sailed recklessly down the corridor, not caring about her trajectory, the urge to flee overpowering all logic.

Those were Scorth body parts. Vesta sensed it in magical vibrations.

The Vision Queen appeared before her.

"How can you think of defeating me when the true enemy is all around you?"

Vesta kept running. Her hamstrings hated her for the wild pace.

She escaped into another room filled with body parts.

And another.

And another.

Rage tore through her, feeding her sprint.

You cannot defeat me. You need me to stop the humans. You can never give me up. The Vision Queen's whisper was loud enough to shatter her eardrums. It was all around her, sucking the air from her lungs.

The cries of the dead Scorth demanded justice. She ran from them. She was no better than Mic Rorren.

She pushed through another door and dropped into a dimly lit room. The wet air clung to her skin with an odd oily feel. Her body adjusted quickly—remembering the familiar climate. The smell of wet leaves and moss with an undertow of rotted vegetation. Like the jungle. Like home.

A dozen oval-shaped objects hung from the ceiling. Giant hibernating bats? They each had a heartbeat that thumped in rhythm to her steps.

Not bats. Scorth pods.

The Galactic Order had Scorth pods!

Vesta tripped over something—a broken pod, unlike the ones from home. The rim of the pod housed a tangle of wires and circuitry. Inside, the half-collapsed command center looked too small to house more than one or two soldiers.

Someone fired a shot.

Vesta plunged behind the pod, dodging the gunfire assault.

She ran for the nearest door and, after swinging it open, smashed into an armada of militants waiting on the other side.

A metal prod stuck her torso. A surge of electricity frayed her nerve endings. She heard a cry she thought was her own and then nothing.

CHAPTER 33

Scorth War

Alpha Moon Military Hospital

9 years ago

RORREN WENT TO THE medical tent and pushed away the curtain, knowing what lay behind was not a sight he wanted to see. He found Lady Layeyre on the cot, head propped up against the pillow, hands folded one over the other.

Seeing her there hurt him. It hurt Freyde, too, by the look of it. The gruff old soldier hunched over her body, looking more like the dying one.

Freyde put his hand over Layeyre's, stirring her awake.

"The General is here."

Lady Layeyre moved to sit up but her strength failed.

"Help me."

Freyde moved her pillows with a gentleness Rorren never thought him capable of. Once settled, the witch touched Freyde's arm.

"Leave us."

Freyde frowned as he left the tent.

"The war is turning in our favor. Command thinks the Scorth may soon surrender," Rorren said as memories replayed in his head.

Obsedei monsters marched through the streets of Tarazi, devouring troops, while the Scorth pods hung between skyscrapers, untouched. A line of slime along their encasings curved into a smile before dripping into the streets.

Rorren remembered in vivid detail the moment Lady Layeyre put away her sword. By conjuring a new magic, she somehow overpowered the pods. She gained control of the Obsedei army at that moment and altered the course of the war.

The woman single-handedly saved humanity and lay there, serene and humble, as comfortable with her approaching death as a kencat in a sand-storm.

Rorren fidgeted in her presence as a distressing sense of the inevitable knotted his stomach.

"They are sending you to Cardinal World Delta," he said. "My mother is a scholar there. I've asked her to look after you."

A weak hand gestured to the table and a satchel containing her posses-sions.

"I wish to give you something."

Under her guidance, he retrieved the tote, unlatched the buckle and reached inside. His fingers wrapped around a chilled, round object, and he knew what it was before he pulled it free.

Streaks of light cascaded through the room in a waterfall of blues and purples. The mesmerizing designs absorbed Rorren, but Lady Layeyre covered it with the edge of the sheet before he fell under its spell.

"You have a solstal?" he asked.

"Now you do," she replied. She slipped it into the bag and removed another object.

"I can't. You know they are illegal and dangerous."

"You will need it."

He wanted to argue but her dazzling magic prevented him.

She ran her aging hand over a tattered, leather-bound book, inhaled, and offered it to Rorren.

"In this is contained all you will need to know," she said, breathing the words into him as much as speaking them.

He took the book, not opening the pages.

"About what?"

"How to become Aux Katan."

She squeezed his hand between hers as if placing inside it some invisible key.

Secret Galactic Order Base
Desandor
Present Day

Thrashing into consciousness, Vesta jarred her shoulder, sending shooting pain along nerve endings to her wrists, which she found cuffed by metal restraints.

Inside the small room, a single lamp hanging from the ceiling assaulted her injured eye and stung the other.

Angling her head to avoid the shine, she discovered her feet tied to a metal chair welded to the floor. The Galactic Order went all out to immobilize her and their fear carried a distinct scent. One she savored.

Her belt rested on a small table across the room. Next to it, something round, covered by a cloth.

The solstal.

Voices carried from outside the door.

She struggled against the bonds in futility, her body aching and her soul tormented by the solstal, Vision Queen, and a jumble of horrors she didn't want to acknowledge.

When the door opened, Sevet Neece stepped inside.

More horrors.

"See, General, unharmed as promised."

Sevet moved to the right, allowing Mic Rorren to enter behind her, flanked by a guard on each side.

"It's not what it looks like," he said. The sting of betrayal became the worst of Vesta's aches.

Vesta forced her gaze from Mic Rorren to the guard. She noticed his bruised right cheek and scratched jaw.

Someone had to pay for permitting intruders to breach base security. Vesta only needed one guess as to who inflicted his injuries.

She looked at Sevet.

"The General tells me the solstal is driving you mad. You're seeing things. We can't have that now, can we?"

The Agent had enough saccharin dripping from her lips to make Vesta rear up.

The cuffs thwarted her attack but Vesta congratulated herself for the effort.

"I see what you mean," Sevet said to Rorren but raked her gaze over Vesta.

"Sevet will let us go. She'll return the solstal," Rorren said. He was probably looking at her but she didn't know. She kept her eyes on the Galactic Agent.

"You trust that witch?" Vesta spat.

"Funny to hear *you* call *me* a witch," Sevet said. She strolled across the room, a kencat in grace and agility but with the soul of a sunwart.

"I explained to General Rorren the purpose of our classified operation here. All Cardinal Worlds have come to expect a certain standard of living. I was sent to recruit planets that would be potential homes for basic operations. Desandor was chosen for our newest manufacturing and research facility."

"Is that why you asked the Chairman to enslave any Sandorian who gets too curious?"

Shaking her head, Severt radiated virtue and purity.

"Are we studying Scorth pods? Yes, I freely admit it. We must understand enemy technology. Whatever else your addled brain saw were lies of the solstal."

Rorren put his hand on Vesta's shoulder. If her hands had been free, she would have snapped it off.

"You are the liar!"

"I told you the Sandorians are primitive," Sevet said, "We struck an agreement with them for the security of this factory. That is their domain and I can't help how they carry out their laws."

Vesta tugged against the metal on her ankles, ready to spring the instant she had the opportunity.

"Just an innocent bystander," Vesta said, glaring at Rorren. "I see it is a human trait."

"Vesta," Rorren chided. His stern tone took some pleasure out of her catfight with Sevet. "Agent Neece will look into any unethical experiments at this facility."

"That should appease your addled mind," the Agent said.

"She has generously agreed to let us go. No charges will be brought even though we compromised the security of her operation," Rorren said. He flicked up his collar—a hidden message to Vesta. Let's regroup and search for more answers, his movements said.

"And if I disagree? Will I end up in pieces like the other Scorth you keep beneath your fortress?" Vesta asked.

Sevet lifted her perfectly arched eyebrow at Rorren.

"Tiresome wench. I don't know how you tolerate her," Sevet said. "I told you, the Scorth can't be reasoned with."

Rorren knelt by Vesta's chair. He rattled her chains and prompted the guard into action.

"Neece assured me that once the Sandorians realize they shouldn't come out this direction, their curiosity will dwindle, and the rest of them will be set free," Rorren explained.

Vesta inhaled, realizing she had to play along.

"I see." Nodding bitterly at Sevet, it was the closest thing to agreement she could manage.

"Uncuff her," Sevet ordered. The roughed-up guard hastened to obey.

Sevet was letting her go.

Surprise and genuine shock coursed through Vesta, a rare emotion that left her uneasy. Hands and legs free, she sat motionless, unsure how to react.

"Thank you," Rorren said.

Smiling with what Vesta thought was an attempt at affection, Sevet opened the door for Rorren.

In a daze of vision and memories, Vesta swam toward the exit, trying to sort hallucinations from reality. The interaction before her seemed like a distant nightmare. She did not know how much of what she witnessed had happened and what had been the solstal's illusion.

"And please, General, keep your Scorth from going mad and scorching the planet. I don't want to regret letting you go."

Rorren hoisted Vesta's belt over his shoulder and Sevet handed him the solstal. Her face sparkled, fingers letting go with too much eagerness. Or was that a delusion, too? Vesta didn't know anymore.

"Guards, escort our guests to the train," Sevet ordered, walking them into the corridor. "It will take you to the edge of the dunes. You can find your way home from there."

Mic Rorren saluted the agent.

"I owe you one."

Sevet clasped her hands behind her.

"My men live on the starfruit you harvested this year. Keep it up and I will—"

"I wish to leave," Vesta said without ceremony. Her cape surged behind her as she strode past them.

CHAPTER 34

THE TRAIN DEPOSITED THEM at the edge of the desert, fulfilling Agent Neece's promise. When the first shadows of dusk rose in waving patterns across the dunes, they neared the outskirts of Rorren's farm.

The Vision Queen, Vesta's companion since Neece gave them the solstal, haunted her footsteps, following just behind as if she were a shadow of dusk.

With shade coating the golden sea like a blanket, Rorren drew Vesta's gaze.

"You have to face the solstal again," he said.

"Now?"

"Now."

Exhaustion threatened to drop her to her knees, but he wanted her to fight and it gave her courage.

"The longer you wait, the more it will affect your mind. You won't know the truth from lies. It's already happening, isn't it?"

Every time she looked at him, it was the same—complete numbness—the watery vision of the Queen diluting Vesta's sense of reality.

"I believe in you," he said. She did not pull away when Rorren took her hands. Her soul was too empty to be coaxed into a reaction.

"You need to believe in yourself," he said.

"You do not know what I must overcome."

"I've never seen the birth of a menti blade. Show me."

He let go and melted into the shadows.

"If I face my demons now, will you also face yours?" she asked.

Rorren lowered his head, moving as if in some invisible conversation. An internal battle commenced, one she could not decide if he won or lost. His face was bright but his jaw skewed off-center.

"Given your mental state, what are the chances I agree and then you forget we had this conversation?" he asked.

Her numbness melted away and emotion returned—annoyance.

She unwrapped the solstal in one stroke and heaved it into the sky. The orb churned in the air, casting prisms of color over everything within a thirty-foot radius.

A wave of sand crashed over her and Vesta squinted through the grains in time to see the Vision Queen barreling toward her. Her hard, quick laughter ushed in the ghosts of moonlight.

Vesta dodged the slashing sword but the Queen dug her shoulder into Vesta's torso, driving her into the sand.

A burst of air exploded from Vesta's lungs as she torqued her hips and rolled out of the sword's path.

"Have you forgotten all the years you spent crafting me? Luha Zyne has not forgotten," said the Queen. The blunt end of the blade clipped Vesta's face, splitting open her cheek.

If it was just a hallucination, it was a dangerous one.

"I can change my future," Vesta said.

The Queen relented the assault, laughing. Jolts of lightning and stars clouded Vesta's vision, foiling attempts to rise.

Her armor and feathered cape vanished in a flash of magic, replaced by rags. A true Aux Katan warrior.

The pointed end of the sword touched her chin and lifted, coaxing her up to face her attacker.

"Only I can destroy the humans who are hurting the Scorth," the Vision Queen said.

"That was an illusion. You deceived me."

"You are weak and foolish. I alone make you strong."

A lie—the first one she'd recognized for days.

Many things made Vesta strong and with that realization, the ground firmed beneath her. Her lust for power and wealth did not make her strong. It was a revelation.

A chorus of Scorth voices clamored for her, crying out not from the immoral lab but from far across the stars: from Ragora.

Above them all came the soothing timbre of her granda.

No longer did the Queen stand before her.

Her eyes beheld sandy shores and snakes dangling from moss-covered branches.

The Palace.

Home.

A little girl sat on a rock by a woman dressed in rags. Vesta saw the robes with a new sight—glittering. Ethereal. Magical.

Her granda was a Fire-Scar Warrior.

"Remember the things I have taught you," Vahza said. She inclined her head toward the image Vesta saw of herself as a child.

"There is no treasure greater than the soul of a living being," Vahza told her that day, unknowingly starting Vesta's journey to the way of the Aux Katan.

Something unlocked inside Vesta. It lurched with physical force, enough to make her lift a hand to her chest.

Her fingers grazed a knot in the pocket of the tattered dress.

Sand—the kind that glowed. She kept it safe in her pocket since her first encounter with the Vision Queen.

She reached inside the fabric and funneled the grains into her hand. The moment the sand touched her flesh, it swirled up into the air, drawing more particles inside, sucking the energy and oxygen from around her.

The grains smoldered and melted together, forming a crystal shell and cooling into an unbreakable alloy.

Where the handle met the blade, a deep purple gemstone sparkled in unison with her heartbeats.

Vesta lunged into battle with a menti blade at her command. Lightning crackled from a cloud that swirled above her, charging her with a fierce determination.

Out of the sand, she swung the fire-laced edge of the menti blade. Vesta struck the Queen's sword, splitting it in two and shaking the foundations of the vision.

The Vision Queen impaled herself on Vesta's blade—knowing it was over—hissing as the blade wedged deep into her torso.

"I will always be in you," she whispered, drawing up to Vesta's ear.

Yes, Vesta thought, pushing the vision off the blade. *A reminder of what I was and will never be again.*

The Queen dropped to her knees, grinning, sand particles that created the vision dissolving in fragments, leaving behind the outline of her visage. Her lips lingered, suspended in time and space, uttering a curse.

"You do not know who I truly am," she said and vanished.

The menti blade had drawn its first blood and it left a lingering metallic taste in Vesta's mouth.

Prisms of light that Vesta forgot filled the air disappeared like someone flipped a switch.

The orb fell out of the sky, landing at Mic Rorren's feet.

The blade returned to dust once more and filled her hands.

Rorren paused—chest lifting—and let a pregnant silence linger before he blurted, "Hot beans with sauce!"

Ignoring him, Vesta deposited the sand inside the pouch and pulled tight the strings. Surprised by its buoyancy, she tied the pouch around her waist and bent to retrieve the solstal.

When she touched it, a gut-wrenching spasm shot through her. Hissing static filled her ears, then a sharp ringing.

The noise escaped its prison, flying up to the stars.

A transmission of unknown origin.

Someone had been spying on them.

***

Scorth War
Alpha Moon Military Hospital
9 years ago

The last time Rorren saw Lady Layeyre, she was leaning on Freyde as they exited the medical station. Freyde helped her navigate a street bustling with military activity. The Scorth woman was upright and that stirred some hope in Rorren.

He didn't have time to spare. His command ship would leave orbit within the day and he had much to do, but he made the time for her.

"General," Freyde saluted as best he could with one arm wrapped around Lady Layeyre. When they stopped, she did not remove her hand from his arm. Rorren took hope in it. She seemed to read his thoughts. She did not comment, exchanging a silent look with him instead. For years that followed, Rorren wondered what happened to the Fire-Scar Warrior and the gruff munitions expert.

"I'm glad to see you up and about," Rorren said.

"She's recovered enough that the doctors finally cleared her for travel. Your mother is going to meet us today," Freyde replied.

A convey passed without stopping and splashed mud on Lady Layeyre's robes. "Idiots!" Freyde yelled. He settled the Scorth against a storage crate, then said, "After I teach them some manners, I'm going to find our ride. Excuse me."

Lady Layeyre let go of his arm and Freyde disappeared.

Rorren sat alone with the woman who saved his life and changed the war.

"I hope you make a full recovery," he said.

She drew him under the shelter of a combat net, overhead holes casting spotted shadows across her face.

"You are called to action, I know, General, but I wished to speak with you one last time."

"I hope not for the last time," Rorren said. He bowed his head with reverence.

"Family is important, is it not?" She placed a hand on his arm.

Rorren had come to expect seemingly random comments from the woman. He found, more often than not, they carried wisdom only distance and the ages revealed.

"Families care for each other," she continued.

To hear those words from a Scorth no longer surprised him. She changed what he thought about Scorth.

"You have become my family. Have I become yours?"

He put his hand over hers, nodding.

She exhaled and Rorren sensed he had made an unspoken commitment to her.

"Then, I shall give you one final gift. When the time comes, I wish to ask something in return."

Rorren's communicator buzzed. He let go of her hand and answered. Once he dealt with the call, he turned to her.

"You name it. I'll do it."

She smiled, reaching for Freyde's arm as he returned to her.

"In time, Mic Rorren. You shall know in time," she said.

She and Freyde stepped into a transport ship and Rorren never saw either of them again. Sometimes, he thought about the favor she never put into words.

He gave up on understanding the mystery that was Lady Layeyre.

CHAPTER 35

Desandor
Present Day

VESTA LOWERED HERSELF OVER the embankment, hearing the clang of weapons before she saw the Sandorians. Slender bodies spread over the canyon floor, wielding crude tools made of imperfect stone and wood. Finding them there surprised her. Tucked away in the secret recesses of Desandor, they prepared to rescue their enslaved kin. She respected them for their courage.

Mic Rorren followed her into the desert, mood sour, chopping on her nerves like some rabid sunwart at her heels.

"If you need to do more investigating, more recon, then by all means, go," she told him just like a thousand times before, but here he was, breathing down her neck, glaring at the Sandorian warriors as if they had sprouted two heads. He adjusted the collar of his trench coat, leather gleaming in the hot afternoon suns.

"What are you going to do? Barge in and say, I'm Aux Katan now and I'm here to save your sorry kitlush behinds?"

She wrinkled her nose at his impression of her. His voice pitched up an octave and he tilted his head with an air of superiority that was far too accurate.

She clenched her teeth and hissed, "Yes, I am," then marched down the ravine into the middle of the secret camp.

The camp fell silent as she approached in stages. Dust stirred by battling warriors settled and the roar of moments ago gave way to an eerie tension. The men stood in a line but just beyond them, Vesta saw women holding children close.

Tribe Chief Yan-hara and a group of older Sandorians, including the chief's son Dusen-hara, whispered to each other in guttural tones.

The intensity of Dusen-hara's fixed stare and the leaden weight of his limbs made Vesta regret her reckless plan.

Vesta stepped toward them, but her sudden gesture threw the natives into battle-ready stances—all but the Tribe Chief and his son.

"I've come to assit you if you will let me," Vesta said.

The assembly kept still as Dusen-hara closed the space between them. Vesta stood her ground, unblinking, grateful Mic Rorren decided not to leave her. The tribe trusted him. That he stood beside a Scorth witch did not go unnoticed.

"Tell us with truth, Rorren-sun, do we stand any chance of driving the Chairman from the Citadel and freeing our people?" the Tribe Chief asked.

Dusen-hara slowed his steps, stopping when he stood a few paces away. It was then Rorren spoke.

"With her, you might."

In one self-assured motion, she flung out her cape and called the menti blade. She ripped the rim across the air and the blade left behind a trail of fire. Some clambered backward, others gasped, but Yan-hara lifted his hands, settling the spectators.

"The Fire-Scar Warrior shall fight with us."

Following a collective mummer of surprise, all the tribe members rushed forward to meet her.

Awkward at first, but in the following weeks, as she trained alongside them—helping and guiding them and taking a few lessons herself—the camaraderie they built blossomed into something exquisite. They were surprisingly good archers. Years of targeting sunwarts in the sands helped hone their skills with bow and arrow. The hidden talents made her think maybe Rorren was right. They might have a chance.

As the time for battle neared, a spirit of joviality swept through the Sandorian camp, catching Vesta in its wake.

Only Rorren seemed unaffected.

He trained with her, mood growing darker with the passing days.

He created a trap within himself and she could not understand why.

She preferred the company of the Sandorian men to the kitlush and avoided Mic Rorren when she could. She also avoided the Sandorian wives. Their social shrewdness and simplistic cheer made her nervous.

A group of them approached her, cornering her in the stone ruins of the main camp, leaving her nowhere to escape within the high pillars. For weeks, she watched them flitting and scheming in preparation for the pre-battle festival set to occur within the hour. For them to abandon their duties to speak to her seized up every muscle in her body.

"Scorth-Vesta," Alta-Ray said, fidgeting, "It is tradition for the warriors to wear a special dress to the ceremony tonight. We have made you a..." She turned, looking at her compatriots.

"Offering?" One of them said.

"Reward?" Another chimed in.

"Delight?"

Altra-Ray lifted the gown in her hands. The gazes of all the women bore into Vesta, ripping a hole in her well-guarded façade.

"We tried to add it with Scorth bits," an older female said. Heads bobbed between bursts of enthusiastic remarks.

"Do you like it, Scorth-Vesta?" Alta-Ray asked.

Vesta scoured the universe for treasure, claiming it for her own by any means necessary. Never before had such treasure been freely offered to her.

She rubbed her forearm and reached out, prodding the intricate textile as if it might grow venomous teeth and bite.

"I shall wear it tonight to honor you," she said.

Smiles found their way to faces, each brighter than the next.

A heavy-set, bright-eyed Sandorian with cherub cheeks asked, "Does that mean she likes?"

Vesta laid her fingers on the native's round arm and then took the dress from Alta-Ray.

As she walked away, she heard Alta-Ray speak.

"Yes, Emme-Sims, she likes."

A chorus of pleased laughter erupted behind her.

The lines of the turquoise dress traveled the shape within boldly, apologizing for nothing. The color was the brightest Vesta ever remembered wearing, making her feel strangely detached from all she knew.

Gathering at the shoulders, a string of gold feathers resembling her cape drew back over silk sleeves. All the fabric moved in billowing sheets as she walked. A formal gown so flagrantly Sandorian would be unsuitable for any event but the one happening just beyond the door. If the galaxy saved any fame for the Sandorians, it was for their handcrafted fabrics. Vesta strode outside, a sacrificial object to Sandorian pride.

She had pulled some of her wild hair into a braided crown. The rest fell to her shoulders, brushing the golden feathers as she followed the sound of laughter out to the courtyard's stone walls.

Lanterns bobbed in the evening breeze over rows of tables filled with rare delicacies and steaming slabs of meat. Savory odors assaulted Vesta's nose. She paused beneath an archway carved with ancient deities, observing a veil of joyous faces, a portent of the approaching dawn.

Yan-hara sat in the center of the main table, Dusen-hara on his right and Mic Rorren on his left. The human wore the navy-colored dress uniform of a Galactic Order General. He shed his trench coat, but the high collar of his undershirt concealed the inky scars of the relheer. He sat deep in the chair, relaxed, legs stretching beneath the table. Upon seeing her, his stillness welled up with violence and he shot to his feet.

The chattering and music stopped.

A hundred curious gazes fell on her, sticking to her with a physical weight as she pressed across the courtyard. The moment felt uncomfortable and lasted an eternity. It shouldn't have been like that. Vesta loved attention. Anything that fed her vanity was welcome.

This time was different but she struggled to know why.

The realization hit her as the Tribe Chief extended his hand: she cared what these people thought.

"Scorth-Vesta would honor the elders to join us here," Yan-hara said.

The excruciating attention ended and the music started up again. Vesta sat beside Rorren, though she wasn't sure she was welcome beside him. After his initial reaction, he melted into the seat and avoided looking at her.

She studied the place setting—a plate, a fork, a knife, and a spoon. Hardly a ceremony worthy of the Scorth.

"Don't be such a snob," Mic Rorren whispered.

She replied with a glare.

"You're welcome," he said. His index finger tugged at the uniform collar.

"For what?"

"You were nervous just then, but thanks to me, now you're only annoyed."

To prove him wrong, she became a paragon of civility for the first three courses, imbuing every conversation she entered with enough life that soon all the attention was hers. This time, she relished the spotlight.

Rorren ate, chewing in slow motion with a maddening crunch now and then.

She was so distracted by him that she failed to notice when the music stopped and the Tribe Chief stood.

Mic Rorren leaned close to her.

"Time to get nervous again," he said.

The Tribe Chief glanced at Vesta and then addressed everyone with the unhurried drawl of a true leader.

"Welcome all to the warrior's feast. It has been sixty-eight red suns since last we needed a warrior's feast. With the help of friends Rorren-sun and Scorth-Vesta, we will return to the old ways that once brought prosperity to our people."

The alien faces of the Sandorians at the surrounding tables turned solemn.

"We share our feast of the warrior with all. And now," he said, turning to Vesta, "they share with us traditional warrior dance."

Some clapped, others whooped.

Vesta wrinkled her brow.

"What?"

Mic Rorren stood and extended his hand.

"Sandorians don't dance," he said. "They aren't built for it. They've always been fascinated by humanoids that do. Yan-hara asked if you would mind."

She folded her arms and rooted herself to the chair.

"I told him you didn't mind," he said with a grin.

"I most certainly do mind."

"I've heard the Scorth are spectacular dancers. It's probably just another Scorth fiction. More unfounded hubris," he said.

Her body turned inflexible in contradiction to her sagging willpower. She knew what Rorren was doing. Still, she had never seen him so open and unguarded. Such behavior appealed to her.

She sighed, loud enough to draw attention.

The simple waltz reverberated through the stone columns, a prearranged melody that excited her as much as it annoyed her. They had learned a tune from the Scorth playbook.

With a hand slipped into his, Rorren lifted her from the table and guided her to the courtyard.

He placed his hand on her hip, raising the other into the air. Supple form perfect, as mother taught, Vesta put her hand on his shoulder, elbow angled.

"I could have performed something much more challenging," she said. She caught the faintest depression of anxiety at the corners of Rorren's mouth.

"I know. But I couldn't."

In all her 143 years, those who passed through her life had been little more than driftwood, useful for one purpose, kindling to burn with the ebbs of her temper. But those people, like her mother, were selfish and portrayed themselves as perfect. Mic Rorren was different.

Gliding in comfort in his embrace, she reminded herself of his many flaws lest she lose herself in the thrill of the dance.

The same thought extended to the Sandorians as she saw three-fingered hands applauding. Despite her training, these people were still pregnable and almost entirely defenseless against the harsh evils of the universe. Yet they had found their slice of heaven. They risked everything to fight for it. Their courage affected her.

She stopped and, taking her arms from Mic Rorren, fled to the pillars at the edge of darkness.

From the high ruins of the Sandorian village, Vesta could see the tops of all the warriors' tents in the camp below. Fires flickered from dots across the sand. The sky was so mirror-clear that sparkling stars looked like a reflection of the lights beneath them.

She sensed a body behind her.

"I do not want any of them to die," she admitted.

Vesta saw pure, ripened guilt spilling over his robust features.

"War turns even the best of us into murderers," he said. Her skin prickled at the coldness of his tone.

"How did you lead soldiers into battle when you knew they might be going to their deaths?"

She pushed him for answers. He had been hiding secrets far too long.

His jaw tightened, profile hardening into stone like the ruins around them.

"My father led the way. He was the real hero."

"Tell me of him."

He shook his head and took a step away from her.

"You shouldn't get close to me, Vesta. I'm not worth it."

The kitlush mustered the nerve to turn and leave. Vesta dug her fingers into his arm, hindering his escape.

"You are afraid I may get hurt?"

"Life doesn't go on for the remaining host. I learned that the hard way," he said.

Her eyes dropped to the mark of the relheer hidden behind the collar. *The remaining host.*

"Did you know there is another translation of relheer? In old Scorth, it means the warrior never surrenders."

Reaching up to touch his face, she wanted to soothe away the pain she saw. Outside movement interrupted her actions.

Two rows of Sandorians dressed in long ceremonial robes traveled up each side of them, filing into the courtyard. Golden bowls dangled from chains wrapped stylishly around each elongated arm, swaying as they walked.

Vesta took Mic Rorren's hand and dragged him into the festivities. More than that, she pulled him into the world.

Males, females, and children all took turns reaching into the offered bowls and retrieving a handful of whatever was inside.

Vesta lifted a brow and obligation prompted her to reach into the mysterious container. Her fingers touched the cool, round grains of desert sand. She took out a handful.

Mic Rorren mimicked her action.

Emme-Sims, apparently Vesta's new best friend, inclined her head, beaming. Joy brightened her face as Vesta partook in the ceremony.

"The widow told me of Sandorian beliefs," Rorren whispered. "She spoke of a ritual traditionally performed before battle. Looks like we get to see it."

Once everyone's hands were brimming, a hundred of them all squeezed together inside the courtyard while the Tribe Chief chanted in his native tongue.

"He is asking a blessing on the warriors from the Great Spirit, God of all the sandstorms of the desert," Rorren said.

The Sandorians in robes placed the golden bowls on top of long poles at each end of the courtyard. The bowls ignited in flames, sending smoke into plumes above them. The Tribe Chief said something else, then flung his hand full of sand into the air.

Everyone around Vesta opened their three-fingered hands, tossing their handfuls into the air. The smoke attracted the grains in waves.

Exciting.

She tossed her sand.

Rorren tossed his.

Her eyes followed the grains as they vanished into the smoke, churning and mixing. Flashes of blue and grey lightning rumbled within the strange cloud.

Emme-Sims giggled, then pointed into the sky.

Vesta couldn't figure out what she—boom.

A sound like cannon fire.

Boom. Boom. Boom.

Shielding her eyes from the sparks, Vesta watched grains of sand explode into fireworks.

The Sandorians cheered, clapping louder at each new burst of color.

Each handful erupted in a unique style enough that Vesta knew which firework belonged to which Sandorian. Her sand erupted into colors of green and purple, lighted in the center by showering sparks in the shape of her menti blade. The barest flash of a Scorth crown emerged, dancing in the sky and Vesta stiffened. She raked her eyes over the multitude, but either no one noticed or they didn't realize its meaning.

Mic Rorren's firework burst next. His explosion earned the biggest cheer as the brightest, loudest, and most dazzling.

It was inside him. Vesta knew it was.

To her surprise, Vesta found the simple celebration and spectacular display enjoyable.

Once the fireworks ended, loved ones and soldiers hugged and said goodbye.

Not for the first time had Vesta become an intruder in the Sandorian family.

She left them to it and came upon Mic Rorren standing above a small fire outside the ruins.

Bold steps carried her to him as she worked up her courage to tell him something—a slew of words she hadn't admitted in a hundred years. The crown came close to betraying her secret and forced her to confront unpleasant things.

Vesta planted her feet in the sand, postponing the moment. He waited, arms relaxed at his sides and mouth tweaked in a half grin as if her hesitation amused him.

"I must tell you who I am," she said.

"I already know."

"You do?" she asked, adjusting the feathers on her dress as casually as possible.

"You're the raven I pulled from the dead river that became a Fire-Scar Warrior."

She cemented her hands to her hips.

"Yes, but there is something you should..."

Mic Rorren raked his eyes over her with enough intensity to make her take her hands from her hips and fold them across her chest.

"Look, we all have a past. Secrets are best left buried there. I'm not sharing mine and I don't care to hear yours," he said.

She watched the flames cast shadows over the sand. She thought of her past. Her mother. Life on Ragora.

"But I think you need to know this."

"All I need to know is that you have my six tomorrow. I'll try to have yours, but don't count on it. I'm no—"

"Hero," Vesta snapped, shedding a few feathers. "You keep saying that, maybe to convince yourself. All of us know you are. The very marks on your flesh tells us so. Stop denying it."

She kicked sand over the fire and the flames perished into smoke. She left Rorren alone in the cold.

CHAPTER 36

Scorth War

Frontlines

Cardinal World Delta

13 Years Ago

BENEATH THE SKY OF wheeling stars, the thunder of a thousand footfalls announced the arrival of Delta's army. Rorren charged into battle against Scorth soldiers who no longer fought with self-assured confidence for the first time since he joined up. He heard the change in the clanging of his staff against Scorth metal. A pure, clear ring loud enough to cut the outer reaches of space.

They were going to win. The humans. The underdogs.

Rorren pinned the Scorth Captain against a boulder. His Scorth forces lay scattered around them, held at gunpoint by Freyde and the rest of Rorren's company.

Rorren waited for the captain to surrender, slipping his diamond-tipped spear under the Scorth man's throat.

"That's another battalion defeated, General," Rorren said. He didn't have to turn around to know who rode behind him. The trot of the resaur as General Harc Rorren strode across the battlefield was unmistakable. No one handled a resaur like Harc Rorren.

"A fine job, Lieutenant," Harc said, "but something stirs in the heavens."

Every Galactic Order soldier stopped and looked to the sky. When Harc spoke, it was prophesy.

Rorren stepped away from his father's resaur, watching a vast shadow roll toward them. Storm clouds swallowed mountain ranges and sky in billowing plumes of unnatural charcoal. There was something in them other than sleet and hail and it churned Rorren's gut like a lingering nightmare.

"Steady," General Harc said. Flashes of lightning reflected in his eyes; a light patter of rain sprinkled his stark white hair. Harc ran his fingers down his coarse mustache and lifted the scope of his veer rifle to his eye.

"Is this it, General? Do we finally get to see this mysterious Scorth weapon everyone's got their panties in a twist over?" Freyde asked, shifting the matchstick in his mouth from one side to the other.

"Maybe our intel was wrong," Rorren said.

Harc lowered the scope and drew the resaur to the front of the brigade. He traveled the line with a valor born of strife and peril, the kind that demands respect.

"We are not wrong. Ready your staff," Harc said. He ignored the boom of thunderous clouds and peered at them all with an intensity that made Rorren quiver.

Down the line of men and women, he rode, shoring up the resolve of each brave soul who, like Rorren, now lamented the victory snatched from them.

"Once in every generation, someone you shouldn't tangle with comes along. Today, here, that someone is us. We know who we are and what we stand for. We didn't go looking for this fight, but we will not falter from it. When a man knows who he is and what he stands for, he will never fall to his enemy, even if he loses the fight. Courage is looking up into that unknown storm and standing through it, come what may. Stand with me now for home, for family, for freedom."

A slab of stone fell from the sky.

The glittering piece of obsidian cracked a nearby boulder.

Rorren jumped aside and others gasped. No one fled.

"Leave the prisoners. Battle formations," Harc yelled across the battle-field. Rorren let the Scorth Captain go. Like the others, he obeyed his father without question or hesitation.

He stepped into line next to Freyde, heart pounding and breathing ragged.

His father yelled again.

"Remove the rounds from your veer rifles."

A strange command but Rorren did as told with the strength and confidence of Harc's voice bolstering his own.

"Set air power and insert standard issue staff into the barrel."

More gasps. Freyde's eyebrows lifted. Rorren brought the makeshift arrow gun up to his shoulder.

The obsidian rain gathered into a mass of black magic across the plains of Mic Rorren's home world. Pieces of magic broke apart, forming silhouettes like men. No, not men. Lanky and deformed creatures marched to them with a gait made uneven by the presence of six arms.

"Forty-five-degree angle," Harc said, looking through the scope of his rifle.

"Fire!"

The diamond-tipped spears sailed into the sky, disappearing into the jaw of the storm and re-emerging across the battlefield. Spears sliced a row of hulking monsters into pieces, but the others lumbered forward. The obsidian army approached, impossible to stop or kill.

"The diamond is the only thing that will cut them down," Harc said. He motioned to hundreds of crates of spears that were instantly cracked open and distributed.

Somehow his father knew. His father always knew.

Rorren clenched a new staff with white knuckles.

"Guess the rumors are true," Freyde said.

"These are the Obsedei warriors," Harc said from the resaur, "but stone monsters will never prevail against flesh and valor." He charged with no fear into the nest of rock soldiers.

Rorren pulled his staff and followed his father. Freyde and the others ran behind him, shouting their victory cries.

Harc showed them the way. He cut down the first monster, old bones still capable of outmaneuvering the attack of six stone arms.

The storm crashed into the fray, wind whipping Rorren's hair against his cheek, the smear of dust rendering the battle in chaos.

With the Obsedei attacking from all sides, Rorren heard his father's voice guiding them through the blinding tempest. They didn't need sight as long as they had that voice. Rorren stepped into the haze, crashing into a stone monster. It stood over seven feet, its body glistening like obsidian, every angle of its frame as sharp as a knife's edge.

Three arms came down on Rorren. Using the staff, he blocked the blow, muscles screaming as they struggled to oppose the inhuman strength.

"They are weakest at the hip and base of the skull," Harc's voice carried on the wind.

With one hand Rorren held off the attack, using the other to pull a knife from his boot. He stabbed the stone creature at the hip. Shards of stone splintered, cutting Rorren's fingers as they fell from its body.

The Obsedei warrior reared, swinging its six swords at Rorren. He spun out of the way, rolling over the stone shards, and landed behind his enemy. With blood oozing down his fingers, Rorren shoved the spear into the base of the warrior's skull just like Dad said.

A high-pitched shriek stung his ears and the monster shattered into pieces. The wind carried away its remains. Rain pelted Rorren in his moment of victory, settling his nerves and some of the dust of battle.

He spotted his father still riding the resaur, surrounded by dozens of Obsedei warriors. The monsters didn't need faces for Rorren to see what was in their minds.

The greatest Scorth weapon pitted against one rough-shod Galactic General and the General would win.

Rorren had always been proud of his father, but at that moment he swelled so high it seemed no warrior of stone or flesh could ever defeat the Rorren men.

Rorren cavorted across the battlefield, downing enemy fighters with almost the same speed and skill as his father. The resaur was not as skilled. The beast took a blow to the hind legs and Harc Rorren tumbled into the dirt.

Rorren reached him in time to shield his father from a death blow. Harc scrambled to his feet next to Rorren. The two of them fought side by side.

Rorren laughed at the Scorth not knowing how misplaced his hubris was.

"They really should just surrender now," Rorren said. He defended himself from swords in the many arms of the Obsedei warrior. The force in those artificial limbs pushed Rorren to his knees. The glowing eyes came near, pressed so close to his cheek he could feel the heat from them.

Its faceless stone of black melted, chin sinking like hot molasses. The face cracked open, sharp fangs growing beneath the glowing red slits of its eyes.

The attack was savage.

Teeth sunk into the flesh of Rorren's neck. After the mind-altering pain, the bite turned his blood cold and numbed him to the world.

All fell into shadow. Rorren heard his father shouting, made out a blur of movement, and the pressure on his neck relented.

"He needs the infirmary. He's been poisoned," Harc shouted.

Blinking to clear the fog, Rorren realized he was on his knees. His father dueled with a dozen of the strange creatures. They all had teeth.

Moving with difficulty, he touched the skin of his neck. He couldn't feel anything. Couldn't understand any of the flashing movements around him.

His father twisted.

Freyde shouted something.

Come over here, Freyde, Rorren tried to say. Tried to move his arm to wave his friend over, but nothing happened.

Strange faceless creatures surrounded them.

Harc didn't let them get close enough to bite.

Good job, Dad, Rorren thought.

Freyde was screaming now—trying to reach them.

Rorren grimaced, seeing the way his father fought. Swords slashed at him and he should have gotten out of the way.

The fang wounds on Rorren's neck throbbed, the sensation clearing some of the mental haze. The poison tore through his veins, coursing down to his shoulder, burning his flesh. He screamed and a hand squeezed his arm.

"Hold on, son, we—"

The sword of an Obsedei warrior ran Harc Rorren through.

Rorren's senses returned in painful splashes.

The wound did not stop Harc Rorren. The General turned and stabbed the rock creature through the chest, the force shattering the stone to rubble.

Another warrior took his place and stabbed Harc again.

His father dropped the staff and Rorren's world came into focus.

Amid the deadliest battle Rorren saw the terror on the faces of the Galactic Order troops. Faith lost. Spirits crushed. General fallen.

Harc reached up and pulled Rorren down to him. Half covered in mud, his broken body sent a shiver of regret through Rorren.

"This moment will decide the war, son. Hold on. Be steady. Never give up the dream."

His fingers lost grip on Rorren and Harc slipped from the world.

The fighting stopped. The Obsedei waited. The troops looked to Rorren.

Rorren welcomed the reprieve. His body ached and his soul anguished. He met Freyde's tear-stained eyes, finding many similar expressions. No one would blame him for giving up.

Hold on.

Rorren stood, every vein in his body burning with the fire of a thousand suns.

Be steady.

He picked up the staff lying in the mud at the end of his father's fingertips.

Never give up the dream.

With a stroke that surprised everyone, Rorren sliced off the head of the Obsedei warrior nearest to him.

The head shattered so loudly that he thought every troop on the battle-field must have heard it.

"The Delta Army will not surrender today. Not today or ever," Rorren said.

The Scorth wasted no time in resuming the attack, fueled now by the victory of a fallen General. It did not matter.

Rorren slashed wildly, taking down stone monsters with a crack more thunderous than the heavens above them. With the poison of the Obsedei coursing through him Rorren fought, becoming more than a leader. He became a symbol. No army, no matter how vast or terrible, could fight the legend born that day.

The poison put him in the infirmary for three weeks. The doctors said he wouldn't live. They said he would never walk again. They predicted he would never wield a staff or shoot a veer rifle again. They were finally right when they told him the scars left behind by the poison would never fully heal.

The scars. Symbol of the human spirit—of Rorren's spirit.

When he recovered and was on his feet, they promoted Rorren to General. No one remembered or cared that he was only twenty-two.

There was not a man nor woman in the entirety of the Galactic Army who didn't know of his deeds. The soldier didn't exist who wouldn't follow him into the fiercest battles. If Mic Rorren trusted a Fire-Scar Warrior, they would too.

Rorren didn't care about any of that.

Looking at the view screen in the infirmary, mouth dry, Rorren waited for her image to appear. The bandages on his neck and shoulder itched. His wounds still sent unpleasant pangs of pain down his side.

His mother appeared on screen. He remembered her eyes softer than that, kinder. He expected them to be red-rimmed.

"They won't allow me to come to you. They said it's too dangerous," Rorren's mother said with a rebellious anger. He half expected her to show up anyway.

"How are you?" she asked, staring at a spot beyond his shoulder.

"I murdered him, Mom," Rorren blurted.

She bit her bottom lip, turning away.

Her tears fell.

He waited for her to deny it.

"You just focus on getting well," she said. Her words stung worse than any wound.

Symbol of the human spirit! Laughable. He was no great General. Rorren was a murderer.

Desandor
Present Day

Vesta led the Sandorian warriors through the empty desert. The shadows in the dune valleys reminded her how Rorren looked while he worked his farm. In his tattered t-shirt and slacks, the sun on his bare arms and hair, turning him into a bronze God. He belonged on this journey with her, but he also belonged to the humans and the tragedy that haunted him.

She didn't want to think about how out of reach he was even so near beside her. His trench coat swallowed him, protecting him from the sun and life. In the stillness of the moments before battle she hoped for a new beginning for both of them.

The Citadel stood on a knoll between rocky plains. The cargo bed of the military vehicle limited her view, but now she saw a second story above the public entrance. The air of luxury and privacy mocked them from the high balcony, a superlative comfort for the elite few.

So often had she seen her mother stand at the edge of a balcony like the Chairman was now, peering with filmy contempt at the dirty denizens below.

Yan-hara's voice overpowered the music coming from the high soiree.

"Let them go."

Simple, powerful words. Typical of Sandorians.

The Chairman and his assistant, draped in expensive robes, groomed impeccably, exchanged anxious glances.

Vesta held Mic Rorren's gaze, neither needing language to understand the message. Silent as the rolling dunes, Rorren pulled part of the company of Sandorians toward the prison cells.

"I am at leisure and cannot be disturbed. The captain of the guard will use force if you do not leave," the Chairman said.

In support of his claims, rows of armored Sandorian soldiers appeared, clutching weapons that the Galactic Order must have supplied.

"Release them," Dusen-hara said. He stepped out of line and to his father's side, a true heir to the tribe. "Or face your fate."

"Do you think you nomads and a Scorth woman scare me? Captain, take no prisoners."

Vesta beamed, flung out her cape, and the menti blade solidified in her hands. The fleet of troops absorbed the scene, mouths gaping.

"They have a Fire-Scar Warrior!" someone shouted.

"Hold position," said the captain.

The battle commenced and the fight seared a tighter bond between Vesta and the natives. Closing on the Citadel's entrance, Yan-hara shouted orders, withdrawing his fighters from exposed positions. The Tribe Chief used Vesta like a scalpel, orchestrating her assaults and advances until she cut through the front lines with a beauty that left all in awe.

Dusen-hara fought next to her, deftly navigating the battle but lacking the improvisation Vesta excelled at. Out of breath, bruised, but grinning, the two stood beneath the stone archway of the Citadel.

Beyond them, inside the building, the Chairman's triple chins filled a holoprojection spanning the breadth of the stained-glass dome.

"You will live knowing that you have sentenced the chattel to death."

Camera angle blocking her view, Vesta couldn't see the controls he fumbled with, only the movement of his arms.

The projection changed shapes, blurring the holographic light until, coming into focus, a clock appeared, digital numbers counting down to something.

Vesta hunted for answers on the faces of the warriors around her but found no clues about its meaning. The energy drained from Dusen-hara's body and he let out a growl she dreaded hearing.

Father and son exchanged looks.

"Whatever it is, we must stop it," Yan-hara said. "You and Scorth-Vesta find the control room. We shall deal with the Chairman."

Dusen-hara nodded and hastily piloted Vesta through the corridors. Shrill notes of hysteria and confusion accompanied the fleeing government workers. Vesta and Dusen-hara navigated Citadel patrons in bouts of failure and success, picking up bruises for their efforts.

The Sandorian moved with the power of a freight train, barreling toward the room at the end of the corridor. Vesta sprinted to keep up with his seven-foot frame.

Charging into a brightly lit room just behind him, Vesta stepped into the glow from a wall of security monitors. Two hundred screens covered the walls, stacked one on the other. Each was a window to a different part of the Citadel, from the sentencing arena to prison cells.

She saw the Chairman pinned in a corner, his broad, languid body defenseless at the end of Yan-hara's weapon. The Chairman's face carried the raw, blank stare of numbness and shock as they latched handcuffs around his wrists.

"This is a victory for Desandor," Dusen-hara said.

Mic Rorren's unkempt hair and broad shoulders drew her attention to another monitor. The lights inside the cellblock shone like feeble insects in a fog, reminding Vesta of the dank odor she remembered too well. None of the patrol guards had been alerted to their presence. Rorren worked in a vacuum, dragging natives out of cells, the hope of freedom spurring their speed.

Vesta glanced away from the screen, conceding that the pleasant warmth overtaking her always occurred when she witnessed Mic Rorren being, well, Mic Rorren.

The numbers in the countdown dropped like a slap in the face, jolting Vesta into the danger of the present moment.

She scanned the other screens. Dusen-hara's long finger directed her eyes to a spot in the bottom corner. A flash of gemstone streaked across her vision—robbers pillaging the Chairman's vault—image fleeting away as her gaze continued downward.

"That has to be the control room," Dusen-hara said. The tangled wires and lights flashing beneath rows of computer servers and consoles were unmistakable. The entrance was the most heavily guarded spot on all the monitors. Of course, that is where they had to go.

Gesturing to the door, Vesta said, "The Chairman treated us like a joke. Shall we now deliver to him a final 'punch' line?"

No, no, no—had a pun come out of Vesta's mouth? She blamed Mic Rorren.

Dusen-hara wrinkled his leathery brow but said nothing as he moved out of the security room and down the corridor.

They dodged random security guards and sprinted through more corridors—no map to follow but instinct taking them closer to their destination.

A company of soldiers crashed out of a door to the right, cutting Vesta off from Dusen-hara and coercing her into battle.

Eight Sandorians swung at her with the ferocity of dying animals, making them challenging to contend with. Vesta darted up the wall, twisting around and into the circle of warriors, blade swinging. The sight of it was enough to scare most of them away. Four more slashes and a roundhouse kick disarmed the others.

She called for Dusen-hara, scanning the area, but the corridor was empty. The ticking of the ever-present countdown and swishing of air through the ventilation systems were the only sounds around her. She hurried past more doors, tension rising, preparing for another burst of soldiers, but the place had cleared out.

Digital display barraged her from various consoles. Each minute they lost sent a wave of unease through her body. She stopped cold, hearing voices, movement, and clanging.

She edged up to the door frame and, peering inside, discovered the Chairman's vault and the pillagers.

Vesta stumbled into a mess of sacks and boxes scattered across the room. A few natives and Aklaren carried armfuls of treasure, plopping the booty into waiting containers.

Vesta glanced at the countdown.

She had time.

She stepped inside, flashing her blade.

"Please don't hurt us," one of the natives said. He and his fellow thieves retreated. That left only the Aklaren. Vesta stood before him, poised for battle and lips pursed in mirth, daring him to choose.

He looked at her and then at the box filled with gold bars and jewelry.

"I'll just take this and…" He retrieved the box and took delicate steps as he squirmed around her and out the door.

The vault was hers.

She sensed something there—a tiny fragment of jewel called to her. Tearing open boxes with a lust she relished, she searched the vault. No luck in the containers, so she pulled sacks from wire racks, opening them to find nothing but gold coins.

With a huff and hands on her hips, she scanned the room and glared at each inanimate object as if its presence was an insult.

A tattered old box on the top shelf caught her attention. She pulled it down along with a blanket of dust that stung her eyes. Ripping the box apart, she found the rare talisman inside.

She removed the jewel from its gold casing and discovered it was a piece from her mother's crown.

A hairline crack ran through the center.

She cursed but, though damaged, her people built entire Rishkas to protect less valuable treasure.

Having a menti blade and being able to transform into a raven gave her more power and confidence than one Scorth ought to have. She would, perhaps, be a force in the universe enough to reclaim her lost birthright.

The thought caught inside her like a clump of sand in her throat.

For the first time since leaving Ragora, a desire to save her home world surged inside her.

She pocketed the jewel and went in search of Dusen-hara.

CHAPTER 37

VESTA REACHED THE CONTROL room and found Dusan-hara and the fruits of his admirable courage. He fought through two rows of trained soldiers, striking with confidence, smooth movements taking him deeper into the onslaught.

A sickening dread pooled in the pit of Vesta's stomach as one of the guards spun and slashed. A blade sank into Dusen-hara's stomach.

He didn't scream or flail.

Vesta rushed toward him, her limbs heavy and steps as lethargic as the sidle of a sandcrawler.

She reached into the air, calling her menti blade but it did not obey her.

The Sandorian guard pushed Dusen-hara off the end of the spear and Vesta's eyes followed him as he sank to his knees.

He clutched his stomach, a confused expression marring his smooth features.

The guards wasted no time in attacking. Vesta rolled beneath their lunging spears and picked up Dusen's sword. Letting rage overtake her, she cut them down.

Blind anger blurred her vision but not for the men she disarmed and defeated. Guilt and shame for her lust for treasure threatened to turn her from the path she committed to. She thought of her mother, sitting arrogantly on the Scorth throne.

Vesta cried out and struck a guard on the head with the butt of the sword. There were many of them but not enough to quench her rage. When the last one fell, she dropped the sword and sank to her knees beside Dusen-hara.

Blood coated his long fingers. He reached toward the command station as the numbers in the countdown turned to zeroes.

"How do I stop it?" Vesta asked.

"You cannot."

She tore part of her cape, using it to put pressure on his wound. His cry of pain seared through her.

"I am sorry I was not here to protect you," she said.

The young warrior's lipless mouth curved upward.

"No blame to you, Scorth-Vesta. I give my life for my people. My mother and Ben-hara might still live."

The jewel hidden in her belt brought the boy here, lying in a pool of blood. Vesta clenched her jaw and squeezed closed her eyes as she recalled Mic Rorren's words.

War turns even the best of us into murderers.

The ground rumbled.

The vibration traveled through her toes and thundered around her, knocking boxes from shelves and toppling computer towers.

Vesta used her body to shield Dusen-hara from the debris.

"What is happening?"

"Find the controls to open the cell blocks. Rorren-sun must hurry," he said.

His wide Sandorian eyes looked at her. They filled with a hope and faith she didn't deserve. With his encouragement, she stood, moving past her faults and refocusing on the mission.

A thousand levers, lights, and buttons swirled across the control panel. Vesta doubted her ability to find the right one. The image shot to her mind with the force of a super-nova. A small, green dot in the console along the wall called to her and she pressed it.

Nothing happened.

She could not call her menti blade.

She closed her eyes.

Her mind carried her out of the Citadel and over the dunes to the arena. The building sank into the sand sea and her concentration faltered. She squeezed her hands into fists, pressing into the vision until she found Mic Rorren. He was running through a dark place, his heart beating fast. Arms were grabbing at him and then he was climbing up, free of the prison cells, confirming she had found the right button.

Opening her eyes, she found Dusen's pale face twisted in confusion.

"Let us get you out of here," she said.

She wrapped his long arm around her shoulders. His body weighed her down but that didn't matter. She would save him. There would be no rest for her again if she didn't.

"Leave me. You go. Save my family."

"Shut up."

Teeth gritted, seven-foot frame crushing hers, she hobbled out of the control room. The shaking was worse now and it tossed them into the walls as they limped for the exit.

Something heavy fell on her head.

She blacked out and then came too with Dusen-hara leaning over her. The leather of his face sagged as his life drained. She sprang to her feet, dragging him with her again.

A draft of warm air carried them down a narrow corridor to a door. Vesta latched onto Dusen's arm to keep him from slipping and kicked the latch until the hinge swung open.

They landed together on hot sand.

They both sucked in lungs full of air. Vesta tried to stand and pick up her companion again.

A hand fell on her shoulder, alarming her, and she snapped at the attacker.

Yan-hara dodged her wild swing.

"Scorth-Vesta, can you slow the sinking?" the Tribe Chief asked. "Rorren-sun and the others are still inside."

Yan-hara hadn't seen his son yet.

"He needs a doctor," she said. The agony on Yan-hara's face tightened her stomach.

The others came quickly and surrounded the boy. Vesta stepped aside, leaning against the building, trying to breathe. She watched them, feeling like a true outsider. Mic Rorren was right. They would never accept her now that she murdered one of their own.

"This is not something I can heal," one said. Vesta assumed he was the doctor. Dusen's hand rested between both of Yan-hara's. The Tribe Chief looked up, eyes glistening.

"You must stop the sinking," Yan-hara ordered.

Vesta brought her fist to her lips, then tore across the sand until she reached one of the military sandcrawlers. She reached inside, switched on the communicator and pressed the transmitter.

"We have an injured Sandorian and request medical assistance. Agent Sevet Neece, this is Vesta. Save him and we will negotiate."

When she turned, she found all the tribe warriors looking at her, a mix of horror and relief on their elongated faces.

"Now, I shall stop the sinking."

The prison looked like a strange boulder jutting up from the plains of sand. Small sheets of glass reflected the sunlight as if the suns were a part of the structure itself. Those shimmering panels called to Vesta with the last glints of light before they sank beneath the dunes—burying alive the people the Chairman had called chattel.

She ran toward the building, slipping down soft surfaces and churning with the turmoil that altered the ground beneath her feet. The native prisoners poured out of the building, scrambling to safety in groups of five and ten.

Vesta dropped through a series of sand shelves until she reached a fissure at the edge of the building. A cascade of sand swept over her and buried her to the waist.

I must give them time, she thought.

Reaching out with her mind, she fought the frantic impulses shocking her system. She wrenched free of the sand and then turned to do the same for the building itself.

Her mind held each grain suspended, forcing it not to give way in the series of explosions the Chairman unleashed at the end of his countdown.

The pressure overwhelmed her mind.

Millions and millions of particles to uphold.

She stilled her mind and suspended herself in time as she did the building over the sand.

The natives shouted and Vesta opened her eyes. Droves of them balanced across roughshod bridges made from hastily assembled scrap wood. They connected the planks to broken windows and doorways of the building, granting escapees safe passage over the ever-widening fissure.

Yan-hara's tribe succeeded in clearing one floor of survivors. The Tribe Chief stood just above Vesta on the dune connected to one of the make-shift bridges. He signaled her and she moved the building with her mind. A new group of doors and windows fell within reach of the bridges, ready for the subsequent rescues. The Sandorians reconnected the planks and the evacuation began all over again.

Each time Vesta adjusted her hold of the stone and mortar, the strain weakened her. She fought the exhaustion, vowing to save all the prisoners.

When she thought of giving in to exhaustion, she remembered Dusen-hara.

No one else would die because of her. She kept control as the last of the explosions rocked the building.

"That is almost everyone," Yan-hara shouted.

Almost.

The fissure widened and swallowed the building. Vesta lost control. Plumes of dust soaked the air in a fog so thick Vesta couldn't tell if she was sinking along with the structure.

She climbed, pumping her legs up the steep dune until they ached. She rubbed the sting out of her eyes and wanted to clear the dust for the air but lacked strength for even the most basic elemental control.

Patches of grey shadows formed against distant hills and revealed silhouettes of bodies with three-fingered hands. She heard shouts of joy.

The dust cleared and Vesta saw a little Sandorian girl. The girl dropped the doll she clung to in favor of running into the embrace of a tearful couple.

Vesta bent, picked up the toy, and turned over her shoulder. The prison cell was submerged and only a broken window was visible above the sand. No sign of Mic Rorren.

Vesta handed the doll to the little girl and those large eyes went larger.

"I do not know why Scorth has helped us, but we thank you," her father said.

A timid thank you tumbled from the child's lips. Vesta touched her head gently and passed many similar scenes until she found Yan-hara, his wife, and their youngest son.

The boy threw his arms around Vesta as he did in the prison cell.

"You kept your promise," he said.

The grains of sand in her menti blade stirred in the pouch.

"Where is Mic Rorren?" Vesta asked.

Yan-hara looked at his wife, frowning.

"He and two of my warriors went inside for a final sweep. Two young are still missing."

Instinct took over and Vesta started for the submerged ruins, ready to charge inside.

Yan-hara gripped her arm.

"No, Scorth-Vesta, you must not."

She glared and he let go. She hadn't meant to frighten him but Mic Rorren's life was in danger and nothing else mattered.

Sandorians, wounded in the battle and their reunited families gathered in groups, but Vesta barely noticed.

She pinned her attention on the pane of broken glass. A thick cloud of dust still circled the building and she watched, trying not to think about her father's murder, being trapped as a raven, or saying goodbye to her granda. The loss then had been as keen in her soul as the loss she faced now.

Mic Rorren. Kitlush.

She was embarrassed by the days after she transformed. Rorren fed her, dressed her wounds, kept her alive, and later made her long to be something more.

Loset kay aux whiff.

Reen-hara put her hand on Vesta's shoulder, a bold gesture considering Vesta's mood.

"This is good work, Scorth-Vesta, with a loss of five. My people are indebted to you," Yan-hara said.

Five lost—Mic Rorren, the two warriors with him, and the two children. The Tribe Chief had not included Dusen-hara in his death count and Vesta wondered if he had told Reen-hara.

Mic Rorren's words kept repeating in her head. *Murderer.*

"Look," Reen-hara said, gazing into the darkest part of the sand cloud.

Out the single, broken window, Vesta watched several figures emerging.

Two Sandorian warriors.

One carried a child in his arms.

A female who must have been his wife greeted one of the Sandorians.

A final survivor appeared, cradling a small child with an unabashed kindness that belonged to Mic Rorren alone.

A kindness Vesta had received without thought or hesitation time and again.

Murderers do not deserve kindness, she thought, watching Mic Rorren hand the child to an eager Sandorian female.

He scanned the crowd and locked his eyes on her.

Rorren swaggered over.

Arrogant.

Reckless.

A hero.

CHAPTER 38

S AND GRITTED AGAINST HIS retina every time he blinked, but the grains did not stop Mic Rorren from seeing. Her cape rustled in the breeze, conforming to her shape before slipping free and flapping against the honeyed dunes.

Her familiar eyes, heavy on him, contained a look he knew too well. Something terrible happened and she was responsible.

He thought of his mother and the first time he'd seen her after his father's death. A critical moment. One he could never undo.

Rorren had to decide then and there how to save Vesta from the cycle of torment that held him as captive as the scars on his neck. They reached the crucial moment and he could think of only one thing to do—drastic, and he'd probably regret it.

He stopped in front of her and kissed her full on the mouth. She squirmed, endeavoring to push him off. Then, she gave in for four seconds.

"I have you worried?" he asked.

She lifted her chin, pretending to care more about the state of her hair.

"Even a kitlush has uses. I was concerned for the children."

Vesta stood as if she had exposed her vital organs to the enemy on the battlefield.

She averted her attention to a worse discovery: the entire Sandorian nation watched her and Rorren embrace.

Something greater drew their gazes to the heavens.

The clouds above them cracked over the metallic hull of a Galactic Order Cruiser. Plumes billowed around its flanks as it descended.

Two more ships landed beside the first with a friction-hiss of gears as metal sank into the sand. Sevet was taking no chances.

Vesta's cape flowed in the wind around her body, her awareness of her menti blade fading to the distance. Everything was about Dusen-hara now. Any risk was worth his life.

"What are they doing here?" Mic Rorren asked.

"I sent for them."

Rorren stared at her with a wisdom that annoyed her.

The Tribe Chief and his natives drew up beside her, their long, tendrilled hands gripping the sides of the gurney that contained the limp body of the young warrior.

Vesta found herself needing to touch the edge of the gurney. Connection somehow helped her cling to hope.

"You were right," she said to Mic Rorren. "This was my fault. The battle, indeed, turned me into a murderer."

His hand landed on her shoulder, lips dropping to her ear.

"All of us know that's not true. You are a hero. Stop denying it."

Her own words thrown in her face rankled and then comforted. She paused, looking into Rorren's kind face and sensed something more. Perhaps those words cost him more than she knew.

The ship's docking ramp descended, cresting the sand where it landed.

A line of armed soldiers marched out and behind them came the undeniably feminine gait of Agent Sevet Neece.

"The boy needs medical attention," Vesta said. She sounded eager, desperate even, and Sevet heard it. The woman was shrewd. Her eyebrow
lifted almost imperceptibly.

"And, in return, you agree to do anything I request?" Sevet asked.

Hell no.

"Yes," Vesta said.

Neece drew her gaze slyly from Vesta to Mic Rorren. Poised in thought,
she seemed to be rehearsing in her head.

"I never had full control of the manufacturing plant. It was a wide
operation. I've told Tage—the Premier—of my failure." She pretended it
was an admission and Mic Rorren seemed to believe her.

"Things were going on I was unaware of," Sevet said. She adjusted the
fabric of each finger of her black leather gloves. "Foolish young scientists
lost control of *it*. Now, *it* threatens the spaceport. I need your help to
destroy *it*."

"What exactly is *it*?" Vesta asked.

Sevet waved her charcoal fingers at her troops.

"Take the native aboard and see he is given what he needs," Sevet ordered.

The troops obeyed but Vesta's irritation at being ignored engulfed any
relief she might have found.

"What did you create in the pits of your depravity?" Vesta asked.

Sevet Neece glared at Vesta as if she had asked the stupidest question in
the galaxy.

"You told me you'd get your Scorth witch under control, General. I see
I'm not the only failure."

Mic Rorren ignored Sevet in favor of helping the Tribe Chief, Reen-hara, and Ben-hara up the docking ramp.

"Only one attendee. This is a military ship in the middle of battle, not a recreation barge for natives," Sevet hissed.

Reen-hara squeezed her husband's hand, leaving him to go aboard alone.

Sevet spun on her heel, angled herself toward the ship and taunted Vesta.

"Are you coming?"

CHAPTER 39

TWO COLUMNS OF BLACK stone peeled against the horizon as Vesta leaned over the pilot in the cockpit.

Mic Rorren stood close to the window, neck craning for a better view, revealing a hint of scar beneath his trench coat.

Sunburnt stone swung through the air, creating a wind tunnel that knocked the ship sideways. Vesta tumbled into Mic Rorren.

A crystal gleam of sand came at them through the heat waves, separating the ship from the monster.

The pilot pulled up at the last moment, evading a crash landing into the mountain's side.

No, not a mountain. A chest.

It stood at least ten stories taller than the largest gantis Vesta had encountered but it was not a creature of flesh.

Two rows of spiked rock adorned its head on either side, connected by horizontal bricks covered in Scorth markings.

Through wide cracks in its body, Vesta saw pools of glistening liquid oozing through valleys and hills in humanoid-like veins.

Like an Obsedei warrior, except it was too clumsy and bulky to be true Scorth.

"What were your scientists—" Vesta asked, grabbing Sevet by the lapel of her uniform, but the pilot swerved to avoid crashing into a stone hand.

Everyone in the cockpit slammed against the wall.

The monster plucked one of the other ships from the air, catching it between fingers and twig-snapping the hull.

Mic Rorren sagged against the wall.

"Yan-hara was not on that ship," Vesta reassured him.

Sevet pulled the pilot from the cockpit and climbed into his seat.

"This is a blood bath," she mumbled, reaching for the com. "Full retreat, that's an order."

Mic Rorren flipped off the com—an action that earned a death glare from the Agent.

"You can't do that. If you do, there will be nothing between that thing and the spaceport," Rorren said.

"I've already lost two air squadrons, not to mention our entire manufacturing operation. I've given enough soldiers. It's your turn."

The creature moved against the sky, threatening all life with a slow but inexhaustible energy for destruction.

Rorren didn't have to say anything to Vesta. She understood what they must do.

"Open the hatch," Sevet yelled to her subordinates. "The witch and the General are descending."

The kitlush fought against the inevitable and Vesta waited, watching the exchange and readying herself for battle.

"I don't care if she is a Fire-Scar Warrior, Sevet. You can't expect the two of us to take that thing down."

"If you don't, then we're all dead."

One of the soldiers held out a parachute harness. Vesta strapped in, pretending not to notice the fear in the eyes of the young soldier. He reminded her of Jon.

Mic Rorren gave up the argument with Sevet. He joined Vesta at the airlock and buckled himself in.

"I'm evacuating the other ships, but I will remain and give you air support for as long as possible," Sevet said.

As the hatch opened, Vesta silently cursed Sevet for acting so heroically.

Mic Rorren nodded and then they fell free into the air.

Explosions erupted around them. Cannon fire exhaust from the escaping ships swallowed them in smoke.

They landed and unlatched their chutes, balancing between the monster's earth-altering steps.

From their insect-like position on the ground, the size and scope of the monster left Vesta gasping.

The monster's heavy stone leg took another step forward, shifting the sand beneath them. They rolled and tumbled at the mercy of rippling waves.

Another round of cannon fire drew a mangled, deafening cry from the creature. Its clumsy fingers grasped at the ship, missing as Sevet maneuvered free.

"She can't distract it forever," Rorren said.

The ground rumbled again, though the stone monster had not taken a new step. A cloud of dust moved across the sand in the distance.

"What is it?" he asked.

Vesta listened, letting the answer come to her.

"A stampede," she replied.

She treaded sand, moving up the dune. At the apex, she found herself in the path of a herd of charging gantis.

Vesta suffocated in the emptiness of the sand-sea for a moment before a tumult of pounding hooves vibrated over the dune.

"They must have escaped when the base was destroyed," Mic Rorren yelled to be heard.

He grabbed her arm and pulled.

"We have to get out of the way."

"No," she said. She focused on the dust storm, "We have to ask for help."

Mic Rorren was brave, but concern skewed his lips as the herd showed no signs of stopping.

His hand was still on her arm. A wild impulse tingled her senses and she slipped her hand into his.

He looked at her, curiosity replacing some of the concern.

"Do you trust me?" she asked.

"Yes."

"Good." She squeezed his hand and then released it. "But you should not trust anyone. Not in these times."

Mic Rorren hunched his shoulders, bracing for impact.

Vesta held up one hand—a single, motionless action in a world of chaos.

The lead beast stopped and the others copied the action. Vesta recognized the scars across its shelled back.

It dropped his head nearer and Vesta touched the scales of a wet snout. Her friend grunted and steam from its nostrils blasted them. Rorren wiped his mouth.

"A nice juicy hello to you, too."

Vesta saw her reflection in its round black eye and surrounding yellow iris.

"Even after everything, these beasts would sacrifice themselves for us. Go with them, Mic Rorren. They will help you stall the creature from reaching port."

"You got all that from a snort?"

"Go!"

"What about you?" he asked, touching her arm.

"My sword can breach the stone but I need time."

"We will give you as much as we can."

The gantis bowed its head. Rorren reluctantly dropped his touch from Vesta and then climbed up.

In a quiet agony, she watched him ride away. The stone monster was ten times the size of the gantis, but Rorren charged fearlessly, leading the herd into the heart of an impossible battle.

Sevet reigned gunfire on the stone chest towering above, but the battle left Vesta no time to question the agent's motives.

The creature took another step and Vesta timed her jump. She landed upright, latched onto its leg and climbed hard, sparing no time to shake off the pain of impact.

Black stone warmed her fingers with a familiar air just like the jagged mountains surrounding Sevet's secret base.

The sharp edges cut her fingers but she ignored the sting and climbed higher.

She kept a constant grip, allowing her to weather the surge of movement when its mass lurched forward to take another step.

She spotted Mic Rorren and the beasts, small dots over the sand, scrambling as the starship-sized foot approached them.

The monster's knee bobbed upward and then sank. Vesta's shoulders screamed as the movement nearly tore bone from sockets. She hung on, adjusting her position, muscles in revolt against the shifting momentum. She jumped again, crossing the gap between leg and torso. The massive head swung sideways as its arm swatted at Sevet's ship.

Rising higher, Vesta thought she was near the heart, though it was hard to tell. Nothing but endless vertical stone stretched before her.

She called the menti blade, power reverberating as the sword formed in her hands.

A shadow blocked the sun and she swiveled, finding a house-sized hand barreling toward her—insect beneath the swatter.

She slashed in frantic spurts and a fissure erupted in the stone. Vesta crawled inside seconds before the rocky hand flattened her. Narrow chutes within the chest cavity swallowed her and sent her roiling over rock clusters. A flash of lightning stunted her vision when she landed. Faint splashing sounds came through the darkness. It was hard to remember the battle happening outside with all the quiet and damp surrounding her.

An oily liquid soaked her skin and clothes. The fabric clung to her when she stood.

The passage was tight but she forced herself upwards, abandoning one chute in dynamic motion to reach for another. Each chimney was tighter than the next and when she finally broke onto a flat plane, she flopped to the ground. Her legs and arms throbbed and she didn't continue until her strength returned.

Smoke stung her eyes. She searched for its source and found a ladder with polished metal rungs leading upward through a hatch.

No. Not a hatch.

Soft and wet. Organic like a Scorth pod.

She cut through the membrane with her blade and flattened herself against the wall to avoid another gross oil bath.

Pushing through and then up more ladders, her boots landed on smooth square tile. She recognized the floor pattern from Sevet's secret lab.

Shattered view screens covered the wall. A few remained intact but sputtered with static.

She found bodies of scientists clad in strange uniforms strewn across the control room. Sparks lit the room from loose wires dangling at intervals in between cave-ins.

Vesta coughed, pressing forward toward the sound of groaning.

One of the scientists was alive.

"What is this place? What happened here?" she asked.

Charred skin covered the side of his face and blood trickled from the corner of his mouth. Vesta jumped with surprise when he spoke.

"We couldn't control it."

Kneeling beside him, she gave in to baser instincts and took his hand.

"We warned Neece but she ordered us to continue. Too big. Too complex. We didn't understand it."

"Neece? Agent Neece ordered this?"

The man's lids eclipsed his eyes and Vesta squeezed his hand to keep him conscious.

"What is Agent Neece trying to do?"

"Agent? No, no. She is the Commander. Head of Galactic Order science division," he said, gesturing toward his uniform. "The Order wants her to harness Scorth power."

"I do tire of always being right," Vesta said.

Loud, hissing sparks showered down on them. Vesta shielded his body with hers, wondering how smart that was as oil trickled down her back.

"How do I stop it?" she asked.

"You can't." His hand went limp and he became just another lifeless body strewn across the room.

Vesta spotted another ladder leading upward and ran to it.

As she treaded metal slats, she could sense the consciousness of another Scorth—a warrior who died at the hands of the Galactic Order, out of control with rage. They dissected him and trapped him in a monstrous body of rock.

She slipped her head through the hatch, then pushing off her arms, she emerged into a room the size and shape of a Scorth throne room.

The energy and light inside the chamber hummed from inside a glass tube. A metallic object floated within the tube, suspended by some clear liquid. Vesta took a few steps forward and understanding washed over her, followed by a hollow panic. She couldn't breathe and her legs threatened to give out. She leaned against the stone of the wall, eyes on the floating object.

The brain.

A Scorth brain, covered in metal sheeting, controlled the monster from the tank.

She moved toward it, soul sickened and nerves frayed.

They thought they could control it.

"You had different plans, my friend," she said and reached out. The instant her flesh touched the glass, a blast of light hurled her across the room. Her upper body slammed against the wall and she crumbled to the ground.

Ignoring the crushing pain, Vesta reached out to the lost Scorth mind. Blinding rage cut through her.

"Please, listen to me. Stop the attack," Vesta's mind said to his.

The monster roared outside, loud enough to reach her through meters of stone insulation.

"I will have to stop you if you refuse to listen."

The room went silent.

The walls moved.

Pebbles and stones conglomerated, metal fragments pulled together by magnetic forces until four—beautiful and terrifying—Obsedei warriors surrounded her.

How long had it been since she'd seen one? Had she ever seen one?

Her awe and delight overpowered her common sense.

One of them charged her and the swords swinging from each of its six arms shocked her into action. She rolled out of the way, using her blade to counter the attacks.

The warriors stood on spring-loaded legs, lunging at her, cartilage crunching as the blunt edge of a sword struck her head. Blood gushed into her hair.

She plowed into the nearest warrior, bruising her shoulder into its stone-slat thighs. Her menti blade cut through and its legs snapped. Vesta fell in unison with the warrior. About a dozen swords sought revenge and flew at her.

She crawled upright, torqued her hips, and drove her sword to a torso. The crystalline stone cracked and the Obsedei warrior split in half.

A trail of fire left by her blade burned in the air.

Vesta wiped oil or blood from her lip, losing track of who was bleeding where.

"Care to try again?"

The last two warriors came at her from either side. All her concentration went into defending herself against twelve more swinging swords.

A stone hand clutched her neck, lifting her off the ground and cutting her air supply. It pinned her against the wall. Her arm went numb but she kept her hold on her blade, fighting the urge to pass out.

The warrior leaned in and she saw her reflection in its red, soulless eyes.

"Please kill me." The voice attacked her mind, whispering with the sting of needles.

Dazed and wedged to the wall, she watched the stone warrior with one clear eye. Its hand relented a fraction. Enough to break free.

Vesta brought her sword around and sliced through the stone arm that held her. She dropped and landed on her feet. She stood motionless for a nanosecond before she charged—sword raised—aiming for the pillar in the center of the room.

The blade sliced through the glass, igniting a fire when it contacted the metal-plated brain, then straight through like a hot knife through tresacoi.

She heard the shatter of glass as the Obsedei warriors crumbled into stone.

The air went still.

She waited, her breathing coming in slow, steady creaks.

Pieces of rock broke free from the ceiling. One or two at first. Then an avalanche.

A loud snap preceded a shift in the room and everything slanted sideways. An earthquake caused by the monster losing its balance.

The room caved in and Vesta sped to the ladder. She climbed down halfway, then jumped, rolling on impact as boulders tumbled after. She caught her breath in time to see the other ladders twist into mangled heaps.

Light appeared through a tunnel ten yards ahead of her, providing her a final chance at escape.

Twenty feet up the tunnel, her calf muscles started burning. She struggled to move against the velocity of a spinning world.

Long shadows appeared, cast by jagged rocks that barred her from the promise of light and fresh air. Her oil-soaked boots slipped and she fell away from the light.

The monster shifted again and momentum pushed her in the other direction toward the pointed stones. She angled her body, shoulder slamming against the edge of one of the snarled edges before she slipped through.

She fell backward into the air, panicking as she came face to face with the monster. The jagged rocks—its teeth—crumbled behind her. The creature's face became distorted as the two of them dropped together. In a freefall two hundred stories from the ground, she knew death was a certainty.

Vesta fought the force of the airstream, reaching for her belt and pulling free the cracked crown jewel.

In a flash of magic, she spread her wings.

She soared above the debris with the wind streaming through her feathers.

The transformation sucked the last life from the gem and it shattered between her talons.

From the vantage point, she watched the stone monster crumble. Its body created a new mountain in the middle of the golden dunes.

Hundreds of gantis littered the ground surrounding the new landmark. Vesta's raven eyes saw that Sevet and her ship had survived despite the thick plumes billowing from the engine.

Vesta circled, lower and lower, small heart pounding with anticipation.

Had he survived?

Unsettled dust limited her sight.

He had to stop doing this to her.

She found Rorren crouched next to the carcass of a gantis, hand resting on its enormous scaled neck, head bowed.

"Thank you, friend," she heard him say.

She perched on the slack jawbone of the fallen beast.

Mic Rorren froze when he saw her. Shaking out some of the sand from his hair, he squinted.

"Vesta?"

Caw.

She wished she had the words to explain.

CHAPTER 40

T HE CEREMONY DREW A gathering of cheerful, somewhat bewildered merchants, farmers, and Citadel survivors. They came to witness the establishment of a new headship.

Yan-hara's warriors soaked in much-deserved adulation.

Perched on a stone column in the shadows beyond the central throne, Vesta lamented her inability to join in. She had been a raven for over half of her life but never minded the isolation until now.

Mic Rorren never let her too far from his sight, but their conversations were only one way. Already her cognitive abilities began to decline. She tried to keep engaged by fluttering or cawing whenever conversation allowed.

She scanned the classical architecture of the Citadel, forcing her mind to focus, watching as sand crept through the open doorways.

A handful of disgruntled Galactic Order troops entered, uniforms pressed and buttons polished. They marched in strict formation around Sevet Neece.

Vesta moved her head sideways, allowing her raven eye to fixate on the Commander.

Sevet folded her arms and four gloved fingers drummed rhythmically over her bicep. When she approached the Interim Chairman, Yan-hara, Vesta took flight, landing on the tallest post of the ancient throne.

Sevet hesitated, distracted by the raven, then forced a bow.

"Chairman, the Galactic Order requests a renewal of our former agreement. We will clean up the factory and then rebuild—"

"No."

His voice carried on the hot, intruding wind from the open entryways.

Sevet tried to hide her emotion, but Vesta saw barely contained rage cracking the corner of her mouth.

"The Order will leave Desandor until we rebuild. Later, we will revisit our treaties with you."

If she weren't a raven, Vesta would have laughed.

Sevet had no choice but to agree. Yan-hara held all the cards. Sevet was lucky he hadn't lodged a formal complaint against her.

Sevet bent her head in acknowledgment as if the action might cause her to snap in two. With the flick of her wrist, her men turned and marched out of the Citadel.

Vesta could not resist the urge to soar over them. She relished Sevet's arrogant steps, knowing the Commander would return to her beloved Tagion as a pathetic failure.

Vesta landed in an open window frame overlooking the decorative stairs to the grand entrance.

As Sevet passed, Vesta cawed at her. Even with her limited capacity for sensation, mocking the Commander brought satisfaction.

"I prefer you as a bird."

With a flick of Neece's wrist, she captured Vesta's feathered body in a painful hold.

"I could snap your little neck so easily," Sevet said, squeezing. "When I think about what I have planned for you. Oh, you're going to wish I had."

The black gloves restricted her movements and Vesta gasped for air, heart thudding.

"Even if you could talk, Rorren will never believe you. He loves the Galactic Order too much."

Sevet brought the raven nearer to her red lips and whispered insidiously, "I win."

She let go of Vesta with a violent shove and walked away.

Vesta cawed, then soared above the crowds in search of Mic Rorren. She found him making his way to the heart of the Citadel. Vesta swooped down and landed on his shoulder. He carried her through an elaborate archway into a room with a vague familiarity. Yan-hara and his wife sat at Dusen's bedside, neither stirring as Mic Rorren entered. Vesta searched for accusations in their expressions but found none.

The accusation was implicit in the room itself, in Vesta being there in raven form, looking down on the boy who might die because of her.

Mic Rorren sat across from them, providing Vesta the perfect angle to see the bed. Dusen's face was relaxed but cold. The long tendrils from his chin looked defenseless, laying slack against his neck.

Sevet unloaded the boy from the Galactic Order medical ship with such rapid violence Vesta's wings stiffened with rage. It was a subtle revenge. Pure and ugly.

"Whether he lives or dies is up to him now," the Galactic Order doctor said before turning tail and retreating behind his master.

It was a lie. The doctor could have waited until the boy was out of danger. Vesta took on another swell of guilt.

She saw a movement in the beautiful textile cloth Reen-hara wore as she gracefully lifted to her feet. Her eyes seemed to tear themselves away from the still body of her son, brightening as they focused on Mic Rorren.

She took Rorren's hand and placed something inside.

"The Chairman did not keep all treasures in the vault," she said. Inside Mic Rorren's palm, small and bright, glistened another piece of Scorth diamond.

Vesta wished she had the voice to tell Reen-hara of her unjustifiable actions that left the Sandorian's oldest son fighting for his life. Rorren rolled his shoulder, forcing Vesta to hop down his arm. She landed in his palm, talon wrapping around the jewel.

In the time it took her to pull in a breath of air, she transformed. She knelt on the ground, hand inside Mic Rorren's, and he lifted her upright.

Vesta cupped the diamond from his hand and then gave it to Reen-hara.

"But, Scorth-Vesta, you can use this to—"

She closed Reen-hara's three fingers around the stone.

"I will take nothing more from you."

Her act of repentance helped some of the sting to go away.

They heard no news of Dusen-hara for a week. Vesta tried to distract herself with chores around the farm, but guilt tainted her every action. Compiling to it, she knew she needed to tell Mic Rorren about Sevet, about the message from the stranger in the Sandorian arena but hideous words played over and over in her mind.

Rorren will never believe you.

And what if Sevet was right?

Her desperation for relief from the ache made Vesta reckless.

While Mic Rorren was busy in the barn tinkering with the sandcrawler, she stole into the cellar. Sand blew in from the door, making the downward steps slippery. She navigated them without caution, slipping on the last one before she reached bottom. The blinds over the windows made the room dark and the dry air scratched her throat.

Beyond the barrels of sandfruit and water, a piece of cloth covered the familiar round orb on the top shelf.

She knew better than to dissect it. Ignoring her common sense, she retrieved the solstal and sprung open the bottom hatch. Jumbled together inside the compartment, she studied a mix of swirling tubes and electronic circuits. She didn't know what she was looking at so if there was some out-of-place transmitter, the chances of her finding it were slim.

Relieved to have her mind occupied with something other than Dusen-hara, she continued poking around.

The solstal reacted. A thick black plume of smoke reared up, blasting Vesta across the room. She coughed and brushed herself off and by the time she moved to the work table, Rorren had appeared.

"For the love of Alpha, what are you doing?"

Ignoring him, she touched each side of the round crystal in a sequence known to every Scorth child of her generation.

The gases in the orb changed color. Rays of light danced on the table, looking almost like—

"A holoprojection?" Rorren asked. He moved further into the cellar, waving his hand to clear away lingering patches of haze.

In the center of the holoprojection, a woman appeared, face shielded by a hooded cloak. Two aged hands pushed the hood away.

Vesta gripped the side of the table. Her throat constricted.

Her granda's image filled the room—a younger granda than she remembered. She looked almost exactly as she had the day she left Ragora. The years peeled away the prejudice of young eyes and Vesta saw her grand-mother clearly for the first time.

Her short hair left no room for traditional Scorth weavings. The clothes Vesta found shabby as a child were actually crystal clean and sparkled like light off ocean waves.

Vahza stared at Vesta, face beaming as if she were in the room.

"I have contemplated for years what I would say to you, my sweet little Vesta, if this message does indeed reach you."

There was something wrong. A yellowish tint in Vahza's eyes. Scorth sickness. Her granda was dying.

"My heart tells me that you might end up on an outlying planet one day. If I can, I will lead you to Mic Rorren. On that belief, I will deliver the solstal to him."

Something in the background distracted her granda. Vesta saw part of a man's head enter the frame. She recognized him from the Sandorian arena.

He said something unintelligible to Vahza and then disappeared.

"I left you over a hundred years ago, yet it seems like yesterday."

Vesta forgot Mic Rorren was in the room. That her granda mentioned his name registered slowly across her consciousness. His attention fixated on Vazha, jaw gaping and brow squeezed with such intensity it looked painful.

"I sense what path your life may take and so my chosen words to you are these: forgiveness for oneself is sometimes the only way forward."

Seeing her granda after so long, hearing the message, felt like a form of torture, one that Vesta relished and endured.

"When you wield the power of the Aux Katan, it seems all your past missteps surround you. Do not give in to despair. Move forward. Know that my love will always be with you."

There was yelling in the distance and Vahza's image went out of focus.

"More than anything, I hope you find love as you knew in my arms when we parted."

Vahza reached for the message controls, hand flashing nearer the lens and stopping. Vahza lifted her elegant head.

"It may be in vain but I am compelled to say this. Teach our people, Vesta. Show them the way, for I believe you will one day fulfill the mission I never could. Free Ragora."

The message abruptly clicked off. The light vanished from the room. For a fleeting moment, Vesta had her granda back. When the message ended, she lost her all over again.

Mic Rorren blew out an exasperated gasp, then looked at the ground. He ran a hand through his hair and when he looked up, he was beaming. The smile was contagious and Vesta found herself returning it.

"Your grandma is Vahza Layeyre?" he asked, shaking his head. "Why do I get the feeling our meeting was no coincidence? She knew all these years. She said that I would train a Fire-Scar Warrior. She said you were her one regret. She—"

"There you are!"

Vesta and Mic Rorren both turned. At the top of the cellar, they met the faces of Yan and Reen-hara. The youngest Ben-hara and—Vesta's heart sped up a beat—Dusen-hara. He leaned on his father's shoulder, his other arm in a sling across his chest.

The family pulled them from the cellar, and Vesta, much to her irritation, was drawn into a string of hugs, playful slaps, and cries of joy.

"You sent no word for weeks," Vesta said. She tried to tamp the emotions running wild through the small gathering.

"We wanted to surprise you," Dusen-hara said. He took Vesta's hand in his and she fidgeted. This encounter brought too much personal contact, especially with her equilibrium already off balance by the hidden message from her granda.

"We have another surprise for you," he said with a sly glance. The Hara family all turned to Yan-hara. He lifted both his arms, a gesture she found a bit grand, given only six people were present.

"In celebration of the success of our tribe and my son's return, we shall have the Unity-exult to honor Scorth-Vesta and Rorren-sun for all Sandorians. Will you participate?"

The power of her guilt left her breathless. If Yan-hara had asked her to dance naked in front of a troop of Galactic Order soldiers, she would not have refused.

She nodded.

Mic Rorren went into some weird spasm but she ignored him. They invited the Haras in for dinner. They ate and exchanged pleasantries, Vesta often glancing at Dusen-hara, unable to ignore the relief in knowing he survived. Rorren kept oddly quiet.

They set a date for the Unity-exult and then the Haras departed, laughing and cheerful.

Mic Rorren leaned against the front porch post, slipped a piece of straw between his lips and shoved his hands in his pockets. The moons of Desandor highlighted his most appealing features. His look caused a shiver along her spine.

"Do you know what a Unity-exult is?"

The heaviness of his gaze worried her.

"I do not," she admitted.

"A Unity-exult is the Sandorian term for wedding."

"*What?*"

The Sandorian women, led by Reen-hara, whisked Vesta to the dressing room inside the Citadel. They moved her to a raised platform in front of a mirror and she endured a parade of Sandorian females. Each one brought in materials of different colors and styles. She suspected she was treated to the display as some ceremonial honor and could not find the words to tell them she had no intention of getting married.

Guilt tied her tongue.

She examined her favorite dress, a dark blue gown with white jewels sewn around the collar and circling the sleeves. Reen-hara and another female undid Vesta's coiled locks of hair, combing out the Scorth.

She watched her reflection in the mirror as the females transformed her from an Aux Katan warrior into a bride. Reen-hara placed her three long fingers on Vesta's shoulder.

"Mic Rorren-sun is a worthy choice for you."

Vesta tried to smile. Underneath the tamed hair and bright clothes, she could still see the eyes of the Vision Queen, watching her, warning her.

"I will never marry a kitlush," Vesta said with a thrill fluttering through her veins at the thought of a new adventure.

Reen-hara dismissed the other females. Once they were alone, the wife of the new Interim Chairman stood in front of Vesta. On the raised platform, Vesta was face to face with the tall Sandorian.

"We need this and so does Scorth-Vesta," Reen-hara said.

And, because of Dusen-hara, Vesta did not protest.

THE CROWN

CHAPTER 41

THE BREEZE OVER DESANDOR'S surface tasted sweet—a grit laced with salt and a hint of starfruit. Savoring the flavor, Mic Rorren walked through the tunnel of the honorary Sandorian spears. The warmth from the fingers wrapped around his arm acted like an anchor, grounding him in the moment.

During the ceremony, he fought the urge to look at Vesta, afraid a single glance might undo the spell. He focused on Interim Chairman Yan-hara and the bits of flesh visible beneath his hide as he spoke the ceremonial words. The twinkle of his delight and the shine of handmade lanterns provided Rorren an excuse. He told himself he, a murderer, had to marry Vesta for the sake of the Sandorians. He couldn't abide disappointing anyone else.

When it was over, the noise and cheers drowned out Rorren's nerves, numbing him to the magnitude of what took place.

He watched grubmite hatchlings swirl up into the lanterns, each tiny winged body called by the light from the desert skies beyond.

Never get hitched to a Scorth witch. His father never said that but he should have.

Rorren related to those insects—drawn to an overwhelming glow and helpless to do anything but succumb to the temptation.

Journeying home to the farm in the sandcrawler gave his new reality plenty of time to set in.

He was married.

Sitting as silent as the horizon was dark, Vesta didn't move despite how hard Rorren watched her.

Her hair fell over her shoulders, small desert blooms woven into the dark strands. The colorful textiles of the Sandorian wedding dress reflected in her pale skin. She almost didn't look Scorth.

He cleared his throat and paused to think of something to say.

"So, wife, when we get home, what are you making me to eat?"

With a scowl deepening her features, she looked like herself again.

"We were not married by Scorth law."

"Sandorian law is every bit as binding and legal as Scorth law," Rorren scoffed, wondering why he was so defensive.

Vesta shifted in her seat, a rare and telling movement for a woman who was usually so controlled and precise.

"But even if we were," she said, "I will never be made to cook for you."

Rorren draped one wrist over the wheel and pretended to be as relaxed as if he was making his weekly market run, except this new territory was anything but routine.

"A marriage in name only then."

"I intend to fulfill the obligations contracted in most Scorth marriages. It will honor the Sandorians."

"Don't sound so excited about it."

"Are you excited about it?"

Rorren decided it best to cease talking for the rest of the ride.

The sky glittered with stars as they arrived at the farm and a chill laced the gentle breeze.

Rorren slammed the door to the sandcrawler, angry for giving into the foolish belief any woman could marry him and be happy.

Trudging around the sandcrawler, he opened the tailgate and retrieved some Sandorian wedding gifts. He hoisted a hand-weaved blanket over his shoulder and picked up a basket of goodies. The weight strained his muscles and his patience.

Once that food ran out, he'd return to desert moss and noodles. So much for his ideal wife.

He didn't bother opening the door for her.

After dinner and chores, he plopped the banket down on the couch, ignoring the creaking bedroom door as she passed through. With fists tucked beneath him, he waited for sleep. His anger was interrupted by the moons, high overhead, casting enough light through the windows to swathe the entire living room.

A delicate hand slipped into his. Vesta pulled him up to his feet.

"You have endured the couch long enough. Come."

He knew better than to give in, but moonlight made Vesta even more stunning.

"Not even a smile, kitlush? I shall change that," she said with a mischievous glint. Following her to the comfort of his bedroom, Rorren smiled.

Rorren Farm

Desandor

3 months after the Unity-exult

Vesta settled into a comfortable routine, as much as any Scorth woman could be comfortable with marriage to a human. She devoted herself to the role—atoning for what almost happened to Dusen-hara. Her devotion allowed her to rationalize keeping secrets from Mic Rorren.

Though she exchanged her traditional Scorth garments for Sandorian textiles, more than a century of Scorth ways had molded her—not undone in a day.

Rorren did not ease her evolution. He prattled now that they were married. At first, it shocked her. He was a kitlush of few words. When he spoke of her granda—of Racer and Captain Cantona and his loyal band of soldiers—it became impossible to tell him Freyde was dead and that he died only months ago.

The things he said did not matter; the quality of his voice, the firm but simple tone with a note close to happiness, meant everything.

Despite her blackened Scorth heart, she listened, wanting him to be happy. It is why she could not tell him about Freyde and the message. She feared he would grow distant and all the work she'd done to draw him near would fade to nothing.

Rorren loaded the sandcrawler with supplies for the neighbors as Vesta stood near the barn door, watching him and feeling the stir of the Aux Katan inside her.

Even that couldn't calm her troubled soul.

Rorren climbed into the cab, looked at her and waited for a beat. The expectant pause came daily. Ever since their marriage, he seemed to be wrestling with words that never came.

She put a hand on the top of Brawn's head. The kencat sat at her side, under orders from Rorren to stay and guard his property. That did not include her, Vesta explicitly reminded him.

"Sandorian law says otherwise." He gave her that lopsided grin. She wanted to slap it off his face.

"Go on then, kitlush. Go be a hero to those who know not of it." She meant it as a caress of encouragement but it sounded hollow. Not impactful enough to reach that place inside him that he let no one see.

Rorren shrugged and climbed inside the cab in a single motion.

Vesta pretended not to be disappointed.

She and Brawn stood together, watching the vehicle fold into waves of sand. She thought how simple things were. How inevitable. From the instant her raven eyes opened on him, she knew fate would come to this. There was a peace in the finality of it. Never would a word of love be mentioned between them. She made the decision never to give in to her emotions and he fought his. Now, all that remained was to watch his slow descent into himself.

She stood straight, head balanced. In the remote recesses of her face, the porcelain precision could not conceal a feminine vulnerability; her hands hung still, parallel with the long lines of her Sandorian dress.

Despite her efforts to suppress it, she anticipated waking up next to him every morning and enjoyed the sensation.

She buried her feelings deep beneath her Scorth heritage and her skepticism. The binding tie between man and woman, valued by so many other cultures, was always elevated to ridiculous extremes. She would never admit she had gained a new understanding of why.

Parting with him now after being so near him bothered her but that was natural. His absence displaced familiar comfort. Nothing more.

Brawn growled.

"Not to worry. Your master will return soon."

Vesta led the kencat up to the front porch and sat in the swinging chair. Brawn draped himself across her feet and they watched dark clouds blow over the dunes hundreds of miles away. A pang of longing for the thick vine-covered trees and salty sea air of Ragora struck her in the quiet interludes.

The vast bareness often unsettled her stomach because it opened the way for thoughts to invade her mind. Sevet Neece. The lost message from Freyde.

She pushed Brawn off her feet and he moaned in annoyance.

No, she told herself. Better to be contented here and leave all else behind.

She was envious of how easily Mic Rorren could bury the past in the sand, snug and forgotten like ripening sand-fruit.

The moons of Desandor appeared in the sky when Vesta decided to go inside.

She saw bits of herself scattered around the single open room of the quaint farmhouse. Her Scorth armor loomed from a rack in the corner. The staff Rorren made for her leaned against the front door. In the window seal were the beginning sprouts of tresacoi that Rorren had imported from the southern shores of Ragora. Her mouth watered at the sight. It was hard to believe three months had passed. Another three and the famous Scorth vegetable would bloom. She wondered if her entire life with Mic Rorren would pass by so quickly—so idyllically despite its imperfections. She fought the urge to smile.

Brawn sprawled in front of the fireplace. He had settled for about ten minutes when his head jerked up.

A rapping on the door filled the room.

The kencat sprang to all fours and Vesta gestured for him to stay.

She opened the door and looked upon a young Sandorian boy she didn't recognize. He was out of breath and purple blood oozed from a cut on his lipless mouth.

"Scorth-Vesta. The Aklaren are attacking my village. Please, help?" His voice shifted upward in pitch. Tears welled in his eyes.

Guilt and contentment made Vesta unwise and trusting.

She glanced over her shoulder to her armor in the corner. She should not leave without it but time was fleeting. She retrieved the sand pouch that contained her menti blade and grabbed the staff Rorren made her. She rushed out after the boy. Brawn bounded beside them and jumped into the motor cruiser before Vesta started the engine.

It took only a half rotation to reach the village. Serval houses lay in an outcropping of sage, framed against a ledge of dark cliffs. Stripes of smoke stretched above the charcoaled structures, a few still engulfed in flames.

Aklaren danced like fools, drinks in hand, laughing and tormenting another young Sandorian.

Vesta jumped from the glider and called on her blade.

Thwat.

Something struck her neck.

She cried out, reaching around, and pulled a dart from her flesh.

The sleek metal tip didn't look Aklaren. Nor did it look Scorth.

Her head spun. She fought the vertigo in vain. Her legs buckled and her body sank into the sand.

The shadows of two Rocbull marauders twice her size loomed over her. Sand particles refused to answer her telepathic command.

A heavy boot kicked her in the stomach.

When she looked up, she saw the Rodilian.

He bent one arm from the elbow, lifting the gun with a short jolt.

"Not so tough without your witch tricks or your soldier boy, are you?"

Hevcar Duronilan spat at her. Mercifully, she didn't feel the grease on her skin.

"Can I get my payment now?" she heard the young Sandorian ask. He and the girl stood together with three-fingered hands outstretched.

Vesta cursed.

Thieves. She could see it now.

"Here, kid. Worth every penny," the Aklaren gang leader said and dumped a pouch full of gemstones into the boy's hand. Vesta watched them scuttle off, feeling the loss of sensation in her arms and legs. She tried to call the power of the Aux Katan, but it was as numb to her as her flesh.

The two Rocbulls and Hevcar chuckled over her.

"Neat little poison, isn't it?" He pulled her head up by her hair. "I told you I'd have my revenge."

Vesta reached for her staff with her last strength. Hevcar stepped on her fingers, mashing them into the sand.

"The bounty on your ugly Scorth head is going to make me rich."

He yanked her across the ground by her hair.

She heard a roar and Hevcar froze.

Brawn soared through the air and his teeth clamped into the arm of the Rocbull.

The sound of ripping flesh was the last thing Vesta heard before darkness engulfed her.

CHAPTER 42

MIC RORREN SURGED AGAINST the sky. He stood rigid, shoulder
blades drawn together and the curve of his neck strained at the
sight before him. He flipped the flaps of his trench coat up and shivered in
the heat.

Currents of smoke rose in layered plains across the landscape. The wind
pressed against the hollow of Rorren's back, driving him down the dune.

He found nothing left of the village below but a smoldering pile in the
center square, ripe with the scent of charred flesh.

His eyes scanned in awareness of every indent left in the sand. Vesta's
boot print. Five-padded paw marks of a kencat.

The battle was drawn in the ground as if just for him, waiting for his agile
mind to decipher each thrust, fall, blow, and retreat.

Vesta went down near the pile of debris. They dragged her forward and
Rorren knelt on the spot. The tracks went wild.

A battle ensued. There was blood. Claw marks in the formless soil gave
Rorren a glimpse of the scene. Brawn's fangs were sinking into some poor
aux rand—more blood on the ground. The kencat reared up on his hind
legs in front of Vesta, protecting her, sailing through the air to defeat the
enemy.

Rorren came across a severed finger.

Beyond the red spray over the ground lay a fur-covered body.

Rorren held his breath. He waited for that familiar form to shudder with life. The closer he drew, the slower his pace became. Too many mortal wounds tore apart the familiar stripes on Brawn's torso.

He reached out, fingers brushing the hide but numb to its feel.

Clutching onto the fur at Brawn's chest, Rorren turned his head and drew in a rapid breath. The Aklaren had torn out his two long saber teeth.

Damn them.

Brawn's friendly face was a mess. Blood from his mouth left a deep stain on the sand surrounding his head.

Mic Rorren didn't remember walking to the sandcrawler to retrieve the old blanket. He worked in a daze. He wrapped the body with meticulous movements, cradling each paw as he tucked it inside. The task reminded him of folding up the flag of the Cardinal Worlds, the symbol of freedom he loved and would die for. Satisfied with the dressing, he carried the lifeless body across the village.

He laid Brawn on the hauling bed, arms shaking from the strain of lifting the two-hundred-pound animal.

The way the kencat glided over the sand—buoyant and eager—flashed across Rorren's mind like unwelcome lightning.

Damn them to hell.

He returned to the battle scene, but his head was fuzzy and his blurred eyes lost track of Vesta's footprints.

"Mister?"

He turned and found a young Sandorian boy fidgeting in the shadow of a half-collapsed wall.

"What happened here?"

The kid was a pathetic sight. In his right mind, Rorren might have noticed he was a bit too pathetic with his soot-stained face and torn shirt.

"Aklaren attacked our village. The kencat and the witch tried to protect us, but they did something to her so she couldn't use her Scorth magic."

Another little one peeked around the boy's arm.

"They killed everyone and took everything. Only me and my sister escaped."

The kid pointed to the smoldering pile.

"They took the kencat's teeth and burned the witch. Even her armor. They must have really hated her not to take it for profit."

Rorren forced himself to the ash pile. He dug in a rage until a powder-thin dust covered his hands and forearms. His fingers latched on hard metal. Out of the rubble, he pulled the mangled remains of Vesta's armor. Some crude instrument etched an insignia into the bottom right corner—Hevcar's insignia.

As he studied it, he heard the mocking laughter of the Aklaren gang leader.

"You saw her die?"

The words were dry and sucked the moisture from his throat as they emerged.

The kid nodded.

He spent nights worrying about this. Ever since the day he met her. Glancing at the pathetic twisted metal, he saw the mistake he made.

He got too close. He let Vesta in.

He hadn't cared that she couldn't say 'I love you.' What mattered was that she was strong enough to survive a life with him. No one else had been. Not his father. Not his mother. To protect his sisters, he ran away.

Now, he had to run forever.

I murdered him, Mom.

There was no one to apologize to this time, not even Brawn.

He kept looking at the ash pile, waiting for some sign. Wouldn't be the first time he'd thought she was dead, only to see her rise out of nothing.

The wind swirled the dust across the barren sand. Still. Lifeless.

He jammed his hands into his pockets and emptied them. He gave what money he had to the kid and the girl.

He walked to the sandcrawler with one longing glance at the ashes.

With effort, he pushed himself into the cab. He splayed his hands over the dash. He knew it was time to go but he waited another few minutes. He glanced through the windshield to the sky and then revved the engine.

Driving into the suns, light blinding on the white dunes, gave Rorren too much time to think.

At the farm, he worked on auto-pilot. He buried Brawn near the harvester, concentrating on the steady rhythm of shovel, toss, repeat. The weight of sand strained his spine, but he went numb to the pain. Between each scoop, he wiped his eyes with the tail of his shirt.

Goodbye wasn't easy so he didn't linger over the grave.

He locked up the house first, then went down into the cellar. He pulled out the dust-covered trunk and retrieved his old uniform.

If being a murderer was his destiny then so be it. He'd put that trait to good use.

Dawn cast an orange glow over the horizon just as he pulled the sandcrawler into the market surrounding the space hub.

So many times he walked these streets. They passed in a blur. If shops opened, if the roads began to fill with pedestrians, he didn't notice. His body and his senses went numb to everything.

He trained his eyes on a single building at the end of the square.

When he reached it, he stepped inside and marched straight to the front desk. He slapped his Galactic Order badge on the table.

"I want to re-enlist."

The man behind the desk, a soldier of no more than nineteen, did not look up from his computer console.

"You'll have to pass some recruitment tests first. Life out here isn't conducive too—"

With a forced smile, he scanned Rorren's badge.

The change was immediate.

The soldier's jaw dropped at the same time his body lifted out of the chair. The salute was awkward but genuine.

"General Rorren. It is an honor, sir."

"At ease."

The officer didn't relax.

"A lot of people were hoping you'd re-up. There is a note on your file from the Premier himself."

"That's nice."

Small talk meant nothing to him. There was only one thing on his mind.

"What brings you back, sir?"

Rorren fisted his hands and leaned over the desk.

"I am going to wipe out every Aklaren marauder on this planet and when I'm finished, I'm going to do the same for the rest of the galaxy."

The young soldier grinned.

"If anyone can do it, sir, it's you."

Rorren frowned at the enthusiasm and adjusted the collar of his trench coat.

"Just one condition."

"Anything, sir."

"I keep the coat."

Rorren walked away from the desk before the officer answered.

Somewhere in the Galaxy
Present Day

Vesta drifted through a dense mental fog. The ship traveled but she could not determine for how long. There was a vague memory of turbulence. Landing gear touching down.

The jab of a needle. Once. Twice. Whatever poison Vesta's captors were pumping into her blurred her vision and made her limbs heavy.

When she awoke, her neck ached and her head was woozy enough to make her nauseous. Her sense of smell returned first. Chemicals. Metallic aftertaste. Her arms were on fire with pain. She realized they were latched to the wall by metal clamps above her head. Her vision cleared. Objects in the room came into focus. A large computer console sat in the corner beside a glass cylinder with large clumps of mossy green blobs floating inside. Men in black lab coats hunched over dissection tables filled with the pink flesh of some poor creature exposed to harsh overhead light.

"Commander, she's awake."

The voice wasn't loud, but the sound reverberated through Vesta's system and made her nausea worse. She heard a click of heels. A hand painfully squeezed her jaw and jerked her head upward.

"I don't understand what he sees in you," Sevet said. She pushed Vesta's chin away. In the cold light of the lab, her uniform took on a shine that made her severe style even more glamorous and terrifying.

A stab of memory flashed through Vesta's mind as it had before. Sevet buried her emotions so deeply that they bubbled up in mysterious ways that Vesta could sense and see.

Sevet's glamor was in vain now—for love had already rejected her—and Vesta mourned when she saw Sevet had not always been empty and cruel.

"You should thank me. I'm about to give you a greater purpose than you ever imagined. Now is your chance to be more than a pathetic nobody."

Something pinched Vesta's ankle. Heavy and metallic. She looked down, expecting to see chains like those on her wrists. A clamp, lights blinking and strange liquid rimming the collar, bit into her flesh with prickly little teeth.

"Brilliant invention that," Sevet said. She clasped her hands behind her and bent to admire the device. Her short blond hair was sleek with gel, making it shine even more than her uniform. "Much better than the drugs. It negates your magic but allows you to be conscious. And, oh, I want you conscious for this."

Vesta pulled at the restraints. Pain coursed from her ankle to her other limbs and made her growl. Whatever the ankle clamp was, it prevented her from calling her Aux Katan power.

"Bring her," Sevet said and turned, heels clicking as she crossed the lab.

Two armed guards unchained Vesta from the wall. She lashed out at them but in her weakened state, one blow to her skull knocked her to the ground. They yanked her up, strapped her to a cold metal lab table and wheeled her into another room. The light—dimmer than before, or was that her head injury—filled a small room that smelled of burnt flesh and mold. In the center of the grated floor, four glass walls encompassed a tank filled with neon-colored water.

By stabbing needles into her flesh, the guards attached wires to her collarbone, to her neck on either side and down her legs. Blood dripped from each entry point, warm on her skin. They released the straps on the lab table. Someone shoved her from behind and she landed in the water with a violent splash. The world vanished for an instant as her head submerged.

Vesta swam up, gasping for air when she broke the surface and the ache settled into her limbs. She wiped the water from her eyes to see Sevet loom over the platform, dry, calm, and half-grinning. The two of them locked gazes.

Even as the guards strapped her wrists to the sides of the tank, Vesta never broke eye contact with Sevet. The evil creature would not beat her. The more the drugs wore off, the more determined Vesta became to survive. Her left foot sank to the bottom of the tank from the weight of the clamp, but the straps on her wrists kept her head above water.

She hovered there, shivering, as a piece of machinery lowered toward her head. The laser tip came into focus when it dipped into the light. Sevet walked to a console on the platform and looked over a man's shoulder. The grin never left her pink lips.

"Take your time. I want this procedure done properly. The product is too valuable to risk damage."

The man nodded and another leaned forward. There was something wrong with them. In their eyes. The dead, blank gaze of a brainwashed helot.

"Commander, should we administer the sedative now?"

"No."

The man trembled but his questioning gaze never left his superior officer.

"I want her awake for all of it."

An audible gasp came from somewhere in the dark room. Sevet turned sharp eyes on each of the workers, seeking out the source of the noise and daring anyone to object further. None did.

Sevet conditioned loyal inmates.

"Proceed." Her voice shuddered with impatience. The laser above Vesta's head hummed, coming to life with a red glow. One of the guards flipped a switch and electricity buzzed through the water just enough to tingle. She called on her menti blade, a last desperate attempt to save herself. Pain bit into her ankle. The clamp had to come off.

She kicked her legs and thrashed but she was strapped so tight the water barely rippled.

For the first time since tapping into the power of the Fire-Scar Warriors, Vesta doubted her ability to triumph in battle. Without the Aux Katan, she was alone and weak. Mic Rorren's face flashed through her mind. The distance between them stung worse than her wounds.

The shadows of regret tasted bitter.

Her flesh burned from the voltage they pumped into the water. She focused on her new husband—the few months they shared—surprised her last thoughts in life would be of him. She wondered if such powerful feelings would linger after Sevet turned her into a floating blob of goo in a tank.

Pockets of water detonated inside the tank. Vesta braced for a wave of pain and then the endless unknown. The guard at the voltage switch shot across the room, thrown by some invisible force. Sparks rained from the laser, smoke billowing from its sides before it powered off.

"What is happening?" Sevet screamed over the rumble of exploding machinery. She grabbed a scientist-butcher by the arm, ordering him to operate the voltage switch. He did so reluctantly. His finger touched the switch and the discharging energy blasted him against the wall. He landed in a lump beside the other worker.

"The ankle binding, is it malfunctioning?" Sevet pushed the man at the command console aside and swept her fingers across the keys. Her smile had finally disappeared. She glared at Vesta.

"You're not that powerful."

Just as confused, Vesta struggled against the clamp on her ankle. The device still prevented her from using her power, but something drained her energy. Her eyes grew as heavy as her limbs, forcing her to kick harder to stay afloat.

Men lifted her from the water, removed her from the lab and deposited her into another chamber. This one looked much cruder and its technology appeared outdated. This place was more Scorth in nature than the prior lab.

In the center of the room, Vesta saw another tube made of glass. The guards prodded her up the metal stairs and forced her inside the tube. They sealed the glass behind her and a swish of air filled the chamber. She found Sevet lurking in the shadows, hovering over another console where two of her butchers worked.

Clamps dropped inside the tube, constricting Vesta's head between them and locking her skull into place. Sevet bent toward a microphone and her voice filled the glass tube.

"I didn't want to do this the old-fashioned way, but you've left me no choice. The vulgarity of it seems to suit you."

Something cool and metal touched Vesta's forehead like a finger drawing a guideline into her flesh.

Strands of blue voltage swept in waves over the glass walls. Vesta closed her eyes to the sound of a bone saw reverberating inside the chamber. She had no power or recourse, but something was there. Her granda protecting her?

The chamber shook and Vesta grasped the glass to stabilize her balance. Smoke poured into the tube, obscuring Sevet from view and filling Vesta's lungs. The blades screeched, stopping just before they reached Vesta's skull. The clamps released and Vesta took advantage of her good fortune.

With her elbow, she pounded at the glass between coughing fits. Whether by her power or that of Vahza, the glass shattered and Vesta tumbled into the clean air.

She fell on her side, pushing the smoke from her lungs with more violent coughs. She turned to see Sevet over her, perfect white teeth clenched and the scowl on her features not half as fierce as the rage behind her eyes.

Sevet's reached for Vesta.

"Not the hair. Why is everyone determined to drag me by the hair?"

Sevet hissed and snatched the first thing she could, Vesta's offered wrist. She pulled Vesta down the metal stairs, each slat clanging painfully against Vesta's body.

Sevet let go of Vesta's wrist and clutched her throat, using her weight to pin Vesta to the ground. Vesta wrapped her hands around Sevet's arms, struggling to relieve the pressure from her airway.

"If I can't have your power, no one will."

Vesta watched someone slip a scalpel-like blade into Sevet's hand. Letting go of Vesta's neck, Sevet reared and then brought the blade straight at her chest.

A loud crack vibrated through the room. Warm blood soaked into Vesta's clothes. Blood that belonged to Sevet.

The knife tip had snapped against some invisible force and lodged in Sevet's flesh.

The Commander screamed. Between them, Vesta watched the remnants of a translucent shield fade away.

She silently thanked Vahza for the protection and wished she could ask Mic Rorren about it. No book or myth ever mentioned protection as a gift of the Aux Katan.

"I am powerful. All I must do to vex you is breathe," Vesta said.

Sevet pulled the blade from her hand, screaming in rage.

Ignoring her wound, the Commander latched on to Vesta's hair and pulled, exposing Vesta's neck. In vain. The strange shield would protect her and they both knew it.

"For you then, a fate worse than death." Sevet's hot breath grazed Vesta's cheek.

Sevet tugged her hair but Vesta laughed.

"Ready the transport." Sevet released her hold once the guards appeared. As they pushed her down the corridor, Vesta made sure to continue laughing loud enough for the Commander to hear.

CHAPTER 43

THE RAIN WAS INVISIBLE against the fringe of clouds, but Rorren heard it pounding the starship's hull as they descended into the capital city of Cardinal World Alpha.

The crisp, white towers of Tarazi were coated in a thin gruel of moisture, but the marble still glistened under the sun as spectacularly as he remembered.

The storm brought them down with a gluey suction that pulled local sky-buses and cargo ships into the flight lanes alongside them. Turbulence made Rorren's passengers restless.

"Quiet down!" He yelled to the prisoners behind the security shield in the aft cargo bay.

"I bet we get a commendation." The young soldier at Mic Rorren's side mentioned for the millionth time since leaving the Aklaren stronghold.

Behind the cell bars, Hevcar Duronilan sneered at them.

Rorren had done what he set out to, gaining nothing for his accomplishments but a soul-crushing numbness.

He insisted on delivering the dangerous prisoner to the Galactic Order personally. Tagion must have caught wind because before Rorren knew it, he received summons to all kinds of formal galas and high-level conferences.

He looked at his com badge, ringing from the same number again. He ignored it for the twentieth time.

Despite his numbness, there was a spec of curiosity growing inside Rorren. He wondered about his old academy friend turned leader of the free universe. He wanted to see the wonders of the Galactic Order and the good they had done since he left them for Desandor.

Instead of landing in the capital city, orders reversed their course to outer space.

Rorren's appetite to explore the human capital went unsatisfied, tainting his numbness with irritation.

They lifted through the rain clouds.

The young cadet must have seen Rorren's curiosity.

"The Lement Shield only lowers twice a day," he said. "It's going back up in twenty minutes, so they want us at Tallum Station."

Rorren heard rumors of the Lement Shield, an intricate network of satellites connected around the planet to protect it from invaders. A marvel of the new Galactic Order. Apparently, its implementation had been successful.

Struck Rorren at that moment, how little difference there was between a shield and a cage.

His com badge rang again and he pressed dismiss for the twenty-first time.

The dark, sleek lines of the Tallum Nebula Space Station filled the ship's viewscreen. The station was enormous and the crescent curve of the hull now almost connected with itself. At the center, lights from the cityscape flickered against an environment of churning gases. The deep reds and purples of the nebula obscured the view of Alpha's nearest star as the ship fell into the station's shadow.

Something about the new design of the station bothered him. The general architecture looked human enough, but the spikes and ridges of black metal whispered of Scorth technology.

The sight of anything Scorth made him sick.

He swallowed his nausea and readied the prisoners for landing.

He relished the mundane task of shackling Hevcar and escorted him down the docking ramp.

The welcome waiting there for Rorren, the pageantry and spectacle, was a conspiracy against him and the numbness inside.

The Premier of the Galaxy, Tagion Krave, stood before a row of soldiers in dress uniform, his white robes a beacon against the charcoal platform. Next to him, in a contrasting black bodice, Sevet Neece smiled as Rorren approached.

"General Rorren, boy, are we glad to have you here," Tagion said. He bypassed the still sneering Hevcar and pulled Rorren in for a hug.

"You wasted no time. Bringing in one of our most wanted after only two months. You make the rest of us look bad," Tagion sent a sidelong glance to Sevet, "isn't that true, Commander?"

Sevet's jaw clenched briefly before ordering her guard to take Hevcar into custody.

"Walk with me." Tagion turned and Rorren followed.

The line of soldiers, though motionless, silently celebrated Mic Rorren's triumph as he passed them, tongues all but physically hanging out when the Premier strutted by.

By his swagger, Rorren could tell Tagion both relished it and took it for granted.

"I was sorry to hear about your wife. Sevet told me. She said the Aklaren murdered her. You've done well to avenge her." Tagion inclined his head toward the marauders marching onto the barge bound for Isken prison.

Rorren pictured the famous compound—surrounded by seas on all sides and home to the galaxy's most dangerous criminals. Rorren found it easier to think about the evil in that place than about the memory of his wife.

"I still have a long way to go," Rorren said.

Tagion stopped.

"Peanuts. We need you here. I have bigger plans for you."

That Tagion shrugged off the violence and killing done by the Aklaren as "peanuts" overpowered Rorren's numbness enough to raise his temper.

"This is the future." Tagion extended his hands toward the windows. "This station is not just the nebula mining operation anymore. It now serves as our military headquarters. No one is getting past that shield unless they stop here first. We know Scorth hate space battles."

Tagion's green eyes flashed as he led Rorren along the corridor windows. The station's crescent curve filled the glass, making Rorren feel as insignificant as when he stood at the shore of the sand seas.

"I want you here, General," Tagion said. Rorren glanced at Sevet but her attention stayed on the path ahead.

"I know what you'll say but we need you here. One of the greatest Generals the Cardinal Worlds have ever known, just like your father. Given your family's history with the Scorth, there is no one I trust more with ensuring the safety of our people."

His father.

The first person he had murdered. Not the last.

Tagion put his hand on Rorren's shoulder and brought his head nearer.

"You don't want to go down there. I know you. Too many memories down there."

Tagion could still read him like a book.

"Sevet is here to keep you company," he added. The comment drew a laser glare from the Commander.

Rorren cared about nothing but had he not been so dead inside, he might have picked up on the underpinnings between the Premier and Commander.

As long as he didn't have to see his family, and as long as he was far enough away to keep them from danger, Tallum Station was as good as anywhere.

He'd cleaned up the Aklaren mess. There was nothing for him on De-sandor or any of the Cardinal Worlds.

"I always did hate space living," Rorren said, "but I could never say no to a friend, especially one that protects the free galaxy."

Tagion grinned, shook Rorren's hand and then slapped his back. Rorren smiled, but it was the smile of an imposter.

"Good, because we have a problem and I know you can solve it."

Rorren ignored the twenty millionth call from his sister and followed Tagion toward the city of blinking lights at the station's center.

Vesta lifted the crate and poured the contents over the edge of the trolly, wishing she could not feel the strain in her muscles or bruised forearms. The dead gray in the wall of the mine coated individual stones in a powder that clung to every inch of her skin as she gathered them into the crate.

When she swiped her hand across her forehead, the powder smeared and seeped in, a constant reminder of the hell around her.

Scorth children all knew of the diamond mines. Parents used the stories to instill fear in misbehaving youth.

But they weren't just stories.

There was little terror for Vesta, safe in her palace bed beneath fresh white sheets. As a child, she knew nothing of the horrors of its reality.

Months passed and time became the enemy.

A fear like she'd never known permeated her tired muscles.

She swallowed, gagging on the soot and dust in her throat.

The Ovokar shoved her along the path toward the upper bed, where men, women and children worked with picks and hammers to loosen the stone.

The delicate diamonds could only be removed and refined by hand—a grueling and dirty process. The Scorth spent centuries refining the techniques. The fact those techniques were akin to sadistic torture became a fringe benefit used by Vesta's mother and other royal families.

"Es arrin lu roe takit he cent," the Ovokar shouted from above.

Her Scorth was rusty but once she relaxed, the words flowed to her.

You need to clear this bed by dusk.

No light ever entered the mines, so Vesta could not tell morning from night.

The Ovokar stalked the edge of the quarry. The Scorth manager didn't carry a whip as some ancient overlord might, but it wouldn't have made a difference to Vesta if he had. That her people had been sentenced to this for centuries turned her blood cold.

The crash of colliding boulders, followed by a string of curses from the overseer, made her turn away from her pick. Across the mine, a young boy and girl, not more than teenagers, narrowly escaped the onslaught of stone from an overturned cart. They emerged, dust and scratches covering their arms and faces.

Luha must have been like those children once. Vesta ignored the pain of that memory.

The Ovokar raised a fist and brought it down, pummeling the boy for spilling the precious stone. The girl tried to pull him off, but the soldier pushed her aside and she landed hard on the stone.

The exhaustion that tore up Vesta's every muscle vanished in the wake of her rage. She willed her body forward, throwing herself between the boy and the Ovokar. His fists attacked her but she dodged left. Gathering her wits, she powered forward and into the protruding gut of the overseer.

He gasped, tumbling over, and cursed again.

Vesta pulled the boy to his feet.

"Run."

The boy nodded, tugging on his companion's torn shirt and the two children fled.

The Ovokar lifted his massive frame and Vesta prepared to continue the battle. Instead, he barked a request for reinforcements into the communicator at his shoulder.

"It's the grinder for you," he sneered.

Too many days in the grinder meant a slow and painful death, but Vesta didn't care. She dug her heels into the ground, straining the strap at her ankle that prevented her from using her power. All Scorth prisoners in the mines wore one. Sevet must have modeled her device after them.

The Ovokar laughed at her actions, at their futileness. His eyes widened, laughter stopping abruptly. The massive frame dropped to the ground, turning into a languid lump.

Behind him, Vesta found the frame of a petite old woman with a heavy stone in hand, face half hidden beneath a tattered hood. The stone had done its job and the woman dropped it.

"You must follow me," she said.

Vesta planted her heels.

"Stubborn girl, I'm trying to save your life."

Vesta folded her arms. Two months in the mines taught her not to trust anyone, especially those who openly offered help.

The woman peeled away her hood, revealing a head of chestnut hair, white at the temples, pulled into a bun. A few curled strands wiggled free of the pins.

"You are human," Vesta said.

"And you are a stater of the obvious."

Vesta stepped toward her, avoiding the limp body of the Ovokar.

"I meant, I am surprised a human would risk her life for a Scorth."

"I've been looking for you. I've come up from tos par loon to fetch you." There was an urgency in her tone. The woman reset her hood and scanned the area for signs of danger.

The human must have been in the mines for ages, at least by human years. Vesta guessed she was in her early sixties, though she looked like a Scorth woman of at least two hundred.

"Tos par loon is a myth," Vesta said.

The woman stepped close, her wrinkled hand latched onto Vesta's wrist. Vesta should have pulled away. Common sense dictated a hasty retreat, but something in the woman's spirit hooked her.

"You better hope it's not because that *myth* is the only thing that can save your unborn child."

Vesta's mouth gaped.

"Sometimes, in the mines, we look out for each other. That wasn't the first time you have helped someone in need. It does not go unnoticed. And besides, I help all the expectant mothers."

The human pulled her forward, but Vesta froze in place. Her mind cranked roughly, busy deciding which part of what just happened most shocked her.

"Come," the woman coaxed.

Vesta's feet listened. In a kind of delirium, she allowed the human to drag her deeper into the mine shaft than any Ovokar dared to go.

The human woman removed a gemstone beneath the rags she wore. The glow from her hand grew and lighted the path before them. *Tos par loon. The diamond light.*

Vesta allowed herself a measure of hope for the first time in months.

When the woman resumed walking, Vesta stopped her by touching her arm. The touch surprised the human.

"Who are you?" Vesta asked.

She smiled, wrapping her fingers over Vesta's. Such a touch was uncommon for Scorth strangers but unheard of between Scorth and humans.

"I could ask you the same thing."

"I am Vesta."

"My name is Lelia but they call me kara zati."

Conspicuous woman.

That she had a Scorth nickname made Vesta more suspicious and confused.

The kara zati held the diamond above her head and the light flickered around them.

"Let's hurry. We have a long way yet and not much light left in this stone."

Vesta stumbled over hidden potholes and scratched herself against jagged stone, endeavoring to decide if the human was right about her condition while at the same time discounting the possibility.

Lelia moved through the darkness with a skill that suggested she'd made the trek numerous times.

Even with the flicker of the diamond growing dim, Vesta caught glimpses of curved beams upholding millions of tons of rock and jewel. The weight oppressed her lungs and the dank air prevented her from adequately filling them.

Her deathshade tainted eye could see under the suns of Desandor, but she struggled to navigate the terrain in the pitch of surrounding stone.

She reached out in blind faith and groped for the robes of the human woman. Finding them, Vesta latched on, hating her dependence on the stranger.

The tracks for the mine carts ended, leaving Vesta no landmarks to tell apart one stone bend from another.

Lelia stopped and Vesta stumbled into her. Vesta apologized and took advantage of the delay by loosening the rags at her neck. Sweat balled up and trickled down her skin as they drew nearer to Parkell's molten core.

"Do you hear that?" Vesta strained to hear the old woman's whisper and then quieted her breathing to listen. No sounds, more like vibrations, started low and sizzled. A few strands of dust powder dropped from cracks in the beams.

Vesta held tight to the rags of the old woman as the light from the stone faded and plumes of dust consumed them. The air choked her but she darted out of the path of crushing rubble. She lost her footing and pebbles struck her arms and back. Vesta reared, pushing Lelia out of the path of danger. Using her body as a shield over the human, she waited until the tremors stopped.

Silence consumed them and Vesta felt a tug on her arm.

Lelia helped her up from the debris. Luck, it seemed, saved them. The boulders left a crevice around them just wide enough to spare their lives.

"This way," Lelia said, coughing. The human guided her through corridors and tunnels, bursts of air filling Vesta's lungs without the taint of mine dust and decay.

A faint flicker of light came at her from the core of darkness at the end of the circular shaft. Like a street light at an intersection that hung suspended in midair, the globes inside the walls brightened the murky caves.

They neared the source and the air crisped to the point it almost smelled fresh.

The light drained from the gemstone and Lelia tossed it aside. The shock of the action sobered Vesta. Here, the light gave gems their value and though a single stone could purchase grand treasures, once used up, Lelia cast it away like garbage.

As they traveled, walls of stone transformed into walls of solid diamond. The diamonds pumped out light and a few tunnels further, Vesta marveled at entire walls surrounding them as bright as day. The kara zati drew her hand across a crevice in the wall, fingers translucent against the light.

"What secrets you are to learn," Lelia said.

Her eyes narrowed, mischievous, and she vanished through the crack in the wall. Vesta steeled her courage, inhaled and slipped in behind Lelia. The narrow tunnel of light led her to an enormous cavern. A breeze of jungle air tossed her hair and filled her lungs. She shielded her eyes from a glow above as bright as a yellow dwarf star.

She couldn't tell where the wind came from but relished its caress against her skin.

Interrupting Vesta's reverie, Lelia brought her to a small Sandorian-looking village. Rudimentary structures made from old mine beams and cart rails littered the landscape—not beautiful but modest and well-built.

Vesta saw two or three Scorth men, some women and many children. She couldn't remember seeing so many Scorth children together since she attended the Advent.

"We call them na see tos par loon."

Children of the diamond light.

Lelia weaved through the various buildings, greeting Scorth women and their children with nods and smiles.

"The Ovokar don't know about the children and they don't keep track of who is who," Lelia said. "We rotate the children, so not all of them work all the time. It's risky, but it buys us some freedom."

A Scorth man approached, his long white hair blowing over his shoulders, his piercing eyes shooting through Vesta. For an instant, Vesta found something familiar about his face.

"Light and air from the surface are channeled through diamonds tunnels and into these caverns, like an oasis in the dark," the old Scorth man said. "Our ancestors stumbled upon this phenomenon, but the kara zati organized them into a refuge for mothers and families sent to the mines."

Lelia lowered her head as if embarrassed by what she had created for the people.

Vesta took in the village.

The people.

Something intangible swelled within her.

Not just *the* people.

Her people.

"The earth moves and the light caverns change. We are constantly chasing the oasis," Lelia said. She smiled at Vesta and then fell victim to a coughing fit. The old Scorth man touched her shoulder, hand swaying to the convulsions of Lelia's body. Vesta wanted to think the cough was residual from the cave-in they had just experienced, but the deep rasp told her otherwise.

The Scorth man bent toward the human woman and a necklace dropped from his shirt. Vesta recognized the necklace. The jem once belonged to Vexen Layeyre, her father.

"Kara zati has brought you here to have your child but you, in return, must keep this place secret," he said.

Vesta locked her jaw and frowned. How did these people know what she had only begun to suspect?

The old man left them and Lelia guided Vesta to a rough but solid shack and cot in a quiet corner of the day-bright cavern. Lelia gestured to a chunk of bread and a pitcher deposited on a crooked table.

"Rest now. Tomorrow, we put you to work."

"Kara zati," Vesta called and the human turned to her. "I am no stranger to human kindness but thank you for this."

Lelia inclined her head.

"Gratitude from a Scorth. You're an odd duck." Lelia left the shack, chuckling to herself. Vesta wondered what made a duck odd and why humans used so many bird references. Mic Rorren would have explained. She missed him.

For the first time since being ripped away from her home and husband, she slept well.

CHAPTER 44

THE PIRATE SHIPS FLEW at Rorren from across the screen and he remembered him how much fun leading a mission could be.

"Open the dock," he ordered.

Ansgar lifted an eyebrow, offsetting his cherub cheeks and full lips with its sharp line.

"Do it," Rorren said.

The pirate ships advanced in curves of gradual descent. They plunged while Rorren watched the dock grow to meet them. The steel beams of the station crisscrossed above the vessels, each shimmering with rays of the nebula's refracted light.

"We are being boarded," Ensign Ansgar growled at Rorren. The kid had a lot to learn.

Rorren leaned against the plush of the command seat and clicked on Tallum Station's PA system.

"Security personnel, join me in docking bay twelve."

Indifferent to the scowl of the Ensign, Rorren grabbed the standard-issue staff and handgun. Ansgar copied the actions.

"Time to put the rebels out of business," Rorren said.

With his team of top soldiers, Rorren stormed the docking bay. He set the trap with precision, just like hunting Rocbulls on Desandor.

He hadn't been in command for years but that didn't matter. Military strategy came to him naturally, more than sand farming ever had. That part of his life seemed like a strange dream that didn't belong.

With soldiers stationed along the overhead catwalks and behind crates surrounding the enemy ships, Rorren waited for action.

The pirate ship extended its landing platform but the traitors failed to appear. He heard no sound of footsteps down the plank. Rorren inched around the steel crate and stole a glance. Empty. These pirates were no fools.

He lifted his eyes upward and saw bodies swaying down zip lines, racing at them and then smashing into his soldiers.

Rorren didn't know how they managed to exit the ship without being detected, but he didn't have time to worry about that. He shouted commands over the private channel.

Gunfire echoed around them, the cackle of bullets dipping in rhythm to Rorren's strategic repositioning of his elite force. Barrels of nebula ore and precious metals crashed in thunderous booms across the tarmac, victims of battle. Sparks flew from the ceiling between flashes of light and dark. For an instant, chaos reigned.

Rorren knew how to command his troops and take charge of the situation. A half-hour longer and the battle was over.

Rorren watched as his soldiers rounded up and then encircled the ragtag group with an expert intensity.

On their knees, hands held behind their heads, Rorren discovered the pirates were just kids. Hardly a triumph worthy of their efforts. As Rorren approached to parlay with the leader, he couldn't help but admire them.

These kids, with their crude weapons, had given the Order problems for months.

"The Premier is not pleased with you," Rorren began. "You've cost him millions with these skirmishes. You'll be taken to Isken. What I can't understand is why you would risk that to fight a battle you were bound to lose."

One of the rebels stood up.

"What I don't understand is how *you* can serve them, Mic Rorren."

Ansgar aimed his veer rifled at the outspoken outlaw. Intrigued, Rorren moved through the kneeling faction until he reached the boy. A familiar face stared up at him. A gut punch. Metra would not be pleased.

"Take them to the prison transport but leave this one with me."

Rorren didn't take his eyes off Jon as the docking bay emptied of soldiers and rebels.

"You're hurting the Cardinal Worlds with these attacks. Is that what you want?" Rorren asked.

Jon was still young, couldn't be more than 23, but his face had aged. He needed a shave and shower.

"So, you believe the lies now?" Jon laughed, a hollow sound to Rorren's ears. "Where's the Scorth witch? I liked her."

Rorren forced himself not to think of her. It was the only way to move forward.

"Isken isn't where I wanted you to end up. Why did you do it?"

Jon's lower jaw jutted forward with a cockiness Rorren remembered.

"I'm going to let you in on a not-so-well-kept secret. Tagion Krave is a murderer and a liar."

Rorren objected but that didn't stop Jon.

"Sevet Neece is a psychopath. Neither of them cares about us or the Cardinal Worlds. Any worlds. They only want power, control, and slaves."

Jon believed what he was saying and his passion left Rorren incredulous.

"I don't know who you've fallen in with but you're wrong. It's because of Tagion that we cleaned up the Aklaren mess. Desandor is free of that threat. I'm here on Tallum to make sure the resources from the nebula make it to the people who need them."

Jon's words continued to pour out like dragon fire.

"Tagion pays the Aklaren to do his bidding. He hordes the resources from the nebula so he and his friends stay rich. He is not a supporter of the people. He is an oppressor and worse. There are rumors of experiments on Tallum Station. Inhuman and wrong. He is not your friend, Mic Rorren."

Rorren clicked his com.

"Bringing the last prisoner up now." Rorren lifted Jon by the arm and pushed him toward the prison transport. "I'm sorry for Metra's sake that I have to turn you in."

"You'd see the truth if your Scorth witch was here. I'm sorry for your sake, she's not," Jon replied.

Rorren heard the words but didn't let them in. He couldn't. If he did, he was afraid he might break. Being General again was the only thing holding him together. He wasn't ready to give it up. Not for some lies from the lips of a naïve kid.

"I'll do what I can to keep you out of Isken," Rorren said as he released Jon into the custody of one of his men. The transport ship doors closed. Even after Rorren could no longer see Jon, the look on the kid's face haunted him.

Vesta traveled to the surface once per moon cycle. The kara zati insisted that expectant mothers not risk working in the deep mines and only surface to appease the Ovokars. Vesta was not accustomed to watching others do the work.

She blamed Mic Rorren for it.

The more she immersed herself in the village of diamond light, the more rage burned inside her.

For this, she also blamed Mic Rorren.

The influence of Lelia on this group of Scorth was noticeable. They were still Scorth, but Vesta could see the fringes of change taking place. They had been forced to work together for survival. As the ingrained desire for riches dissipated, Vesta could see it replaced by a serenity she knew well.

These people, *her* people, had the fire sword inside them. She knew it.

"You never saw Ragora in its glory," Vesta heard a woman tell her young child as she passed.

"It used to be filled with lush greenery and fresh salt in the air from the seas." The woman's porcelain face turned sullen. The way Scorth usually looked. "Until the humans took over and scorched everything."

Vesta entered Lelia's tent with hands fisted.

The old Scorth man nodded when she entered. She'd learned his name was Nalex Zyne. A familiar name she refused to acknowledge.

Lelia gestured for Vesta to sit on the other side of her small, half-moon table. She brewed a batch of hot tresacoi tea and poured it into each glass. Vesta savored the sweet taste as it lingered on her lips. Where the old human had gotten such a treat was a mystery.

Nalex must have seen her curiosity because he said, "They sometimes give gifts to kara zati for saving their lives."

Lelia smirked, waving her hand through the air.

"Unnecessary."

"You rescue Scorth and they give freely of their wealth. This does not sound like the Ragora I remember," Vesta said.

Nalex set his cup—chipped on one side—on the table. He crossed his legs beneath him and his hands rested on his knees. He looked like pictures of wise old Fire-Scar sages Vesta had seen in banned books in the royal vault.

"How old were you when you last saw the home world?" Nalex asked.

"It was nearly a century ago."

"Ah, then we were still under Scorth rule. Talie was Queen. Our last Queen."

Vesta took another sip of tea as the mention of her mother unsettled her stomach.

Nalex leaned forward.

"You are Vesta Layeyre, are you not? Heir to the Scorth throne."

Vesta snapped her eyes to the old man. From the corner of her vision, she saw Lelia's mouth drop.

"I am not."

Nalex reached around and unchained the necklace. He placed the jewel in the palm of his hand and extended it toward her.

"Then, this is not your family jewel?"

Vesta hated how much she wanted it. Unable to fight the urge, she snatched her necklace from him. To touch it again, her last connection to her father and granda, stirred emotions in her that she loathed.

"That line was broken long ago." The admission caught in her throat.

The intensity of his gaze reminded her of another. The look of a young girl the Queen had sent to the slave mines. Luha Zyne.

Vesta wanted to ask about her, but in the mines to speak of family meant putting their lives in danger. Too many had been sent here for refusing to denounce loved ones already sentenced. Deep inside the moon's core, Vesta understood that naming names was forbidden. It awoke something inside her. Perhaps her people cared more deeply about each other than anyone realized.

"Yes. I am Luha's father," Nalex said. "She died here shortly after we arrived. They sent her to work in the grinder because she was small enough to pick stones from the gears. The humans seduced her brother. He is Ovokar now, but at least he lives."

Lelia reached across the table, fingers searching but stopping before touching Nalex. They both knew the danger Nalex had just put his son in by uttering even that much.

Still reeling from the guilt of having caused the death of her childhood friend, Vesta wrapped her fingers around the jewel. A jewel once meant for Luha's escape.

"You are the Queen and Aux Katan," Nalex said.

He looked at her with new eyes, his sorrow replaced by what Vesta hated even more. Hope.

"I am no one and nothing except the murderer of your daughter," Vesta said.

Lelia withdrew her hand from the table, gaze fixated on Vesta.

"You are no murderer, Queen of the Scorth," Lelia said, her passion draining her face of color.

The human and the old Scorth sat there, motionless, burdening her with a painful truth. Vesta left them, withdrawing to a dark corner of the cavern. The light trailed through the walls, following after her.

She already knew her destiny. Vesta glimpsed Vahza's image reflected briefly in the sparkling diamond walls.

"You wonder how we knew you were pregnant?" Lelia approached, her voice causing the image to vanish. "Your unborn protects you. I watched it happen many times when you arrived. It happened during the cave-in."

"What?" Vesta asked the question but suspected the answer.

"There are legends about the Fire-Scar Warriors. You may not be able to access your power but your child can. The child protected you even before you came here. Is it not true?"

Vesta put a hand to her stomach. The bulge wasn't noticeable beneath her rags, but she carried Mic Rorren's child. The magnitude of that fact threatened to knock her on her sideways every time she thought about it.

"There is an evil human woman who dissects our kind for power. She tried with me and failed," Vesta said.

Lelia nodded and then coughed. What an agonizing death Luha must have endured, Vesta thought. The curse of the grinder. A fate awaiting the kara zati.

Vesta watched families gather in the distance. Mothers chatted as Scorth and human children played together.

"I cannot lead them. I do not know how."

Lelia took Vesta to the middle of the village square. The old human woman was as conspicuous as her Scorth name suggested. The moment Lelia appeared, a crowd collected around her, drawn by mysterious magic.

"This is Vesta Layeyre," Lelia said.

Vesta heard gasps and a low murmur travel through the crowd. Then, the first knee dropped. Others followed.

"The rightful ruler of Ragora," someone shouted. The murmur turned into a buzz of excitement.

"She abandoned us," another said.

"She is a traitor."

The crowd argued until Lelia spoke again.

"She is Aux Katan."

Everyone went quiet. All knees bent and heads bowed to Vesta, including Lelia's. The actions left Vesta's head spinning. Looking down at the old woman, she remembered everything Rorren taught her.

"We must first understand that no one is above anyone here." Vesta extended her hand to Lelia and helped the old woman from her knees.

"You must next understand that you all have the power of the Fire-Scar inside you."

The crowd grew, now reaching to the outskirts of the makeshift shacks. All eyes were on Vesta. All filled with hope. Nalex appeared by her side.

"Teach us, my Queen. Tell us, what do we do?"

She met the gaze of each one of her people as far as her one good eye allowed. She had run from her birthright for a century.

No more.

"We take back Ragora."

CHAPTER 45

THE SILENCE OF THE refuge in the middle of one of Cardinal World Beta's famous farming communities filled Rorren with relief and desolation. The silence gave the illusion of safety and that the Premier was in no danger. Sevet, seated next to him around the oblong negotiations table, reminded him of the beauty and feminine companionship he had lost.

The remnant of daylight pouring through massive skylights coated fields of cabbage and mint beyond the windows with a shine worthy of images he'd seen of Ragora. Beta was a slice of heaven and the reason his youngest sister, Ivy, chose the planet for her home.

Rorren stood for long, blank minutes at the edge of the room, scanning for threats and reassuring himself his sister had no way of knowing he was there.

"General Rorren resolved our most immediate rebel problem, but we can't risk any more factions popping up on Beta or any Cardinal World, would you agree?" Tagion was saying to the elite leaders of government. There were only half a dozen diplomats in the room, all nodding.

"The threat of a Scorth attack is still real. We continue to have skirmishes with them, so we must stay united."

Clouds wrapped the sky and descended into a fog, drowning out sunlight and causing a shadow to creep between cultivated farm rows and over Rorren's mind. Skirmishes with the Scorth? He scanned his memory for reports of such attacks. None had found their way to his desk.

News from Ragora was sparse, save for the imports of goods and jewels that flowed without interruption. These reports made Rorren think trade between the two worlds was thriving and without incident.

Either he was out of the loop or Tagion was lying.

The meeting concluded with a real-estate deal guaranteed to make Tagion and the others at the table rich at the expense of Beta's rural slice of heaven. He could hear his sister's rant already and expected another message from her as soon as the deal went public.

He watched the Beta officials exit and positioned his troops around the Premier, just out of sight but vigilant. He thought how different being a Field General during the Scorth war was, being part of the action instead of a stooge to his best friend. *You*—he thought—*whoever you are, I will never find you again. The one that kept me alive. The one that struggled and cared and believed in something. You found me on Desandor but now you are lost forever.*

He'd never given in to hopelessness but standing at the window next to Sevet, he understood her completely for the first time. She had given up long ago.

They walked into the fog, side by side, behind the Premier. Rorren mustered only an indifferent astonishment when the low clouds parted and the wings of a takdull knocked them down. Its fanged snout snapped at them, capturing one of his men by the arm and throwing its head back as it swallowed the man whole.

Rorren, first to his feet, raised his head and his gun to face the winged scourge of Beta's farmers. Sevet held her ground beside him, corralling the creature while Rorren's soldiers worked to unfold a Betanese takdull net.

Sevet was a competent fighter, though not as physically powerful as Rorren's dead wife. Still, to have her there shook him. He faltered and the takdull lunged, wing hitting him. The impact shot him across the field. Through the fog, he saw its fang sink into Sevet's leg. The beast pulled her up into the air.

Rorren was too far away to intervene. Across the fog-laced field, he spotted Tagion. All masks were gone. The Premier set intent eyes on the monster, muscles tensed, body and mind disciplined and working together. The most un-Tagion-like pose he could remember. Rorren recognized the determination. There was no way *that* man was letting *that* woman die.

He watched Tagion charge forward and stab the beast through the leg with a Galactic Order staff. The creature screamed, stunned by the action as much as everyone else. The takdull lost its hold on Sevet and she fell through the air into Tagion's waiting arms.

They looked at each other, a gaze that pulled Rorren through memory. He should have focused on the battle. He should have directed his soldiers as they forced the takdull into the net. Instead, he watched Tagion caress Sevet's cheek and kiss her tenderly.

She fought him off but not in a cute, maddening way as Vesta had the first time Rorren kissed her.

Sevet raged. Her scowl swallowed a deep heartbreak. The medical team carried her away. Tagion was left alone, helpless, shoulders slumped with guilt.

Rorren pulled himself upward, finding a bittersweet satisfaction in the fact that love seemed to deceive everyone in the universe.

Any thought he had of visiting his sister vanished at that moment.

───────

Vesta worked the mine with a new purpose. The dust that stung her eyes didn't bother her as it had when she first arrived. She hammered away at the diamond spikes in the caves, driving the tool with the same drive growing inside—a drive to free her people. An urge like on Desandor with Reen-hara, but deeper and more urgent than before.

The kara zati worked by her side. The human woman refused to let Vesta venture more than ten paces from her when their turn to work the surface arrived. The old human woman knew how to work hard. Though she looked thin and frail, she had surprising strength in her, visible in the still-toned muscles of her arms.

The human toiling in the harshest conditions was a pathetic sight, considering she should be enjoying her golden years on a beach somewhere. As much as it wounded Vesta to see Lelia like that, witnessing the soot and grim caked to young children as they crawled through suffocating tunnels was most unbearable. The Ovokar afforded them no mercy because they were children.

Norn, Ovokar of the South Beds, descended from his perch and lifted one of the children by the arm.

"Et gliten el tos Hecick," he ordered.

You are needed in the Grinder.

The boy, not more than ten, did not take his eyes off the Ovokar but did not answer. Vesta abandoned her post and moved to interrupt, but Lelia arrived first.

"I will go," the kara zati said. "I am more experienced than the boy. I will increase your output."

Norn frowned, rubbed fingers over his smooth, square jaw and nodded. He released his hold on the boy and gestured for Lelia to follow.

Vesta grabbed her arm.

"You cannot go. The Grinder has already tainted you."

The wrinkles of Lelia's face smoothed—a kind of mirth replaced them.

"Never argue with a stubborn human woman." She winked at Vesta and then stumbled after the Ovokar.

Vesta balled her hands into fists, debating the merits of a physical fight.

She barely noticed Amul Torat when he appeared at her side.

"Why do you think we listen to a human? Why do you think we call her the kara zati?" Amul asked. He stood nearly as tall as Rorren, a physically impressive man with a deep scar near the cleft in his chin.

She heard him speaking, but concern and anger blurred everything except the thought of attacking the Ovokar.

"This is not the first time she has spared one of our children. Nor the hundredth."

His hand touched her shoulder. Startled, she turned, curious to see what could inspire such a hardened Scorth man to show affection.

"Our young have a future free from sickness because of her. We owe her much."

"She needs a doctor. There may still be time to save her if we can escape," Vesta said.

Amul nodded, dropping his hand from her shoulder.

"That is dangerous talk."

Vesta's dangerous talk did not stop there.

Two days later, she sat at the head of the circle of elders, eyes trained on the small fire. Despite the danger, she gathered them, assembling the strongest of those trapped in the mines in the same place.

Few Scorth were amiable to her words, but those who had been touched by kara zati gave her the courtesy of listening. As Vesta spoke to them, she found the people she remembered. Empty, hard and bitter because the riches they worked to attain all went to the humans.

"It is impossible," said Amul Torat. The Torat family had long been known for producing strong and clever warriors. She needed him in her council of the new republic if they had any chance of success.

"Even if you somehow disable the shackles and overtake the mines, you cannot go up against the Galactic Order on Ragora. They outnumber us and outgun us two to one."

Vesta drew in a breath to calm herself. The shackle at her ankle blocked her from using her power, but it could not stop her from feeling it. Her people would feel it too. It would grow inside them just like the life growing inside of her.

Nalex handed her a worn book like the one Rorren used. She opened the wrinkled pages and smiled. Her actions drew curious glances.

"This was smuggled to us by the kara zati. A banned text on the Aux Katan." She held up the pages for all to see. The creed of the Fire-Scar Warriors written in the language of the ancients caused a quiver of silence in the circle.

Vesta read the words.

"Lualth tu'ah. Treasure the spirit that gives us strength."

She turned the page.

"Lualth comen daxu. Treasure the bond of comrades."

Aware what she spoke would have labeled her a heretic by her mother and Scorth society, she pressed on. No one objected. A new dawn was upon them.

"Lualth ukish zall, camu, cree wyze. Above riches, treasure truth, virtue, and freewill."

Amul tossed kindling on the fire, shaking his head.

"Outdated and disproven rubbish. Truth, virtue, and freewill will not feed our bellies or shield us from gunfire."

Many nodded. Too many.

"This shall be the creed of our new republic. It will not fail us. I will not fail if you join me," Vesta said.

She stared into a dozen grave but calm faces. She stood before them, letting them study her—showing them she had nothing to hide, not even her weariness from life in the mines.

Nalex stood first and then Lelia almost in unison. Others followed.

Amul moved to the edge of his seat but one of the elders stopped him.

"No, Amul," he said, "if you join her, you betray your heritage. There is no room for doubt."

Vesta closed the book and met the eyes of each around the fire. Lelia looked as though she wished to speak but she said nothing, instead encouraging Vesta with a nod.

"There is always doubt. Without it, there is no courage," Vesta said. "Many feel as Amul and the elders do. But our Scorth heritage includes the Aux Katan, try as you wish to deny it."

Vesta extended her hand to Amul.

"Doubt now, but join us and find your courage."

Vesta heard gasps among the group of forward thinkers. To extend such an open invitation to a rival had not been seen in a thousand years.

Amul hesitated and glanced away as if hoping the move would end the struggle visible in the tense muscles under the skin of his face.

He took her forearm, sealing the pack with a slap.

"Better to pin our hopes on a rag warrior than to have no hopes at all," Amul said.

Vesta smiled and found her expression to be contagious. Nalex copied her smile and Lelia's eyes, dulled by years of living in the mines, brightened.

With her small council of allies, they faced the difficult days and weeks with a growing perseverance.

Vesta never refused her turn to work the mines, much to the chagrin of the kara zati. As the time drew near for the birth of her child, Vesta knew she would no longer be able to complete her shifts. She determined to show her people that she cared by lightening their load in other ways—by watching the children, cooking and cleaning, or training warriors to use a menti blade. No domestic task was beneath her. No Queen had ever been a servant of the people.

The rewards came step-by-step, day after day, with painful slowness.

Undoing the violent and selfish culture of Ragora drilled into each of her people was not a small task, even for a Fire-Scar Warrior. As Vesta trained them—as she taught them to treasure intangible things and tap into their own power—she gained a new appreciation for Mic Rorren.

Mic Rorren.

She cradled her stomach when she thought of him. She longed for his embrace and held bitterness at bay because he knew nothing of his child.

The Ovokar must have sensed something brewing because the electric ends of their prodding sticks bruised more often and with more aggression. Aching muscles, empty stomachs, and outbreaks of disagreement between Vesta's squabbling counselors tempted her to give up.

Mic Rorren never gave up on her.

She kept fighting.

The spirit of the *tu'ah* touched not only those living in the chamber of diamond light but also began to spread. The cavern attracted people from the western and northern mines. Soldiers willing to fight in Vesta's army.

Growing numbers forced them to seek out immense caverns of diamond light and expand operations.

The time to overtake the mine drew near.

"You must wait until after your child is born," Lelia said one quiet night. Even the human sensed that the time to strike was upon them.

Vesta squeezed Lelia's arm.

Like Mic Rorren, the human had wormed her way into Vesta's affections.

Lelia had become a more trusted advisor to Vesta than even Amul Torat. If the people cared that their Queen took advice from a human, she heard no objections.

The kara zati had become one of them.

Vesta weighed Lelia's words carefully.

"Bring him to me," she told Nalex. Lelia sighed and frowned. Nalex visibly swallowed.

"I do not know, my Queen. He needs more time."

She looked between her friends, astonished that the word friend so naturally entered her mind.

"The time is now. You both know it."

Lelia laced her fingers together, scowling. Nalex dropped his head in reverence and then vanished into the tunnels.

Vesta sent messages to her Generals in the other chambers to prepare for battle.

She and Lelia waited for Nalex's return. Lelia, never able to sit still for long, paced the shack.

"You never speak of him but think of him, don't you?" Lelia said with a downward glance to Vesta's stomach.

"Yes." It was easier to admit than Vesta thought it would be.

"Who was he?" Lelia asked.

"Who *is* he. He lives still and if we are successful, I hope to find him again."

"You love him?"

Vesta met Lelia's gaze. The kindness in it reminded her of the Haras and Metra—and all those others who had shown her compassion.

"I never told him. I was a fool. Worse than any kitlush."

Lelia took in a deep breath, chuckled and then coughed. Whenever a coughing fit overtook her, Vesta knew Lelia preferred it if they all ignored it. If they retook the planet, Vesta vowed to have a top doctor see the human as her first task. One of the few things she and Amul agreed on.

"I'm sure he'd be proud of you if he were here now," Lelia said.

Before Vesta could respond, Nalex returned. Two of Vesta's new warriors followed him. A young boy and girl, trained to be Fire-Scar Warriors, had never tapped into the power because of the shackles at their ankles.

They pushed a third Scorth down to his knees. They had covered his head with a cloth sack, but the uniform of an Ovokar Commander was unmistakable.

Nalex poised to lift the sack and looked to Vesta. She drew her robes around her to conceal her pregnancy and nodded.

They were in the darkest part of the cavern, but Norn Zyne's eyes filled with the dim light as they removed the sack. His earnest expression turned into a plea once he saw his father's face.

"What have you done?" Norn asked.

"He has brought you here at my request," Vesta said, stepping into the light. Norn pulled at the ropes that tied his hands.

"Who are you?"

"Vesta Layeyre, Aux Katan and your Queen," Nalex said.

Norn's skin pulled tight and Vesta saw the emotions fight across his face.

"You! It is because of you my family was enslaved. How can you stand beside her, Erra? It is because of her that Luha is dead."

The Ovokar glanced at the wall as if his mind were following countless hidden trails in the darkness, each leading to more fury than the last. Nalex shielded Vesta, using his old, bent body to protect her from some perceived danger.

The shackle was still around her ankle, but whether because of her child or not, the sparks of her old power returned.

She eased Nalex away and then called upon the truth inside her. Let it grow into an intangible force that encircled the young man.

Something happened then she did not expect.

They paused there, silent in the glare of a faint light refracted from particles of diamond dust. A swirl of magic formed into the glassy silhouette of a child.

"I am sorry for your family. If I could restore Luha to us, I would. I must live with this regret all my days," Vesta said.

Luha smiled at them from the dust. The sight hit Vesta with a sudden, sharp pang of sorrow. Norn turned away, tears cutting his work-hardened face. Luha's delicate hand fell over her brother's shoulder.

"We must free our people. We must reclaim Ragora so no family ever endures again what the Zynes have," Vesta said.

Luha wore the graph of a lifetime's worth of hope on her youthful face and then the ethereal vision vanished. Vesta clutched the jewel on the end of the necklace. Pungent emotion beat at the fortress of her heart at the open forgiveness on that tiny face before it disappeared.

Vesta dropped to her knees, a problematic action in her current state. With her index finger under his chin, she drew Norn's eyes to meet hers.

"I make you a promise. If you help us, if you free our shackles, no one will ever work the slave pits again. Ragora will be free."

"It is true, my son," Nalex spoke with compassionate serenity and disregarded all concern for showing too much emotion. "The new creed of Ragora is truth, virtue, and freewill. Lualth comen daxu. Come back to us, son."

Norn raised his head, looking at his father and not Vesta.

"We will all die if you fail," he said through locked teeth.

"We are already dead," Nelax said. "Time to live again." He unexpectedly cut the bonds on his son's wrists. The look of admiration and strength on Nalex's face seemed to be the balm of healing for Norn. One Vesta saw him visibly begging for.

Son took father's hand and rose to his feet.

"Tomorrow, a new day begins," Vesta said.

CHAPTER 46

Tallum Space Station

8 years later

DOWN IN THE BOWELS of the space station, a musky heat poured out from the air shafts and its condensation clung to Rorren's neck like the rank breath of a sunwart.

"You won't regret this," Jon said, face illuminated in shades of blue and green from the console he hunched over.

Rorren looked through miles of computer servers and his senses honed for signs of stray guards to whom he might have to explain himself.

"I already do."

When Rorren refocused, he found Jon still leaning over the female hacker at the console. Jon hadn't given her name and Rorren hadn't asked. The less he knew about Jon's operations, the better.

The annoying kid from Desandor was now a man. His merry band of rebels sprung him from Isken Prison shortly after Rorren put him there.

Over the last eight years, what surprised Rorren most wasn't that Jon had asked for his help but the numerous occasions on which Rorren had given it. He didn't like the direction Tagion was taking the Galactic Order. Every day, it seemed even in his position as General, he was privy to less and less pertinent information.

"What's taking so long?" Rorren moved up behind them. The hacker couldn't have been more than twenty. Rorren felt old.

"There are a lot of archives to search," she said.

Rorren scowled.

"This was a bad idea."

Jon kept his gun hooked in its holster around his waist, but his eyes blazed with the fire to do whatever was needed to keep his rebellion alive.

"You know how important this is."

Rorren wanted to argue but the more they talked, the greater the chance of being caught. He growled and stalked to the edge of the console.

Tagion had total control of the flow of information, so when Ragora expelled all Galactic Order troops, few details emerged about how and why.

Rorren glanced at the time on the computer console. He'd been in the habit of doing that lately. He hadn't seen any Scorth since Desandor.

In three days, an envoy from Ragora would dock at the station.

A peace mission, they said.

Tagion didn't believe them.

Sevet chomped to launch a counter attack, though her hubris in thinking they could easily squash a Scorth uprising bothered him.

He knew better than anyone that Scorth were powerful.

He frowned.

He also knew better than anyone their offer of peace could be legit.

"Here we go," the girl said. She plugged something into the console and Rorren saw a download status bar appear.

"So, what does it say?" he asked.

The kid tucked her bottom lip under her teeth and pushed up her glasses, eyes never leaving the screen.

"It's encrypted. It will take time to decode."

"Great. So all this was for nothing?"

"I thought age brought patience. Not true in your case," Jon said, arms folded and looking grave.

"I'm not a fan of treason," Rorren said.

"Look, we know what we owe you. We are not wrong about this. Tagion takes power in darkness and we must expose that."

"You've never given me anything concrete."

"I have. You just don't want to believe it."

They locked gazes, the staring match ongoing until the girl said, "got it."

She unplugged the device and pushed off the console, the chair screeching over the tile.

"Sorry," she said.

"Time to go," Jon said and Rorren moved halfway down the row of servers.

Voices echoed through the corridor.

Rorren cursed.

"Go, I'll handle this."

Jon hesitated.

"I'll be alright," Rorren said, "but don't ask something like this of me again."

Jon gripped Rorren's arm, gave a determined nod and he and the hacker disappeared in the other direction.

Rorren sprinted forward and headed off the two patrol guards.

"General, sir." They both saluted. Rorren saluted. For a moment, Rorren thought they might pass without a word.

"With respect, sir, why are you down here? Are you supposed to be at the gala?"

Anxiety filled the young guard's expression over questioning a superior. Rorren used it to his advantage.

"Special mission for Vice Admiral Neece."

Anxiety turned to flat-out terror.

Mentioning Sevet had that effect.

The two guards saluted again and Rorren passed.

He walked silently through the dead tunnels of the station, up to the better smelling air, rolling his shoulders at intervals to shake off the unrhythmical sense something was amiss.

Neece had always been a bit terror inducing, but since her rise to Vice Admiral of the Galactic Order Science Council, nasty rumors grew in frequency and depth. Jon hadn't given Rorren any substantial proof, but Rorren wasn't a fool.

She was up to something.

If he hadn't spent the last eight years trying to forget everything about the love of his life, he might have given credence to the solstal hallucinations Vesta secretly believed.

Her death still hurt as much as the day he found her mangled, scorched armor in the pile of bones.

Those memories slammed into him. They forced him to stop.

He leaned against the wall, drawing in an uneven breath.

In a few days, he'd face a room filled with Scorth and reminders of what he'd lost. He didn't know if he had the strength.

A fitting punishment for a murderer, he supposed.

He braced himself and carried on to the station's Domu Center.

The open ballroom had been decorated with glittering chandeliers and tables covered with embroidered cloth, elegant enough to rival the Sandorians, though not nearly as colorful.

Women were dressed in the finest evening gowns, men in ceremonial robes. Rorren smoothed his uniform and parted his way through the crowd.

Everywhere he looked, he saw smiles, most of them insincere.

Glasses clinked.

Smug laughter drifted from the four sparkling corners of the room.

The Domu Center had the best view of the Tallum Nebula of anywhere on the station, second to Tagion's private office.

Through lavish windows, Rorren saw the active section of the nebula suspended against starless space. Far below, a thin thread of neon gas fell from ledge to ledge and splashed at the base of the Essex Moon, where shimmering pools of minerals seduced nearby mining ships.

A rock wall shot upward against the Tallum Star, casting a shadow against the nova like talons ready to sink into prey. The moon was so close and so familiar it seemed impenetrable to even the slightest touch of time.

Lost inside the coils of green-blue gases, Rorren remembered his childhood fear of the strange moon. The endless drilling over the years had made its shape more sinister.

"There you are," Tagion yelled, motioning for Rorren to join him inside an elite circle of celebrities. Sevet Neece stood on his right, a place she seemed to be uncomfortable with.

The Vice Admiral glittered like the room.

She wore a slender gown of midnight blue—the luxurious texture transformed her typical severity into an elegance laced with a strained sensuality.

Tagion couldn't take his eyes off her.

"Enjoying the celebration?" Tagion asked and lifted a long-stemmed glass toward him.

"You certainly went all out," Rorren said.

Tagion offered his arm to Sevet, not for the first time and not for the first time she snubbed him.

"The passing of the Purgate Agreement is the crowning achievement of my time as Premier. It required something special," Tagion said.

The waiter offered Rorren a long-stemmed glass, but he held up his hand and the man moved on.

"I'm glad to see you here," Tagion continued, "it does me good to know you support me even if you disagree."

Rorren's smile was as insincere as the rest.

"Punishing citizens who want peace with the Scorth is a fool's way to quash a rebellion."

Sevet rolled her eyes.

"That's right. Mic Rorren thinks we should invite the enemy to dine with us," Sevet said.

Tagion's face turned ashen except for the pink of his nose colored from his drinking.

"That's what we've done with this convoy. Tell Rorren, Sevet."

Sevet stepped close to Rorren, her voice lowered and her minty breath came out as cool as her tone.

"Look at this."

Sevet flipped on the holoprojector around her wrist and images of Scorth practicing battle moves filled the space between them.

"We smuggled this out of Ragora's capital city. As you can see, the Scorth are preparing for battle."

Tagion said, "We believe this peace meeting is a front for an attack on the station and, more specifically, a chance to assassinate me. You have a good heart, Mic, but peace is not possible with the Scorth. People need to stop having false hope."

Tagion leaned forward and the light from the holoprojection pushed half his face into shadow.

"If this station falls, it leaves Alpha open to attack. We will not let that happen," Tagion said.

Rorren, unsteady on the motionless ground, watched the projection. The Scorth were not wearing expensive armor. He saw no pods, no Obsedei. Still, they were not dressed as he remembered the Aux Katan. Something caused his senses to ring with a warning.

Then he realized what it was.

The images came from Alpha's prime broadcast channel.

Sevet leaked the footage, inciting fear on purpose.

The alarms inside his head somehow made him relax his outward stance. His wits sharpened.

"And if this is a legitimate peace mission?" Rorren asked.

Tagion and Sevet stood close together but did not look at each other.

"Then we will meet with them as planned," Tagion said, and took a sip from the glass.

Not the first lie Tagion had ever told him.

The most dangerous lie.

"With precautions," Sevet said with a clandestine look over her shoulder, then she whispered to Rorren. "We will have eyes on the new Scorth Queen."

Rorren marveled at the ever-growing boldness of his influential friends. They no longer tried to confine their strategizing to the command center. They had become so comfortable in their absolute power it surrounded them like a shield.

They were conceited.

Vesta was the same way when he first found her.

He reasoned that if she could shed that vice, so could they.

"I'm no assassin," Rorren said.

Tagion gave Sevet a look, but then, despite how attractive Sevet was standing there next to them, Tagion's attention was drawn away by the two beautiful daughters of one of the visiting diplomats.

Once he was gone, Sevet turned on the charm. The empty smile on her lips was designed to tempt even the most loyal husband. Her arm snaked around Rorren's as she guided him to a secluded corner of the ballroom.

"Something else came to light during our spy operations on Ragora."

Sevet slipped something from a hidden compartment in her gown. Like a child lashing out for attention, Sevet's movements carried a desperation.

"This message was meant for you but your Scorth witch kept it from you."

He succumbed to the sweep of an emotion he could not contain. It burst upward even as Sevet pulled his ear down to her tantalizing lips.

"They can't be trusted. When are you going to learn that? Even the ones that seem harmless are pure evil. Take it," she wrapped his fingers around the chip, "then call me when you're ready to accept the mission."

She left him in the middle of the ballroom. There were dozens of conversations around him, but Sevet reduced his world to a single question. What was in the message?

The glittering assembly never noticed his absence.

Ragora Royal Fleet
En Route to Tallum Station

The view from the bow of the Scorth Starship gave Vesta the sense that some unthinkable disaster awaited them inside the star-covered blanket of space.

The captain did not question her when she retreated to her quarters. Her people accepted the way of the Aux Katan, but they had not been able to give up some traditions. The elaborate, jeweled robes of the Queen trailed behind her, heavier than they should have been.

She stood in the quiet of her quarters and listened to the dead whirl of metal as sterile air from the ventilation prickled across her exposed neck. Sometimes, she forgot she sacrificed her coiled tresses to symbolize her commitment to her people.

She didn't miss them.

She missed Mic Rorren.

She thought of Valor safe and asleep beyond the bedroom door and found contentment for a fleeting instant.

The bulkhead opened. The bent but sturdy frame of Nalex Zyne appeared against the corridor lights.

"You better come now."

"Should I wake Valor?"

"Let him sleep. The kara zati asked for you."

She followed Nalex outside and nodded to the royal guards at the door as she left her sleeping son in their care.

At this hour of the night, the dim flicker of light would not have been sufficient to see by had Ragora's liberated doctors not restored her deathshade tainted eye.

That, too, had become symbolic for her people. Like the green jungle that had regrown over the palace grounds, things that had once given her people hope now gave them hope again.

The kara zati's quarters were down on level two, the same floor as the medical sector. When they arrived, the doctor was waiting for them.

He was a roundish man with an awkwardness of movement made worse by Lelia's insistence that he vacate the room.

He scuttled out, bumping into the door, bowing lopsided at Vesta and muttering. A laugh from the kara zati turned into a coughing fit.

A swell of bitterness constricted Vesta's movements. She hated the mines. Hated the grinder and greed for what they had taken from her people.

Vesta reached the bed. Nalex bowed and closed the door as he exited.

"He respects you. They all do," Lelia said.

Vesta wrapped her youthful fingers around the aged ones.

"I will never get used to that."

"You must let them show their respect. You have earned it."

"I have earned nothing."

"You are strong."

"As are you."

Lelia grew weaker by the day but she hid it well, especially from Valor. The human lifted her hand up to Vesta's cheek, an action that took more energy than it should have.

"You have given me so much already. More than I could have imagined."

Vesta put her hand over the one pressed to her cheek.

"Not enough. I can never repay you. Valor and I would both be dead if not for you."

"Listen to me." Lelia drew in a breath and the coughs wracked her body.

Sympathetic agony invaded Vesta's own chest.

She placed a hand on the old human's arm and, with her power, eased the woman's suffering as well as she could. Some secrets of the Fire-Scar still eluded her.

She wished the solstal hadn't been lost.

But then, she wished for many things.

She never used to wish.

She never used to hope.

Now she did both and didn't like either.

"There was a legend among the Aux Katan. A prophesy lost to the ages that I've longed to understand for years," Lelia said.

She pointed to the stand beside her bed and guided Vesta to a notepad with human scribbles. Vesta pulled it from the stand and read the ancient Scorth written in Lelia's hand.

"I saw an original only once. I committed it to memory," Lelia said.

Lelia put on her readers and spoke the words aloud. Vesta saw the kara zati struggle but refused by sheer willpower to give into more coughing. Vesta read along as Lelia translated.

"For the Raven Star warrior, past is present and present is past, but hope is everlasting. Gift of the Raven Star," Lelia recited and took off her glasses.

"The raven star?"

"I think that's you." Lelia propped herself against the pillow, unable to keep still. The surge of eagerness and excitement when she spoke of Vesta's path was heartbreaking in its innocence.

"According to legend, the kira tahu appears once in an age to restore freedom."

Vesta smirked and pulled her jeweled robes around her.

"I see you've entered the babbling and delusional stage."

Lelia laughed and then bent over in bed when the coughing became violent. Vesta helped to settle her once the fit was over.

"Rest now. I will call Valor to see you in the morning."

"But—"

Vesta held up two fingers.

"Yes, the morning. You will not die tonight. Your Queen commands you."

"Just like a Scorth. Thinking you control life and death."

Lelia grinned, then closed her eyes and sank into the plush pillow. Vesta had been praying daily for her friend but she prayed even harder now. The kara zati had to live to see Tallum Station.

CHAPTER 47

THE FIRST THING RORREN noticed was the flash of a waiting message on his com station. A message so urgent he was forced by protocol to listen to it before he could plug in the chip Sevet gave him.

Tarza's face appeared.

Ah, gingersnap.

She paid for an emergency military channel. That could not have been cheap.

"This has gone on long enough." Not even a hello. Tarza Rorren Alterson was three inches shorter, four years younger and every bit as stubborn as Rorren. The core difference between them was Tarza's immaculate grooming and ballroom grace—every inch her mother's daughter. Her language, however, had been tainted by her naval officer husband.

"Shut your gaping piehole. Yes, I paid for it. If there is another Scorth war coming, then it's time for an intervention. Aux rand kitlush! They said you were married and your wife died? Eight. Years. Ago? Son of an aux-whiff! Stop shutting us out. We miss you. We are coming to see you. *All of us.* And if you don't like it, you can go kiss a Deltanese stinkworm!"

The message clicked off.

Just like that, the room went silent.

Tarza usually barreled out as she barreled in.

He forgot how much he missed her but pushed that aside. He spared himself no time to think about that now.

He plugged in the chip and fiddled with the programming to get the system to recognize such an old code.

The hazy holoprojection took up the length of his desk.

He wasn't sure what he expected but Freyde's face was far from it.

His former munitions officer had never been young but in the message, he looked younger than Rorren remembered him.

The images came through cracks in the static. Rorren saw what looked like a barge ship of some kind—a less than savory one from the glimpses of rotting cargo and huddled stowaways.

"General, I don't have much time. An Aklaren warship is attacking us and I may not have another chance to record a—"

The transmission cut out, followed by a screeching. When it reappeared, Rorren watched stowaways scramble out of the way of the Aklaren gunfire.

The camera bobbled and then Freyde reappeared.

"...the Cardinal World from a wayward Scorth pod. She died to save us."

The gruff and tough munitions expert had real tears on his face. Vahza. He had to be speaking of Vahza.

Rorren sensed the power of their love even through a degraded message from years ago.

The message was a painful reminder of what he lost to the Aklaren.

"The point is," Freyde drew the recorder near and lowered his voice, "your mother is alive and the Scorth have her. They are bound for the diamond moon. Find her. Save her. I wish I could have. Goodbye, my friend. My General." Freyde ended with a salute.

Rorren heard blasting in the background. A few screams followed and the message ended.

He sat motionless. His breathing sounded heavy. The stars outside his office window seemed frozen in the moment. Anger trembled within him, the devouring, helpless anger that tears all common sense to shreds.

Beep.

He leaned toward the desk.

Beep. Beep.

He opened a drawer and found the secure transmitter Jon gave him.

Red light flashing. Beep. Beep.

Code for an urgent message.

They might have translated the stolen data.

Rorren reached into the drawer and took out the small oblong device. He positioned it in the center of his desk.

He hunched to eye level with its tiny light and watched it blink.

The light reflected off the polished stone paperweight on his desk. Sevet had given it to him as a gift for arresting the rebels. The stone came directly from the mines on Parkell, she told him.

His mother might have mined the rock with her blistered fingers.

Rorren slammed the rock on Jon's secure transmitter and the plastic components splattered across his desk. He pushed them into the trash dispenser and dropped the moon rock on top.

The Mines
Parkell - The Diamond Moon of Ragora
8 years ago

The kara zati handed the baby to Vesta.

Her failure to free her people grew into a tower of self-loathing when stacked against the gurgles of her son.

Norn Zyne tried to release the shackles, but security measures were more complex than any of them knew. Nalex had warned her that Norn hadn't had enough time to plan the escape, but–like a stubborn headed aux lant–she hadn't listened.

She put freedom above common sense.

Because of it, her son was born under the diamond light instead of Ragora's yellow dwarf star.

"You are full of surprises," Lelia said.

The wall of the hut flared open against the mine, allowing in light from the largest diamonds.

Funny how the soul cradled in her arms was worth more to her than all the jewels on the moon.

She touched the single blond curl on his bald head. The curl that gave away her secret.

"Do you think they will accept the half-human child of the Queen?"

Vesta kept her eyes on her son while waiting for Lelia's answer.

"They accepted the creed of old. They accepted the way of the Fire-Scar. They will accept the son of the Queen."

"How can you be so confident?"

Tiny fingers wrapped around Lelia's callused ones, undaunted by the roughness.

"Because the forces of good in this universe have always been stronger than the forces of evil."

The tense, scornful laughter of the Vision Queen pounded in her head, mocked Lelia and tainted Vesta's heart with doubt.

"It is hard to believe that."

"But you must believe it, now more than ever. Let this miracle in your arms be a constant reminder."

He had Rorren's eyes and chin. Vesta rested her cheek against his soft forehead.

"Valor is courage in the face of doubt and danger. I shall call him Valor. Prince of Ragora."

Lelia squeezed Vesta's shoulder and then sat. The presence of a human at such an intimate moment comforted Vesta.

Over the next four years, Lelia's presence in Valor's life continued to comfort her. Vesta watched the old human instruct the boy under the light of the diamonds. With one eye, she watched. With her other—deathshade injured—she focused on leading her growing army.

There was no Advent for their children.

The new rite of passage became the shackling.

At the age of seven, when children could no longer be hidden from the Ovokar, they were brought to the surface and put to work.

The older Valor grew, the longer hours Vesta worked to ensure he and his peers would not spend one moment of their lives enslaved.

Norn Zyne weaved a plan to set them free.

This time, Vesta gave him years.

The rebellion would succeed. So confident was Vesta that her plans extended far beyond the recapture of the mines. She had her eye on Ragora's white shores and the castle she grew up in.

On Valor's fourth birthday—the eve before the second attempt to escape the diamond moon—the loset jumped into her arms, leaving Lelia panting behind him.

"Edda," he said, "kara za says 'gora is beautiful. When can I see it?"

Vesta glanced up at Lelia, who shrugged, guilty face feigning innocence and then coughed.

The cough upset Vesta more than tales of Ragora's former glory ever could.

"It used to be. It will be again."

She pushed a brown curl around his ear. The loset had never been to the surface nor basked in the sun's glow that his father loved so much on Desandor.

"When can we go?" he asked again. He snuggled his head against her arm. She indulged the boy with physical affection, very unlike her Scorth mother.

Vesta blamed Lelia for her human influence on both of them.

The woman seemed to have that effect on the whole of the mine. Leadership through uninhibited kindness and patience. Like Mic Rorren.

The kindness part, anyway.

"I promise you will set foot on the home world within the year."

Lelia's eyebrows shot up, her mouth dropped, but she said nothing.

Vesta's answer satisfied the boy and he left her lap with the wild energy of youth, joining a group of children playing near the market shacks.

"Was that wise? Norn hasn't succeeded yet," Lelia asked.

"The mine will be free tomorrow."

Vesta's rags, pieces of cloth sewn together, seemed incapable of holding together as she stood.

At peace, holding her mind still, Vesta thought about her family. Her rags transformed into the silken robes of the Fire-Scar Warriors.

"And then, Ragora herself."

Leila's eyes reflected the glow from Vesta's new apparel.

To her credit, the woman brought no attention to the change.

"You'd do anything for him," she said, her expression wistful as she watched Valor.

"As would you."

"I had four—a boy and three girls. I don't know whether they live. I would do anything to see them again, especially my son. The last time I saw him, I..." She turned away and tears fell.

A click at Vesta's ankle drew a gasp from Lelia.

"You shall see him again. I promise you this as Queen of Ragora."

Vesta did not need to look down to know the shackle around her ankle had split in two.

Excerpt from 'The Scorth Enigma: Complied Logs of the First Ambassador'
By Professor L. Rorren
Published Circa 33-86-5 (Chapter 53 repealed in Editions 5-8)

Chapter 53: An Alternative Ethos

The Scorth would have us believe their cities are as pristine as their beautiful coastal realms. There is, I discovered at my peril one night, an impoverished community just as in most large cities. I found a different sort of Scorth there. I would not venture to say it was an outright rejection of Scorth culture but scarcity of food and shelter is a natural humbler of the humanoid condition.

A young aux na approached me there. The literal translation of aux na: a dirty rag child below even contempt. As a side note, aux is a derogatory term in the Scorth language. In our tongue, it would be the equivalent of the four-letter curse word for feces. The literal translation of Aux Katan is ragged or dirty warrior beneath contempt. The enemies on the battlefield witnessed the awe and prowess of the Fire-Scar Warriors and dubbed them as such. They hold no place of honor in the Scorth tongue.

This precious gutter child handed me some ancient text I can only assume was banned from every corner of the planet. I dared not show it to anyone else and returned it to the child by proxy after I committed it to memory. I dared not risk smuggling it off the planet.

I provide below the original Scorth text and my translation. This text is written in old Scorth and there are parts that I couldn't fully grasp even after consulting with my peers. We have attempted to capture the beauty of the language, though we are scholars and not poets. The original Scorth I find quite beautiful. My colleagues have debated its merits as a poem, though I believe its original context was set to music.

Only the Aux Katan of old know its true purpose. It would be so easy to pigeonhole the Scorth as I have done for the last 52 chapters as vile, uncaring, wealth-obsessed galactic conquerors. The ethos here suggests something else. The word Aux Katan might be derived from the Old Scorth word "aukata." In Old Scorth aukata meant freedom.

ᒐᘓᗑᕵ ᒐᕽ ᗒᘓᎱᎢᘓ ᕽᕽᘓ Ꭲᘓᗑᕵ
ᕵᏞ ᕽᕽ ᘓᕽᒐᘓ Ꭲᘓᘓ ᕽᕽ ᕽᕽᘓᗑᕵᕵ ᎢᎢᘓ ᗒᗑᕵ
ᏞᎢᘓ ᕵᘓᎢ ᒐᎢᘓ ᒐᘓᘓ ᘓᗑᎢᒐ ᒐᗑᗒ Ꭲᘓᗒᘓ ᒐᘓᗑᕽᕽ
ᘓᕵ ᕽᘓᎢ ᘓᘓᘓ ᘓᘓᕽᘓ ᘓᘓᘓᘓ ᒐᕵᎢ
ᎢᕵᏔ ᏞᕽᎢᒐᎢ ᗒᘓᘓ
ᎢᘓᏔ ᒐᕽ ᕵᗒᘓᕵᎢ᛫

ᗒᕽ ᕵᏔ ᗒᗑᎢᒐᕵᕽᗒ ᒐᗒᗒ Ꮮᘓᘓᘓ
ᕵᕵᗒᎢ ᒐᗒᗒ ᕽᗒᗒᘓᕵ ᘓᕵ ᒐᘓᘓ
ᗒᕽᎢ᛫ ᕽᕵᘓᗒᎢᘓᘓ ᕽᕽᒐᏞ ᕵᕵᎢᒐᘓ ᕵᗒ ᎢᕵᎢᒐᗒᎢ
ᕵᕽ ᕽᕵᗒ ᘓᎢᕵᕵ ᘓᘓᘓᘓ ᕽᕵᗒ ᕵᕽ
ᕵᕽ ᘓᕽᒐ ᕵᕽ ᕵᕽᕽᎢᘓ ᒐᕵᕽᕽ
ᗒᕽ ᕵᏔ ᘓᕵᒐᏞ ᘓᗒᘓᘓ ᕵᕽᎢᕵᒐᕵ

ᗒᕽ᛫ ᗒᕽ ᕵᏔ ᗒᗑᎢᒐᕵᕽᗒ ᒐᗒᗒ Ꮮᘓᘓᘓ
ᕽᕵᒐᏞ ᕵᕵᗒᎢ ᒐᗒᗒ ᎢᕽᕽᗒᒐᒐᗒᎢ ᕽᕵ Ꭲᘓᘓᘓ
ᗒᕽᎢ᛫ ᕽᕵᘓᗒᎢᘓᘓ ᕽᕽ ᘓᗒᏞᏞᏞ ᗒᗒ ᕽᕵ
ᕵᘓᕵ ᕵᎢᎢᕵ ᕵᗒ ᕵᕵᎢ Ꮮᕵᗒᕵᘓ
ᒐᗒᗒ Ꮮᘓᗒ ᒐᕵᕵᏞᕵᕽᕽᒐᕵᎢᒐᕵᘓ
ᗒᕽ᛫ ᗒᕽ ᕵᕵᎢ ᕽᕽᕵᕵᒐᏞ ᕽᗒᒐᒐ ᕵᕽ ᒐᕵᘓ

Translation of the ancient text <u>Kira Tahu</u>:

<u>Raven Star</u>

I worship riches by royal design.

Steal every treasure, till the universe is

mine.

But souls are haunting me, asking me

to turn

From ways I can't unlearn.

Taught by a good man who under-

stands

If he offered the sea

Cured the wasteland in me

Then, destiny could never be denied

No longer to fight

Lost in the dark night.
A raven unable to soar.

All of my misdeeds I must atone
But I never knew I can't do it alone.
Will he help me find the courage to
stand
In storms of wind and sand?
A menti blade
At my command!

If he offered the sea
Cured the wasteland in me
Then, destiny could never be denied.
I'd fly long and fly far
To that far distant star,
If he tried and set me free.

Oh, if he offered the sea
He could cure the darkness in me
Then destiny, I'd welcome you in.
Born again with new grace
Like the wise, ancient race.
Oh, if his love was meant to be.

Note: there is no Scorth word for love, but in the context of the above passages, I believe the word lualth (lü-əlth) is its substitute. The modern translation of lualth is to worship or adore something based on its monetary value.

CHAPTER 48

Tallum

Space Station

Present Day

THE DIGITAL CLOCK ON the weapons console stole Rorren's attention.

Time is up, it seemed to say. Every number marked the progression to the moment Rorren knew would change his life forever.

"Late. Just like Scorth."

Captain Ansgar sneered whenever he said the word Scorth. It was an involuntary action, an instinct that seemed as much a part of him as his weak jaw and cherub cheekbones.

The young captain, now a hefty man with a disposition for complaining, enjoyed a meteoric rise to the rank of Sevet's favorite soldier. The Vice Admiral handpicked Ansgar for the mission and he glowered from the rafters, smirking like a man who relished his own self-importance.

"All groups check-in," Rorren ordered.

His com lit up as each squadron answered and he spotted his soldiers spreading across the hanger floor and along the catwalks. They were good men and women, even the untested rookies.

Like his company during the Scorth war, Rorren made friends with them. Ansgar was the exception, but a mole planted by politicians was nothing new.

From the elevation in the rafters, Rorren watched the platform about half a kilometer away. The Premier's guards appeared, just beginning to filter into the key areas.

Rorren glanced to the podium, noting Tagion's bald spot as he scooped up his robes en route to his designated seat.

He wondered if the Scorth Queen would recognize the honor the Premier paid her by dressing like that.

All for show.

Sevet lurked in the shadows behind the stage. She must have sensed his eyes on her because she looked up. At a strange angle from his high position, he saw only the tip of her nose and the reflective gel that sleeked her hair.

He couldn't see her lips moving but he heard her voice in his ear.

"Are you prepared to act if required?"

Rorren dropped his shoulders and aimed the scope of the veer-rifle at the spot where the Scorth Queen would soon stand.

"I serve the Galactic Order."

His answer must have satisfied her because she left the shadows and went to Tagion's side.

Vesta took in the dying body of the kara zati, marveling how yet another human wormed their way into her heart. Even in the mines, ill humor never soured her features, nor did an inconvenient turn in the grinder displace her composure.

Lelia lay silent and still. Her tranquility calmed Vesta but came with the alloy of unavoidable sadness.

The com at Vesta's waist buzzed—an incessant vibration—and Vesta switched it off with such force that it snapped from its clip.

The humans would have to wait.

"You must linger, kara zati. Let me find your children. I can negotiate that when I meet with the—"

Lelia turned her head, the action draining much of her fading spirit. Vesta resisted the urge to flee but the presence of death near the one she loved terrified her.

"Just give them my messages. Tell them I never gave up. Tell Mic I don't think he is a murderer. I never did. I was in shock. That's no excuse. I've regretted my reaction every day since. In a way, those regrets kept me alive. Correcting them was a powerful reason to go on each day."

Black feathers from Vesta's high-collared cape tickled her cheek as she listened to the rhythm of words. The vowels came out so strong. They made Vesta cling to the hope all her best doctors were wrong.

"What? What are their names?" Even now, out of the mines for years, a chill crept up her throat as she asked. To speak of such things still seemed dangerous.

Lelia's shoulders shivered, her face thin, but her expression brightened.

"Jane, Tarza, Ivy, and Mic."

Vesta's mind raced into a cutting static, followed by a haze of understanding that left her undone.

"I am satisfied. When I am gone, you must not grieve. I am going to God and the tu'ah."

Lelia spoke too fast and then coughed in a way that accentuated her fierce angelic grace in dying.

"Mic Rorren?" Vesta's throat constricted, making her tone tight and breathy. She hadn't dared utter his name in the mines.

With new eyes, she saw Lelia—the solid cheekbones, gentle eyes, an unbending resolve.

His mother.

"Professor Rorren?"

Surprise pumped life into Lelia's trembling lips.

"No one has called me that in a lifetime."

Vesta shuddered, her mind grinding to produce meaningful sentences.

A soft knock drew her attention and she watched her son enter through blurred vision. He stood, hands shoved in pockets, foot tapping at the ground.

"I-I wanted to... Nalex said to come see her."

As sorrow swept his face, Vesta found a revelation of joy affecting hers.

"Kara zati, what was your husband's name?" Vesta asked.

"Harc Rorren."

"Come, Valor Harc Rorren," Vesta said, "and say hello to your granda."

The boy stopped at the foot of the bed and his hands came out of his pockets.

"My name is not—what do you mean, my granda?"

"The kara zati's son, a former General in the Galactic Order, is your father. I just named you after your grata, Harc Rorren."

The gaunt lines in Lelia's face shocked themselves straight as if she knew what Vesta meant but couldn't fathom it.

Lelia turned her failing sight to the boy in gradual motion.

"My grandson?"

Joy filled her colorless face as her lips curved.

"But that would mean, no, Mic would never fall for a Scorth witch."

"Perhaps not, but he married one."

"Not just anyone. The Queen," she half coughed, half scoffed, "he always did go for the prize."

Valor jumped onto the bed and threw his arms around Lelia's neck.

"I do not want you to die, granda," he said, tone thick and soft.

Lelia studied his innocent face. Vesta wondered if she saw Mic Rorren in it, as she did every day.

"We had so much time together, didn't we? Time we never thought we'd have. You won't forget me, little prince. And I will always be with you. God brought us together and we will never truly be parted."

Lelia used the last strength in her fingers to banish the tears from his cheeks.

With a sigh, Lelia released him, head indenting the pillow. Her fingers sought Vesta's one final time.

"My family."

Her eyes drifted closed, peaceful but permanent.

Vesta had never known what it was to mourn. She had never cried, not even as a child. Not for Metra or Luha.

She cried now.

Valor snuggled into her arms and they stayed that way, clinging to each other over Lelia until the royal guard interrupted.

Vesta left her son and readied to meet the Premier.

CHAPTER 49

T HE DIGITAL READOUT THROUGH the scope of the veer-rifle said: 0900 hours. Rorren leaned across the rail, shoulders pulling taunt. He figured out why he'd been keeping one eye on the clock for months. He watched the march of life to the rhythm of numbers.

They reminded him of his mother.

The first Scorth snapped up to the podium and Rorren set his sights, scope blurring then becoming better focused as he adjusted the range.

Seconds rang through his body like a life age.

He drew air when necessary and held himself in perfect stillness.

He waited for her.

A void filled his sights.

Then, feathered plumes.

They draped her shoulders, cascading over diamonds welded into the silver armor around a lithe bodice.

Rorren did what he did best.

He watched her.

The robes were ornate. The woman was as beautiful and hideous as any Scorth Queen before her.

"General," he heard through the com. Sevet's voice betrayed strain. Unusual. Rorren swept the scope in search of her. She wasn't on the platform.

"It is a trick. The Scorth have disabled the Lament Shield. We are receiving reports they are attacking Alpha," Ansgar said.

Rorren heard scuffling around him and saw his soldiers on the ground abandon posts, taking new orders from Ansgar.

"Take the shot. That is an order. Cut off the head of the snake," Sevet said.

The Queen greeted Tagion. The Premier and the Scorth stood side by side, smiling for the cameras.

But Rorren was a watchman.

In tales of old that his mother told him, watchmen stood on high towers, appointed by the king to protect legendary herds of gantis against marauders. Men called to sound the warning at the first sign of the enemy on the horizon.

Everything was clear to him—his chosen path set long ago, even though he had left his post for a time. He wanted to laugh.

"Kill her now!" Sevet hissed through the com with a force that seemed aware of its own futility.

When the watchmen of old fell asleep or joined round the campfire, that is when the invaders came—in shadow in the night, snatching prey unfettered and in secret.

The invaders, Rorren, realized, looking through the scope down at the scene, were not the people he had thought. Those watchmen of old must have been stunned when they, too, discovered friends, not foes, looting the stables.

He saw his wife in those purported to be the enemy—in every Scorth woman—like the one below. The veil of darkness hiding the enemy lifted from his gaze. Not even the Scorth banishing his mother to the diamond moon could encumber his new sight.

"I'm no murderer," he said to Sevet.

A hand fell over his shoulder and he recoiled.

"Mic Rorren." Jon coaxed him from the railing and into the dusty rafters of the hanger. "Sevet and her minions disabled the shield. She's unleashed her experimental pods on Alpha. The people need your help."

"What is going on up there?!" Sevet screamed in his ear.

Rorren ripped the com from his uniform.

"What do you need?" Rorren asked Jon.

"We have proof. We decoded the transmissions from the servers. Tagion has allied with the Aklaren. The Galactic Order paid them to capture your wife. The people need to know."

"Show me."

"I'll do more than—"

The blast shattered the space between them, shooting up in a thin line of fire to the heights of the station. Rorren kept his footing, suspended for an instant, then descended, falling in spirals of chaotic ringing alarms, down through floor after floor.

Steam gushed from holes in the vents, burning his hands as he grasped for anything to hold onto.

His shoulder caught on a sharp piece of metal and tore his flesh. He groaned. The ground continued to open beneath him, layers of acrid smoke blinding him to what came next.

He lost consciousness.

He woke in a pool of liquid, his trench coat and uniform soaked through.

He groaned, skull pounding, and rolled to his side. Water filled the corridor from a broken main overhead. Just enough light flickered from a fractured fixture, allowing him to examine his wound. Not as bad as he feared. Ignoring the pain, he pushed himself upright.

The place was unfamiliar. Rorren hadn't been this far below the station's main decks before. Loose wires and pieces of debris splashed into the ankle-deep water as he made his way down the only unblocked passage.

"Jon?" He waited, but he saw no one else in the wreckage.

Wading toward a strange blue glow at the end of the dark tunnel, each step forward sent his mind a step backward.

Back to the Scorth Queen.

No, he thought, *stop seeing ghosts.*

Rorren's mind conjured displays of light and color that increased in vibrancy the longer he traveled the dark hallway. A haunting radiance swirled up in the darkness, hinting at a secret ready to be discovered. Small fires popped up around him. The creeping water line soon swallowed the flames.

He knocked over a piece of steel, sending it down another blast hole in the ship. He craned his neck up. Water dripped from more broken mains and landed on his face in annoying trickles.

He wiped it away and continued toward the heart of the ship. The soft blue light shot up from behind shattered glass. He pushed open a mangled door and listened. No voices. He heard the gush of fuel and water. Glass crunched beneath his boots, strewn across the deck from damaged tubular containers.

Organic matter spilled out over jagged shards, like insides from the guts of a slain monster.

He didn't look at it long enough to make out shapes of organs or limbs.

He didn't want to.

A ball of dread bounced around in his stomach.

He pressed further into the destroyed lab.

The door locks fizzed, disabled by the blast and Rorren quickly passed through. The explosion must have blown out the entire security grid. Rorren braced himself before he opened each door, unsure what he might find on the other side. He hated to admit this could be the secret lab he never believed in.

Vesta believed it years ago.

She tried to tell him it wasn't the solstal.

A digital display on the computer console read *Holding Brig*.

Rorren crept inside and hunted for voices in the shadows. With aching caution, he peered around the wall. Two or three poorly dressed men used the butts of their guns to try and pry free the locks on the cells. The prison locks must have been on a backup generator.

Rorren studied the men and the clothes gave them away.

Jon's rebels.

From the shadows, he couldn't see what was inside the cell. With a fist clenched, he decided to risk it.

The barrel of three guns pointed at him. He lifted his hands.

"It's only the General," one of the men said. Rorren nodded and the rebels returned to the futile pounding.

Rorren peered inside the cell.

He saw Scorth.

Men, women, and children—some huddled together and some working with the rebels to open the gates.

Rorren drew the attention of one of the Scorth men. His hair was buzzed to the scalp, revealing a raw scar above his ear.

"Who did this to you?" Rorren asked.

"You did," the Scorth sneered.

"Admiral Neece?"

"The devil dressed as a human wench." The Scorth man turned his head, showing off the imposing scar.

The truth of what Sevet had done slammed into Rorren. His trench coat, soaked and heavy, irritated the scars on his neck.

He took a breath and balanced himself against the wall.

He loved the Galactic Order and what it stood for.

Freedom. Peace. Justice.

The way Sevet and Tagion twisted it, using their sacred power to abuse and torture, sickened him. Worse, they made him an involuntary part of it.

Because of his inaction, this Scorth man bore the scars of their evil.

Rorren reached beneath the lapel of his coat and tore the General stripes from his uniform. He didn't watch as they sank beneath the pooling water.

Vowing retribution, Rorren pried open the security panel and cut the wires. He'd hotwired enough farm equipment to know how.

Five minutes later, Rorren and Jon's rebels led the prisoners through the ship. He gleaned from the rebel chatter that Jon had purposefully set the charges to free those in the lab, one of many across the station, but that there had been some unexpected chemical in the mix. The explosions erupted through the station, causing heavy damage, as evidenced by the flashing alarm lights in the corridors.

Rorren's drive to reach the surface—to see the hanger—wasn't just for the sake of the prisoners or bringing the Premier to justice.

A gnawing curiosity pervaded his thoughts.

The face of the new Scorth Queen lingered in his mind's eye while he helped children navigate fallen debris.

Was her familiarity real or a mirage? He had to find out.

CHAPTER 50

T HE SAVAGE EXPLOSION DROVE the Galactic Order soldiers from
their posts, but none of Vesta's warriors left her side.

Strong arms pulled her upright.

"You were right. The humans set a trap," Norn Zyne, the Ovokar turned
royal guardsman, said.

A cold draft from the gaping crater rattled over broken hulls of docked
ships—all blown into mangled heaps inside the station's hanger.

The distant chatter of Vesta's re-grouping guard sounded lower than
usual, making the howl of wind drafts louder.

"I do not think this was Sevet," Vesta said.

Beyond the rubble, she saw a few dots of human troops scattered verti-
cally toward the exit bulkhead.

Around her, menti blades formed in the hands of a dozen royal guard
members led by Norn. He slashed the blade through the air, allowing the
fire scars to sizzle deliberately. The human troops observed, yelled franti-
cally, and climbed over each other to escape the path of Vesta's armada.

Norn put his finger to his ear com.

"Alpha is reporting that we disabled their Lament Shield. Our sensors
show the shield is still up."

"That is Sevet's trap," Vesta said.

She accounted for all her guards. All there, but the absence of one aggravated her. Amul Torat. She sent a glance skyward, thinking of him in space with the full force of her Fire-Scar army.

"We continue with our mission. Let Amul worry about the planet," she said.

The steel around them rang with the aftershocks of the explosion and her guards raced to meet the troops attempting to escape.

Norn Zyne called to Vesta, his voice stilling her in the center of chaos. She watched the swift Aux Katan figures streaking through stretches of smoke and falling debris.

Norn Zyne rushed up to her and then dropped his gaze to his waist.

There, cowering behind him, the frame of a small boy.

Norn caught the boy's wrist in his grasp.

"I found a stowaway."

"I came to protect you, Edda," Valor said, pulling a knife from his boot. A dark, serrated blade that Amul had given him on Ragora.

Vesta knew Norn, her son, and her people always carried with them the impulse to protect her.

Her son's dust-covered face held such conviction that it tempered her anger.

"This is not the way," Vesta said.

Valor dropped his head, turning the knife over in his hands. Vesta knew he had another reason for disobeying.

His father might be here.

"Go," she said to Norn, "return to your post. Valor will come with me."

Valor started to speak, but a volley of gunfire drove them behind a storage container. Vesta pulled her son to her, protecting him from the onslaught. One of her guards lay fallen near a broken structural beam.

Norn and another of her guards jumped into the fray to save the wounded Scorth.

Vesta swore and addressed her son.

"Stay here."

With menti blade slashing, Vesta deflected the bullets, shielding her kin while they carried the fallen warrior to safety.

Through broken coils of steam around them, Vesta observed the fighting style of this new band of humans. Their mismatched clothing and well-cared-for but outdated guns set them apart.

They fought with a conviction that eluded Galactic Order troops.

"We are on the same side," Vesta yelled. A few more rounds came at them. Vesta's blade deflected the shots back at their masters.

The hanger fell silent, amplifying the sound of steam from broken pipes.

One of the humans appeared out of the fog, rifle aimed at Vesta's head. He didn't look at his feet as he stepped over torn hull fragments.

Norn tensed and Valor lifted the knife. Vesta glared at them, warning them not to barrel into an unwise battle.

A woman appeared but she lowered her weapon.

"Vahza?"

The man flexed his grip on the rifle.

"It's not her," he said.

The woman took tentative steps. She put her hand on the man's arm and kept it there until he lowered the rifle.

Vesta faced skyward, taking in the peaceful darkness inside the blast fissure above them.

"Vahza was my granda," Vesta said, unsure why. It wasn't something she went around announcing.

These were not strangers.

Vesta observed the streak of white across the woman's eyebrow and her short, dark hair. The missing ring finger on the hand of the man that clutched to the rifle.

"Cantona and Racer."

The man re-aimed the rifle at Vesta. The woman huffed and pushed it away.

"You are the Scorth Queen. How do you know us?" Racer asked.

"I am married to Mic Rorren, your General during the—"

"We know Rorren," Cantona interrupted. "We came here to find him. Jon called us."

Another familiar name.

"Jon," Racer said, "the resistance leader."

Jon, who she once rescued on Desandor. Jon, who Vesta thought was lost to the Galactic Order forever.

"Plans were set in motion I could not foresee," Vesta told herself.

The two human fighters exchanged glances at her cryptic words.

"Have you found Mic Rorren? Is he here?" Vesta asked.

They answered with silence. Valor tugged on Vesta's cape and gazed at her with hopeful eyes. What would Mic Rorren make of their son? This was not the first time the question plagued her, nor the first time she ignored it.

"Sevet must be stopped," Vesta said.

Racer snorted.

"No kidding. We set charges to free her test subjects. Something went wrong. The blast wasn't supposed to reach up here."

Cantona pressed the com at her ear and turned aside, listening.

"They are bringing up the prisoners now. We need to dig out our transport ships," she said.

Racer stepped toward Vesta and asked, "You coming with us?"

Racer, Cantona, Norn, and Valor seemed suspended in a single breath, waiting for her reply.

Mistrust was there in the human faces, but also awe and curiosity.

"If Sevet is not stopped here, she will only rebuild. I must do what I came here to do."

Vesta bent, placing her hands on Valor's shoulders.

"You need to go with them."

He opened his mouth to argue but one look from her silenced him.

"This is my son. Mic Rorren's son. Will you take care of him?"

"Hot beans," Racer said, running a hand through his silky hair, "Mic Rorren has a son with a Scorth witch?"

Cantona punched his arm.

"And Mic Rorren would laugh at us if he knew we got married and had a daughter." Cantona, gaze intense, addressed Vesta. "We will protect him with our lives."

Vesta believed them because they once protected her granda with their lives. That qualification enticed her into trusting them with the life of her son.

"I will hold you to that."

If they failed, she had what Mic Rorren called Plan B.

"Stay with them, Norn," Vesta said to her guardsman.

"But—"

"There is more honor in this request than any other I could give," she told him.

"Yes, my Queen," the son of Nalex said, head bowing.

"Be careful, Edda," Valor interrupted. He wrapped his arms around her waist. She hugged him and mused over the shocked expressions on the faces of the humans.

She kissed Valor's head and said, "Get used to it. It is the new Scorth way."

Cantona reloaded her weapon and then handed cartridges to Racer.

"No. It's the old Scorth way. The way of the Fire-Scar Warrior," she said.

Vesta and Racer sealed their pact with a firm handshake. Norn guided Valor, hand on the boy's shoulder, in step behind the humans. Vesta watched until they disappeared into the steam. When their silhouettes vanished, she commenced with the hunt.

CHAPTER 51

Rorren fought through a pocket of Sevet's most loyal troops as they attempted to reach the transport. One of the Scorth prisoners had been shot in the shoulder during the skirmish and Rorren helped him navigate the debris until they stumbled into the docking bay.

Chaos surrounded them.

Resistance and Galactic Order troops—led by Ansgar—attacked each other in rounds.

There was a twisting pain in the muscles of Rorren's legs and back as he balanced the weight of the large Scorth man.

He pressed through the battle with an eagerness, scanning for signs of the Scorth Queen.

She had vanished with the rest of the Scorth envoy.

Resistance fighters directed them through a secluded ventilation passage and to a secret transport barge far away from the main docking area.

Rebels worked on rudimentary scaffolds just above the right flank of the ship, pulling chunks of steel and concrete away from the partially buried hull.

Rorren set the man down and medical staff arrived with lightning haste.

When he looked up, he found Jon and an intimidating Scorth man standing before him.

"Jon, glad to see you are in one piece."

"Norn Zyne, this is General Rorren," Jon said.

Rorren nodded at the Scorth and those dark eyes went a little overkill in their intense scrutiny.

"We have a problem," Jon said.

Jon activated a holo device and Rorren recognized the skyline of the capital city of Tarazi in the moving images. Scorth pods littered the landscape, crashed into skyscrapers and wedged into alleyways and pavement.

Another Scorth General appeared this time through the projection—a living nightmare of a brute, older and bigger than the one glaring at Rorren.

"Our Fire-Scar army is waiting," he said. "The Queen foresaw this, but your people will attack us if we enter."

"This is Amul Torat," Jon said. "We need his help. My team will not be enough to defend Alpha."

Rorren tried to focus on the problem. His mind only saw her. The Queen. All the reasons not to believe flooded him.

She had both eyes.

Her hair wasn't coiled in braids on her head.

She was the Queen.

Rorren folded his arms and forced himself not to demand information about her.

"Have your ships follow us in," Rorren said.

Jon turned off the projection, frowning.

"You sure about this? Will they believe you?"

"Only one way to find out."

Rorren rolled up the sleeves of his trench coat and started grabbing at rocks. Scorth and human worked side by side and a swell of laughter rose inside Rorren. He winked at Norn Zyne, his fellow conspirator. The man shared a camaraderie with Rorren but refused to acknowledge it, just like a Scorth.

When the transport was free, they all looked to Rorren. He couldn't deny the pleasure of taking charge. His confidence grew as he ushered the refugees on board, interacting with everyone with a parental disposition.

He was where he was meant to be, doing what he was meant to do and not murdering anyone.

Norn left them to go in search of his beloved Queen. The rest of them prepared for flight.

The ship wobbled, engine sputtering as the entire barge went airborne. The starship floated out of the docking bay with the debris and Rorren praised the rebels for their ingenuity.

The celebration was short.

"Open a com-link to Alpha base," Rorren ordered as he entered the bridge.

The pilot was stretched in a poise of untidy relaxation, his legs on the console, arms resting behind his head, grinning at a woman. A green glow from the command station washed over her face and hair, highlighting a streak of white across her eyebrow.

"Piece of tresacoi-cake," the pilot said.

Rorren read the scene outside of himself as if he wasn't a part of it. Years ago, in a muddy war trench and these two were horsing around like they did now.

The woman's mouth gaped when she saw Rorren. She pushed the pilot's feet off the console.

"Hey, what are you..."

The man saw Rorren, blinked twice, and then jumped from the seat.

"You old kencat! You look as gruff as Freyde." Racer pulled him in for an embrace, knocking the cockpit controls. The ship lurched and Rorren's old friend returned his attention to navigation.

"What are you two doing here?" Rorren asked.

"Looking for you," Cantona said, shaking his hand, "Jon said his plans were big. We had no idea he meant taking down Tagion and the Order."

A flash of light on the console caught Rorren's attention. Alpha Base was answering their call.

"This is Mic Rorren?" asked a young voice.

In search of the owner, Rorren scanned the bridge and, dropping his gaze, discovered a kid standing next to Cantona.

The boy, maybe eight or nine, glued his gaze on Rorren. The astonished curiosity and hint of admiration on the face of the onlooker flummoxed Rorren.

The kid wore exquisite clothes tailored to perfection but not, in essence, completely Scorth. His brown hair seemed out of place against the even lines of his face.

The image of the Galactic Order troop appeared on the holoprojector, drawing Rorren's focus from the young spectator.

"Alpha Base to incoming transport. State your purpose and clearance code," Alpha Base said.

Rorren saluted, wishing he hadn't ripped his rank patch from his uniform.

"What is your name, soldier?" Rorren asked.

"Private Temis Grant."

"Listen up, Private Grant, I'm about to enlighten you. You won't believe me but the fate of the universe depends on you."

The private's chest swelled and he leaned into the camera.

Rorren explained what was happening—about the Scorth pods Sevet controlled, her attempt to frame the enemy and the Fire-Scar Warriors waiting in the wings to assist. The story sounded phony even to Rorren's ears.

He stood, every inch a General, permitting nothing to exist but his determination and one nervous private.

"Lower the Lament Sheild. That is an order," Rorren said.

Everyone on the bridge stilled, waiting on a private who only looked slightly older than the strange Scorth kid on the bridge.

"Is it true that the Fire-Scar Warriors helped you win the last war?" Grant asked.

"It is."

Cantona moved into the projection beside Rorren.

"I was there. The woman who led us, Vazha Layeyre, is the granda of the Queen. This new Queen is a Fire-Scar Warrior herself. I trust her and I trust Mic Rorren."

The world swam to Rorren through a veil of static.

The granda of the new Scorth Queen.

Cantona's words attacked him, cutting him into apprehensive pieces.

Vesta is the Queen?

He ran the statement over again and again until it soaked through his brain and pooled in his chest.

Rorren ripped off his trench coat and the leather crumpled into a humble pile. He assigned his scars no limits, allowing them the freedom of infinite possibilities. The transmission shot his image across hundreds of channels and into a future he felt worthy to claim.

"The mark of the relheer took us to victory once before. Will you let it again?" he asked.

The private studied the alien ink swirls, saluted, and said, "Yes, General."

There is still some magic left in this old kencat, Harc Rorren used to joke.

"Me too, Dad," Rorren whispered, but cheering on the bridge shut out the quiet interludes.

"The Scorth are with us. Fighter ships stand down on order from General Rorren. Yes, *that* General Rorren. You saw it yourselves," Private Grant said.

"Thank you, Private." Rorren returned the salute.

"I can't guarantee they will listen," the Private said.

"Keep the faith, soldier."

The Private nodded and Racer ended the transmission, replacing it with a new one. The face of Amul Torat appeared on the encrypted channel.

"You heard that?" Rorren asked.

Torat nodded and they locked eyes.

Both of them knew the Scorth were not space-faring people.

Torat put the lives of his soldiers in Rorren's hands. An honor he didn't feel ready for.

"It is not you that I trust," Torat said as if reading his thoughts, "it is Vesta Layeyre."

The projection ended with Rorren still processing the mention of his wife's name. The ship angled sideways, beginning the descent to Alpha. Behind them, Rorren heard the rumble of a hundred Scorth ships. He gripped the command station, knuckles white as he waited for an attack he hoped would never come.

"Rorren," Cantona said. Her arm was around the kid, steadying him against the swaying movements of the ship.

Captain Cantona could be reckless on the battlefield, but to bring her kid along? That was just plain crazy.

Rorren's chest tightened with excitement as they entered Alpha's air space. Without the constraints of his trench coat, he breathed decently for the first time in years.

Single pilot fighter ships, each bearing the Galactic Order insignia, formed a row on each side of Rorren's armada—a gauntlet of safe passage or doom.

"Rorren!" Cantona demanded his attention and then flinched oddly at the kid.

"Yours?" Rorren asked.

"Our daughter is home on Beta with her grandparents."

She glanced at Racer.

"You and Racer got married?" Rorren chuckled, grateful for a release of some tension between his shoulder blades.

Racer shrugged at Cantona with a you-were-right expression, but Rorren lost its meaning.

"No," she growled, "this is your son."

"I'm picking up coms," Racer said. "Patching them through."

"This some kind of joke?" Rorren asked, looking at the boy for the first time.

The messy hair. Rorren had hair like that when he was a kid.

The striking eyes. Those were Vesta's.

"I was born on Parkell and we lived in the diamond mines for a while until Edda freed us and reclaimed the throne," the kid said.

The ship righted but Rorren wobbled. He leaned against the command center.

Racer routed coms from Alpha's fighter pilots over the speakers. Their intense arguing only half registered in Rorren's head.

–General Rorren is onboard the transport.

–I don't care if Kenny Kencat is on board. We can't let more Scorth in. They are slaughtering us on the planet.

–These Scorth are Fire-Scar. They want to help.

–You really believe that?

–My father fought under General Rorren. Yes, I believe him.

–So do I.

–Good enough for me. How about you, Z5?

The coms fell into a deafening silence.

Rorren dropped to one knee, looking the kid in the face.

His kid.

"Your mom," he said, "edda, is Queen of the Scorth?"

The kid nodded.

He had Rorren's chin.

"And she said you are my erra...um...father," the boy replied.

–I can't let this happen. Not on my watch. I'm taking them out.

Rorren ran a hand through his hair and studied the kid as if he were a figment.

"I always wanted a kid."

The boy gave him a roguish grin that reminded him of his father.

"I always wanted a father."

–Stand down, Z5, or I will open fire on you.

–No way, Kal. You'd fire on one of your own before the Scorth? They are the enemy.

–Not these Scorth. Can't you feel it?

–Feel what?

–Let go of your fear for a second and listen. Look at coordinates 4.64.

Registering at last, Rorren trained his eyes on the spot the pilot referenced among the stars. He saw her over his son's shoulder.

In a glittering kind of shadow, against the dark of space and stars, appeared a vision of Vahza Layeyre.

She beamed at them, the radiating light a guide through the darkness.

He heard gasps from the coms.

Rorren wondered how many pilots looked at the vision without believing—how many lost their capacity to believe, replaced with a dim insolence by those who told them it was foolish to believe.

Vesta taught an entire army how to tap into the power of the Fire-Scar and that miracle thinned the veil of death.

No one seeing it could deny it.

The kid looked over his shoulder but by the time he did, Vahza had already vanished.

"What's your name?" Rorren asked.

"Valor Harc Rorren, after my grata."

"Nice to meet you, Val," Rorren said, extending his hand.

The kid jumped into his arms.

Rorren spent years digging in the sand, wondering what was missing. He didn't wonder anymore.

"I hate to interrupt this tender moment but we are entering orbit," Racer said, with the mockery Rorren remembered from the old days.

"Fighting is worst in Tarazi, Sector 24," Cantona said.

Rorren untangled himself from Valor but kept one hand on his son's shoulder.

"Take us in. Open a com to the Scorth."

Rorren watched as the holoprojector scanned him, scars and all. In seconds, his image would appear before an army of Fire-Scar Warriors. His life prepared him for the moment and he owned it.

"Sevet Neece has been using your people as lab rats. I don't know what is in store for us down there, but I know this. You are Fire-Scar. Aux Katan.

God and the tu'ah will guide you. Courage will see you through. My people might try to attack you. They don't know any better. Try to protect them. When they learn the truth, they will thank you. I thank you now. We will meet in battle. Lualth comen daxu."

The holoprojector clicked off.

In the expressions of Cantona and Racer, Rorren found what he had years ago on the brink of another battle that decided the galaxy's fate: fear, courage, and hope.

CHAPTER 52

VESTA AND HER ROYAL guard swept through the corridors, each
armed with a menti blade, each dealing mercy and justice in a relay
of blows. Some of Sevet's men surrendered on the spot, staring into the
faces of a dozen Fire-Scar Warriors. Others, thirsty for blood, met their end
at the hands of the Scorth Queen's warriors.

Vesta did not allow herself to fear the label of murderer. She kept
those she protected—those innocent lives that would no longer be Sevet's
lab-warts—in the forefront of her mind.

In a blaze of fire and dust, they reached the command center.

The enemy cowered just beyond the thick steel impact doors.

Vesta transformed her menti blade.

The sword disintegrated into grains from the dunes of Desandor. Particles swirled, coiling straight up, holding in the air before diving into secret
microscopic cracks in the walls.

Norn and her other guards flanked her, unmoving, intent on the blast
doors as if studying some revelation about to appear. Rays of light grew
stronger across their faces, illuminating a distinct look of patience.

Vesta had only ever seen it once before in the eyes of her granda.

The metal sagged. Bolts shot out from the edges of the steel doors, leaving scorch marks inside empty encasements.

The walls shook and bulbs in the corridor burst, showering them in glass and a million sand pellets.

With the force of a Cardinal World bomb, the doors exploded from the wall and the whole command center lay bare to them. Vesta let the wind and dust wash over her until the air settled enough to see through.

She pulled her blade back into existence and stepped inside.

The soldiers in the room stood, some slack-jawed, all with weapons raised.

She heard the rising, accelerating sounds of the charge until human and Scorth met in the clash of battle.

Blades clanged, defecting bullets, and the brute force of Tagion's guardians fell upon them. Vesta went toe to toe with a man twice her size. He pushed her up against the wall and pinned her leg painfully against a sharp piece of debris.

The face of her enemy drew near, breath tingling her skin in hot waves, eyes power-crazed with a look she recognized in Sevet. Some unnatural strength coursed through these men, and its source had to be the Vice Admiral.

Vesta rallied, shoved him and freed her blade from the tangle of metal. She sliced his staff in twain down the center. Another man lunged at her. She spun and kicked him to the ground. Three more came at her in unison, but even their anger was not enough to stop her.

When the last soldier dropped, Vesta surveyed the room. Shivering behind a console, as if amid an ice storm, the brave Premier of the galaxy looked up at her.

Vesta lifted him by the lapels of his costume.

"Where is she?"

Tagion quivered. Hard to believe the former friend of Mic Rorren could be such a coward.

"I...I don't know. I swear."

Vesta let go of her anger and loosened her grip just as Norn lifted his blade to destroy the communication console.

"No."

The single word stilled his hand. Vesta released Tagion and he dropped to the ground with a cry of pain.

"It's time the Premier did something useful for his people."

"I will not help you."

Vesta wondered, not for the first time if his drive for fame and cowardly means of taking freedom from everyone were the opposite of what she took them to be—not the actions of a dictator mad with power but a confession of his guilt, a defense for a betrayal so cutting the despair could only be filled with the universe.

She probed into his mind in search of answers.

She found memories of him and Sevet together.

They laughed together, happy and in love.

And then Tagion strayed from her. Again and again, Vesta watched it happen until Sevet developed a mask of her own. A mask of spite and insults delivered with a smile, seeking pleasure in the twisted faces of men and prisoners she tortured—people in worse pain than she was.

Tagion's resolve melted into an intenseness and his first response was to laugh. As Vesta telepathically played those happy memories for him, she saw his face fill with the pity, waste, and shame of it all.

She broke him.

And now, the universe was hers.

Rorren always tensed when a ship entered orbit—anticipating the unknown as the landing gear rocked the hull on touchdown, wondering what secrets awaited beyond the bulkhead.

And in war, what horrors.

The metal doors swished open to a scene of fire. Flames spread through streets, catching onto cars, buildings, and the wires attached to green and red lights, hanging like drops of color in the distance.

A web of destruction greeted them, weaved by line after line of Obsedei warriors.

These were not the warriors Rorren remembered. Each of the six insect arms no longer carried an elegant blade of Scorth design.

The black shape of the first shot flames down the streets, exploding parked cars and rupturing tapestries.

Another arm, barely visible against the pavement, pinned down a company of Galactic Order soldiers with a volley of gunfire.

The hum from the third arm reached them even from 20 yards away. The stone turned molten red and blasted some projectile into the air that exploded an armored tank like the cracking of an eggshell.

These new monsters had to be Sevet's handiwork.

Rorren didn't wait to see what the other arms did.

He jumped onto the pavement. The change in gravity made him feel light, lifted, and ready for action.

He moved fast, leading his son by the wrist, dropping behind the cover of a cement highway divider as if speed could erase the disaster happening to the capital city.

Blasts from energy bursts created a splitting pressure in his head. His ability to fight, his will to defeat the invading enemy, consumed him so strongly it was paralyzing.

Tiny fingers touched his arm.

"A nosk pod."

Valor pointed intently into the atmosphere.

A massive oblong object dangled by wires between two skyscrapers. Not like any Scorth pod Rorren remembered. The Scorth used elemental technology. Their pods were slimy, riddled with moss and vines. This pod was sleek and metallic and the blinking lights on the wires glowed brighter as the lights from the buildings dimmed.

Sevet's work again.

Cantona was on one knee beside the boy, gun drawn, her brow wrinkled. "Nosk?"

"The Scorth work for fake," Rorren said. "Looks like they are drawing energy from the city to power their army."

An oncoming armada blocked the view, filling the streets with a rushing smear of noise, a desperate attempt by the Order to drive the Obsedei back.

Rorren studied the scene and the translucent light erupting from the fourth arm.

A shield generator.

Rorren learned two things: Sevet's Obsedei were not as impenetrable as they appeared and they were definitely not Scorth.

"General, we are ready to strike on your command," Torat's voice in his ear tore through his racing thoughts.

"Hold, Commander. If you come down now, the Order will think you are the enemy." He turned to his small band of soldiers and one young boy. "We have to get up there. Show them it's not Scorth running that thing."

One hell of a dangerous task, he thought but didn't say.

Racer rested his customized automatic over his shoulder. Cantona nodded.

"We're with you, boss," Racer said.

"What about the kid?" Cantona asked.

Valor disappeared, racing into the battlefield. Had the kid ripped out Rorren's heart and taken it with him, the General couldn't have been in more agony.

How he could love and worry so much about someone he only met five minutes ago was an uncomfortable mystery.

Rorren watched his son dodge gunfire and leap over Obsedei flame throwers with the agility of a kencat. He raced up the hood of a parked hovercar and jumped in the air, catching a grenade launched by one of the Obsedei.

Valor palmed it so softly it didn't explode until he hurled it at its owner. The blast broke through the shield and the fake Scorth warrior shattered.

"That sure is your kid, Mic," Racer said.

"With a dash of Scorth hutzpah," Cantona added.

Rorren set aside the immediate danger and drove them forward into battle, stopping under cover of a trash bin, then a rail car, keeping Valor close to his side. Vesta would kill him for allowing the kid to come with them.

Vesta.

Alive.

Rorren charged into battle, propelled by rage at missing the last eight years. He speared an Obsedei warrior through the torso without mercy and cleared a path to the base of one of the skyscrapers besieged by the pod.

"Gotta be twenty stories up," Cantona said, craning to see.

Rorren followed her gaze.

The nosk pod cast a faint purplish glow against the skyscrapers that appeared in spasms, giving the illusion the structures were exhaling and inhaling under its weight.

"They have shields," Valor said.

The kid was intuitive.

A Galactic Order ship launched a missile at the skyscraper. The bomb erupted in midair, stopped by a purple ripple before it was within fifty feet of the nosk pod.

Racer yanked on the glass doors of the building and cursed each time they refused to give. He used the butt of his gun to break the glass, unsuccessfully, then cursed again, and gripped his shoulder in pain.

"Looks like they also put shields around the buildings," Racer said.

Cantona tapped the keys on her gauntlet and studied the map that appeared on the screen with her bottom lip tucked between her teeth.

"Ah-ha."

"Ah-ha, what?" Rorren asked between firing shots around the wall of the building.

His arm pinned Valor to the wall, protecting him while the reality sank in. Rorren fumbled to reload, shaking with internal haste. He had to hurry. He had no right to let a single second pass until he made the universe safe for his kid.

"I have a plan," Cantona said and hearing it calmed Rorren.

She left them, maneuvered between cars, paused, and vanished.

A few seconds later, her head jolted up and her arm pumped as she waved them over.

They rushed across war-torn streets—Racer firing off rounds to cover them, ground vibrating in rhythm to encroaching Obsedei.

They arrived in time to hear Cantona grunting. Racer bent and, together, they pushed the cover off a manhole.

Cantona dropped inside.

Rorren followed and then reached, balancing Valor as he jumped down. The kid's polished boots splashed in the water.

"Gross."

Rorren glanced up, expecting Racer next.

Cantona shook her head.

"He will make sure we aren't followed."

The rank tunnel led them to a rusted ladder, rungs sagging under slats of light from another manhole.

Rorren made quick work of the cover and coaxed his son up.

Valor climbed methodically with a style worthy of a trained soldier.

Rorren never expected a son to come with healing power—a medicine capable of supplying nutrients he didn't know he missed. He surged with new energy.

In the smooth glass tile of the parking garage, the reflection of a dozen expensive flight cars streaked by.

The three of them raced to the elevator.

Music inside contradicted their urgency.

"Just so you know, I'm going to tell Edda you made me go down there. That was disgusting," Valor said.

Cantona muffled a snort.

"Well, just so you know," Rorren said, but the kid flummoxed him, "it's good for you."

"Going into a sewer?" Cantona lifted her eyebrow.

"Yes, it builds character," Rorren replied.

The door chimed open and Cantona directed them to the stairwell, guided by read-outs of troop activity on her wrist console.

They sprinted upward.

By floor twenty-six, Valor's breathing grew labored and his short legs wobbled with exhaustion.

Rorren slowed the pace without drawing attention to the fact.

Cantona offered to scout ahead and disappeared up the stairwell.

"I am not fast enough," the kid said, gazing at his boots.

"You don't have to pretend. I know you are just giving me time to think of a plan. I don't think very fast, you know." Rorren tapped his temple and Valor brightened.

Cantona met up with them on floor thirty-seven. The holoprojector on her gauntlet shuddered to life and displayed a map of the area she scouted.

"The cables connect to the building on the floor just below us. It is guarded by about ten Obsedei and two dozen of Neece's science goons."

"What is that?" Valor motioned to a dark spot on the holo-projection where the cables from the pod tapped into the building's electrical lines.

"The air vent," Cantona replied.

Cantona and Valor both grinned, looking at each other mischievously.

"Oh, no." Rorren reached over and clicked off the holo-map. "Your mother would kill me if I let you."

"Please, Erra, I'll be careful."

"No."

"What the Scorth Queen doesn't know won't hurt her," Cantona said and Valor enthusiastically nodded.

"You're not helping," Rorren said to Cantona.

Cackling, spontaneous laughter resonated through the corridor. Rorren grabbed Valor and Cantona and drove them into a damp storage closet. Rorren fought his conscience, ripped apart by his desire to fight and his need to protect his son.

The noise died and the troops passed. Rorren waited for a full minute before he cracked the door.

The hall stretched into a maze of black channels, the only light from a glaring bulb about twenty paces away.

Rorren turned to give the all-clear but met with the shocked and guilty slouch of thieving bandits.

Valor had one foot on Cantona's shoulder. The other was in her hand as she hoisted him up into the air duct on the rear wall.

They both froze and Rorren had to take a few steps toward them to ensure they were still breathing.

He glanced between them, sighed, and then pushed Valor the rest of the way with his hands.

Once Valor scrambled inside, Rorren glared at Cantona.

"If she asks, we tell her it was *your* idea."

Cantona smirked and then winked at Valor. She offered him a small knife from her mobile arsenal.

I'm in so much trouble, Rorren thought.

"I have my own," the kid said. He pulled a knife from his boot ten times more menacing than the one Cantona offered. The ugly dagger assuaged some of Rorren's guilt.

Cantona pulled up a small holo-projection map generated from a chip she plucked from the gauntlet.

"Cut the lines here, here and here," she said, motioning to red x's on the readout.

Valor nodded and took the chip.

"Be careful," Rorren told him, but the kid disappeared into the vent with head-strong arrogance, just like his mother.

Rorren marched back into the corridor.

"Where are we going?" Cantona asked.

"To give him all the help we can."

Five minutes later, the two stood on a balcony, looking to the floor below and two dozen men in constricting lab coats—all protected by more Obsedei than Rorren cared to count.

"Hey, stinkworms, up here," he shouted. "I bet you couldn't hit the broad side of a space hub."

The scientists shouted and gunfire hammered over Rorren and Cantona. He dodged to the left and Cantona went to the right. The Obsedei responded this time with a blistering stream of flame.

The fire fell short by a good half story.

Cantona lay on her side, twisting her wrist to track Valor's progress on the holo-map.

Son of an aux rand! The kid already cut three of the five massive cables that connected the nosk pod to the building. He was good. Hot beans, he was good, just like his mother.

The Obsedei burst at Rorren, crashing through the balcony door, shrieking their rage in some strange mechanical harmony.

Shadowy forms shambled forward, scraping claws along the floor, backing Rorren up against the windows that fell forty stories through tangled nosk wires to the street.

He saw the pod sway when Valor cut another cable free.

Cantona fired at the creatures defensively, instinctively. Their distraction bought Rorren a few seconds. They threw Cantona against the wall. She picked up a nasty gash on her forehead for her efforts.

Two warriors charged Rorren.

He looked at his gun.

A joke. No match for what Rorren faced.

The Obsedei stopped. Static danced across their faceless heads. Something mesmerized them into inaction.

Rorren glanced out the broken windows.

Not just the Obsedei.

Everyone stopped.

Heads craned up.

The image of Tagion Krave appeared all over the city, a massive twenty-story holoprojection that turned everything in range an odd shade of blue.

"Citizens of the Cardinal Worlds," his voice vibrated through the steel foundations.

"We have failed you. Vice Admiral Neece has been experimenting on innocent Scorth. Instead of war, they have extended the hand of friendship. The Fire-Scar Warriors will help rid us of the plague that is Sevet Neece. She wishes to enslave you."

Rorren saw his friend visibly cracking like a fatal wound had split open his soul.

"This is not all her fault. Please don't judge her too harshly," Tagion said, moving closer to the projector. "Sevet, I'm sorry. For all of it."

The hissing energy projection faded and darkness swallowed the image.

"Vesta," Rorren said, relishing the sound on his lips.

A boom rocked the building and knocked the Obsedei off balance. Rorren plowed into them, unable to break their shields, but that was not his aim. He slammed against the forcefield hard enough he knocked the creatures over the railing. Scientists scrambled out of the way as stones crashed around them.

One of them screamed, "The boy is in the vents!"

The last cable of the nosk pod snapped. The crushing weight swung on a pendulum, slamming into the building across the street and then raining concrete and steel on the warring factions below.

Rorren pressed the com in his ear.

He'd been waiting for the right time.

Now or never.

"Torch tal aukata, Torat!"

Fight for freedom.

Out the window, he watched a hundred Scorth ships descend from the sky.

Torat himself jumped from the docking doors in mid-flight.

Another Scorth showoff.

He fell through the air, menti blade drawn, edge cutting through the hull of the nosk pod as gravity hurled him down. Galactic Order scientists spilled from inside like lab-coated spiders from an egg sack.

The game was up.

"Let me go!"

A pencil-neck scientist had Valor by the scruff, ghost-white fingers clutching to Valor's clothes and forcing him toward the exit.

A line of Obsedei blocked Rorren's path.

Arms burning with flame. Shields flickering as the nosk pod lost power.

Rorren grinned at them.

One of the monsters tilted its head like a curious kencat.

"That's right, aux rands. Come get it."

Six Fire-Scar Warriors slipped into the building from shattered windows, all swelling behind Rorren with power so palpable it made his hair tingle.

One of the warriors gave Rorren a staff.

"Say hello to the cavalry," he said, twirling the weapon.

The Obsedei fell in chunks of stone, each shattering like Sevet's façade once they hit the ground.

"They have my son," he told the Scorth.

These warriors he'd never seen before each gave a single nod.

It was all he needed.

They jumped over the balcony railing. Rorren followed them without a plan, with complete trust.

He latched onto a Galactic Order flag and rode it down to the floor.

When he landed, a half dozen Fire-Scar Warriors were busy annihilating the remaining Obsedei.

The scientist that held onto Valor looked at the scene before him, dropped the kid and ran.

He didn't get far. Rorren tripped him with the staff and the Scorth handled the rest.

Rorren knelt next to his son.

"You okay?"

Grease smudges from the vent streaked his face and arms.

"Did it work?" the kid asked.

Rorren rubbed his head and messed up his hair. He looked better that way.

"Yeah, son, you did good."

"General, the nosk forces are retreating," he heard Torat's voice in his ear.

Fire-Scar Warriors escorted them out of the building and the honor of being in their company put a pretty adorable bounce in Valor's step.

In the chaos, Rorren lost track of Cantona and Racer, so he was relieved when he spotted them unscathed across the street.

There were pockets of fighting around them, but they were minor skirmishes, cleaning up the remnants of the Obsedei and scientists.

Racer and Cantona made their way over to him just as Torat appeared.

Rorren had never seen the Scorth General in person, but just by how he moved toward them, Rorren knew something was off.

A colossal ship broke through the atmosphere. Scorth were not known for their prowess in space, but seeing how easily the new ship destroyed Scorth star-cruisers surprised Rorren. A tail of fire and smoke trailed behind the falling vessels. Escape pods dotted the sky like stars.

"What new villainy is this?" Torat asked Rorren.

The Obsedei were Sevet's thugs.

The real threat arrived now.

Rorren's staff caught the glare of the sun as he stepped forward.

"Aklaren."

CHAPTER 53

Vesta was alone and closing in on her prey.

Her royal guard thought they had left her to chase Sevet.

Vesta knew better. She knew Sevet's tricks.

Fits of cold water pounded her face and forehead.

Pipes leaked all over the station, coating the railings and stairs in a slippery glaze. A treacherous climb took her to the top of the stairs. Her hand shielded her eyes from the light blasting through enormous windows.

The Tallum Nebula and its dwarf star were so close she could see the gases churning and the crescent shadow cast by the Essex moon.

A flat platform stretched before her, its marbled tiles glistened like water, holding a stillness—the moment in battle before the Titans charged.

Vesta moved forward down the expanse. The viewing glass wrapped around her, a thin veil between the abandoned tourist area and the Astro-storm in space.

Beyond the light's touch, in the far corners, she sensed her rival lurking in the shadows.

"Come face me. Or do you fear me without shackles?" Vesta asked.

"I fear nothing."

Vesta turned, but the echo in the room made it impossible to tell where the voice originated.

"He thought you were dead. He never even questioned it."

Vesta ignored the taunting and scanned for the enemy.

"I guess love isn't stronger after all."

Vesta dropped to one knee and flung a handful of sand into the air. It swirled through the shadows until the grains pelted against something.

The form of a woman appeared.

Sevet laughed and stepped into the light, gracious elegance of her figure wasted on the wrong audience.

"You think your pathetic fire sword is enough to stop me? Your abilities are nothing compared to the power I have unleashed."

"You will not be able to control it," Vesta said. Up close now, looking at Sevet, she pitied her.

The power-hungry scientist. The heartbroken lover. Spiraling down a path that led nowhere good. A path Vesta herself had been on before Mic Rorren saved her. Her granda and the spirit of tu'ah showed her the way.

"Tagion has surrendered. He doesn't think it is too late for you. Let me help you," Vesta said.

Sevet shuddered as she looked at Vesta's outstretched hand. Her gaze filled with the murky secrets amassed from a lifetime of dark deeds.

"Tagion served his purpose. Feckless coward. He never had the stomach for it."

"It is over, Sevet."

"Poor little, naset. What would your mother say? Is it too harsh, or shall I kill them all where they stand?"

Sevet's voice changed. Queen Talie's vocal inflections tainted the words in a way that still made Vesta tremble. The sounds brought her to the throne room on Ragora all those years ago when Talie sentenced the Zyne family to the mines.

"What have you done?" Vesta asked.

Sevet pulled a vile of glistening liquid from her uniform.

"The essence of the former Queen delicately squeezed into this vile. I wouldn't have discovered how had your solstal not transmitted the secrets to me." Sevet stroked the test tube with a disturbing semblance of joy on her face.

"This is the crowning achievement of years of research. One more sip, these last drops, and your Scorth power will be mine."

Sevet pressed the vile to her cheek for long moments in nameless emotion.

"I was disappointed at first—that I had to settle for Talie and not her daughter—but now that we are here, I can see this is better. This way, I can destroy you with the strength given to me by your mother. Fitting, don't you think, little naset?"

Sevet tilted her head and the liquid vanished in one swallow. The empty glass broke against the marbled tiles.

"I'm going to relish telling Mic Rorren all over again that you are dead."

Sevet reached into the shimmering air and drew down a cylinder of black marble about half the length of her forearm. With a hiss, an artic blue sword crackled into existence.

A menti blade.

Vesta pulled her blade from the sand grains tied in the pouch at her waist. The ship rumbled like it knew what was about to happen. The air around them turned thin and hissed.

Vesta sprinted at her rival. Sevet ran toward her. Blade met blade in a clash of fire and ice.

The blast from their convergence snapped Tallum Station in two.

The Aklaren dominated the skies from the cockpits of starfighters and the hides of harnessed takdulls. The beasts screeched through the air, clawing at Scorth vessels while fighters blasted them with sophisticated weapons.

Survivors from the fallen ship gathered to Rorren: three hundred Galactic Order soldiers and half that many Aux Katan. Scorth banners blew in the wind alongside Cardinal World flags.

The darkness shrouding the Aklaren forces broke under the light of the Tallum Star, shedding some hope for victory against the vast forces that covered the far plains.

Rorren climbed up a rock and stood before them, his scars and staff complimenting one another. He became like the illustrations of ancient Scorth chieftains. The ones rendered by human artists that sparked his imagination all those years ago.

Rorren often dreamed what those heroic men might have said posed there on the edge of battle.

"Loren tos tahu el es."

Ignite your power. Rorren willed his words into the hearts of Aux Katan and the human soldiers.

"Do not lose courage," he said.

The sun burned hotter and the mangled roar of the enemy echoed louder. Rorren shouted above it.

"They may be twice our number but they are not fighting for freedom."

A hundred pairs of eyes, both Scorth and human, looked beyond his scars and into his soul. He picked Racer and Cantona from the crowd, but the gaze that penetrated most came from a young half-Scorth kid.

"Stand your ground. Trust the countryman at your side."

There had been an unease between the Fire-Scar Warriors and the Galactic Order troops, but now, in the face of the Aklaren army, old tensions faded.

Trust grew in the eyes watching him from across the plains. Whispers between human and Scorth about the sign of the relheer reached his ears.

"Our fathers sacrificed on the battlefields. Let us honor them now. For the Cardinal Worlds." Rorren spun his staff around his body. "For Ragora."

He charged headlong into the approaching legions. The clash of menti blades and Aklaren clubs against the green of the far plains sent vibrations through the earth. Boulders rolled down the mountains of Tarazi. The ship-sized stones, barreling at high speeds, found victims on both sides.

"Get him out of here," Rorren shouted to Cantona.

Valor threw a fit worthy of a spoiled prince.

Racer kissed his wife and then she pulled the kid by the arm. The two of them disappeared into the ranks and after that, for Rorren, all that remained was war.

They were few, but they hammered against the hordes. The power of their alliance ran through Rorren's veins with fire. They all channeled the fire. The assaults pounded them in relentless waves.

The enemy fled into the horizon like a storm escaping from the morning suns across the sand sea.

Shouts of praise and cheer flooded the plains, prompting those Aklaren who remained to drop weapons and surrender.

Rorren's gut prevented him from joining the celebration. Acid and adrenaline constricted his muscles as a low rumbling shook the ground.

A storm thundered over the Tarazi mountains, causing the peaks to move. White snow tumbled from cliffs that became arms. Grassy hills turned to legs.

Rorren knew before the others. Déjà vu struck him as the monster emerged. A creature of rock also controlled by the twisted power Sevet designed.

Five rose from the mountain range.

Dust from the upheaval swirled and soaked up the retreating Aklaren.

From out of the plumes, Rorren saw the first enormous hoof, as wide as the base of the Tarazi skyscrapers and sprinkled with crystalline specks that sparkled when the sun struck them.

A plated head appeared, embellished by dark spikes, eyes dull under a crown that used to be part of Rorren's favorite mountain peak.

Above the stone creatures, circling on the back of a takdull, Rorren made out the gray-skinned hide that belonged to Hevcar Duronilan.

Wild with terror, Rorren's troops reassembled. The Scorth and humans fought for balance against the raw air, the movement of the approaching mountains a blow to morale.

Amul Torat pushed his way to the front line. He was bleeding from several gashes on his face and arms.

"We cannot stop them this way, General."

"What do you suggest?" Rorren asked.

"The Queen said you were wise. Trustworthy. We shall see."

Torat sprang up, tall and proud and shouted to his warriors in a voice clear as the shores of Ragora.

"Hac anit tim el tos aux marie."

We fight now in the ancient way.

The Aux Katan dismissed their blades and formed a circle, one hand on another's shoulder. With heads bowed and bodies exposed, they were like one of those idioms Rorren knew Vesta detested. They were sitting ducks.

"Defend the Scorth," Rorren ordered.

In a searing second, the monsters stood before them, dazzling in spectacle but murderous in every lumbering movement.

Rorren swept out his staff and sprinted toward the massifs. The nearest monster roared when Rorren stabbed the diamond tip into the base of its hoof. His troops followed him. Their courage in the face of such odds visibly alarmed the Aklaren.

Mounds of dirt rippled up around them, knocking Rorren off his feet. He rolled onto his spine, heard a scream and watched the sunlight blotted from the sky.

The thirty-ton rock hoof rushed at him, poised to stomp him flat.

He braced for impact, thinking of Vesta and his son, preparing for the end.

Darkness engulfed him like the jaws of a black serpent.

Then, a light.

The blue glow hovered about him and reminded him of the shield of Sevet's Obsedei creations.

The hoof of the behemoth lifted and Rorren scrambled out of the imprint. His troops and the Aklaren staggered over each other at seeing him alive.

He didn't understand it, but he used it to his advantage.

"We can win!" Rorren shouted.

The Galactic Order soldiers rallied and reformed the line, surrounding the Aux Katan with new hope and determination.

Five enormous shadows descended like falling clouds, ready to trample them all.

Soldiers on both sides lay slain around them, but Rorren's faithful company refused to abandon the Aux Katan. The bond, Rorren knew, was true power.

The hoof of the monster destroyed a distant farmhouse, sending a storm of dust cascading over the landscape.

Chaos prevented him from gaining a clear picture of the battle.

Men shouted.

Rorren peered through the haze, breath hitched and staff stretched before him, waiting for the final assault.

Silence engulfed the battlefield and then amazement.

Somehow, Rorren didn't know how, the mountains turned on their masters.

Large chunks of stone crumbled in a swirl of blue light—a light originating from the circle of Aux Katan warriors.

Rorren heard Torat's voice in his head.

They are yours to command.

The human troops must have heard the same voice because Rorren saw them climb even as the monsters fell to pieces. The humans rode the last remnants of life in the five stone creatures. Into a final battle with the Aklaren, they rode.

Limbs made of cliffs swatted Aklaren star cruisers out of the air. Rock and metal rained from the skies. The takdulls were better at out-maneuvering the clumsy stone, but they did not last long. When the last life pealed from the rocks, new mountains rested inanimate on the plain. Rorren turned skyward.

One winged gantis remained.

The takdull spiraled down, shrieking when its claws touched the ground about ten paces from Rorren.

Its rider dismounted, steel armor scraping against the hide of the winged giant.

"We may have lost the war, but I can still take the head of the General," Hevcar said, lifting a machete into the air.

He swung.

Dodging the blows and mounting an offensive after all Rorren endured drained him to his breaking point. Hevcar landed a fist on Rorren's jaw and the smell of blood jarred loose the memory of his loyal kencat.

Hevcar torqued his waist and drove Rorren's face into his armor-plated knee.

The pain fueled Rorren's rage. He breathed in dirt near his mouth, eyes blurred. He fought his way into focus and noticed a boulder teetering on top of a pile of debris the fallen rock creatures created.

Rorren righted himself an instant too late.

The machete came at him and he reared to action. His staff stopped the blade from slicing him in half. He took an uppercut to the chin that left him vertical against the rock debris.

Hevcar let out a gloating laugh and his shadow fell across Rorren.

"I'm gonna enjoy this."

He lifted the machete.

"Up here, stinkworm!" Valor's voice carried across the sky. The boy hurled a piece of starfruit over the side of the motor cruiser and hit Hevcar in the head.

Rorren took advantage of Hevcar's momentary distraction and reached for his staff. He jammed it into the stone, prying open a crack that split the wall up to the unstable boulder at the top.

By the time Hevcar turned, an avalanche of rock descended on him.

Rorren rolled out of the way.

Cartilage crunched.

Hevcar's feet protruded from the ruins, the only part of his body visible beneath the stone.

"A fate too good for a kencat murderer," Rorren said and stuck his staff in the ground, marking the scene of his triumph for Brawn.

Rorren waited, panting from the fight, while Cantona landed the spacecraft. Valor rushed up to him, face beaming.

"Erra, that was so cool. You kicked his butt."

"I told you to keep him out of here."

Cantona rolled her eyes.

"We were safe. The battle is over. Besides that, he was about to Scorth magic me if I didn't bring him here."

Rorren glared at her and then took in the battlefield.

He discovered she was right. Medical teams escorted the wounded to make-shift tents. The last of the Aklaren surrendered and soldiers hand-cuffed them in between burning scars of fire and piles of stone debris.

A shadow dimmed the Tallum Star and all looked to the sky.

Rorren shielded his eyes and squinted, realizing Tallum Station had dropped orbit and was eclipsing the sun.

Cantona shoved the ignition key of the spacecraft into his chest.

"Go."

"Edda is up there," Valor said.

Rorren took the key and shouted to his son as he raced away.

"I'll find her. I promise."

CHAPTER 54

THE SPACE STATION SWEPT in wide curves around the nebula, clinging to its orbit while being pulled in two.

Vesta slid along the observation deck, catching glimpses through windows of dismembered hull fragments. She saw no lights or forcefields, just long bands of wires left holding the crescent together, a tangle of mechanical cords like spilled intestines.

Sevet struck at her with wild, frenzied madness.

Her icy blade chipped sand particles from Vesta's, creating streaks of black flame that burned through oxygen with a sickening rubber smell.

Dust swirled about them. The entire platform succumbed to a storm worthy of Desandor.

Lights went out section by section, signaling a doom overtaking the station, a warning that the wreckage would soon reach them and expose everything to the lifelessness of space.

Vesta wiped the blood from her cheek where Sevet had split it open with the tip of her menti blade.

They both knew Sevet was stronger.

With a spinning kick, Sevet dropped Vesta to her knees.

A vision appeared to Vesta out of the sand. The robes draped the Scorth Queen like in her vision. This time, Sevet wore them.

She fought the darkness inside of herself and came out victorious. Sevet embraced her inner darkness.

Sevet let the blue blade drag behind her and she sauntered toward Vesta, the anticipation of the killing blows curving her lips.

Vesta heard her mother's voice in her head.

The evil inside me has made her strong.

The first encouraging thing Talie had ever said to her.

It gave Vesta enough strength to rise and meet Sevet for another round.

The sand washed over them.

Flashes of Queen Talie appeared in Sevet's deformed shadow.

"She is fierce," Vesta said. "But I will free you, Edda."

Her mother's face overtook Sevet's, cunning brilliance shining and then vanishing into oblivion.

Sevet pounded Vesta repeatedly—steel clanging against steel—with a strength beyond anything natural.

The endless pummeling forced Vesta to drop to one knee. She lifted her menti blade to meet the overwhelming blows.

She envisioned this moment on Desandor.

She knew then this battle would claim her life.

Still, she fought fate with all she had, refusing to lose until Sevet was defeated.

The station dropped orbit and slipped into a free fall toward the Essex moon.

Vesta stumbled off balance and Sevet took advantage. She landed her boot in Vesta's stomach.

The force launched Vesta into the air. Her bones cracked against the observation window before she slid to the floor.

Sevet jumped after her in defiance of gravity itself.

Vesta lifted her blade. The sword blocked the attack and then shattered into a million sand particles.

Blue steel of Sevet's sword glistened, reflecting all the colors in the encroaching nebula.

Sevet yanked Vesta by the hair.

"You've always been a disappointment, haven't you? To your mother and especially to me."

Sand engulfed them.

———

Rorren didn't care that the station was heading for certain doom.

He crash-landed the ship and raced through the station corridors, blocked by the appearance of a sandstorm.

The golden cotton of clouds reminded him of Desandor.

He wrapped a cloth around his face and stepped into the storm. The winds whipped around him, turning sand grains into painful needle pricks.

He pressed on into the madness. The glaring light from the nebula highlighted every swirling pattern, isolated and magnified shapes that weren't real and obscured the ones that were.

He ran into a wall, tripped over an office chair and tore through every oncoming obstacle.

He melded with the constant flux as Brawn once had. Rorren channeled the spirit of his fallen pet.

He thought of the prince from the stories, traveling through sandstorm castles to find his lost love.

Rorren broke into a clearing in the center of the storm.

Sevet and Vesta appeared before him, locked in a death duel. Sevet towered over his wife, enhanced somehow by Scorth magic.

One slice of a serrated edge and Vesta's menti blade shattered. Its sand particles scattered to the winds.

A small mound of sand gathered at his feet.

He knelt and scooped up the grains.

Any other weapon would be useless.

Rorren closed his eyes. He envisioned the Scorth war with Vahza, then Desandor, training with Vesta between rolling dunes.

With sand in hand and stealth as his ally, he charged at Sevet.

The scars on his neck tingled and a strange light cut through the haze in the shape of the alien markings along his skin.

He neared Vesta as a sword formed between his fingers.

Sevet drew her blade above her head, exposing her mid-section.

Rorren ran her through with Vesta's menti blade.

For fleeting seconds, Rorren controlled the fire sword. All he needed. The blade crumbled to dust between his fingers. The light from his scars vanished and left behind a strange throbbing.

Sevet's sword clanged on the tile and she staggered after it. She scoffed at Rorren and fell to her knees, eyes wide with alarm, face cold and lovely.

"You! Traitor."

Rorren ignored her. He hadn't seen his wife in eight years. Everything else faded from existence.

He offered his hand. Vesta looked up at him with both eyes, no sign of deathshade. Her skin was blemished with a few new battle scars but her beauty overtook his senses.

He pulled her to him and kissed her with violent desperation. Between kisses, she caressed him with whispers of *I love you*.

He did not pause to grasp the magnitude of the moment because every-thing slipped away in the flooding brightness of joy, even a world that was falling apart around them.

Arms clung to him.

"They told me you were dead. I swear if I would have—" Vesta silenced him with her fingers to his lips. Her eyes reflected the pure joy he felt inside.

"Your mother kept me alive. Me and Valor."

His mother? The words came first like a jab to the abdomen, then a follow-up right hook. His guts ached and his jaw smarted.

The ship groaned as the gravity of the Essex moon frayed the outer hull.

"We have to get out of here," Rorren said. He pulled on Vesta's hand but she didn't move.

Sevet was watching them, a mix of bitterness and horror on her tear-stained face.

Something like regret caught hold of Rorren.

What a waste.

Sevet hissed through her teeth, a mangled cry of pain and rage, and then her body disintegrated into a liquid somewhere between an inkblot and a dense fog. It floated above them in turmoil against an emerging silver smoke.

Vesta extended her hand and the sparkling silver gases floated toward her while the black fluid oozed through seams in the metal sheeting.

The silver smoke danced between Vesta's hands and formed into some-thing solid. A shape he recognized. A raven.

Light flashed and then a living creature burst from the smoke. Wings flapped with vocal cords belting: caw, caw!

The bird perched on Vesta's arm. Unlike Vesta in raven form, this bird had a grey body and neck, with a black ring circling its head and wings.

"Mic Rorren, this may sound odd, but this is my mother. Or, at least, what is left of her."

The bird tilted its head and glared at him, he thought, like a disapproving mother-in-law.

"Nice to meet you, ma'am," he said, "Now can we go?"

The corridors were lined with unseen dangers, rising in tiers, igniting gas leaks from broken mains and raining metal shards from shattered windows. A constant, dry suction of air left them both panting.

The bird flew ahead, squawking directions that echoed through the halls.

Rorren pressed the length of Vesta's arm to his chest, their bodies running in motion together, driving toward a single point. Escape.

The heat from the nebula made the walls slick with sweat.

"The shield is giving out," he said.

They were half a section from his crash-landed ship in the docking bay when Vesta stopped and gazed out the window.

The dark, inky cloud drifted toward the dwarf star. It entered orbit like oil spilling into the water until a dark spot formed within the yellow sun.

The shadow turned the sweat on the walls into small balls of ice.

Blasts of sun-heat tried to escape the dark cloud, but it trapped them, pressure building inside red veins that cracked through the ink spots.

"She will destroy all the Cardinal Worlds, every world, in one blast if I do not stop her."

The room was cold, but the tone of Vesta's voice froze Rorren's bones.

"There has to be a way to use the station..." He tried to think. His world depended on an alternative, never mind the Cardinal Worlds.

Her hands gripped his.

"You know I am right. I thought the universe was meant to be mine to rule. But it is mine to save."

Rorren squeezed her fingers—no way he would let her out of his sight again.

She drew his forehead down to meet hers.

"It was your father, was it not? But your mother told me she never thought you a murderer. A father would sacrifice anything for his son. As yours did. As you must do now. Let me go."

"I came here to save you."

"Always bragging, kitlush. You have already saved me an obnoxious number of times."

Rorren rested his forehead on hers, relishing the warmth in the growing cold around them.

"You should know, I let him fight the Obsedei and taught him to say stinkworm."

She laughed and the music in it made his soul sing.

"You are going to survive. Promise me you will try," Rorren said.

"I will. I know who awaits my return."

Rorren kissed her palm.

"And besides," she said, "as your peasant wife, I still owe you a meal cooked by my hand."

She grinned and he pulled her in for a hug.

"Go. Mother will lead you out," she said as they parted.

The gray raven cawed and flew through another door.

Vesta pulled the royal jewel from around her neck and placed it in Rorren's palm with her hand in his.

She transformed into a raven and—like he had seen her do years ago on Desandor—she flew out of the station with a beam of white light in her wake.

The next moments became fused into a blur of falling objects, flames, bird calls, and fumbling with controls.

Rorren couldn't process anything until he strapped himself into the shuttle.

Engines strained against gravity as he tore away from the space station.

He won his fight for freedom but watched the crescent station crash into the Essex moon out the window. The impact ignited dormant volcanos. Molten red bled over the man-made metal, fusing to it forever.

Beyond the destruction, the yellow dwarf star struggled to fight the darkness. Life-giving light grew dim.

CHAPTER 55

RORREN WALKED THE TARMAC in the shadow of a fading sun. The second ship he crash-landed smoked behind him and the raven Queen, Vesta's mother, circled above. In the chaos, no one noticed him or his spacecraft.

Med techs and ground crew raced across the pavement, seeming directionless.

Rorren searched for Valor.

He stopped at the base of a pole and looked up to the Cardinal Flag.

He loved that flag beyond death, just like he loved Vesta. The way he loved his son.

"I won't abandon you again."

In response, the flag caught the breeze, a brief ray of sun touching its colors before dimming.

"Mic—the mighty General—Rorren."

Of the people left to greet him, the last he expected came at him—his sisters Tarza, Ivy, and Jane and a swell of spouses, nieces, and nephews.

Jane looked most like their mother.

"No more running, General," Tarza scolded even as she hugged him. A bombardment of affection came after that. He embraced it. It wasn't like him. He avoided them for years but he didn't want too anymore.

"Did you hear about mom?" Jane asked, brushing a hair behind her ear.

"That's she's alive? I can't believe it. Where is she?"

Stunned expressions stared at him and Jane swallowed. His gut tightened.

"She died en route to Alpha beside the Scorth Queen and your son." Jane raked her gaze over him. "The Scorth Queen." She lifted her eyebrows but let the words sink, thickening the air.

"What happened to your scars?" Tarza asked.

Rorren glanced at his reflection in the window of a nearby command station. The inky designs no longer lined his neck, erased somehow by the burn of the menti blade.

Jane placed a half dozen holo-chips in his palm.

"Mom recorded hours of messages for all of us. Imagine our surprise when they were hand delivered by a member of the Scorth Royal Guard," Jane said.

"The Scorth Royal Guard," Tarza added with a playful scowl.

"Not that we have hours. They say the Tallum Star is dying," Jane said, shielding her eyes as she glanced to the sky.

"Don't give up hope," Rorren said, latching onto Jane's shoulders. "Never give up hope." He squeezed for emphasis, then returned to scanning the tarmac. "Where is my son?"

"I am here, Erra." Valor appeared from among his cousins. A violent and sudden clarity of perception surged through Rorren. Valor with his cousins. His aunts and uncles. His family. Their family.

"At least we will all die together," Jane said.

"Families never die," Rorren replied, watching Cantona and Racer approach. The two humans flanked Amul Torat and Norn Zyne.

"You speak the truth, Mic Rorren, but your she-kin is also correct. The Aux Katan have tried, but we cannot stop the evil that darkens the galaxy." Torat glanced at the sun when he finished speaking.

"Only she can stop it now," Rorren said.

"I should have stayed with her. We were forced to flee when the station cracked," Norn said, eyes guilt ridden.

Valor scowled, eclipsing all the human in him for a moment. He left them for a quiet corner near the barracks and sat cross-legged, arms folded and eyes closed. The grey raven landed on Valor's shoulder.

"Who is that?" Norn asked.

"It's a long story," Rorren muttered.

He excused himself from the horde of depressed faces and joined his son, mimicking the boy's posture as he sat.

"I will never stop searching for her. She will succeed and then we will comb the galaxy to find what remains of her. She will be with us always, just as your granda is. Just like Freyde and my troops are. Death is not the end."

The raven cawed at him and fluttered into the sky, but Valor remained motionless.

Rorren placed his hands on the boy's slender shoulder and bowed his head. He didn't know if Valor prayed, but it was all that remained, so Rorren did. His sisters and their families surrounded them, copying the solemn pose.

As the dwarf star dimmed, it cast deeper shadows over Amul Torat. The tip of his menti blade rested against the pavement, his thick hands gripping the handle so tightly his muscles flexed. Cantona and Racer gripped each other and Rorren saw the emptiness in their faces, stranded so far from their child as Armageddon arrived.

"I've always given up a moment too soon. Not this time." Rorren lifted, resolved not to despair and focused on the horizon. "Look."

Beyond the city skyscrapers, sunlight returned, mile by mile, chasing away the shadows. Faces watching the dwarf star had to be shielded when its full brightness reached them. The rays warmed them, thawed away the despair, and a murmur of relief grew until it became shouts and cheers.

"She did it," Valor said, rejoining them from his trance.

"She did," Rorren put his arm around Valor's shoulder. "And now, we find a ship and go get her."

"She is coming to us," Valor said. The kid's hope cut Rorren like a blade. "I know she is alive, Father, because I protected her. I can do that. I protected you, too. That big, ugly mega 'sedei stinkworm could not crush you. I would not let him."

Rorren scarce allowed himself to hope, but the grin on Valor's face was contagious.

"General," Cantona said, pointing skyward. Rorren snapped his head to see a streak of white light shooting from the heavens. The beam came straight at them, leaving a burning trail of flame in its wake, just like the slash marks of a menti blade.

Valor started for the pavement where the beam touched down but Rorren held him back, unsure what to make of it.

The beam blasted a hole in the ground, showering them with steam and pebbles. A few soldiers ventured up to the edge.

Through the steam, Rorren made out the movement of shadow. A raven blasted from the smoke. Rorren tossed the jewel into the air.

The talons caught it and the bird landed, taking on the form of the Queen of Ragora as it did.

In royal robes, unscorched and unmarred, Vesta appeared, chin lifted in arrogance.

"Edda!" Valor sprinted and threw his arms around her. Hands gripped his mother's waist as he glanced over his shoulder to Rorren.

"I told you I protected her."

Rorren shoved his hands in his pockets and walked over. He tried to be casual but joy exploded through his body.

"You're full of surprises, kid." He met Vesta's eyes. "You'll cause me as much trouble as your mother."

Rorren engulfed his family in a hug. Vesta's tears wetted his bicep, but she quickly wiped them away.

"Are you going to introduce us?" Tarza interrupted. Rorren almost forgot how much his sister annoyed him.

Vesta took Tarza's hand and said, "The kara zati, your mother, saved my life and hundreds of my people, mostly children. She will forever hold a place of honor in Scorth history."

No one ever managed to shut Tarza up. Vesta succeeded in less than a minute. Rorren's sister was left teary-eyed and speechless, which served her right.

"Look, Erra. The Raven Star," Valor said.

Above him, as if it had always been, the crescent of the Essex moon fused with the remains of the Tallum Station and formed the silhouette of a raven, wings spread, rising against the dwarf star.

***

Desandor

Six Years Later

Rorren stood next to the stone column of the ancient village courtyard, eyes tuned to every facet of the festivities. Vesta watched him from the chaos of the kitchen, ignoring the clink of dishes to appreciate the orange light from Desandor's suns as it softened the edges of sand and stone.

The galactic treaty with the Scorth seemed a minor achievement compared to the peace Rorren and Vesta secured even among the outer planets like Desandor.

He was a beacon to the universe, a lighthouse pouring its truth over the darkest seas, exposing evil and rooting it out before it corrupted again.

She was proud of him.

"She is a lovely child-ling, Scorth-Vesta," Emme-Sims said as she handed Vesta's daughter to her.

A tangle of dark hair already reached the two-year-old's shoulders. Vesta rested her daughter on her hip and wiped the smudges from the girl's cheeks.

"They let you at the chocolate, I see."

Emme-Sims dawned a guilty frown, but Jane remained ever serene. She was Vesta's favorite of Rorren's three younger sisters.

"I told them it would be alright. It's hard not to spoil my niece," Jane said and reached out. The baby wrapped her hand around Jane's finger with a drooling grin.

A pleasant scent reached them on the wings of unexpected breezes carried beneath a cloudy sky. The startling suddenness of it reminded Vesta of home.

"These tresacoi pies smell delightful," Reen-hara said, balancing a tray in each of her hands. "Do they taste as delightful?"

"Time to find out," Vesta said as a string of women poured out of the kitchen doors carrying trays. Vesta followed them but sank into a deserted corner, marveling at the way freedom rang in the sounds of laughter, the sparkling of ceremonial attire and the excitement of a visit from the newly elected Chairman.

The women carried the food along a stone wall that led along the columns to the feast table. Beyond its brightly colored stones, Valor played with his cousins. He was determined to show off the tricks he'd taught Queen Talie, but the raven refused to perform in public.

Somehow, no matter how obstinate Talie acted, it only strengthened Valor's bond with his granda.

Strange but comforting, like the power of the Aux Katan.

The power had been with Vesta all her life without her realizing it. It was there when her granda left. Luha, the little girl who just wanted a friend, possessed it. Despite his smelly sunwart breath, Brawn used it. The kencat was the first to wake Vesta from her slumber of indifference and hatred.

Her mother winged to Valor when the boy called. Vesta watched, feeling her heart had grown enough to forgive the one who wronged her most. She even lauded the small measure of peace her mother might have found with Valor.

Rorren surveyed the landscape and stopped when he spotted her. He sought her out with a wily half-smirk.

"They let you bake all those pies and you didn't burn the place down?"

"That was one time and I was not provided the proper tools."

Rorren placed a lingering kiss on her lips. As much as she hated public displays of affection, she enjoyed it enough to let it slide.

"How's my girl?" Rorren hoisted his daughter and a string of giggles followed.

Everything her father did was hilarious.

Vesta wasn't jealous.

Rorren was true to his word. He was a good man who became even better and taught her how to unlock her potential. Naturally, giggles followed him now.

The gray raven swooped on the crowd and plucked a necklace from the wife of one of the human politicians. She carried it overhead with a caw, ignoring shouts, and dropped the jewel in Vesta's hands.

There would always be a dark side to her soul and Vesta found herself grateful for the presence of her mother. The raven was a necessary reminder of what she had learned to live with about herself.

As she returned the jewel to a blond woman, the owner, and a bitter swell of remorse invaded her thoughts. Images of Sevet's final moments overcame her—poor lost Sevet, who should not have died alone.

Without Mic Rorren, Vesta might have become Sevet.

The desert was not a wasteland anymore. Sandfruit had not been Mic Rorren's path to redemption but had set her on hers.

Stuck in different ways, she the raven, and he with his scars, her granda brought them together, knowing just what the other needed before they did.

Mic Rorren pretended to fly their daughter like a ship, pulling another burst of giggles from the baby. He hadn't realized yet that he hadn't aged since he picked up Vesta's menti blade. At that exact moment, the Aux Katan power healed the mark of the relheer.

Looking up to the clouds, between breaks in the plumes, Vesta discovered twinkling stars.

She saw the heels of an elusive vision in a fleeting thrust of motion. A vision of Vazha and Freyde, Harc and Lelia, and others that had gone before, smiling on them with a galactic message.

At last, Mic Rorren burns with Scorth fire.

ACKNOWLEDGEMENTS

With gratitude, I must thank the many friends and family who encouraged me in my endeavor to write this book. Your support has meant the universe to me while I rambled about galactic queens and tattooed former generals. To my brother, Lee, for lending me his incredible artistic talents and insights. The only thing more impressive than your visuals is your kind heart and brilliant sense of humor. You and Alyssa are a dream design team!

My parents, the rock in the center of my sandstorm-laden world, are fire-sword-wielding warriors who inspire me daily.

Jenel, thank you for being my lifelong writing cohort. You nourished the seeds of a beginning writer. I can't repay you for reading the early stuff and the pain you must have endured. You are a legend.

Writing a book takes a village of support, so thank you to my friends, Susan, the M&M queen and loyal reader, and Vicki, the wise-sage of all things publishing.

A lot of life happened in the eight years it took to bring this book from thought to reality. We lost some along the way and gained a few more. To all of you, both here and up there, you are the reason I know there is no greater treasure than the soul of a living being. I plan to continue treasuring you all...and writing more! Ready for blast off.

ABOUT THE AUTHOR

Nikki Root grew up on fantasy books, sci fi reruns, and heroes leaping off the comic page. She has a fully functional geek engine which must be fueled with comic cons, cosmic comedy, and compelling characters. She lives in the western deserts of the USA with adventure and almost enough jigsaw puzzles. *Taming of the Fire Sword* is her debut novel. For more by Nikki visit www.storieslikethat.com

Made in United States
Troutdale, OR
12/26/2024